PRAISE FO
OF A

Assassin's Gambit

"In a strong debut launching an Ancient Rome–inspired romantic fantasy series, Raby offers a captivating tale of an assassin who falls for her target.... The main characters have excellent chemistry, meshing right from the start. In addition to a richly imagined world and a delightfully entertaining tale of magic and intrigue, Raby also delivers an understated yet versatile magical system."

—*Publishers Weekly*

"A great read."

—*Dear Author ...*

"An exquisite debut novel. The scope of the novel is ... epic, as it roams through counties and territories, introducing us to dozens of strong and dynamic characters. The setting is beautiful, and the story line is one that will instantly attract readers searching for everything from a sizzling romance to a vast adventure filled with mystery, intrigue, and murder." —*Night Owl Reviews* (top pick)

"Raby's debut heralds the arrival of a terrific new fantasy romance voice.... [Raby] has a gift for storytelling."

—*RT Book Reviews*

"There's nothing quite as sexy as a woman who can be both assassin and love.... The hot tension between [Vitala] and Lucien will keep readers eagerly turning pages."

—*Coffee Time Romance & More*

"A great setting and protagonists worth rooting for."

—*All About Romance*

Also by Amy Raby

Assassin's Gambit
Spy's Honor

PRINCE'S FIRE

THE HEARTS AND THRONES SERIES

AMY RABY

A SIGNET ECLIPSE BOOK

SIGNET ECLIPSE
Published by the Penguin Group
Penguin Group (USA) LLC, 375 Hudson Street,
New York, New York 10014

USA | Canada | UK | Ireland | Australia | New Zealand | India | South Africa | China
penguin.com
A Penguin Random House Company

First published by Signet Eclipse, an imprint of New American Library,
a division of Penguin Group (USA) LLC

First Printing, April 2014

SIGNET ECLIPSE and logo are trademarks of Penguin Group (USA) LLC.

ISBN 978-0-451-41784-8

Printed in the United States of America
10 9 8 7 6 5 4 3 2 1

For Jessica and Julie. Cupcakes forever!

ACKNOWLEDGMENTS

My agent, Alexandra Machinist, and my editor, Claire Zion, for championing these books and making them stronger.

Jessi Gage and Julie Brannagh of the Cupcake Crew, for their aid in shaping and perfecting this book, not to mention their much-valued support and friendship.

The talented people at Writer's Cramp, who never let me get away with anything: Barbara Stoner, Kim Runciman, Steven Gurr, Tim McDaniel, Amy Stewart, Thom Marrion, Janka Hobbs, Michael Croteau, and Courtland Shafer.

And my readers, who make this all worth it.

Thank you.

1

Celeste followed her older brother, Emperor Lucien of Kjall, down the sun-drenched pier at the docks of Riat. Shielding her eyes, she gazed at the Inyan ship *Magefire*, which rode at double anchor in the harbor. It looked like an interloper among the heavy Kjallan warships. Its masts were higher, its lines sleeker, its hull paler in color.

Sailors and dockworkers moved aside to clear a path for them. The emperor was an infrequent visitor to the docks. He moved at a brisk walk, limping almost imperceptibly on his wooden leg, his eager eyes fixed on the barrels rowed in earlier this morning.

Beside Celeste gamboled a large black-and-white dog, who darted longing glances at the ocean waves that lapped at the sides of the pier. And on all sides were the Legaciatti, their bodyguards and security staff.

"You're going to love this," said Lucien. "A stone that burns."

Celeste smiled; she knew his real reason for dragging her out here. Celeste wasn't naturally sociable except with a few trusted people. She had a tendency to lock herself with her work in her rooms, where the hours slipped by faster than she intended. Her brother interrupted her now and then, when he thought she needed sunshine and conversation.

The dock guards before the barrels stood straight and stiff, awed by the presence of the emperor. Lucien studied the label of the first barrel and signaled the nearest guard to open it. Celeste ran forward to see its contents revealed.

Inside was a bright yellow powder. Celeste scooped up a handful and let it sift through her fingers. "This isn't stone."

"It's brimstone." Lucien dug into the substance and cupped a handful of it, staring reverently as if it were powdered gold. "It's been pulverized into this powder. Do you know where the Inyans gather it? Along the edge of a volcano."

"What poor sod gets stuck with that job?" She had no personal experience with volcanoes, since there were none in Kjall, but everyone knew a volcano had destroyed the nation of Dori.

"A well-paid sod, I hope. But Inya's volcanoes are more manageable than Dori's. The Inyans have a system for controlling them. Ask the prince about it when you meet him."

Celeste was trying not to think about the prince. He'd come in the *Magefire* to negotiate a trade agreement with Kjall and had brought the barrels of brimstone as a demonstration of good faith. What the prince didn't know was that Lucien wanted more than a trade agreement. He wanted an alliance, and to secure it, he meant to offer Celeste's hand in marriage. Celeste had never met the Inyan prince, and in a matter of months, he could be her husband.

Scooping up a double handful of brimstone, she asked, "Does it really burn?"

"Absolutely. Come and see." Carrying his own handful, Lucien gestured her to follow. The black-and-white dog wagged its tail beseechingly, and he addressed it. "Oh, just get in the water, Patricus. Everyone knows you want to."

With a joyous bark, the dog leapt off the pier and splashed into the ocean.

As they walked the length of the pier, passing by the staring dockworkers, Celeste cradled the powdery treasure in the folds of her syrtos to shelter it from the breeze. At the end of the pier, they descended a wooden staircase to a sandy beach.

Lucien found an open space with nothing flammable around and, with the foot of his wooden leg, dug a crude hollow in the sand. "In there."

Celeste poured her brimstone into the hollow, and Lucien added his. Though the brimstone had a consistency similar to the sand, it was a brighter yellow.

Lucien took Celeste's hand and backed away from the hole, drawing her with him.

A bit of movement caught her eye—a dark shape appearing and disappearing among the white froth of the breakers. "Don't light the brimstone yet. Patricus is coming."

"I see him," said Lucien.

Patricus burst from the waves and loped up the beach.

"He's sopping wet," said Lucien. "Shake it off, Patricus!"

The dog kept coming. His feet sank into the soft sand, but he pumped his legs and scrambled on, sending the sand flying out behind him.

"Shake it off!" Lucien commanded.

Patricus galloped to Lucien and shook, spraying sand and seawater all over him.

"Pox this animal." Scowling, Lucien brushed sand off his imperial syrtos and turned to the Legaciatti, who were covering their faces to hide their grins. "Where were you? Some security detail."

"We don't interfere with the imperial dog, Emperor," said one of the Legaciatti.

Lucien muttered to Celeste, "I don't get half the respect Florian did."

"They love you. Everyone does." This was not true, of course. Lucien had numerous enemies. But Celeste felt that if those people truly *knew* Lucien, they would love him as much as she did.

Lucien grabbed Patricus by the scruff and gestured to the fire mage in his security detail. "Light the brimstone, Jasper."

The fire mage waved his hand, and the yellow powder ignited.

Celeste gasped. The flame was *blue*. "Three gods, that can't be right. It's unnatural. Like a Vagabond fire."

"It stinks like the Vagabond's breath." Lucien waved away the smoke.

Celeste got her first whiff of the fumes and choked. He was right; the burning brimstone smelled like something rotten. She backed away and so did Lucien, dragging Patricus with him.

Lucien beamed like a delighted schoolboy. "Have you ever seen the like?"

Holding her nose, Celeste shook her head.

"Only the gods could devise something so strange and wonderful. No wonder it's needed for making the most important substance in the world."

"Chocolate?" said Celeste.

Lucien gave her a look. "Gunpowder, as you well know. Put the fire out, Jasper." When the fire was out, he released Patricus, who fell into step at his side, wagging his tail. He offered his arm to Celeste, and they headed to the carriage, followed by the Legaciatti.

"Where are the Inyans?" asked Celeste.

"Up at the palace," said Lucien. "They've had a long sail. They need to rest, freshen up. So do we, I think, after that brimstone."

"I wish you had told the prince in advance that you were going to offer him my hand."

"And spoil the surprise?" Lucien grinned. "Trust me, it's better he should see what he's getting. If you can't sell this alliance, no one can."

Celeste shook her head. Lucien thought the world of her, but he was her brother and obviously biased. She was not as pretty as he suggested. "When will you make the proposal?" Her stomach knotted at the thought of seeing her potential marriage partner for the first time at a formal event, with everyone's eyes on her. She'd heard a few things about the prince: that he was twenty-two years old, a good match to her own age of nineteen, and handsome. Those were points in his favor, but they were surface traits and told her little about whether she would be happy with the man. Or whether he would be happy with her.

"I don't care for official presentations," said Lucien. "The last one I attended turned into a fiasco. Instead I've arranged a small dinner party. You and me and Prince Rayn, plus a few officials to balance things out and keep the conversation flowing. What do you think?"

She let her breath out. "That sounds less intimidating."

They had arrived at the imperial family coach, an imposing blue-and-gold conveyance that comfortably seated six and was drawn by a quartet of matched grays.

Lucien took her hand and squeezed it as he lifted her into the carriage. "Courage, sister. It will all work out."

Celeste smoothed the folds of her gown, wishing her tumultuous insides could be similarly brought to a semblance of order. She was waiting in the anteroom for Lucien, who had trapped himself in a conversation with his adviser Trenian. Celeste drummed her fingers against her gown. When those two got going, they could prattle all night. It was unfortunate that the empress was out of town. Celeste would have taken some comfort from Vitala's presence.

At length, Lucien disengaged, stepped to her side, and took her arm. "Ready?"

She nodded. "As I'll ever be."

Lucien called over his shoulder, "Trenian, let's meet the Inyans." He nodded at the guards, who opened the doors, and they headed in to dinner.

State dinners were normally held in the Cerularius Hall, but Lucien had selected the west dining hall—a family room—for this meeting. While the significance of this gesture would be lost on the Inyans, Celeste understood it perfectly. It meant he was more interested in cultivating intimacy with his guests than impressing them with opulence. The west dining hall lacked the Cerularius Hall's cavernous size and decadence. Still, it would hardly insult their guests. It was lavish on a smaller scale, with sculpted walls, silk tapestries, and a chandelier hung with a thousand colored light-glows.

The glows were dimmed, but Celeste had a clear view of the three Inyans as they milled about the room. They'd separated. One man stood alone and the other two stood next to each other, admiring the tapestries. Though they were the only people in the dining room, she'd have identified them easily even if they'd been strewn among a pack of Kjallans. Inyans stood out. Most were blond, and they wore their hair long, the women in a variety of styles and the men in a braid down their backs. Celeste looked these men over, hoping to pick out the prince.

The one standing alone she wrote off immediately. He was an older man and sallow-faced; he couldn't be the twenty-two-year-old prince.

Next, the two who were together. Her eyes fixed on the leftmost figure. Tall and muscular, with his golden braid falling to his waist and a furred cloak slung about his shoulders, he put her in mind of a lion, maned and regal. His features were pleasant and honest, and he moved with an easy confidence. Though he did nothing to call attention to himself, she had the impression that everyone in the room was subconsciously aware of him and in his orbit.

Celeste's heart made a strange little jump. She clutched at Lucien's arm, feeling dizzy. *That one,* she pleaded. *Let the prince be that one.*

In the interest of fairness, she studied the third man. He was handsome too, but in a different way. Long and lean, older by at least a decade, with well-defined features. She could learn to like him, but the man in the furred cloak—he was the one she wanted. It ought to be him. He was the only man who looked the proper age.

Lucien led her toward the two younger men. "Prince Rayn Daryson," he said, speaking diplomatic Kjallan.

The man in the furred cloak stepped forward and clasped wrists with the emperor. Celeste's heart leapt. The young lion *was* the man Lucien wanted her to marry! But it remained to be seen how well he liked her. Or whether his character matched his good looks.

"Your Imperial Majesty," said the Inyan prince, answering in diplomatic Kjallan. "An honor."

She liked his voice: a pleasant, rumbly tenor.

"Allow me to introduce the Imperial Princess, my sister, Celeste Florian Nigellus." Lucien held out Celeste's hand.

Rayn's eyes slid over her with interest. He took her hand and bowed slightly. "Imperial Highness. Your beauty lights up the very room."

"Thank you," said Celeste, her heart doing little flip-flops. He'd obviously prepared the compliment in advance, but she appreciated his courtesy. Nervous, she pushed her hair back from her face. "I've heard much about you, Your Highness. The stories don't begin to do you justice."

His eyebrows inched upward, as did the corners of his mouth. "Let us hope you heard the right stories."

The onlookers chuckled.

Lucien waved Rayn and the others toward their seats. "Let's finish the introductions at the table. I don't want this to be formal. Are you comfortable speaking in Kjallan, or would you prefer we spoke Inyan?"

"Magister Lornis and I are fluent in Kjallan," said Rayn. "Councilor Burr knows enough to get by. I've always felt that when abroad, one should speak the host's language."

"Very well," said Lucien. "We'll translate if need be. Celeste and I speak passable Inyan."

Celeste took her seat directly across from her might-be future husband. Lucien introduced his adviser, Legatus Trenian, and Prince Rayn named the two men in his company. The man Rayn had been walking with when they'd entered the room was Magister Lornis, apparently a royal adviser or teacher or judge—she was not clear on the exact role. And the older man was a member of a Land Council on Inya that drafted laws and operated in some sort of power balance with the king.

The servants placed before each of them a white soup sprinkled with pistachios and pomegranate seeds. Celeste stirred and sipped at her soup, wanting to talk to the prince but feeling shy. Kjall needed this alliance, and she'd have gone through with this proposed marriage even if the man had been a toad, but there was nothing amphibian about Rayn. He was handsome and charming.

Lucien opened the conversation. "Prince Rayn, I hear you're involved in Inyan volcano management."

"Indeed," said Rayn, settling into his chair. "I wouldn't say we manage the volcanoes so much as we try to minimize the damage they do. We've eight smokers at present, three of which are on inhabited islands."

"Smokers?" said Lucien.

"Active volcanoes," said Rayn. "But ours aren't the same as the ones on Dori. Dori's smokers are taller and more conical in shape. And when they erupt, they're more devastating, as you know by the recent catastrophe."

"The year with no summer," said Lucien. "Of course."

"Our volcanoes erupt frequently," said Rayn. "Some of them more than once a year. But they're rarely explosive. Occasionally they belch a little steam or ash, but mostly we have lava flows."

"Which it is Rayn's job to manage," said Magister Lornis.

Celeste wondered exactly how a lava flow could be managed, but her tongue was in knots. She couldn't bring herself to speak in the company of the man she might one day marry.

Councilor Burr said, "Rayn and the other fire mages use their magic to halt the lava flow before it makes its way into the lowlands."

A flicker of annoyance crossed Rayn's face. "Sometimes we halt the flow, if the volume of lava is small and we find that to be feasible. More often, we have to direct it away from the city, to a safe location where it will do no harm."

Burr, after downing the dregs of his wineglass—his second of the evening so far—shook his head. "Fire mages of old used to stop the flows entirely rather than shunting them elsewhere. So the old texts say."

Rayn grimaced. "Councilor Burr and I are in disagreement on this point."

Magister Lornis spoke. "Prince Rayn is a fire mage, along with all his extended family. For generations it has been their collective job to manage the volcanic eruptions, exercising their best judgment on how to accomplish that aim."

Warm emotion welled up in Celeste. She wanted to tell Rayn how touched she was that the royal family of Inya served the people in such a direct and important way. But she felt too shy to intrude upon the conversation.

"As for their judgment," slurred the councilor, "I cannot call it sound. The land onto which Rayn intends to direct Mount Drav's lava flows is now settled with civilians."

Rayn set down his soup spoon. "Our petty squabbles bore you, I'm sure," he said to Lucien. "Burr and I disagree about whether that land should be settled."

"I find Inyan politics fascinating," said Lucien. "I understand that power is shared between the king and the Land Council?"

"Yes," said Rayn. "The Land Council is responsible for land management and some aspects of taxation. My father, the king, handles justice, international relations, the military, and other things. I am empowered to act in his stead in some of these areas."

"Such as the negotiation of this treaty," said Lucien.

"Precisely."

"I believe you and I are in a similar position," said Lucien. "I am still in the early years of my reign—gods willing. You are not yet king, and your father may rule for many years to come—"

"Gods willing," said Rayn.

"Nonetheless, the day will come when you must take up the reins of your kingdom. Have you considered what you hope to accomplish as a ruler? What legacy you hope to leave your people?"

"I think on that often," said Rayn.

"As do I," said Lucien. "I want to give my people the legacy of peace."

Rayn was silent as the servants delivered their second course, a steak of sturgeon with capers. He picked up his fork. "Peace is something we all desire," he said blandly.

"Before I ascended the throne, my country had a long history of war," said Lucien. "But not in recent years. Leaving aside a brief conflict that took place entirely within Kjall, I have presided over eleven years of peace. Still, no emperor rules forever, and I often ask myself what will happen when my successor ascends the throne."

Rayn plunged his fork through a caper and a flake of fish. "By the very nature of succession, no one can know such a thing."

"Yet predictions can be made," said Lucien. "Your country neighbors Mosar, yet there has been no war between Inya and Mosar for centuries."

Rayn nodded. "There is much trade between Inya and Mosar. And intermarriage among the noble houses."

"I have observed that," said Lucien. "To ensure a

long-term peace between Inya and Kjall, perhaps we should consider what has worked so well for Inya and Mosar: trade and intermarriage."

Rayn stopped chewing.

"My sister, Celeste, is of marriageable age," continued Lucien. "She is beautiful and intelligent, and I've had many offers for her hand."

Rayn's eyes flicked over her. "I do not doubt that."

"I understand you are not yet contracted for marriage yourself," said Lucien. "I think you could do no better than to ally yourself with the most powerful country in the world."

Rayn was silent, obviously stunned by this overture.

"Do I understand you correctly?" said Magister Lornis. "You propose a marriage between your sister and Prince Rayn?"

"That is exactly what I'm proposing," said Lucien.

There was a moment of awkward silence.

Magister Lornis finally said, "Your offer is most generous. We shall consider it carefully. A decision such as this would have tremendous impact upon Inya."

"Take what time you need," said Lucien. "The princess and I are at your disposal for the duration of your visit."

Celeste felt the prince's eyes on her again. Her cheeks warmed. She looked down at the table. It was embarrassing to be bartered like a cask of brimstone.

"Princess Celeste." Magister Lornis nodded in her direction. "You're so quiet—we'd love to hear from you. The emperor and empress are known for their prowess at Caturanga. Do you play the game?"

"I do not," she said softly.

"Celeste is extremely intelligent," said Lucien. "She's

involved in the Mathematical Brotherhood of Riat. And like all women from the imperial line, she's a mind mage."

"The Mathematical *Brotherhood*?" said Magister Lornis.

Celeste grimaced. This was embarrassing to explain. "They don't normally admit women. They made an exception for me."

"What sort of math do you do there?"

"A variety of things." Mostly cryptography and cryptanalysis, which she wasn't at liberty to talk about, since she was working with Lucien to upgrade Kjall's ciphers to a higher level of security. She'd also broken Inya's ciphers as an exercise. It was probably best to abandon this subject. Her love of math wasn't likely to endear her to Prince Rayn.

"She's writing a treatise," said Lucien. "What's it called again? *Linguistics and Mathematics*?"

"*Linguistics and Probability Theory.*"

"We're terribly proud of her," said Lucien.

Magister Lornis smiled. "I think it's wonderful that we live in a world where there's something everyone can be passionate about. For the emperor it's Caturanga, and for you it's mathematics."

"And for the prince," slurred Councilor Burr, "it's volcanoes and blondes."

An uncomfortable silence fell over the table. Celeste was raven-haired like her brother.

Magister Lornis steepled his hands on the table. "It's well-known that Rayn dotes on his mother and sisters. And Councilor, you've had more than enough to drink."

2

Prince Rayn preceded Magister Lornis, his friend and onetime tutor, into the stateroom they'd been assigned for their visit. The guards shut the door behind them, granting them some well-earned privacy. No more Kjallans. Finally he could relax.

"That was a fiasco," snapped Lornis. "Could Councilor Burr have been any more undiplomatic?"

Rayn shrugged. "He did what he came here to do—make a mess of things."

"Indeed," said Lornis. "I don't think he was nearly as drunk as he was pretending to be."

"What do you think about that marriage proposal? Here's my sister. Would you like to marry her? Surprise!" The audacity of the Kjallans, assuming that just because they had the largest land army in the world, he would leap at the opportunity to marry their princess.

"The emperor ought to have warned you in advance instead of springing it on you with the poor woman sitting right there," said Lornis. "Nonetheless, you should take the offer seriously. You're unlikely to receive a better one."

"Thanks," said Rayn dryly.

"I'm not insulting you," said Lornis. "There simply are

no better prospects. The Mosari royal line has been almost entirely wiped out. You could take a Sardossian princess, but Sardos is increasingly unstable these days. If there's a coup, you could end up allied to the wrong family."

Rayn collapsed onto a couch, rubbing the back of his neck. "Or I could marry at home. Why not an Inyan queen for once?"

Lornis shrugged. "Won't help you at court. Kjall is the strongest alliance you could make. Surely you have no objection to the woman herself."

Rayn frowned. Celeste was beautiful. She seemed rather shy, but he didn't mind that; he liked the idea of being the one who might coax her out of that shell. But she was, after all, Kjallan, and he refused to be tempted. "She has freckles."

Lornis snorted. "Only you could find fault. I thought her lovely."

"Really, you notice such things?"

"I'm as capable as any man of appreciating aesthetic beauty."

"She likes math," Rayn observed. "She's writing a treatise."

"She's smart, like her brother. It's a good thing."

"And I don't like math. So I'm stupid?"

"This is a one-way bit of logic." Magister Lornis took a seat across from him. "All people who like math are smart. But not all smart people like math. Nonetheless, you *are* stupid."

"Oh?"

"You *will* be, if you decline this opportunity. She's arguably the most powerful woman in the world outside of the Kjallan empress. She's beautiful, she's smart, and she seems agreeable, if a little quiet. Why hesitate?"

"Because she's Kjallan. Do you realize these savages don't drink coffee?"

"Who cares what they drink?"

"Lack of coffee is doing nothing for my mood."

Lornis shrugged. "I'll have some sent up from the ship. Be serious. You can't object to the Kjallans because of that."

"I have more substantial concerns. Tell me, Lornis, why is it that the Mosari royal line is almost entirely wiped out?"

"Do you think me a sapskull? Because of the Kjallan invasion."

"Exactly! Shall I marry into a line of thieves and murderers?" said Rayn. "Aunt Vor-Lera was among those killed—remember Vor-Lera, who wove those beautiful tapestries? The man who ordered her death was Emperor Florian, Celeste's own father. You think I should ally my line with *that*, maybe sire a few grandchildren for Florian?"

"She's not a *that*. She's a *her*."

"She's Florian's daughter, and I'd be a traitor to Vor-Lera's memory if I married her."

Lornis grunted. "The whole point would be to prevent Kjallan invasions from happening in the future."

"The Kjallans haven't changed their ways. They attacked Mosar, they attacked Sardos, they *destroyed* Riorca—"

"All under the previous emperor Florian," said Lornis. "You heard what Lucien said. He's held the throne for eleven years and hasn't started any wars. Jan-Torres of Mosar likes him."

"Jan-Torres married Lucien's cousin; he's hardly unbiased. Open your eyes and look at the details of the trade agreement," said Rayn. "What are they asking from us? Brimstone. For gunpowder! Why don't we *hand them the gun* so they can shoot us in the head? This deal smells, Lornis, and I don't care how beautiful that princess is—she's not going to make it smell any better. We should handle our problems ourselves. Trade amongst ourselves and with trusted allies like Mosar. We don't need to go crawling on our knees to Kjall—"

"We're not crawling on our knees!" Snorting in exasperation, Lornis rose from his chair and paced to the other side of the room. He glanced out the window, and then aimed a disapproving stare at Rayn. "I know you'd like to do everything yourself, but you can't. You have powerful enemies in the Land Council, and if you hope to outmaneuver them, you need stronger allies. Ask yourself, why are you here in the first place?"

Rayn glared at him, refusing to answer.

Lornis returned to his chair. "Because your father sent you here. And why did he do that?"

"I don't want to talk about this," Rayn growled.

"Because he's not thinking clearly anymore, and the council convinced him to send you. Because you *scare* them, Rayn. They want you away from Inya. You're a thorn in their side—the only person left with the ability to oppose them."

"So I go through the motions on this ridiculous trade agreement, which is not going to happen, and then sail home. They can't get rid of me forever."

"They'd *like* to get rid of you forever," said Lornis. "And they will if they can manage it. To fight back against the kind of power they have, you need to swallow your pride and find yourself a strong ally."

Rayn cocked an eyebrow at him. "Are you proposing I actually go through with this trade agreement?"

"Yes," said Lornis. "And you should seriously consider the marriage as well."

"They sent me here to get rid of me, not because anyone actually expects the trade agreement to happen."

"Surprise them," said Lornis. "Make it happen. Make them regret sending you."

"I do not make deals with Kjallan warmongers."

Lornis shook his head in exasperation. "There is no family more powerful and more resourceful than the Kjallan imperials. If they back you at court, the balance of power will shift in your favor."

Rayn sniffed. The Kjallan imperials were frightening. Also peculiar. The emperor and empress were obsessed with some war game, plus the empress was a former assassin trained in combat and other techniques that were the subject of tawdry speculation. Celeste was apparently writing a math treatise. Lucien's cousin Rhianne, now married to King Jan-Torres of Mosar, seemed to be the exception to the family's peculiarity. Rayn had met her a few years ago and liked her. But she was from a slightly different bloodline, as he understood it, and not a representative example.

"Are you listening to me?" continued Lornis. "You had better get used to freckles. This opportunity has landed unexpectedly in your lap, and you will not throw it away."

Rayn looked him in the eye. "Would *you* marry a woman for the good of your country? If she were the daughter of a murderer?"

"I would do it in a heartbeat," said Lornis.

"A woman, Lornis?"

"I would do it," Lornis insisted. "And for you, she's more suitable than she would be for me. Your objection to freckles aside, I saw you casting your eye at her. You like her."

Rayn sank onto the couch with a growl of frustration.

He could never fool Lornis; the man saw through him every time. And he ought not to bait the man. Lornis hated traveling alone and pretending he was a bachelor just because foreign dignitaries might not approve of his lifestyle. Yet he did so, for Rayn's benefit and no one else's. Rayn's trust in the man was absolute.

Still, he was never going to ally himself with the Kjallans. The trade agreement for brimstone was worrisome enough. But the marriage? He was not going to share a bed with the daughter of the man who'd murdered his aunt, no matter how beautiful and smart she was. "Sorry, Lornis. You're wasting your breath on this one."

Celeste headed along the footpath to the Imperial Stables, trailed by her bodyguard Atella. She shivered in the cold. As a girl, she'd been curious why the stables, when viewed from a distance, swarmed with activity, yet when she arrived, the grooms met her at the doors idle and ready, with the aisles cleared, as if they had nothing in the world to do but attend to her needs. Even at that age, she could not let a mystery go unsolved. She'd discreetly observed the stables and learned that they employed a spotter, always the least senior groom, who sat high in the hayloft and watched for approaching imperials. The lesson had stuck with her: because of her rank, the world presented to her was distorted. Sometimes, to see things as they truly were, she had to cultivate relationships with people outside the palace's inner circle and come at things a little sideways.

Since she was shy by nature, this was difficult. But as an imperial princess, she could not afford the luxury of isolation. She would always, whether she liked it or not, be involved in high-level politics—either Kjallan politics or perhaps, once Lucien married her off, those of some other country.

The head groom, flanked by a pair of his underlings, met her at the stable door and bowed low. "Your Imperial Highness. Shall I have Raven brought out?"

"Thank you, no," said Celeste. "I'm here to see Tatia. Is she working today?"

"I believe she's in the second wing. May I show you the way, Your Imperial Highness?"

Celeste shook her head. "I know where it is, and you've enough to get on with."

She headed down the main aisle, past stalls and little alcoves where horses stood in crossties to have the dust whisked off their backs and the mud picked out of their hooves. It was blessedly warm here—the grooms kept it so. Down the side aisle and into the second wing. A loud bang startled a trio of barn swallows into frenzied flight.

Atella stepped up to her side, alert and ready.

"I think it was just a horse kicking the stall," said Celeste.

A stall door rattled open, and a woman darted out into the aisle, slamming the door behind her. Celeste caught a glimpse of a chestnut horse's head snaking out over the stall door and striking, teeth bared, but the woman was out of range. The head disappeared, and there was more banging.

"Tatia," said Celeste.

The woman turned. She started at the unexpected sight of an imperial, and dropped into a curtsy. "Your Imperial Highness. Always a pleasure."

"Patient giving you trouble?" asked Celeste.

"He'll kick himself lame if he keeps that up," said Tatia. "But he's already lame, so it doesn't make much difference. He's in pain, and when he starts throwing a tantrum, he just makes it worse." She cupped her hands around her mouth to amplify her voice. "Sunny, knock it off!"

The banging continued.

"I can help," said Celeste.

Tatia's forehead wrinkled. "He's a stallion. I'm not sure your magic can handle him, but I can get Pilian on the twitch. Pilian!" she cried.

A distant voice called back, "What you need, Tatia?"

"Twitch!"

A sturdy-looking groom appeared from around the corner. "Tell me we're not twitching Sunstorm."

"Your favorite horse!" she called cheerily.

With a groan, he disappeared into the tack room.

Celeste had seen the twitch in action. It was a metal clamp that a groom could place on a horse's nose, which for reasons nobody fully understood tended to quiet the animal. It was painless and humane but didn't work reliably on the most challenging horses. Furthermore, for her purposes, she preferred to be alone with Tatia. "The groom doesn't need to twitch that horse. My magic works on any animal."

"Your Imperial Highness—" began Atella.

"There's no danger at all," said Celeste. "But, Tatia, I'm asking a favor in exchange."

"What's that?"

"I need gossip."

Tatia perked up. "I'd give you that for free—especially if you have some to offer in return. What kind of gossip?"

"I heard you were among the party chosen to entertain a group of Inyans last night."

Tatia's eyes sparkled. "I heard *you* entertained the prince."

"I did," said Celeste. "And something happened. . . ." She trailed off as Pilian the groom approached, carrying the twitch. He looked as grim as if he were marching to the execution block. "We won't be needing you after all, Pilian. Thanks very much."

Pilian bowed and retreated with a spring in his step.

"Let's start on the horse," said Celeste.

Tatia went to the stall door, snapped, "Get back" at the stallion, and drew the door open.

The chestnut stallion stood in the middle of his stall, blowing from exertion, his ears flicked halfway back in suspicion. His left foreleg was puffy and swollen, leaving no doubt he suffered. As she approached, his ears flattened against his mane, and he bared his teeth. She reached out with her mind magic and seized him forcefully with a suggestion. *I like these people. I want them to come into my stall.* Instantly, the stallion's ears flicked forward, and the expression on his face changed. He lowered his head and chewed, a submissive gesture. "We can go in now," said Celeste.

"I love it when you come around here. It's a miracle what you can do with a vicious animal." Tatia entered the stall and knelt by the stallion's foreleg.

Celeste followed, trailed by her bodyguard. The praise embarrassed her a little. What she did wasn't miraculous; it was just typical mind magic applied to an animal. Most mind mages could only ply their skills on people, but a few women could apply the magic more broadly, and Celeste was one of them.

Healing magic, which Tatia possessed, seemed less particular; it worked equally well on people or animals regardless of the mage's degree of talent. While Tatia worked on the swollen foreleg, Celeste kept her eye on the stallion's ears and body language, making sure he didn't get any ideas.

"So you're looking for gossip about the prince?" asked Tatia.

"Yes. You may have heard that Lucien offered him my hand in marriage last night."

Tatia looked up. "Well, *that's* news. Did he accept?"

"It was sudden. He's thinking about it."

Tatia's eyes twinkled. "And what do you think of him? I caught a glimpse of him in the hallway. He's a fine-looking man."

Celeste had a feeling Tatia hadn't run into the prince by chance; in all likelihood, she'd deduced where he would be and deliberately stationed herself there. That was what made Tatia so useful to her, not just as a friend but as a source of information. Tatia's family was well-off but not of noble lineage. She moved in different circles than Celeste and was privy to a brand of gossip that Celeste was not. "He's handsome, yes. But he seemed . . . distant. It could just be the suddenness of the proposal." And hopefully not the fact that she wasn't pretty enough for him. She motioned at the chestnut's foreleg. Tatia was hanging on her words with such interest that she seemed to have forgotten about the horse. "Have you heard anything about Prince Rayn's romantic life in Inya? Have there been other proposals? Can you think of any reason he'd be disinterested in this one?"

Tatia probed the chestnut's foreleg. The swelling began to diminish in response to her healing magic. "I'm not aware of any other proposals, but I did hear something. A couple of years ago, Prince Rayn was—how do I say this?—indiscreet in a relationship."

"What do you mean?"

"He impregnated a girl."

"He has a *child*?" The stallion laid back his ears, and Celeste threw a suggestion at him. *I'm perfectly happy just standing here.* He relaxed.

"A daughter," said Tatia. "You didn't know? Everyone was talking about it. He apparently slept with some palace servant, and they must have been lax with their wards, because now he's got a bastard."

"Three gods." She had about a million follow-up questions. How serious was his relationship with the servant woman, and who was raising the illegitimate daughter? In a day of near-universal warding, how had he managed to get someone pregnant?

This could be the reason Rayn had made no response to the marriage proposal, leaving Lornis to smooth things over. He might be in love with the servingwoman. Since she was lowborn, he couldn't marry her. Perhaps he was delaying his royal marriage as long as he could in order to maintain that relationship.

Why hadn't Lucien said anything? There was no way he did not already know about the illegitimate daughter.

Tatia glanced up from her work. "Was that the gossip you were looking for?"

Celeste took a deep breath. "I don't know for sure, but it's an important piece of information. A good starting point. Thank you."

"I appreciate your coming," said Tatia. "You've done His Nastiness here a great favor and saved Pilian and me a good deal of trouble."

Celeste had a feeling Tatia was more grateful for the gossip she'd handed her, about the marriage proposal at dinner and Rayn's lack of response. No doubt Tatia would begin sharing that news about with relish.

But she was pleased about the horse. She rarely had cause to use her mind magic, and for good reason: it was invasive and frightening. She certainly wouldn't enjoy someone entering her mind and making magical suggestions that she had no choice but to obey. Yet in this case its use had been compassionate and kind. The horse had been too mad with pain to allow Tatia to treat him. Now, with his leg healed, he was quiet.

She organized their exit from the stall as if it were a controlled retreat: first Tatia, then Atella, then herself. Once the stall door was rolled into place and latched, she released her magical hold on the stallion and watched him, curious to see if he'd lunge at her. Instead, the animal yanked a tuft of hay from the net hanging in his stall and chewed contentedly.

3

Rayn's trade negotiations with the Kjallans began poorly. While he was open to the idea of trade in general, what the Kjallans really wanted was brimstone, which he would not grant them. The Land Council had sent along a gift of the substance, which had made the Kjallans think he'd be more amenable than he truly was. The council was desperate to diminish Rayn's popularity among the Inyan populace; thus they constantly tried to set him up for failure. In this case they might succeed at it.

Coffee, citrus, chocolate, and iron—he offered them all, but the Kjallans did not budge from their demand for brimstone. Their already-established trade agreement with Mosar supplied the tropical goods they could not produce in Kjall. He was wasting his time.

When he'd had enough of the day's negotiations, he left Lornis and the others to continue the fruitless arguing and returned, annoyed, to the state apartment the Kjallans had granted him for the duration of his visit. There he found a woman trying to speak to his door guards—in the Inyan language, which the guards didn't understand.

He was not in the mood for this.

"Zoe," he said in Inyan. "What do you want?"

"This woman is known to you?" asked one of the guards in Kjallan.

"Yes," answered Rayn, switching to Kjallan himself. "She's one of my servants."

"She says she should have access to your chambers," said the guard.

"That is not true." He frowned at Zoe, who stood looking innocent and confused, with her hands at her sides and her shoulders hunched. She couldn't understand a word they were saying. "Don't let her in without my permission. But I'll speak to her now."

"Yes, Your Highness," said the guard.

He ushered Zoe into his stateroom and, when the guards had shut them in, rounded on her, speaking in Inyan. "This is a bad time. I've had a terrible morning, and I'm not in the mood."

"I could get you in the mood," said Zoe.

He sighed. Zoe was interested in only two things: sex and Inyan whiskey. "That is not what I was talking about."

"It could be."

"Is this all you came for?" Sometimes he wondered what he'd ever seen in her, aside from the fact that she was nice to look at. Before the pregnancy, she'd been waifish, almost boyish. Now she had more curves above and below, a change he found agreeable. Her hair was long and lustrous, blond and straight as hay stalks, though far softer, framing a delicate face and round hazel eyes. She was soft, submissive, and completely unstable.

"I needed to see you," she said. "I'm lonely."

Tired of standing still, he turned and paced to the other side of the room. Years ago, he'd tried to rescue this woman—a foolish notion if he'd ever had one. He'd met her in a bar: beautiful, fragile Zoe sporting a black eye given to her by her drunk father. Rayn had downed a shot of *uske* and ordered her to take him to her father's farmhouse. There he'd found the man and given him a black eye to match his daughter's. Then he'd offered the woman a service job at the palace. It was easy work: fetching and carrying.

A few days after beginning the palace job, she'd seduced him in his rooms. He'd been amenable. Why not? He'd slept with servant women before. But the others had understood that there were no implied promises.

Zoe had ended up pregnant, an event so unlikely that she saw it as miraculous, a sign from the Vagabond that they were meant to be together. Despite all that, Zoe had essentially abandoned the girl. After witnessing the child's neglect, Rayn had hired a wet nurse. He visited baby Aderyn on a regular basis, but Zoe had stopped visiting entirely. It seemed the woman was more interested in her *uske* than in her daughter.

And though he'd broken things off ages ago, she wouldn't leave him alone. He thoroughly regretted ever sleeping with her.

"You're a beautiful woman," he said. "I'm sure you've no shortage of interested suitors. But please, I'm here on business. Leave me alone."

Celeste found Lucien in his office, going over contracts with his legal and language advisers. He looked up at her, bleary-eyed. "Is this urgent?"

She leaned on the doorway. "There's something you didn't tell me about Rayn."

He winced, which told her he knew exactly what she was talking about, and waved away the advisers. "We'll resume in an hour," he told them. "It's time for a break anyway." To Celeste, "Tea?"

She nodded.

The advisers vacated their chairs, and Lucien called to his door guard. "Send up some Dahatrian. And whatever else they've got in the kitchen that's good."

Celeste slid into a chair on the opposite side of Lucien's desk. She waited until the room was empty and said, "Prince Rayn has a daughter."

"I was going to tell you," said Lucien.

"When?"

"After you got to know him a little. I didn't want you jumping to conclusions. He's a good man who ran into a difficult situation at the worst possible age and did some things he now regrets."

"How old is the baby?"

"About a year," said Lucien. "Maybe a little younger."

"Are you sure he regrets what he did?" said Celeste. "Because he didn't seem very interested in the marriage proposal."

"I sprung it on him," said Lucien. "Give him time to get used to the idea."

"Maybe he's still in love with the mother of his child."

"I doubt it," said Lucien. "From all accounts, it was a meaningless affair with a palace servant that resulted in a pregnancy through ill luck."

A servant arrived, bearing a tray with two cups, a pot of Dahatrian tea, and a plate of lemon cakes. Celeste poured for her brother and then for herself. "How did Rayn get her pregnant? Don't they use wards in Inya?"

"Of course they do," said Lucien. "Nobody knows how it happened."

Celeste tipped a sugar cube into her tea and stirred. "What does his family think about it?"

"From what I understand, they're not much in the picture. Rayn's father, the king of Inya, is unwell."

"In what way? Is he dying?"

"I'm not sure. I just know that it's serious, and he's unable to run his kingdom or manage his family. The Land Council has been ruling in his stead for years."

"You mean Councilor Burr, that awful man at dinner? He's been running Inya?" Celeste sipped her tea. It was rich and nutty with a cinnamon finish. "Good Dahatrian."

Lucien raised his cup in agreement. "Him and others. Did you notice the antagonism between Burr and Rayn last night? There's a reason for that. Inya's supposed to be ruled cooperatively by the king and the Land Council. But lately it's been all the Land Council, because the king isn't able to govern, and they've taken advantage of the situation by trying to pass some unpopular laws. Rayn, though he has no official power until he inherits the throne, rallied the people and stopped some of those laws from being passed. Now the Land Council is out for his blood. They'll do anything to stop his rise to power."

"He sounds like he'll make a good king. But I don't understand his being careless with wards."

"Neither do I," said Lucien. "But mistakes happen. I don't think it makes him unsuitable as a marriage partner."

"He sounds like a womanizer."

"I don't get that impression," said Lucien. "As I understand it, there was only one woman."

That wasn't exactly reassuring. One woman would be worse than a hundred women, if Rayn loved her. "Are they still together?"

"I am told they are not."

"What about the baby? Who's raising her?"

"I didn't ask."

Celeste sat back in her chair. "How are the trade negotiations going?"

"Poorly. Rayn doesn't want to give us any brimstone, which is odd since he brought all those barrels as a gift."

"Does he think we're going to turn around and attack his country?"

"He might think that," said Lucien. "And it's hard for me to convince him otherwise. He simply doesn't trust us, and if we can't change his mind about that, the negotiations will fail."

Celeste sipped her tea. Maybe that was the reason Rayn lacked enthusiasm for the marriage proposal.

"In fact, I think we need to end the negotiations, at least for the time being," said Lucien. "We're going round in circles. I'd like to encourage Rayn to do some looking around Kjall. He needs to get to know us better."

"I invited him to go riding. He said he was too busy."

"I was thinking an overland trip or a sea voyage," said Lucien. "Kjall is a big country. There's plenty for him to see."

"Where were you thinking, in particular?"

Lucien shrugged. "Wherever he wants to go. But here's the catch: I want you to go with him."

"Me?" She set down her teacup.

"You," said Lucien. "The marriage may be the key to all of this. If he accepts you, he'll accept our trade agreement."

"You want me to . . . charm him, then, on this trip?" She swallowed. She was good at math and linguistics, not at making small talk with strangers.

"Yes, exactly. Win his trust."

"I think someone else would be better suited for that role."

"Hardly," said Lucien. "You're the only one who can do it."

"I'm not skilled at this sort of thing."

"You'll do better with him than I would," said Lucien. "Please say you'll try. For the sake of Kjall."

How could she deny Lucien when it was for the good of her country? "I'll try."

Prince Rayn was bored. The negotiations this morning had gone nowhere, and they'd disbanded the meeting in mutual frustration. Now he was back in his stateroom with little to do and wondering how long he'd have to stay in Kjall before he could in good conscience return home.

His stateroom had a bookshelf, but the books were written in Kjallan. He could read Kjallan, but it was a tedious translation process, more work than it was worth. He'd tried it for about half an hour and given up. Then he'd watched out the window for a while, but his view was of a garden. Pretty, but it got old. Full of pent-up energy like an unexercised colt, he began to pace.

A knock sounded at the door.

He froze, his muscles knotting with tension. "Who's there?"

"Lornis."

At least it wasn't Zoe. "Come."

Magister Lornis entered. "Why do you act like a caged tiger? Nobody's locking you up."

"Because nothing is being accomplished here. We should go back to Inya."

"You were ordered here by the king to negotiate a trade agreement," said Lornis.

"Not by the king. By the Land Council."

"Via the king," said Lornis. "You can't talk to the Kjallans for one day and then give up and leave."

"Then what am I supposed to do?"

"Come to an agreement with the Kjallans."

Rayn snorted.

"At the very least, stay here long enough to look like you tried."

"This Emperor Lucien—he's a bad king," said Rayn. "Have you seen how he's accompanied constantly by an escort of four or five guards?"

"You can't judge him by that," said Lornis. "Kjallan culture is different from ours. All their rulers have bodyguards. Even the princess has one."

"So they're all bad kings," said Rayn. "The princess included."

"Didn't she invite you to go riding? That would get you out of your stateroom at least."

"I'm not marrying her, so why bother?"

"It would be better than pacing your rooms."

Rayn wasn't sure about that. That princess was a Kjallan temptress; he wasn't getting anywhere near her. He wouldn't let a pretty face trick him into trading brimstone to the Kjallan warmongers.

"Well, the emperor's offered you an alternative," said Lornis.

"What's that?"

"He suggests you take a sightseeing trip."

Rayn halted midstride. "Why?"

Lornis shrugged. "I think he wants to play for time. Let you get used to Kjall while tempers cool. He means to send the princess with you."

"Ah," said Rayn. "That's his angle. He thinks she'll seduce me."

"You should accept," said Lornis. "We can't go home yet, so why not spend our time more productively? You could get a look at the country."

"Where does he want to send me, exactly?"

"Your choice."

That was surprising. He'd thought for sure the emperor would maneuver him toward some particular location, one that best showed off Kjall. "Riorca, then."

Lornis's brows rose. "The frigid north? That's a long trip."

"By sea it's not bad—five or six days each way," said Rayn. "I want to see this country that Kjall conquered, enslaved, and then supposedly liberated. I have my suspicions that the Riorcans are not as well treated as he claims they are."

"If you travel by sea, you'll be trapped in the small confines of a ship for upward of twelve days, with this princess who intimidates you."

"She doesn't *intimidate* me," said Rayn.

Lornis smiled. "So you say."

"Convey my answer to the emperor," ordered Rayn. "I'll go to Riorca by ship. Six days north, we take a look around, then six days back. We go through a couple more horseshit days of negotiations, throw our hands in the air, and head home to Inya."

"Surely you don't want me to tell him *all* of that."

"Just the first part."

"Look, on this trip—" began Lornis.

A blast of trumpets silenced him.

Rayn turned, trying to locate the sound. It was coming from above his head, probably from atop one of the towers. He went to the window and spotted a pyrotechnics light show above the middle tower. "Look there."

Lornis joined him at the window. "The Kjallans are celebrating. I wonder why. Some sort of holiday?"

"They probably just declared war on someone," said Rayn.

4

Celeste quivered with excitement. The palace was astir with the news. Empress Vitala had returned! Celeste was part of the small welcoming party who greeted the empress when the carriage arrived at the palace gates. Vitala looked exhausted—not a good thing, in the state she was in—and Emperor Lucien whisked her away for the remainder of the day. Celeste didn't expect to see either of them until the morrow.

It was not until past lunchtime the following day when a knock came at her door. "The emperor and empress," called Atella.

"Enter," called Celeste.

The door opened.

"And hangers-on," added Vitala, as two dogs trotted into the room ahead of her and Lucien. One was the black-and-white Patricus, the other the gold-and-white granddam Flavia. Tottering at Vitala's side was Imperial Prince Jamien, Lucien and Vitala's three-year-old son and heir to the Kjallan throne.

Celeste's eyes went to Vitala's belly, searching for a bulge. It wasn't there—too early yet. But it would be there soon. She was three months into her second pregnancy. "Sit down. Make yourselves comfortable. How was your trip? Are you rested?"

Vitala plopped onto a sofa, and Lucien sat beside her, slipping an arm around her. "The trip was, shall we say, interesting. And I'm rested enough, even if some people"— she glared at Lucien—"might have woken me up a little early this morning."

Lucien grinned. "Some people were eager to hear details about your trip."

"They were eager for something," said Vitala.

Flavia curled into a ball at Vitala's feet while the younger Patricus trotted about the room, sniffing everything. Jamien wandered off in search of shiny things to destroy, which made Celeste's stomach tighten, but Lucien reached forward and scooped him up—obviously a well-practiced motion—and settled him on his lap.

"Were you able to install your new agents?" asked Celeste.

Vitala nodded. "They're in place."

One of the empress's projects over the past five years had been the establishment of the Order of the Sage, a covert organization whose mission was to collect information and promote peace within the empire. Before becoming empress, Vitala had been an assassin working for the Obsidian Circle, which at the time had been an underground resistance group, so she knew about secret societies and how they operated. When she'd come to Kjall, she'd discovered the Kjallan intelligence infrastructure was shockingly primitive, and she was taking steps to correct that.

Little Jamien pointed at Flavia. "Horsey."

"Not a horsey," said Vitala. "That's a doggy."

"I ride the horsey," announced Jamien, trying to squirm out of Lucien's lap.

"She's not a horsey, and you cannot sit on her." Lucien turned to Vitala. "He's been doing this lately—climbing on the dogs. I'll send for his nurse so we can speak without distraction." He carried a fussing Jamien to the door, conferred with the Legaciatti outside, and returned to his place beside the empress. "I believe you had something to tell Celeste?"

"Indeed." Vitala turned to Celeste. "You heard that Prince Rayn requested a sightseeing trip to Riorca?"

"Yes, I'm to go along. We're taking a ship to Denmor."

"Well, I've a message I need delivered to my agents in Denmor. Recruiting for the Order of the Sage has been slow, and I haven't many couriers yet. But I don't trust the signal network. You've proven amply that our ciphers can be broken."

"Easily," said Celeste.

"I was thinking since you're going there, you could be my courier."

"I'd be happy to."

"Excellent," said Vitala. "One of my agents in Denmor will approach you. He or she will use the code phrase *lemons in winter*. When you hear that phrase, I want you to give him two names: Aulus Helividius and Gaius Cinna."

She blinked. "Can I write them down?"

"Absolutely not. You must memorize them."

"All right." *Aulus Helividius and Gaius Cinna. Aulus Helividius and Gaius Cinna.*

"Got it? Repeat the code phrase to me, and the names."

"Lemons in winter. Aulus Helividius and Gaius Cinna."

Vitala smiled. "You're all set."

Celeste loved being part of Lucien and Vitala's inner circle and knowing things that no one else did. Vitala was one of two people in the world she trusted absolutely. When she was thirteen years old, there had been a palace coup. A distant relative named Cassian had deposed Lucien, seized power, and forcibly married Celeste—a political marriage only, never consummated, thank the gods—to legitimize his claim to the throne. Vitala had been one of a team of Obsidian Circle agents who had broken into Cassian's tent, assassinated him, and rescued her.

Vitala's mouth twisted a little. "Lucien told me you heard about Prince Rayn's history."

"You knew about it too?" That stung. She'd thought Vitala would be on her side in wanting her to know as much as possible about her husband-to-be.

"I did, and I told Lucien he was making a mistake in keeping it from you."

"Rayn doesn't seem to trust us," said Celeste.

Vitala straightened her skirts, protectively cupping her not yet bulging belly. "I actually see that as a point in his favor. He shouldn't trust us until he gets to know us a bit better. With this sea voyage, we've bought a little time. You'll bring him around. How could he resist a woman as lovely as you?"

Celeste looked down at the floor. She wasn't *that* lovely. No man had ever loved her for anything more than her wealth and her position as the emperor's sister. She'd had only one romantic relationship so far, not counting Cassian, and it hadn't turned out well. She wasn't skilled at enticing men or winning their trust. Her talents were in mathematics and linguistics, and they wouldn't do her much good here.

"Don't think of this as needing to charm Prince Rayn and win him to our side," said Vitala. "Instead, think of it as an intelligence mission. You're good at research and solving problems. So solve the problem of Prince Rayn. Find out what motivates him so that when you come back, we can bring him into the fold."

That sounded a little less intimidating. "I'll do it."

5

Celeste gazed out the open window, swaying in her shipboard cot and sipping her morning chocolate. Below, the ocean undulated, flecked with foam. On the distant horizon, dark shapes swam in the haze: the cliffs and lowlands of the Kjallan shore, which the *Goshawk* was skirting on its northward journey to Riorca. The captain had granted his commodious quarters to herself and Rayn, although they were not rooming together. A partition had been constructed between the two halves, and they used different doors to enter and exit. She liked that Rayn was sleeping so near, near enough that she might hear him breathing, and sometimes she sat quietly and listened, hoping she might hear him moving about. But the partition was thick and the ship noisy, with the wind groaning in the sails and the sailors calling as they went about their work.

Atella sat cross-legged on the cot across from her, crocheting a tablecloth. The cots were clever contraptions, not mounted upon the floor, but hanging on ropes from the ceiling, so that when the ship heeled over, causing the floor to slant, furniture didn't slide across the room and nobody fell out of bed.

Celeste returned to her treatise in hopes of losing herself in a world of mathematics, where everything was systematic and logical. This wasn't the problem she was supposed to be solving; she was supposed to be solving the problem of Prince Rayn and his reluctance to make any kind of alliance with her family. But the prince was ignoring her. From the beginning of the voyage, he'd claimed seasickness, a plausible assertion except that Celeste saw and heard no signs of illness. On two occasions she'd knocked at his cabin door and been turned away. She'd approached him on the quarterdeck several times, only to watch him retreat to his cabin. And when the captain had invited both of them to dinner, Celeste had attended but Rayn had declined.

Nearby, a door squeaked open. Was Rayn going out on the quarterdeck? She met Atella's eyes and they froze, trying to silence their cots, which creaked on the ropes. Voices outside the cabin—Magister Lornis, and, yes, Rayn as well.

Atella set her crocheting aside. "Are we going out?"

"In a minute," Celeste whispered. "I don't want to look too obvious."

She reread the page she'd just written. Then she set aside the treatise, put down her chocolate, and hopped out of her cot. She left the cabin, flanked by Atella, and emerged onto the quarterdeck. Pale midmorning sunshine spilled over her. The ship was driving upwind and heeling over, giving the deck a slight slope, but Celeste was accustomed now to maneuvering on a surface that didn't stay horizontal. Where was Rayn?

There, on the opposite side of the ship. He stood at the rail, looking out at the open ocean with Magister Lornis at his side. Loose hairs from his braid danced in the wind.

Atella sighed. "That is one handsome man."

"One aggravating man," said Celeste. But Atella was right. Rayn had that effect on women. He wasn't vain. She never saw him striking poses or showing off; if anything, he seemed oblivious to his good looks, though he had to be aware of how women responded to him. If she were an artist, she would paint him where he stood, pensive and looking out over the water.

"You're so lucky," breathed Atella.

"Not really," said Celeste. "He's not interested in the marriage."

"He'll change his mind."

Celeste doubted it. But she'd promised to do her best for Lucien and Vitala. As she braced herself to step forward and open a conversation with the prince, somebody else walked up to him. It was a woman, young and blond and pretty.

"Who is that?" she whispered to Atella.

"I've no idea."

Celeste watched as the woman spoke. Rayn's body language was not open to her; he folded his arms and took a step back when she intruded into his personal space. His movements were stiff and unwelcoming, which Celeste found perversely satisfying—at least she wasn't the only woman having trouble approaching this man. But who was this woman? All the sailors on the *Goshawk* were men. She looked Inyan rather than Kjallan. Probably she was part of Rayn's entourage, but then why did he seem not to want her around?

Her heart thudded in her chest. Was this the servant woman he'd impregnated?

There were indications of an intimacy that went beyond the relationship a prince would normally have with a servant. The woman's manner was soft and enticing; she stood closer than she ought. Even Rayn, though he clearly didn't want her around, was not behaving in a businesslike manner. He looked more like a man rebuffing an unwanted advance.

Curious.

The blond woman walked away and took the ladder that led belowdecks.

Now it was Celeste's turn. She headed for the rail. Rayn glanced over and saw her coming. After a word with Lornis, he left the rail with his adviser in tow and took a wide circle around the ship. Celeste felt hot all over, flushed with humiliation. The other woman was worthy of a few words of conversation, but apparently Celeste wasn't. She considered following him, but decided she'd look ridiculous. Instead, she went to the rail where he'd been. Rayn and Lornis returned to their cabin. Gods curse them. "I can't believe this," she said through gritted teeth.

"He'll come around," said Atella. "He has to."

He wasn't going to come around; she could see that. But even if he didn't like her, he could show her a little respect. And she was going to tell him so. "I'm going to his cabin."

She marched across the deck to Rayn's side of the captain's quarters, knocked, and spoke loud enough to be heard through the door. "I wish to speak to Prince Rayn."

"He's indisposed," someone called from inside.

"He was fine just moments ago," replied Celeste.

No response.

"Rayn!" She banged on the door again. "You're avoiding me, and I feel I should know why."

The door opened. Celeste shivered with anticipation, nervous at the possibility of actually speaking with the prince, but the man who stepped through it—and closed the door behind him—was Magister Lornis.

"Your Imperial Highness, I'm terribly sorry," he said. "Prince Rayn is seasick. He went out on the quarterdeck in the hopes that it would help his condition, but unfortunately it did not."

"Seasick," Celeste repeated doubtfully.

Magister Lornis bit his lip. "It's been a problem this trip. He offers his most sincere apologies."

If Rayn was seasick, she had the pox. She pushed her way past Lornis. "I don't care if he's sick. I must talk to him."

"Your Imperial Highness!" Lornis protested. He reached out as if to grab her arm, but pulled back. One did not manhandle the Imperial Princess of Kjall.

Celeste yanked the door open and stormed into Rayn's cabin. The prince was sitting on his cot, eyes wide at the unexpected intrusion, and obviously not sick since he was drinking from a steaming mug. "I must speak with you," she said.

Rayn eyed her. "Speak, then."

Lornis slipped into the cabin beside her, spreading his arms in a gesture of helplessness.

Celeste took a deep breath. "I understand this marriage proposal came as a shock. And I'm aware that you have a previous relationship with another woman, who might be on this ship with us."

Rayn swallowed and lowered his mug.

"This isn't easy for me either," said Celeste. "I wish to be perfectly frank. We are both from royal families. You understand, as I do, the privileges and the costs of rank. Neither of us will marry for love."

"Your Imperial Highness—" began Rayn.

"Allow me to finish." Without being invited, she took a seat on a nearby chair. "I don't think I need to point out to you the political advantages of an alliance with

Kjall. You already know them. But perhaps you hesitate because you are uncertain about me personally." She swallowed. "I'm aware that I might not be as enticing as some women. But I'm sensible, and I know what to expect from this type of marriage, and what not to expect. I have a mathematical treatise I'm working on, and will probably write another when it's finished. I don't ask for much. Only a quiet space where I can continue my work."

Rayn's forehead wrinkled. "You just want to work on your treatise?"

"I'll give you heirs, of course. I realize that will involve some . . . physical activities." Nervous, she licked her lips. In truth, she was looking forward to the physical activities, even if he didn't like her much.

"That's all you want? Sex and time to work on your treatise?"

Her cheeks warmed. "Yes."

"Are you suggesting that I take lovers on the side? Because that doesn't sound like much of a marriage to me."

"Well . . . that would not be my preference," she admitted.

"No wife of mine will take lovers on the side," said Rayn.

"I cannot see myself being so tempted," said Celeste. "Think it over. And stop avoiding me; I don't have the pox."

"I apologize," said Rayn.

Celeste's hands shook. She rose to her feet. "Perhaps we can talk more later, once you've had a chance to mull this over."

"We'll talk more later, yes," said Rayn.

Celeste turned and headed for the door.

"Princess," called Rayn.

She turned.

"Pardon me for saying so, but I believe you do yourself a disservice," said Rayn. "You should expect more from your marriage partner."

"What I want and what I can reasonably expect are two different things." She left his cabin, standing as straight and proud as she could manage, hoping he wouldn't notice her trembling.

6

Rayn stood on the quarterdeck, enjoying a beautiful, star-studded evening. He couldn't stop thinking about the Kjallan princess and the conversation they'd had in his cabin. Given whose daughter she was and how she'd been raised, he'd expected arrogance. Demands. His country was no match for Kjall militarily; if the Kjallans chose to make an issue of it, they could force this "alliance" on him.

But Celeste was not what he'd expected. He sensed that she didn't think much of herself or her merits as a marriage partner. This was the daughter of mass murderer Florian?

For now, she was leaving him alone, no doubt giving him the space she'd promised so that he could think about what she'd proposed. He had promised they would talk again. He wasn't ready to make a decision on the marriage—he couldn't imagine allying himself to Florian's family—but he was curious about her and eager to learn more.

Zoe, sadly, had not given up. She'd finagled her way onto the ship—she always managed to do that; for a woman who was inept at many things, she was shockingly competent at sticking close to him. He kept telling her off, sending her away. And she kept coming back.

Lornis slipped to his side, wearing his customary disapproving glare.

"What have I done this time?" said Rayn.

"You said you'd talk to the princess," said Lornis.

"I intend to."

Lornis's brows rose. "Have you made a decision?"

"About marriage?" Rayn laughed.

"There's nothing funny about this," said Lornis. "This marriage would help you politically. And you heard what she said—she's not asking much of you."

"She should ask for more." He'd heard the pain in her voice as she'd proposed a politically expedient marriage of birthing heirs and writing treatises. Who had hurt her before, to make her say such things? Why was she so eager to throw herself into a loveless marriage?

He'd kept a surreptitious eye on her since the moment she'd boarded the ship, and he knew that every evening she climbed the ratlines to the platform halfway up the mainmast that the sailors called the top. There she sat for hours, alone.

"Talk to her," said Lornis.

Rayn strode casually to the rear of the ship where he could view the platform without it being obvious he was doing so. Lornis followed. A vigorous breeze was whisking the ship northward, allowing it to carry light sail. Above him, the stars were spectacular. He could make out several constellations: the Pike, the Hammer, the Fortress. He turned to the mainmast. What was so fascinating that called her up there every evening? "Very well. I'll do that now."

"Excellent," said Lornis.

Rayn crossed the deck and approached Celeste's bodyguard, who stood at the base of the mast. "I wish to speak to Celeste." He eyed the pistol holstered at her belt. "May I climb up?"

"Go on." The bodyguard smiled. "She'll be glad to see you."

Rayn swung into the shrouds and hauled himself up the ratlines. Beneath the platform was a square hole next to the mast. He seized the edges of the hole and hoisted himself through.

Celeste was crouched on the platform, looking up at the stars through a telescope. The shiny brass instrument was about the length of his arm. She hadn't noticed him yet, and he hesitated a moment, just watching her. She was so much like her brother Lucien. They had the same black hair, fine build, and aristocratic features. But there was something about her—a wistfulness, a longing. A sadness.

"Your Imperial Highness," he said softly.

She started, jerking her head up and almost dropping the telescope.

He flung a hand out to steady the instrument. "Didn't mean to surprise you."

Her eyes softened as she recognized him. Then she turned wary. "This is where you've chosen to speak with me?"

"I'm curious what a Kjallan princess does up here in the tops every evening." He gestured to the instrument. "You look at the stars?"

"Sort of—well—" she stammered. "There's a better telescope at the palace, but the night sky is more visible here."

"Can I see what you were looking at?"

"It's a comet. You can look, but you might have a hard time getting the position right."

"A comet?" He looked up at the sky. "I don't see one."

"Very faint. Can't be seen without this." She handed him the telescope.

He took the eyepiece and turned the instrument to the sky, searching for the comet without success. "What do your scholars say about comets? Why do they have tails when nothing else in the sky does?"

"They're said to be the pyrotechnic signals of the gods," said Celeste. "But that doesn't make sense considering how long they remain in the sky. One of our scholars believes they're entities that trap light from the sun and spill it out, forming the tail. Another believes they're not solid at all, but made of some material denser than ether, which forms a tail. And still another believes they are small planets venting steam as they travel."

Rayn blinked. He'd never heard any of those ideas, except the signals-of-the-gods one. "Which do you think is right?"

She shook her head. "The scholars are only speculating. We know nothing. Perhaps one day a comet will pass nearer to us and we can learn more. In the meantime, there are other things to study. We've got a Major Reconciliation coming up in less than a week—did you know?"

"I did not." He lowered the telescope and looked up at the moons. It amazed him that astronomers could figure out when a Reconciliation, minor or major, was about to happen, because there was nothing in the current position of the three moons that suggested to him they would all be rising full at sunset some nights hence.

"The sailors are planning a feast," said Celeste.

This was what Rayn got for not talking to anybody. He was probably the last person on the ship to know. "When you look through this"—he indicated the telescope—"at one of the moons, do you see any sign of the god?"

Celeste shook her head. "Not at all. I've never met an astronomer who believed the moons were the gods incarnate."

"But they're said to be."

"By some," said Celeste. "But if you think it through, it doesn't make sense. In our stories, the gods are always in human form, yet the moons are spheres. No, I think the moons are symbols only, placed there by the gods as reminders of their presence."

"What do you think of the notion that the gods live on the moons? Or in them?"

She shrugged. "I can't disprove it, but the moons look barren. Why would the gods want to live there? I think they live in the spirit world. Can I show you something that will boggle your mind?"

"Certainly," said Rayn.

"You may not like it," said Celeste. She pointed at a spot in the night sky. "Aim the telescope there. See the extra-bright star just to the right of the Pike's base? That's the planet Curio."

He aimed the telescope at Curio. It didn't look like much. Just a bigger point of light.

"Do you see the four little specks around it?" asked Celeste.

Now that she pointed it out, he did. They were like dust motes. "Yes."

"Those are moons," said Celeste.

Rayn set down the telescope. "They can't be. There are *four*."

"I told you it would boggle your mind," said Celeste. "What does it mean? Is there a fourth god? Why do we have three and Curio has four?"

Rayn's mind struggled with this new information. It raised all kinds of questions about the gods and the spirit world and what Curio truly was. And all he'd seen were some tiny specks of light through a telescope. "I didn't realize you were an astronomer."

Celeste took the telescope back and set it in her lap. "My interest is in mathematics. But the disciplines are closely related."

"What do you do in the Mathematical Brotherhood? Solve math problems in your head?"

"No."

"Seventy-nine times forty-five. Can you do that in your head?"

She shook her head. "I don't do parlor tricks. Math calculation is basics. It's like learning the letters of the alphabet and the sounds they make. As you progress, you can turn those sounds into complete words, and then you become fluent and you don't even think about the letter sounds anymore. They're background noise."

Rayn was silent. He'd underestimated this woman. He'd imagined she'd had some sort of mathematical tic, a habit of working math problems in her head or reciting the digits of pi. But Celeste was a serious thinker. "Give me an example of what you do."

Her brows furrowed. "Uh—how much background in mathematics do you have?"

"It's not my strong subject."

"My treatise would probably not interest you," said Celeste. "So here's something else. Are you familiar with cicadas?"

"The insects?"

"Yes. There are two species living in Kjall. One emerges from the ground every thirteen years, the other every seventeen. Naturalists report that in other nations, there are other species of cicada, one of which emerges every eleven years, and the others, thirteen and seventeen years like our local species. What do you observe about those numbers?"

He felt a little at sea. "Those are long time periods."

"I mean the numbers themselves," said Celeste. "Eleven, thirteen, seventeen. What's similar about them?"

"They're odd."

"They're *prime*," said Celeste. "Do you notice that fifteen is not among them?"

"Remind me what a prime number is again."

"A number divisible only by itself and one. These numbers are prime: two, three, five, seven, eleven, thirteen, seventeen, nineteen —"

"Okay, so cicadas have life cycles associated with prime numbers. What's the significance?"

"We don't know." Celeste shrugged. "This is just a minor problem of the sort we deal with. It's a curiosity, an odd little puzzle we'd like to work out. I know you must think it strange, my interest in such things. Most people do. But mathematics is the language of the universe." She turned her head, taking in the heavens above and the ocean below. "The planets and moons move according to strict mathematical formulas. The ocean waves below follow a pattern described by mathematics. Are you familiar with the golden mean? It's a ratio between quantities that appears over and over again in nature: in the stems and veins of plants, the geometry of crystals, the construction of spirals. It's the gods' *signature*, something they wrote into creation over and over again."

Rayn regarded her in reverent silence. Her eyes were alight with passion and yearning. He'd never known a woman so deeply engaged in the world around her. Like so many of the mountains in his homeland, Celeste had fire inside.

She lowered her head, tucking a lock of stray hair behind her ear. "You probably find all this silly."

"Not at all," said Rayn. "I think if someone had described mathematics to me that way when I was a student, I'd have paid more attention. Do you know, I've always felt that Inya's volcanoes should be studied. More so than they are."

"So that you could predict when they erupt?"

"Exactly," said Rayn. "It would save lives. And if we could predict tremors as well, so much the better. If I weren't destined for other things, that's what I'd do. Learn the workings of the volcanoes."

"That's a wonderful area of study. I'd like to know that too."

Gods, she was beautiful, especially when her eyes lit up and she was excited about something. Soldier's Hell, he wasn't supposed to like this woman. He couldn't have a casual dalliance with a Kjallan princess. If he wanted her, he'd have to sign the papers and ally himself with warmongering mass murderers.

A breeze whipped the edges of Celeste's syrtos, and she wrapped her arms around herself.

"Are you cold?" asked Rayn.

She nodded. "A little."

He brightened. "I can warm you."

She raised a suspicious eyebrow.

"Not like you're thinking. With magic. May I demonstrate?" He reached for her hand.

After a moment's hesitation, she placed her hand in his.

Her flesh was soft, delicate, and chilled. He called to his magic, kindling the fire that simmered within him. He brought it flaring to life and channeled its heat through his own body, up his arm and through his fingers, into her hand. His magic was versatile; he could have warmed her from a distance without touching her. But it was easier to channel it through touch. It took less out of him, and in this case was more enjoyable.

Her hand warmed rapidly. She drew in a breath, then offered him her other hand. He warmed it too.

"That feels amazing," said Celeste, leaning toward him.

Rayn took her words as permission and worked his way up, using his touch to send fire into her wrists and arms. When he reached her shoulders, he found himself contorting his body. "Can you sit closer?"

"Where?"

"Here." Rayn spread his legs and pulled her into the space between them, placing her back against his chest. She shivered in his arms, and probably not from the cold. He laid his hands on her, warming her shoulders, her neck, her back. She slumped boneless against him, tilting her head onto his shoulder. He avoided her breasts but placed his hands on her stomach and then her legs, spreading fire from his touch.

Finally she was warm all over, a snug little body cocooned in his arms. And he was ridiculously hard. Not a thing he could do about it—he didn't even dare kiss her, though he suspected she would welcome it. "I think I'd better go now," he said.

"Must you?" Her head sagged against him.

"If I stay, I'll do things I shouldn't."

"I don't mind."

He *really* needed to go. "Good night," he said, and scrambled off the platform.

7

Rayn avoided her the next day, and the next. She'd spooked him with that last comment, about not minding if he did things he shouldn't. Was she luring him, intending to entrap him in a marriage? Or expressing a sincere physical desire? He stayed away, and to his relief she did not pursue him. Either she was a patient temptress, or she genuinely respected his space.

After last night, he had a hard time seeing her as a temptress. Her body lured him, yes, but not because of anything she did. It just happened, because she was beautiful and smart and passionate, and she intrigued him.

On the third day, he was beginning to miss her. She hadn't been on deck all morning. He kept seeing her dog, a big, fluffy black-and-white creature who ran about the deck, sniffing everywhere. He approached the dog, which was now intently sniffing the back deck where, in the wee hours of the morning, the sailors had landed a fish.

The dog ran to him as he approached and pressed against his leg.

Rayn switched his coffee to his other hand and stroked the dog's head and ears. "You're an affectionate fellow." He couldn't remember the dog's name. Probably he'd never learned it. "I don't suppose you know where your mistress is."

The dog grinned at him, opening his mouth and panting.

"Do you know where Celeste is?" asked Rayn. "Where's Celeste?"

To his astonishment, the dog took off running. At first he just stood and watched him go—surely the creature had been distracted by something. But the dog stopped at one of the ladders leading down to the lower decks and barked. He looked back at him and barked again.

Was the dog leading him to Celeste? Rayn walked to the ladder and watched as the dog leapt straight down into the hold. Rayn wasn't keen on six-foot drops, so he went down the ladder, whereupon the dog took off running again.

The dog led him to the cargo hold, where Celeste leaned on a rail, sipping something from a mug and feeding hay, one handful at a time, to a pair of live steers. Rayn rubbed the dog's head and stepped alongside Celeste. He took a handful of hay and offered it to the steer with the white blaze. "Your dog led me here."

"Did you, Patricus?" Celeste looked down at the animal. "It's a game we play with him. Hide-and-seek. What's that you're drinking? It has a heavenly smell."

"Coffee. Would you like to try?"

"Is it like chocolate?"

He gathered that was what she was drinking. It looked the right color. "It's different. Taste, if you like." He offered her the mug.

She sipped it and made a face. "Ugh. It doesn't taste at all like it smells."

"It does when you get used to it. You prefer chocolate?"

She raised her mug. "Every morning. My little habit."

He found he enjoyed knowing that about her.

"Tell me something of yourself," added Celeste. "Do you have family? I know about your father, and I'm sorry he's ill. But what about your mother? Any brothers or sisters?"

"No brothers," said Rayn, "which is good for the succession. I have two sisters. The eldest is married and living on Mosar."

"Does your mother still live?"

After a brief pause, he said, "Yes."

"Why the hesitation?"

"She's . . ." He grimaced. This was his least favorite subject. "She hasn't handled Father's illness very well. She won't stay with him or try to help him. Instead, she takes to her bed and doesn't emerge for days."

"I'm sorry to hear that."

"Tell me about yourself," said Rayn. "Your brother is your guardian. Does that mean your parents are gone?"

"My mother passed away when I was four. My father, the old emperor Florian, was deposed by King Jan-Torres of Mosar and lives in protective custody on that island."

He met her eyes. "And how do you feel about that?"

She shrugged. "He's where he belongs."

"Why do you say that?"

"He was a bad emperor."

"He is responsible for countless deaths on Mosar," said Rayn.

"Indeed," said Celeste. "None of us are proud of that."

"Have you seen him since he was imprisoned?"

"No."

"Do you miss him?"

Celeste paused to think. "I miss the *idea* of him. But even leaving the invasion of Mosar aside, Florian wasn't a good man. He terrorized Lucien and Rhianne. Less so me, because I was young and pliable, and I had little cause to displease him. Still, he frightened me. I loved him, but I love my brother so much more. Lucien is intimidating, but I'm not scared of him. There's a difference."

"I didn't realize you were so fond of your brother."

"When Lucien became my guardian, my world opened up in every possible way. Florian used to keep me confined, and I was educated in only a few subjects he deemed suitable. But Lucien gave me the run of the palace. He had me educated in the way a young prince would be: in languages and history, mathematics and science, strategy and war. And the empress taught me swordplay. Not that I'm terribly good at it."

"You approve of the way Lucien rules?"

"Lucien is the best of men, and the best of emperors. I would do anything for him."

Rayn frowned. "Whether he's the best of men or not, I cannot approve of one man having absolute power over a nation."

"His power isn't absolute," said Celeste. "There are governors for each province."

"Even so. The Inyan archipelago is collectively about the size of one of your provinces, yet we divide governmental power."

"You mean between the king and the Land Council?"

"Precisely," said Rayn. "Our leaders serve at the will of the people."

"It seems to me you fight a lot with the Land Council."

"Our disagreements are aggravating but healthy," said Rayn. "You believe Emperor Lucien is a good ruler. And if that's true, Kjall is lucky. But what will happen when Lucien dies and the next man inherits? What if he's another Florian?"

Celeste hesitated before speaking. "I don't think the next man will be another Florian. Lucien's heir is his son, Jamien, and I'm sure Lucien and Vitala will raise him well."

"But you can't be sure." Rayn shook his head. "I don't think any country's welfare should depend on the luck of the draw."

"I see your point," she said. "But it's not likely to change."

Rayn was silent. He liked this woman, liked her a lot, but they had some serious political differences. He made his excuses and left.

The next day was the Major Reconciliation. The sailors slaughtered one of the steers that morning in preparation, and by midafternoon the smell of its roasting meat permeated the ship. Celeste had spent most of her life in the Imperial Palace, where her meals were prepared in a distant kitchen and brought to her. She had little experience with cooking aromas and the delightful slow torture of anticipating one's meal hours in advance of its readiness.

As the sun dropped low over the ocean, the festivities began. Corks were pulled, and wine poured into glasses. The feasters availed themselves of roast beef, rice salad, fried blackfish with greens, cheese breads, sliced oranges, and onion pie. As the sky darkened, every eye turned eastward to the Kjallan coast on the distant horizon. A red sheen appeared over the distant hills, which resolved into the Soldier, the largest of the moons. Normally orange in color, it often appeared red when it rose full on the horizon. When it was halfway up, the Sage and the Vagabond ascended. The Sage was pale yellow instead of its usual white, and the Vagabond a cobalt blue that almost blended into the night sky. The moons sat on the horizon, one next to the other, in a display of divine harmony.

Minor Reconciliations, when two of the moons rose full at the same time, happened frequently enough to pass without notice, but Major Reconciliations of all three moons were rare. As the moons climbed higher in the sky, a group of musicians struck up a tune, and the ship's pyrotechnic signaler lit up the sky with streamers and bursts of color.

Rayn caught Celeste's eye in silent invitation. She took her plate and sat beside him, directly on the deck since there were no chairs. While they ate and drank their wine, the sailors began a lively dance. They stamped the deck as they moved left and right, then spun in unison and began anew. As they danced, they sang:

> *There was a ship came home again*
> *Oh-o-o! Roll and go!*
> *There was a ship came home again.*
> *Toban's on the topsail yard!*

After she'd watched for half an hour, a pair of sailors pulled her and Rayn into the line and she danced with them—or tried. It was harder than it looked, and she'd had two glasses of wine. Sometimes she turned the wrong way, and once she bumped into Rayn, but he laughed and straightened her out. He seemed to be catching on to the rhythm faster than she was.

After two songs, she gave up and retreated to her spot on the deck. Rayn joined her, flushed with exertion, and nestled her into the crook of his shoulder. The weather was getting colder as they approached Riorca. Soon she'd need to break out some warmer clothes, but for now Rayn's body was the only heat source she needed. She let her eyes wander over the crowd—the dancers, the men filling their plates—and froze when she saw a pair of eyes watching her. They belonged to the woman with the straw-colored hair, the one who'd been talking to Rayn on the quarterdeck a couple of days ago.

A chill ran down Celeste's spine. Those eyes were not friendly.

She nudged Rayn and whispered, "Who is that woman?"

"Where?" He followed her gaze. "One of my servants. Pay her no mind."

"She doesn't like me," said Celeste.

"She's jealous," said Rayn. "But she has no cause for such feelings. Ignore her."

It seemed likely that the woman with the straw-colored hair was *the* servant woman, the mother of Rayn's illegitimate daughter. Celeste snuggled closer into Rayn's embrace and tried to think of other things.

The ship's officers were exchanging stories. One lieutenant told the tale of a band of sailors who caught a talking fish that begged to be set free. The sailors killed it and were cursed forever. The captain told a story about the cannibalistic ghosts of Dori. And the bosun spun an oft-told yarn about the Soldier, Sage, and Vagabond digging holes in a field as they searched for buried treasure.

"Are our stories known to you in Inya?" the captain asked Rayn.

"Some of them," said Rayn. "We have our own stories as well."

"Tell us one," blurted out a drunken lieutenant. Someone punched him in the arm, and he added, "If it pleases Your Highness."

Celeste shifted within his arms. "I'd love to hear an Inyan story."

Rayn shrugged. "All right. Let me think." His brow furrowed, and after a moment he began. "In days long past, when the gods lived on the islands, the Sage was walking along the beach. He came upon a man who was throwing stones into the sea. 'Good fellow,' said the Sage, 'who are you, and why do you throw stones into the sea?'

"'O Lord, my name is Drav. I have sworn vengeance upon the sea,' said the man. 'Yesterday the waves drew back so far that they bared the seafloor. My people ran out to scoop up the fish and crabs that lay helpless on the wet sand. But the treacherous sea returned in a great wave and drowned every one of them. I survived by clinging to a piece of driftwood, but what use is my life now, when everyone I loved is dead? I will destroy the sea for its crime. I will fill it up, stone by stone, until it is no more.'

"The Sage said, 'You cannot fill up the sea. There are not enough stones in the world.' Drav replied, 'So long as stones remain, I shall throw them.'

"Days later, the Sage returned and found Drav building a bonfire. 'What now?' asked the Sage. 'Have you run out of stones?'

"'There were not enough,' said Drav. 'I have decided to burn the sea. I will boil it away until it is no more.' The Sage sighed. 'You cannot burn the sea,' he said. 'The water will extinguish your fire.' The man piled more sticks on the fire and said, 'I will build the fire so hot that the sea cannot extinguish it.'

"Days later, the Sage found Drav in the highlands, where he leached the poison from wolfsbane roots. 'Have you given up on boiling away the sea?' asked the

Sage. 'Yes,' said Drav. 'My fire was not hot enough. I will poison the sea.'

" 'You cannot poison the sea,' said the Sage. 'You will only kill the fish.' 'I will make my poison stronger, until it is strong enough to poison the sea,' said Drav. 'I am worried for you,' said the Sage. 'Can you not forgive the sea for its sins?' 'I cannot,' said Drav. 'My kin are dead, and my heart has turned to stone. Rage boils within me like a great fire.'

" 'Stand, Drav,' commanded the Sage, and Drav stood. 'If your heart has turned to stone, be stone.' Drav's limbs and body turned to stone. His shape changed, and he grew and grew. Where once Drav had stood, a mountain now towered over the island. 'Let your rage boil within. Quench the sea, if you can.' Drav erupted in fury, spewing fire out his top. He flung boulders into the ocean. Poisonous gases poured forth from cracks in his rocky surface. Now centuries have passed, and Drav's rage continues to burn and sometimes to boil over. But he has yet to destroy his mortal enemy, the sea."

"Excellent!" cried the captain, and they raised their glasses in a toast. Then the lieutenant began a new story, a true one about a fleet action they'd been involved in some years ago.

Rayn did not seem much interested in this story, so Celeste took the opportunity to snuggle closer. He was big and warm, and her body fit nicely into the crook of his shoulder.

Rayn turned to her and spoke softly. "I believe you lied to me."

She bristled. "About what?"

"You said you wanted a loveless marriage."

"I didn't say I *wanted* that. I said I would accept it."

"You are not so passionless as to accept a marriage of

political convenience," said Rayn. "You want to love your husband and be loved in return."

Celeste shivered. "What do you know about what I would accept?"

"You want love," said Rayn. "In my language there's a word for people like you."

"What do you mean 'people like me'?" said Celeste.

"The word is *karamasi*."

"That's Inyan for *volcano*."

"It has another meaning," said Rayn. "*Karama* means *fire inside*. It can describe a mountain with fire inside—so, a volcano—or something else, such as a person. Add the *si* to the end and you get *karamasi: one with fire inside*."

"I have fire inside, like Drav?" She was bewildered.

"Not like Drav. His is an angry fire. Yours is quieter," said Rayn. "I see it in your love of mathematics. The way you look up at the stars. Your loyalty to your family."

"This *karamasi*," said Celeste. "Is it a good thing?"

Rayn ran his hand down her arm. "A very good thing."

She leaned against him and watched the sailors dance. Hours passed in a dizzy happiness. If Rayn's affection was feigned, she couldn't tell it from the real thing. Even if he never loved her, she could be satisfied, perhaps, with an occasional evening like this. As the hour grew late, she felt sleepy and chilled. She snuggled into Rayn's chest, and he warmed her with his fire magic, melting the tension out of tight muscles. "The other woman I see you with," said Celeste. "Do you love her?"

"No," said Rayn. "She's a palace servant."

"I think she's more than that."

A moment's hesitation. "I had a brief affair with her."

"Is she the mother of your illegitimate daughter?"

He sighed. "Yes."

"Is your daughter important to you?"

"Of course," said Rayn.

"Where is she? Did you leave her in Inya?"

"Yes."

"Why did she not come with you?"

Some of the conversations around them had ceased, and Celeste was aware that Atella and Magister Lornis were listening in, along with quite a few sailors.

"I will tell you about Zoe and my daughter," said Rayn, "but only if we go someplace more private."

"Where do you propose we go?"

"To my cabin," said Rayn. "Or yours."

"Now?"

"Yes, *karamasi*. Just to talk."

Celeste unfolded her legs and stood. She was getting tired anyway; soon enough she would have taken her leave and headed to her cabin. This was better. Rayn was finally trusting her enough to speak candidly.

Rayn rose and made his good-nights.

He took her hand, and they headed to their quarters in the back of the ship. She was happy to leave the noise of the party behind—all those boots on the deck, the music, the conversation.

As they crossed the wooden deck, someone approached them. It was the woman with the straw-colored hair.

Rayn's hand tensed inside Celeste's. "Zoe."

Zoe curtsied to Celeste. "Your Imperial Highness." Then to Rayn. "Your Highness. I need to speak to you right away. In private."

"Another time." Rayn walked around Zoe, tugging Celeste with him.

"No." Zoe hurried in front of him again. "Please—it's important."

"If you have something to say, say it," said Rayn.

Zoe hesitated, biting her lip. "It's complicated. We need to be alone."

"Tomorrow," said Rayn, shouldering his way around her.

He opened the door to his cabin and ushered Celeste through. Atella took up her position outside the door.

Inside, Celeste noticed a flash of movement. She blinked and looked around. The room was still. Perhaps she was tipsy from the wine and seeing things. Rayn closed the door behind them.

But as soon as he did, a hand clamped over her mouth, and someone seized her from behind. She tried to scream, and then to bite the hand, but her attacker held her so firmly she couldn't get her mouth open. She struggled and kicked backward at him. He dodged each blow and pulled her tight against his body. His clothes were wet.

Nearby, two more attackers had grabbed Rayn. They appeared to be a pair of the *Goshawk*'s sailors. One of them grappled with him from behind, with a hand clamped over Rayn's mouth, while the other assaulted him from the front, punching and kicking. Rayn was big, and he fought like a brindlecat in their grasp.

I want to let the woman go, she projected into the mind of the man who held her. No effect. He was probably a war mage, given how easily he'd dodged her blows.

She threw confusion spells and suggestions at the men attacking Rayn. Nothing stuck. The sailor who'd been punching Rayn pulled a knife from his belt. He raised it to strike, but then suddenly shrieked and dropped it. The hilt glowed red-hot, a shining beacon on the cabin floor. The sailor went back to bludgeoning Rayn with his fists. He slugged him again and again.

Rayn struggled in the other man's grip, twisting his body this way and that, managing to dodge some of the blows.

"Get the knife," snarled the sailor holding Rayn.

"It's on fire," gasped the other.

The one holding Rayn glanced at Celeste. "Get rid of the girl."

Adrenaline surged, and Celeste fought harder, but to no avail. The man who held her was stronger. He dragged her across the room, kicking her feet out from under her when she tried to plant them on the cabin floor. What was he going to do? He couldn't use the knife.

The cabin window loomed ahead of her. Through it she saw the sea swirling dark gray in the moonlight. The sailor who'd been slugging Rayn disengaged, ran over, and hauled the window open for his companion. Oh, gods—were they going to throw her out of the ship? She flailed desperately in her captor's arms.

As the other sailor returned to help with Rayn, the cot hanging next to him erupted into flames. The sailor jumped back with a terrified yelp. The cot's ropes parted, and it dropped to the floor. A wave of heat and sparks flew at Celeste as the flames ignited the floorboards and snaked across the room.

Celeste's captor shoved her at the open window. She caught the edges of it with her feet and braced herself.

Noise behind her—a swinging sword. Atella was in the cabin now, shouting and wreaking havoc.

Her captor gave her another desperate shove, and she resisted. Then he kicked her foot away from the edge of the window. Her other leg buckled. She fell forward sickeningly and found herself flailing in the open air, hurtling toward water.

8

Rayn had a chance now that Atella was fighting by his side, but it was hard to keep his head where it needed to be. The image of Celeste struggling and being thrown out the window had seared itself on his mind. Next to him, Atella fought two men at once, leaving him a single attacker, the man holding him from behind, who was trying without success to wrestle him to the ground. How could Celeste survive in the open ocean? Even if she could swim, the water was freezing cold.

He flung himself forward and down, tossing the attacking sailor over his head. The sailor hit the cabin floor and grunted as the impact knocked the wind out of him. He flailed, and as he tried to rise, the fire caught his ankle, and he screamed. Atella was holding her own against the other two sailors, who were obviously war mages in disguise. One of them held a sword. Rayn called fire into the hilt. The man screamed and dropped the weapon, and Atella skewered him on the end of her blade.

Celeste was going to die out there if he didn't help her.

Rayn leapt over the screaming sailor and the line of flames, ran to the window, and dove through it headfirst.

He fell two stories before plunging into the water. The

shock of the cold stole his breath. His muscles seized, and he was lost in a morass of heavy, frigid darkness. Couldn't see, couldn't swim, couldn't tell which direction was up. He called on his fire magic, not the gentle breath of warmth he'd used with Celeste, but a blistering inferno that radiated from his core like a pyrotechnic starburst. His muscles began to uncramp. His boots were weighing him down, so he kicked them off. A sheen of moonlight showed him the way to the surface. He swam for it. Bursting through, he gulped the cold night air.

Where was Celeste? With all three moons high in the sky, he had sufficient light to search for her. He glanced at the ship and swam in the direction opposite its movement. After a dozen strokes, he paused, trying to spot her in the vast, roiling surface of the ocean. The undulating waves dropped him into a trough, then raised him six feet only to drop him again. He felt tiny and insignificant. As each wave crested, giving him a momentary height advantage, he searched frantically.

"Celeste, where are you?" he cried.

"Over here!"

Her voice was weak and thready. How she was staying afloat in the frigid water without fire magic to keep her warm, he had no idea. He swam toward her voice. "Keep your head above water," he called. "When I reach you, I'll get you warm."

"I c-can't . . ."

"You can!" He sputtered as a wave swept over him. "Signal me! I can't see you over the waves."

He looked all around him. There it was—a glowing blue ball of magelight, hovering just over the waves. It was hard to see against the dark ocean and sky, but he could follow it readily enough. He swam in the direction of the magelight.

"Over here!" she called.

He saw her head poking out of the water, rising and falling with the waves. She was staying afloat reasonably well, but the cold would take her soon. He swam toward her, struggling against the waves as they washed him back. The ocean was stronger than he was; fighting it was only sapping his strength. When the waves pushed against him, he rested, yielding to their power, and when their strength dragged him toward Celeste instead of away, he swam hard, throwing all his energy into great sweeps of his arms. She was closer; he could see the fear in her eyes. He rested through another swell of the waves, and the next propelled him into her. He grabbed her. Celeste's flesh was so icy, it burned his skin, but his fire magic bled through and overcame it. "I've got you, *karamasi*."

"Gods," she said, clinging to him. "I thought I was going to die."

She still might. Both of them might. As they washed through the crest of a wave, he cast about for the ship. It was even farther away than he'd thought it would be. A knot of terror gathered in his belly. Had Atella dispatched the remaining assassins and called for help? Did anyone know they were missing? "Throw up another signal for the ship. I can't do it. I need all my concentration to keep us warm."

Celeste summoned a blue ball of magelight above their heads and sent it upward. She moved it back and forth in the sky.

"That's good," he said. "Keep it up. They may see it." He wasn't sure that they would. Blue on blue wasn't as visible as he would have liked.

Now that he'd warmed the water around them, he released Celeste from the body hug and, treading, grasped her hand. His muscles were burning from his frantic swim. To rest them, he thrust himself onto his back to float.

Celeste kept signaling, but the ship dwindled until it disappeared into the darkness.

"They don't see us," said Rayn. "Save your strength."

Land lay somewhere to the east. He could find it, orienting by the stars. But how far away was it? Was it within swimming distance? Maybe they should wait here in the water. Even if Celeste's bodyguard had been killed, Magister Lornis still lived. He'd look for Rayn, and when he couldn't find him, he'd probably call for a search of the ship. Or would the assassins kill him too? The sailors ought to figure out something was wrong and turn the ship around—if nothing else, the fire he'd lit in the cabin would draw them. But ships the size of the *Goshawk* were ponderous to turn.

"What are we going to do?" said Celeste.

"I think we're too far from shore to swim for it," said Rayn. "So we tread and hope the ship comes back for us. Float on your back if you get tired. Are you still wearing shoes?"

"No, I kicked them off."

"Good."

Celeste's face was taut with fear, but she wasn't panicking. He appreciated that about her. Still holding his hand, she flung herself onto her back with a splash, floating neatly, her breasts poking out of the water.

Rayn coughed as a wave splashed over him. "Keep hold of my hand so we stay together." He closed his eyes, trying to rest.

He wasn't sure how much time had passed when Celeste nudged him. "I see the ship."

He splashed upright, but his heart sank when he saw it wasn't close. It was sailing southward, so it had indeed turned around, but it was far to the west of them. The sailors didn't know their exact location.

"Help!" cried Celeste. "We're over here!"

"They can't hear at this distance," said Rayn. "Signal."

Celeste signaled them with blue magelight. She tried again and again, but the ship did not alter course. Finally it disappeared once more into the darkness. Rayn wondered what it was going to feel like when he finally became exhausted and drowned.

Celeste couldn't rest, not with the never-ending motion of the waves and the need to constantly adjust her position. When one set of muscles began to ache, she shifted to transfer the work to another set, but she couldn't keep this up indefinitely. If the ship didn't return soon, her strength would fail.

At least she wasn't cold. She had Rayn to thank for that.

Rayn tapped her palm. "Celeste?"

"Yes?"

"Straighten up—slowly—and come closer. There's a shark looking us over."

Her muscles burned as she stopped floating and began to tread. "How big a shark?"

"I can only see the fin. Not *too* big, I think. It may just be curious—I'm hoping it'll leave us alone."

A shark was exactly what she wanted. She searched the surrounding waters, hoping it was enormous. There! A medium-sized fin. Probably good enough. Sharks were fishes. Simple minds, easy to control. "Rayn, I'm going to take us to shore. I think it's safer than waiting for the ship." She projected her suggestion to the animal: *I want to stop swimming and let these people grab onto me.*

The fin kept moving. She wasn't sure why.

She tried something else: *I want to swim very slowly and let these people grab onto me.*

The fin's movement slowed.

"Quick," she said to Rayn, "swim to the shark."

"What? Why?"

"I'm a mind mage. I can control it—it won't hurt us. Grab hold of it, very tight." She swam to the shark and seized it around fin and body. She'd never touched a shark before. She'd expected sliminess, but the animal's skin was rough like sandpaper. When she moved her hand in the direction of the shark's tail, her hand passed smoothly over the bumps, but when she moved her hand in the opposite direction, the bumps caught against her hand.

"You can't be serious!" cried the prince.

"I'm quite serious. I've got him, and he isn't hurting me. This shark can swim us to safety."

Prince Rayn swam to the opposite side of the shark and wrapped his arms around it.

Celeste sent another suggestion: *I want to swim to shore, fast.*

The shark took off like a bullet, dragging them through the water.

Rayn stumbled onto the sand, exhausted, pushing an even more defeated Celeste in front of him. This was a disaster, every bit of it. They'd reached land; he no longer had to worry about drowning. But the ship was gone, and they were stranded gods knew where, possibly many miles from civilization. Staggering, he tripped over a piece of driftwood. "Let's stop here. Sustaining fire magic that long drains me. I've got to sleep."

Celeste trudged onward, her clothes sodden, her shoulders drooping. "We can't stop yet. The tide line."

He blinked, bleary-eyed, at where she pointed. She

was right. High tide would flood them out. He picked up the piece of driftwood beneath his feet and lurched forward. "Grab some wood. We'll need a fire."

When they'd reached a suitable spot beyond the tide line, he dropped their driftwood into a pile and went to fetch more. She added hers, and in a short while they had enough for a small fire.

He eyed her bedraggled dress and began to strip off his clothes. "Get undressed."

She raised a protective hand to her chest.

"I'm not taking advantage. Your clothes are wet. You need them off so you can warm up without my magic, because I'm going to be asleep in a minute."

She blushed, though her lips were nearly blue from the cold. "Turn around."

Ridiculous. As if he wasn't going to see her one way or another. Even so, he turned his back on her. He set the driftwood alight with a last gasp of his magic. Then he stripped off his clothes and laid them on the sand to dry.

"I'm ready now," said Celeste. "Don't look."

How could he not look? They would be sleeping together. "Just come here. I'm falling over from exhaustion, and right now I couldn't care less what you look like. Political marriage, remember?"

Tentatively, she approached. He bade her lie as close to the fire as she safely could, and settled himself behind her, spooning her so that he blanketed her back with the warmth of his own body. He wrapped his arms around her, avoiding her breasts. He intended nothing untoward. He just wanted them to survive the night.

Within moments, he dropped into unconsciousness.

9

When Celeste woke, she was aware of a couple of things in quick succession. First, she was lying naked in the arms of an equally naked Prince Rayn. And second, he was no longer in the flaccid state he'd been in the night before. She couldn't see him now, since she was facing away from him, but she felt him, huge and hard against her bottom.

He had exactly the body she'd imagined: sturdy and muscled, powerful from head to toe. Now those strong arms hugged her close, one of them snaking under, half-burrowed in the sand, the other encircling her waist from above. A breeze feathered the smattering of blond hairs on his forearm. She wanted to touch him, run her hands over the fascinating contradiction that was the male body—*his* body—all softness and hardness, vulnerability and strength. But it wouldn't be fair to wake him. The man had found her in the ocean, warmed the water, and saved her life. He'd earned his rest. Besides, if he woke up, he'd see her own naked body.

The fire had died down. She was chilly where her skin was exposed to the air, which made her anxious. She hated being cold. But it wasn't so bad that she couldn't bear it. And Rayn might warm her when he woke, or if his magic needed more rest, they could build up the fire. For now, she shivered and waited.

Rayn shifted. Not from waking, she thought—he seemed to be making himself more comfortable. Muscles flexed as he rolled in their nest of sand. He lifted his arm and dropped it again, placing his hand on her breast.

Celeste froze, trying to decide if it bothered her to have his hand there. She decided it didn't bother her; in fact she liked it. It would be even better if his hand moved, stroking her rather than just sitting in one place. Perhaps if she moved, she'd get the same effect—but that might wake him.

He shifted again. "You're cold," he murmured. She felt the rumble in his chest against her skin as he spoke.

"A little."

He raised his head. His braid was falling apart, and the stray hairs tickled her shoulder. He jerked his hand off her breast. "Sorry. Didn't mean to touch you there."

She didn't want him looking at her, but the touching was nice. "It's all right. I don't mind." She took his hand and guided it back.

He took her breast. Stroked it, kneaded it. She melted into him, loving every sensation. His hand wandered, running along her shoulder, her side, then her other breast. With a groan, he pushed her onto the sand on her back and climbed atop her. "I'll warm you, *karamasi*." He kissed her.

Not a gentle kiss. His tongue swiped at her lips— *Open,* it commanded—and she complied. The warmth of his magic flooded her, through his tongue, through his hands on her body. She moaned at the sensations and arched upward. He was fire against her skin—not the controlled flame of the hearth or campsite, but a grass fire, unpredictable and uncontained, smoldering quietly one moment and flaring to immensity the next, licking across her skin in a wild rush.

Yes, she urged him, not with her voice but with her body. *Don't look. But kiss me. Touch me.*

She no longer needed his magic. Her body was responding to him with a heat all its own, pooling deep in her core and spreading outward until it enveloped her from toes to scalp. Her skin pebbled, sensitized and craving him, answering his touch like a stroked cat.

Rayn's eyes were fogged with desire. He didn't close them when he kissed, but drank her in, watching her every reaction. She didn't love being watched, but she could tolerate the scrutiny if he kept his eyes on her face.

His tongue invaded her, and she welcomed him, wrapping her arms around him and drawing him in deeper. He shifted his hips. She spread her legs, opening, and in a single thrust, he entered her. They moved, one body fused together in the sand. She ran her fingers at liberty over every inch of him, tracing the hard muscles of his arms and shoulders, the ridges of his stomach, the smoothness of his lower back. His strokes were long and powerful. Each one sent a dizzying flare of sensation through her that left her moaning and grasping at him, feeling his heartbeat through the wall of his chest as it thumped against hers.

Her orgasm came, sweet and full-throated, and he drove her through it, accelerating his rhythm until he joined her in rapture. Afterward, Celeste lay wrapped in his weight and his warmth, delirious with pleasure, afraid to say anything lest she break the spell.

As Rayn lay on the sand with the Imperial Princess in his arms, he reflected on just how immensely he'd fouled this trip up. He'd been determined not to marry the Kjallan Imperial Princess, and what had he done? Slept with her on the beach. The Kjallan emperor was going to break out his musket if he learned of this, and by musket Rayn meant *massive and well-trained invasion force*.

He couldn't regret the act itself, which had been transcendent, a fantasy made manifest. He'd woken rested and potent, his magic returned to its full strength. After he'd nearly drowned last night, his joy at being alive was fierce, and when Celeste had turned her naked body toward him and put her breast in his hand, his desire overwhelmed him. Any remaining shreds of self-control had fled, along with his common sense.

He understood why she'd tempted him. She wanted the marriage, after all. Her brother had probably ordered her to seduce him, if that was what it took. And without really trying—just by being herself and in extraordinary circumstances neither of them could have foreseen—she'd succeeded.

He had no one to blame but himself. She hadn't forced him to put his cock in her.

Who were the men who'd attacked them in the cabin? They were war mages disguised as sailors, obviously, but beyond that, he hadn't gotten a good look at them. Had they been Kjallans?

"We'd better get moving." He extracted himself from Celeste's arms and climbed to his feet. The fire had died down. He gave the burned-out wood a kick and goaded the flames with his magic. They responded with an anemic sputtering and dropped back to a flicker.

Celeste stood and brushed the sand off her body, naked except for the riftstone on a chain around her neck. Rayn stared at her, unable to help himself. Even bedraggled, she was beautiful. Black hair spilled over her shoulders, unkempt and wild, framing full, round breasts. The shape of her—gods, he wanted to run his hands down her body and feel those curves, especially that glorious one between the waist and the hip. She was like a sea spirit come out of the ocean. His blood rushed south. Given the tiniest bit of encouragement, he would take her again.

Her eyes rose and met his. She started. "Don't look. Please." She turned around.

She was shy. Too bad. With a body like that, she ought not to be. He found his clothes on the sand and wished he'd thought to hang them on something last night. They were mostly dry, but not completely. He pulled them on, making a face as the salty grit rubbed his skin. He needed freshwater for bathing and washing his clothes. Not to mention drinking. He was dry-mouthed and becoming uncomfortably thirsty.

He heard a rustle of fabric behind him. Celeste was getting dressed too.

Where had they washed ashore? He saw no signs of civilization. The beach was gray rather than tan, its sand coarse and spattered with logs, jutting rocks, and pieces of driftwood. Beyond it the ocean was a leaden blue expanse stirred, in places, to peaks of white froth. Not a ship to be seen.

He turned. Celeste was fastening the hooks of her sadly ruined dress. Behind them was a forest, scattered and bare in patches where the sand had taken over, but thickening farther in.

"Shall we wait here?" he said. "The ship may still be looking for us."

"But will they find us?" said Celeste. "We're pretty far from where we went overboard."

"They might explore the shoreline." He frowned. There was an awful lot of shoreline for them to explore.

"We shouldn't go back to the ship. The assassins may have survived. Do you know who they were?"

"I assume they were Kjallans, since it was a Kjallan ship."

"I doubt it," said Celeste. "Why would a Kjallan want to murder you?"

"Any number of reasons. I can't speculate as to motive when I know so little."

"You have enemies in Inya, don't you?" asked Celeste.

"Of course." He swallowed. His mouth felt like cotton. "If we're not getting back on the ship, what then? Do you have any idea where we are?"

"Some," she said. "We're definitely in Riorca. We were only a few days out from Denmor when we went into the ocean."

So walking wasn't entirely out of the question. An overland journey might even be shorter, because the ship had to first go north and then turn east, following the coast, while they could head straight for Denmor. But there was a problem. "Without water, we won't last long."

"I believe I can find water," said Celeste. "I'd rather take my chances walking to civilization than waiting."

"How will you find water?"

"I'll show you." She headed off into the trees.

"We have no shoes," he pointed out.

"I think we can manage without them."

Rayn reached out with his mind to extinguish the dying campfire and trailed after her. "I hope you have a better plan than just walking and looking around, because I wouldn't bet on our finding any water that way."

"I've a plan." She slowed as she entered the forest, looking everywhere. Down at the carpet of leaves, straight ahead into the bushes, up into the treetops.

He couldn't imagine how she would find water by looking up at the trees, but he held his tongue, trusting that she knew what she was doing.

A jaybird popped out of a bush and onto a nearby branch. Not the blue-and-white kind he knew from Inya, but an unfamiliar variety, dark blue with black points. Celeste stared at the bird, and the bird stared back. Then it fluttered away to another bush. "Follow the jay," she said. "And don't frighten him."

"You think the bird will lead us to water?"

"I've commanded him to," said Celeste.

Impossible, he thought, but then he remembered the shark. Had that been a dream? No, it had been real— how else would they have reached the shore? Clearly she could control animals. He wouldn't question it; the skill had saved their lives.

When the bird had led them farther than a mile into the forest and he hadn't seen a droplet of freshwater, he was less certain. "He's leading us on a merry chase. Are you sure this will work?"

"It ought to."

She kept moving. Having no better solution to offer, Rayn followed, picking his way carefully and trying not to step on anything sharp with his bare feet. Half an hour later, he heard the finest sound in all the world: the prattle of water over stones. "Forget the bird—I can hear it." He broke into a run, and she hurried after him.

It was a small stream, no more than a trickle, furrowed deeply into the ground and almost completely hidden by ferns and leafy cabbagelike plants. Rayn dropped to his knees and lowered his mouth into the water. It was ice-cold. His lips numbed as he drank, but he gulped greedily. When one was thirsty enough, water was finer than whiskey.

He came up gasping, refreshed and a little chilled. At the same time, Celeste lifted her head from the water. Her lips were blue.

"Come here," he said, pulling her into his arms. He called fire, sending it spiraling up through his body and into his mouth and lips, and kissed her, sharing the warmth. She moaned, worming her way closer. She tasted exquisite, a mixture of clean, pure water and woman.

"I'm starving," he said. "I don't suppose you could command a rabbit to come over here and stand still while we slaughter it."

"Uh." Celeste looked uncomfortable, and he guessed from her expression that it was actually possible. "There's a spinefruit bush." She pointed at a low, sprawling plant cowering in the shade of a nearby tree. It had several spiny fruits on it, all of them green.

"Those are edible?"

"No, they're still green," said Celeste. "We need a yellow one."

Rayn sorted through the branches. "All the fruits are green."

"Find another plant, then." She wandered about the forest. "The Riorcans cultivate them in these forests. Mushrooms too, but I don't trust myself to pick the right varieties. Here's one." She plucked something from the bush beside her and held up a spiny yellow orb.

Now that Rayn knew what to look for, he saw that the plants were everywhere, tucked up close to tree trunks and shaded by ferns. He moved to the next plant, searched it with no success, and tried another. A glint of bright yellow winked at him from behind the leaves. He plucked the fruit. "Got another."

Between them, they found four. Not a feast, but better than nothing.

Rayn sat on the bank of the creek and studied his prize. It was hard and spiky, not something he could sink his teeth into. "How is this eaten?"

"We have to get the spines off—we'll need a sharp stone or something." She looked around her feet.

Rayn's hand went to the knife holster at his belt. Had the blade survived its dunking in the ocean? The scabbard was damp on the outside and wrinkled, but he could feel the knife within it. He tugged at the hilt, working it back and forth a little, and the blade popped free, tossing a few drops of seawater into the air. "Will this do?"

"You've had that with you the whole time?"

He grinned.

She took it and cut into the fruit, peeling away the spines and the hard outer rind. She struggled with the task—clearly this was not something she had much experience with—but managed to expose the soft fruit within. She cut the edible part in half and offered Rayn a piece.

He bit into it and chewed. It was mildly sweet, like a watery potato with notes of pear. "It's not bad." He'd have preferred rabbit.

"They taste better cooked," said Celeste.

When they finished eating, Celeste captured a crow with her mind magic and tasked it with leading them to the nearest village. The creature took the job seriously. It fluttered to a nearby tree and looked back, fixing them with sharp, black eyes, scolding raucously when they were slow to catch up.

"I'm still trying to figure out those people who attacked us," said Celeste as they walked. "You said you had enemies at home—"

"I can't see them infiltrating the ship," said Rayn.

"These enemies at home. Are they the Land Council?"

"Yes," said Rayn. "Councilor Worryn especially. He's head of the council."

"I was told they hate you because you opposed some laws they tried to pass."

Rayn eyed her. "You've got your ear to the ground, haven't you? Yes, they tried to pass some laws that my father would have opposed, had he not been ill. I rallied the Inyan people and managed to defeat the laws."

"Tell me about your father's illness. Can the Healers do nothing?"

"It's incurable."

"What is the nature of his illness?"

Rayn balked. He didn't want to talk about this. He didn't like to even think about it. "Physically, he's healthy. The problem is with his mind."

She turned, startled. "He's mad?"

"It's more that he . . . forgets things."

"That doesn't sound so bad."

"Important things, like the names of people he's known for years. Details of how Inya's government is supposed to work. When I was a child, he was a wise and thoughtful ruler. He gave me lots of advice, things I'll never forget. But now . . . he's not the same man."

"I'm so sorry. Do you know the cause?"

Rayn shook his head. "I don't. It happened gradually. We first noticed when he began forgetting important meetings and misremembering the councilors' names. Then he started getting lost in the palace. A year later, he set his bedsheets on fire—he's a fire mage, like me—and we had to take away his riftstone."

"Three gods, I can't imagine. How long ago did this start?"

"When I was eleven," said Rayn. "By the time I was fourteen, he was helpless, and the council was quietly issuing decisions through him. Bad decisions he would never have made when his mind was intact, decisions he would have advised me not to make. That's the worst of it. He had friends. I *thought* they were his friends. But when he became weak and needed help, they abandoned him or turned on him."

"What were these bad laws the Land Council tried to pass?"

"They require some explanation. Do you have King's Lands in Kjall? Perhaps you'd call them Emperor's Lands."

"I'm not sure what you mean," said Celeste. "My brother owns a great deal of land, most of it surrounding the Imperial Palace. But we don't call it anything special."

"In my country, the King's Lands aren't for the royal family. They're for everyone. Nobody owns them—well, technically my father does—but they're maintained for the benefit of all Inyans. They are lakes, beaches, forests, mountains. Nobody is permitted to settle in them or build structures on them, but many of our poorer citizens hunt and fish in the King's Lands. Otherwise they might starve. You have something like that in Kjall?"

"I don't think so," said Celeste.

"The Land Council wanted to sell the King's Lands off to private buyers—wealthy farmers and merchants who I'm certain were lining the councilors' pockets with bribes. They tried to do this in secret, without the Inyan people knowing. But I knew. I made some speeches on the subject, and the people rose up in opposition. Land councilors are elected. They cannot afford to anger the people, so they stopped trying to sell off the land."

Celeste was quiet for a while, considering his words. "Before all this happened, you had promised to tell me about Zoe and your daughter."

"So I did." He frowned. This wasn't a subject he liked to discuss; he knew it reflected badly on him. But hiding it from her didn't feel right. Against his better judgment, he was beginning to take this marriage offer from Lucien more seriously, not because he was convinced it was the right move for his country, but because he really liked the woman. "I helped Zoe when she was in trouble— rescued her from someone who was mistreating her and gave her a job at the palace. Later I slept with her. I didn't think anything of it at the time. It was a casual thing, and I thought she understood that. But then she got pregnant."

"Weren't you warded?"

"I thought I was," said Rayn. "She ought to have been warded too. I can't explain it, but we know that wards sometimes fail."

"If they are mislaid," said Celeste, sounding skeptical.

"My first assumption was that the baby wasn't mine," said Rayn. "But Zoe submitted to a truth spell on that account, and it turns out I was her only partner at that time. So there is no doubt. Unfortunately, the fact that I'd sired a child on her led Zoe to believe there was more to our relationship than I'd intended. I had ended things with her already. But since she's the mother of my child, I have to keep Zoe at the palace."

"Does she take care of your daughter?"

"Oddly, no." Rayn frowned. This was something that bothered him. "I thought she would want to. But Aderyn—that's my daughter's name—didn't gain much weight during her first few weeks of life, and it came out that Zoe was neglecting to feed her. So I put Aderyn in the full-time care of a wet nurse. I come by to see Aderyn from time to time, but the nurse tells me that Zoe never visits."

"That's . . . disconcerting."

"Let's talk about something else," said Rayn. "I want to hear more details about this marriage of convenience you suggested for us." He glanced at her to see if he'd made her blush. Yes, he had.

"Oh—well," she stammered. "I think I was pretty clear on the details."

"Not at all," said Rayn. "The deal was that you would have time to work on your treatise, and I would sire heirs on you. But the siring of heirs requires bedroom activities."

"Of course it does." Her face was pink all over.

"How often would these bedroom activities take place?"

"I don't think we have to specify. We would take care of the business as needed."

"I beg to differ. The contract must lay out all the details."

"Twice a week?" she offered.

"What about when you're pregnant? Obviously you have no need for my seed then."

"That is true," she said.

He glanced at her. Did he hear disappointment in her voice? "I'm afraid such contract terms won't be acceptable to me. I expect my wife to be in my bed every night."

She glanced at him shyly. "Every night?"

"And sometimes during the day," he added. "We should also discuss the sorts of relations that don't result in pregnancy. I will want those frequently."

"Do you always tease your women like this, Prince Rayn?"

Rayn said nothing because, in truth, he did not. There was something about the Kjallan princess — her demureness, her tendency to blush like tinder sparking — that inspired him to tease. Zoe had been so eager, so forward, that she'd have his pants down around his ankles and his cock in her mouth the moment he'd closed the door to her rooms. But Rayn found that teasing a little, whetting his appetite and his partner's, made him more eager for the action when it came.

He clambered over a root that grew between two trees, and halted. The ground dropped away, and below them shimmered a crystalline pool ringed by spongy green moss. A tiny waterfall trickled, crisp and clean, from the high ground. "Look where your crow has brought us," he said.

Celeste entered the clearing and gasped. "Three gods. This is beautiful."

"Are you thinking what I'm thinking?" He was in desperate need of a bath to wash away the salt and sand, and Celeste needed one too. Perhaps they could scrub each other's back ... and who knew where that might lead? He was already in trouble for making love to her on the beach. What difference would it make if he made love to her a second time?

"That water will be freezing," said Celeste.

Rayn grinned. "Not for a fire mage."

10

Though she knew he'd seen her naked before, Celeste felt a little shy as she stripped out of her clothes. Their unexpected lovemaking on the beach seemed like ages ago, yet it had taken place that very morning. Then, she'd been disoriented and emotionally wrung out after their harrowing adventure in the open ocean. Now she felt more aware and in control.

She felt Rayn's eyes on her back as she slipped the last bit of fabric over her head. She wanted to turn and drink in the sight of his amazing body, but that would mean exposing herself to his gaze. "Turn your back."

"I've seen you already," said Rayn. "Why be shy around me?"

"Just until I get in the water."

She heard leaves rustling and glanced over her shoulder to see that he had, indeed, turned around. She moved to the pool. Icy water stung her toes, but she gritted her teeth and waded to the center of the pool where the water was deepest. Gasping at the cold water's bite, she folded her legs and sank in up to her neck, perching on the smooth rocks at the bottom of the pool. "I'm ready."

Rayn turned. He'd shed his pants and tunic, and wore nothing but his riftstone, a bright ruby that rested on his collarbone. He looked as impressive as he had the night before. More so, now that his cock stood at attention. Clearly he wasn't the least bit ashamed of his body, and why should he be? If she looked that perfect, she wouldn't be shy either.

"Aren't you freezing?" he asked.

She nodded, her teeth chattering.

Rayn entered the water. As he waded toward her, a blast of his fire magic preceded him. The water became as warm as an imperial bath.

Like most Kjallans, Celeste bathed daily when she had the opportunity. The feeling of grime on her skin was unfamiliar and unpleasant. She had no soap with her, so clean water would have to do. She rubbed at her arms, loosening the salt and sand.

Rayn sank into the water next to her. "Allow me." He grasped her about the waist and pulled her into his lap. His erection pressed against her backside. He found her arm beneath the water and ran his hands slowly up and down her skin. He removed the grit as he went, yet his touch wasn't all business. He was exploring. Separating the fingers on her hand, he paid each one personal attention, stroking its contours, measuring its length. He worked his way up to her palm and then her wrist. She was fine-boned compared to him, and his hand easily encircled her forearm.

Despite having a loving family, Celeste was seldom *touched*, and never in so delicious a way. Beneath the water, she was safe from the scrutiny of his eyes and could relax completely. Moaning with pleasure, she laid her head on Rayn's shoulder. He moved to her other arm, paying it the same attention. Then her feet, separating each toe. The soles of her feet were scraped and sore from walking barefoot through the forest. He gently rubbed the rawness out of them and moved on to her legs, then to her torso. He seemed to particularly enjoy the spot where her waist blossomed into her hips, and stroked the contour of that curve long after her skin was clean.

He ran his hand up her back. "Let me wash your hair."

She lay limp in his arms and didn't stiffen when he tipped the back of her head into the water. She closed her eyes. He supported her with one hand behind her neck while his other hand ran gently through her hair, freeing trapped salt and sand and sorting out the tangles.

When he finished, he restored her to an upright position. She turned in his arms, looking again on his handsome face. "Your braid's falling apart," she said. "Let me fix it for you."

"You can undo the braid. There's a clasp at the bottom."

She circled around him. Rayn was too big to pull into her lap, so instead she knelt at the bottom of the pool, pressing up against his back, and found the bottom of his braid. She undid the clasp and handed it to him. Then she unraveled his hair from base to scalp. She separated the strands, and his hair flowed long and free, the bottom half of it darkened by water. She wasn't used to men with long hair, since most Kjallans kept theirs short. Rayn's fell nearly to his waist, and as she ran her hands through it, she couldn't help but feel that Kjallans were missing out. "Lie back," she said.

She slipped a hand under his neck and massaged his scalp. She ran her hands through the long, thick strands of his hair, teasing them apart. "Shall I braid it back up now?"

"Later, *karamasi*," said Rayn.

She left his long hair swirling in the water and ran her

fingers up his back and shoulders. His body fascinated her—broad in the upper torso yet narrow at the waist. So different from her own. She traced the contour of each muscle, marveling that he could be so strong and also so delicate, especially along his sides where his skin was soft and ticklish. His legs were thick and powerful, but the skin between his toes was tender. She rubbed the salt off him everywhere she touched, acquainting herself with the body that had made love to her this morning.

She avoided what was between his legs and worked her way up his chest. Running her hands through the smattering of hair, she found one of his nipples and stroked it, enjoying the way it pebbled beneath her fingers.

Rayn twisted around. "I haven't finished with you yet," he growled, grabbing her and hauling her in front of him. He set her back on his lap.

"I'm clean everywhere," she said.

"Not here." He slipped his hand into the wet hair on the back of her head, tipped her head back, and kissed her. His tongue swept into her mouth. "Nor here," he murmured, stroking her breast and thumbing her nipple until it stiffened to a peak. Slipping a hand behind her back, he lifted her chest out of the water until her nipples emerged. He took one in his mouth and thumbed the other, not gently, but gods, she didn't want gentle right now. Each stroke sent a shiver of pure pleasure through her, radiating to her core. "Here's another spot I missed." Still tonguing her breasts, he moved his hand down her belly, and still farther until he found her sex. She gasped in surprise and pleasure.

He parted her with gentle fingers and stroked.

So powerful was the sensation that she thrashed in the water, but he hugged her close and continued to stroke, tenderly and with a circular motion. "Touch me," he ordered. He took her hand and placed it on his cock. His boldness shocked her, but she was too curious to shy away. She explored his cock with her fingers, tracing the head and the hard shaft, even taking his cods into her hand. He groaned. "I'd love for you to keep doing that. But we're not going to finish this way."

He slipped both hands underneath her and lifted her out of the water.

She gasped. "Don't look at me."

"Don't be silly," said Rayn. "Everything I see, I like." Carrying her to the bank, he laid her on the soft, mossy ground so that her body rested on dry land while her legs were still in the shallows. She stiffened, anxious about her naked body being exposed. But there was no one to see but Rayn, and his face had disappeared. He'd dropped into the shallow water where she could barely see him. There, he parted her and touched his tongue to her softness. A thrill like no other ran through her.

"Gods, Rayn," she moaned. He stroked her with his tongue, sending a delicious fire through her, not of the magical variety but far more enjoyable.

"Tell me you like it."

"It feels so good." She arched her back as he continued to tongue her. *"So good."*

When her pleasure had grown to almost unbearable levels, Rayn rose from the water with a growl. He lifted her and placed her farther back on the moss, giving himself some room, and climbed atop her. Water dripped off his face and chest, and his cock hung hard and heavy between his legs. He leaned down and kissed her, but she couldn't bear it. She needed him, and she wasn't going to wait.

"Now," she whispered.

He lowered his body and slid into her, warm and glorious. Water glistened on his shoulders as his powerful muscles flexed. His thrusts were ungentle, but they were what she needed. Noises she had never made in her life emerged from her throat at the completion of each stroke. She grasped at him, needing something in her hands, and kissed him so hard she almost bit his lip.

"Come for me," he said.

She did, gasping, her entire body contracting at the unbearable flood of pleasure. He unleashed a series of vigorous thrusts and finished inside her.

Celeste panted, flushed and overheated. For once she didn't need Rayn's fire magic.

Rayn kissed her again, gently this time. He was covered in a light sheen of sweat. "You know what?" he said. "We need another bath."

Rayn felt refreshed as they set off through the woods again, and not just because of the sex. His body was clean and his hair freshly braided. His stomach was making some entirely valid protests about the inadequate diet of spinefruit, and certainly he missed his coffee, but these were minor complaints, which he could ignore for a time. Celeste had captured a songbird with her magic, and they were following it, hopefully to civilization.

How far was it? Lornis had to be in a panic by now. Once the ship failed to locate them, word of his death might be dispatched to Inya. And who knew what Lucien might do when he learned Celeste was missing? They needed to contact their people as soon as possible. "Can you summon us a couple of horses to ride? Or whatever's in this forest. Elk?"

"I can't summon things." Celeste stopped and squinted at the trees, searching for her songbird, which was drab gray in color and hard to spot.

"You've summoned birds."

"No, I just found them and gave them magical suggestions. If you see any elk, let me know. I probably could control one if it were close."

"How far away does your magic work?"

"My range is about to that tree." She indicated a large fir about thirty feet away. "I could extend it if I practiced more."

"Can you control two animals at once?"

"I've done it. It depends on the animal. Simpler minds are easier to control: fish, reptiles, some insects. Mammals and birds are the hardest. People can be challenging. Mages are impossible."

"I have a question about your past," said Rayn. "You don't have to answer it if you'd rather not."

Celeste glanced back at him. "All right."

"You were married once before. Was it . . . I mean, did he . . ." Rayn hesitated, uncertain how to ask such a question. She'd been thirteen at the time and had been forced into the marriage.

"He didn't sleep with me," said Celeste. "And it wasn't a real marriage. Lucien had it annulled."

That was a relief. He'd slept with her twice now, and while in some ways she was uninhibited, in others she was tense and nervous. Clearly, she didn't like it when he looked at her body, which was a shame, considering she was so beautiful. He wasn't sure shyness could entirely explain her reactions.

"I don't mean to imply that it had no effect on me," offered Celeste. "He was cruel and frightening. He used to . . ." She trailed off.

"Used to what?" prompted Rayn.

"Beat me," said Celeste. "When I argued with him."

She turned to her songbird as if to dismiss the subject.

Rayn was pretty sure she'd been about to say something else.

"You might as well know this too," Celeste continued after a minute. "When I was older, I had an actual lover. One of my choosing."

"Oh?" He shouldn't be surprised. She hadn't behaved like a virgin either at the beach or at the forest pool.

"I feel like a fool for ever getting involved with him."

"So you chose the wrong lover," said Rayn. "We have that in common."

"I thought he loved me, but he didn't," said Celeste.

"What happened?"

"He was from the Mathematical Brotherhood," said Celeste. "I wasn't very welcome there—they don't accept women."

"You said they made an exception for you."

"Because Lucien offered them a donation of imperial funds. I don't feel like a real member. I bought my way in."

"Did the other members have to prove themselves in some way to get in?"

"Most were educated at the University of Riat. Or Worich, or elsewhere. Those who didn't have a formal education could get in if they'd published papers on mathematics."

"Did you have a formal education? Or was it all tutors?"

"I had tutors for a while, but I outgrew what they could teach me," said Celeste. "I did end up going to the University of Riat. And I've published some papers."

"So you were as qualified as anyone else in the organization."

"Technically, yes."

"I have little experience with women like you, who go

to universities and such," said Rayn. "I only had tutors myself. But any fool can see that studying math doesn't require a pair of cods. I should say you were a real member regardless of what the others thought." He didn't care how supposedly smart those men were; they were idiots if they couldn't see how gifted Celeste was.

"Most of them felt I didn't belong," said Celeste. "I'm glad you feel otherwise. So did Gallus. He was different from the others. He was friendly and welcoming, and he taught me all kinds of things. I've never known a smarter man—well, except for Lucien."

Rayn wished he'd taken his math studies more seriously in his youth. She loved brilliant men: her brother, this Gallus fellow. He couldn't measure up to either of them. Not that he was stupid. He'd been competent at his studies, and he could speak three languages. He could tame an erupting volcano, but this woman had grown up in a land without volcanoes; his talent meant little to her. "You still love this man Gallus?"

"No," said Celeste. "And he never loved me. I used to take him back to my rooms at the Imperial Palace. I felt pleased with myself at the time. I knew we could never get married because he was a commoner and I would eventually have to make a political marriage, but it was a lovely affair—so I thought. Then things started disappearing."

He looked up. "Things?"

"Jewelry." Her voice was small. "Statuettes. Valuables."

Rayn's jealousy fled. He wanted to sweep her into his arms. Zoe had been a terrible choice of lover on his part, but at least she wasn't a criminal. "I hope you caught him and threw him in prison."

Celeste shook her head. "I let it go on for quite a

while before I said anything. I didn't want to believe it was happening. I didn't want to believe it was *him*."

"But you reported him eventually," he said, hoping it was true.

"When I couldn't deny anymore that it was happening, I told Lucien. That was the most humiliating conversation of my life. Lucien dispatched Legaciatti to arrest him, but Gallus had left town. He hasn't been seen since."

"I hope you get him someday." Rayn was quiet for a minute, considering what she'd said, and how it might make her feel about men. "Is he the only lover you've had?"

"Well," she said shyly, "there's you."

And would she one day look back on this affair with regret? He'd never imagined that this Kjallan Imperial Princess, sister to the much-feared Emperor Lucien, could be so fragile inside. He'd envisioned her as imperious and spoiled, but instead she struck him as lonely, even a little sad. She'd been betrayed by one lover already, someone she seemed to have had genuine feelings for until she'd discovered his true nature. Was Rayn about to betray her a second time? He'd slept with her on impulse. He hadn't made any promises, hadn't accepted the marriage proposal or even taken it very seriously.

But one didn't sleep with an imperial princess and walk away as if it meant nothing.

He took her hand. "That Gallus fellow knows nothing about valuables. He left the most precious one behind."

Her forehead wrinkled.

He grinned, tickled that she didn't see it coming. *"You."*

Her eyes misted, and she pulled away. "I don't think so."

"I know so." He swept her into his arms and kissed her, holding her fast and giving her no reprieve until he was certain she believed him.

11

That night, Celeste slept by the fire in Rayn's arms. In the morning, she captured a robin, and they resumed their travels. The weather was getting colder. Sometimes, now, they saw patches of frost on the ground. Soon they noticed signs of civilization: paths through the woods, stumps where trees had been cut. By lunchtime, two of the smaller paths converged into a wider path that looked like it might lead somewhere. She conferred with Rayn, and they decided to release the bird and follow the path.

Less than an hour later, she spotted the first pit houses of a Riorcan village. Riorcan houses were sunk into the ground for warmth; she'd seen them on previous visits with her brother. Though they looked squat and unimpressive from the outside, she knew from experience that they could be roomy on the inside.

In front of the nearest house, a woman tending her flower patch glanced up at them. She called to a slim, bearded man who was pushing a handcart down the road. He left his handcart, and the woman rose to her feet. The two of them converged on Celeste and Rayn, calling out in Riorcan—names rather than words. More villagers appeared. A gaggle of children arrived, with a gold-and-white dog in tow, and stared at them. Celeste realized that, barefoot and in filthy, ruined clothes, she and Rayn looked disreputable, like a pair of vagabonds on the run.

"We've been shipwrecked," said Celeste in the best Riorcan she could manage. "We need help." When she tried to take a step forward, the villagers held up their hands and stepped in front of her. They talked so fast, and with such a strong accent, that she couldn't make out all their words. She had the idea they were telling her to wait.

More villagers arrived, surrounding them. Celeste waited nervously. If she got desperate, she could use her mind magic. But she preferred not to.

Three men came forward. One of them addressed Rayn. "Why do you come here?"

Rayn turned to Celeste helplessly. "I don't speak Riorcan."

"We were shipwrecked," said Celeste to the man in Riorcan. "We walked here from the beach. We need to get to Denmor."

These words elicited mumbling and whispering among the villagers. Celeste caught the word "Kjallan," which was uttered several times. Her stomach fluttered. These villagers didn't look violent, but rural Riorca did not hold Kjall in high regard.

The three men conferred among themselves. One of them beckoned. "This way."

He led them farther into the city, and where two roads crossed, he pointed at the ground. "Next wagon comes through, you get a ride."

Celeste looked where he was pointing. The road was clearly rutted, with hoof marks between the ruts. She said to Rayn, in Kjallan, "They want us to get a ride on a wagon." Then to the village leaders, "When does the next one come through?"

"Tomorrow morning," said one of the men.

"We need help, then," she said. "Food and shelter. Maybe shoes and a change of clothes." She realized uncomfortably that she had no money with her. She asked Rayn, "Do you have any coin?"

He shook his head. "Wasn't carrying any when I went overboard."

"I'm afraid we've no money with us," said Celeste to the village leaders. "But when we reach Denmor, we can send you some—"

The villagers began to protest, insisting that they would accept no payment for their hospitality, although Celeste detected an undercurrent of reluctance. Perhaps because she was so obviously Kjallan.

"Your husband," said the village leader. "He is Riorcan?"

"He's not my husband," said Celeste. "And he's Inyan."

There was much discussion of this, including some disapproving clucks in Celeste's direction. Then the village leader said, "Sabine will give you a place to stay tonight."

"Sabine?" Celeste looked around.

A woman came forward. She was blond, middle-aged, and a head shorter than Celeste.

Celeste told Rayn, "This woman is putting us up for the night."

"How do I say *thank you* in Riorçan?" asked Rayn.

"*Kelem de,*" said Celeste.

Rayn clasped wrists with the woman. "*Kelem de.*"

Sabine answered with a rapid flood of Riorcan that Celeste didn't understand. Then she beckoned, and Celeste and Rayn followed.

The woman led them several blocks down the street to a pit house. They descended a staircase to the front door and entered. The house had but a single room with a hearth, a table and chairs, and a large bed. Celeste supposed they'd all be sharing the bed, or else she and Rayn would be on the floor. No privacy here. But it beat sleeping in the woods.

Sabine looked them over as if gauging their usefulness. "You help with supper. After, you wash your clothes."

Celeste exchanged a look with Rayn. "She wants us to help," she told him in Kjallan. This was going to be awkward. She'd had servants looking after her all her life; she'd never before even tried to cook or do laundry. She doubted Rayn had either. But she would do her best.

"We'll help, then," said Rayn.

When Celeste had imagined her trip to Riorca with Prince Rayn, she had not envisioned standing beside him at a laundry tub, taking turns stirring their clothes in the water with a wooden bat. Sabine had loaned her a clean syrtos to wear. It was scratchy and slightly oversized, but warm.

"Have you ever done anything like this?" she asked Rayn, stirring once more and wondering how long it took clothes to get clean.

"Never," he said. "You want me to stir for a while?"

She handed him the bat.

Celeste and Rayn were in the yard behind Sabine's house, where they'd hauled the water up from the stream and mixed it with lye. Several of the children had found them and were watching from a short distance.

Rayn stirred vigorously, and the children giggled.

"What's so funny?" called Celeste in Riorcan.

More giggles. Celeste shrugged, and accepted the bat from Rayn for her turn.

"You're doing it wrong," said one of the children.

"What do you mean?" asked Celeste.

The child, a little girl, ran up to the laundry tub. "You don't just stir it. You *beat* it."

Celeste swung the bat at the clothes in the laundry tub. Water splashed over the rim.

The girl laughed and said, "Like this." She grabbed the bat and began to beat and rub at the clothes in the water.

Celeste could see that the girl was an expert at the task. It shamed her to be shown up by a child. "Thanks. I'll take it now." She took the laundry bat and imitated the girl's movements.

The rest of the children, encouraged by this exchange, crowded around. Celeste grinned at Rayn. At least she was learning something.

The evening passed pleasantly enough and that night they slept, as she'd predicted, crowded together in the same bed, the children snuggling up to their parents.

In the morning, Celeste went outside to fetch her gown off the line. It was clean and dry, but unfortunately spoiled, the texture of its fabric destroyed by its ocean dunking. There were a couple of small tears and places where the stitching had come undone. So be it. She could hardly complain about a ruined dress after an ordeal that had nearly taken her life.

Rayn emerged from the pit house. "I'd give anything for a cup of coffee right now."

"I'd do the same for chocolate."

"We should head up to that crossroads and look for a wagon," said Rayn. "There's no telling how early one might come."

Celeste nodded. "Let's get dressed." She looked around uneasily. Sabine and her husband and children were still in the pit house. She hadn't realized before how much of a privilege privacy was. The clearing they stood in was surrounded by trees. She could either strip off her clothes in front of Sabine and the others in the house or do it here in front of Rayn.

"Turn around," she said to Rayn.

He scowled. "I've seen you before."

Not up close and in good light, he hadn't. "Turn around."

"After I get my clothes." He pulled his tunic and pants and smallclothes off the line and turned his back on her.

She knew she ought to immediately turn around herself and put on her ruined dress. But she stared, mesmerized, as he pulled off his borrowed Riorcan tunic, baring his back. Muscles rippled beneath his sun-bronzed skin. He was comfortable in his motions, as if he knew how fortunate he was to be blessed with the body he had, and enjoyed every second of being inside it. She was disappointed when he flung on his tunic and covered himself.

When he pulled down his borrowed pants, still unaware of being watched—or perhaps he knew and didn't care—she blushed and turned around. With trembling hands, she unhooked the borrowed dress and pulled it off over her head. She heard a rustle of leaves behind her and froze. "Not yet."

"I haven't turned round," said Rayn.

She put on her own dress. Gods, it was a mess. The fabric was so stiff, she couldn't hook it in the back.

"Ready?" called Rayn.

"I need help."

He came up behind her and drew the fastenings with fingers that were warm on her neck.

They went back into the house to thank Sabine for her hospitality and say good-bye to the children, and headed out into the village proper, toward the cross-roads where they'd seen the wagon tracks.

"Do you have plans for when we reach Denmor?" asked Rayn.

"I'll contact Lucien," said Celeste. "He'll arrange passage home for both of us."

Rayn eyed her. It was plain that something was on his mind.

"You don't like that plan?" she asked.

"What if Lucien was behind the assassination attempt?"

What a ridiculous accusation. Not only did it make no sense; it was offensive. "He wasn't."

"It happened on his ship."

"He obviously didn't intend it to. Aside from the fact that assassination isn't the sort of thing Lucien does, why would he put his sister in danger?"

"I think that part was a mistake," said Rayn. "The assassins obviously expected just me in that room. They didn't know what to do with you."

"Don't sidetrack yourself with this line of thought," said Celeste. "It will get you nowhere. I am absolutely certain my brother had nothing to do with it."

"I think you might be a little naïve about Lucien. Maybe he's not the wonderful person you think he is."

"He *is* that wonderful. I know him well."

"He's the son of a man who launched a bloody invasion of Mosar, which resulted in tens of thousands of deaths."

Celeste's face heated as she took that line of reasoning to its logical conclusion. "Yes, he's the son of that man. And I'm the daughter of that man. You know that, do you not?"

"I am well aware of it," said Rayn.

She looked into his accusing eyes. Where was this hostility coming from? She certainly hadn't seen it when they'd been alone in the Riorcan wilds. "Are you an exact copy of your father, Rayn?"

"In some ways, I'd like to be."

"But *are* you?"

"No," he said. "I am not an exact copy of my father."

"Then why do you assume Lucien must be the same as his father? Do you think that of me as well? Do you believe that if I'd been emperor of Kjall at the time, I'd have launched that Mosari invasion?"

"One of the people killed during that Mosari invasion," he said through gritted teeth, "was my aunt Vor-Lera. She was beheaded and her head placed on a stake outside the fortress of Quedano."

Celeste could feel his anger falling off him in waves. It caused her an almost physical pain. He wanted to make her feel guilty? She'd been eight years old when the Mosari invasion had taken place; she had possessed neither the wit nor the power to stop it. She supposed that in Rayn's mind, Florian's stain spread over his family like a bottle of spilled ink. "I'm sorry about your aunt."

"I'm glad someone is," said Rayn.

She rounded on him. "If it makes you feel better to heap scorn on me, go ahead. My father invaded Mosar, and I did nothing to stop him. I was eight years old. Maybe that excuses my inaction and maybe it doesn't. But don't take out your anger on my brother, because he was older, and he *did* try to stop it. Lucien is the very opposite of his father. He saw firsthand every mistake Florian made, and has been determined ever since not to make those mistakes himself."

"You say so—"

"I *know* so," said Celeste. "I don't tell this to many

people, but Florian hated Lucien. He used to hit him, knock him down. Those two were never on good terms. Lucien is *not* his father. And neither am I."

Rayn looked skeptical. "Do you know what we say in Inya, about how to tell a good king from a bad one?"

"No."

"The bad king is surrounded by bodyguards."

Her mouth fell open. "You think my brother is a bad ruler because he has bodyguards?"

"A good king doesn't need them."

She shook her head. "Any ruler of a nation of significant size, whether he's a good ruler or a bad one, will have enemies. *You* have enemies. Does that make you a bad king? If you'd had a bodyguard on the ship, we might not be here right now having this argument."

"So you're saying the attack is my fault?"

"You were the target." Her feelings were in a tumult. She had not realized that Rayn harbored so much hostility toward her brother, her family, and even her country. In his eyes, she was tainted by her nationality and lineage. "I understand now why you haven't accepted the marriage proposal."

"Celeste—" he began.

"Don't give me excuses now," she said. "I want to know why you slept with me, if you hate me so much."

"I don't hate you," said Rayn.

"What is hate, if not this? You're angry at me not for anything I did, but for who I am." Had he possessed ulterior motives when he'd slept with her on the beach? Now that she thought about it, it was ludicrous to think that Rayn had found her so appealing that he'd simply lost control that morning. He was a prince and the most handsome man she'd ever laid eyes on. He could have any woman he wanted. Why would he think her anything special?

Maybe he'd slept with her as a form of sick revenge. Love and leave the daughter of the man who'd murdered his aunt. Her emotions were spinning out of control when Rayn's words captured her attention.

"Here comes our wagon," said Rayn.

12

Rayn wasn't sure what to do about Celeste's pensive silence; he was so uncertain of his own feelings that he couldn't give her the answers that he knew he owed her. So it was a relief when he spotted their potential ride to Denmor trundling their way, loaded with copper ore and drawn by six shaggy ponies. He'd seen dogs larger than those ponies. They were sturdy animals, with thick legs and barrel chests, but he could see why six were needed. He waved down the driver and learned that the wagon was going to Denmor. It would reach the city in several days. The driver had no objection to their climbing onto the back of the cart, as long as they didn't expect to share his provisions.

Celeste struggled within the confines of her ruined dress to lift her leg high enough to get a foothold on the wagon frame. When that didn't work, she tried pulling herself up with her arms.

Rayn stepped forward and seized her about the waist. She shuddered at his touch.

She weighed practically nothing. He lifted her gently onto the ore pile. "Why struggle when you don't need to?"

She gave him an irritated look and, when he released

her, climbed farther up the pile to put distance between them.

He climbed up and settled on top of the copper ore himself. Celeste had tried to find a spot where she wouldn't be in close contact with him, but there wasn't enough room. They were only inches apart, and he felt highly conscious of her warm presence. The driver called a *hey-up* to his ponies, and the creatures strained at their harnesses, setting the wagon in motion. He'd hoped the ponies would be fast, but he saw now that their accustomed gait was a plod. This was going to be a long trip.

What could he say to her? Certainly he didn't hate her. His feelings were more complicated than that. She obviously thought it unfair that he judged her and Lucien by the actions of their father, but what else was he to do? She'd had the benefit of growing up with both men and knowing them intimately. Rayn had met Lucien on a handful of occasions, and Florian never. He was working with limited information. He could hardly stake his country's safety on vague assurances.

Of course sons didn't necessarily follow in their father's footsteps. But quite often they did. It was not unreasonable for him to worry about the possibility. He had seen men rebel against their fathers early in life, only to change as they aged, becoming more and more like their fathers over time.

It was hard to sit so near the woman and not touch her. Her perch was precarious—she could use a steadying arm about her. But the expression on her face told him his touch would not be welcome. The wagon lumbered over a tree root. She swayed dangerously as the cart rocked, and brushed his shoulder with her arm. But she caught herself and inched away.

He shouldn't have slept with her.

But gods above, that lovemaking session at the forest pond was something he could never regret. He'd been with women who had more sophisticated bed skills, including Zoe, who could suck a cock like nobody else. By the tentativeness of Celeste's touch, he knew she was relatively inexperienced. But the way she responded to him! It was as if she'd been dying of thirst and he'd held a waterskin to her lips. Celeste *drank* his touch, like she'd never experienced such a thing before. She made him feel like a god come down from the sky, when every move he made elicited moans of rapture. He was getting an erection just thinking about it.

He glanced at her and caught her looking at him. She flushed and turned away.

There was nothing simple about his involvement with Celeste. He was a prince, and she was a foreign princess. He couldn't marry her just because he liked her and enjoyed going to bed with her. She came with strings attached, and those strings could be disastrous for his country. He was not going to betray his people just so he could have a good time in bed.

But gods, he wished he could.

It took three days for their wagon to reach Denmor—the longest three days of Celeste's life. Rayn had turned taciturn, and she took this to mean that he was distancing himself from her. So be it. She would have nothing further to do with him until she had a better idea of his intentions. Never again would she allow her physical desire to override her sense of reason.

They'd camped nightly by the side of the road, building a fire and scrounging spinefruit and mushrooms. On one guilty occasion, when they were desperately hungry, Celeste had used her mind magic to still a rabbit, which

Rayn had killed with a blow to the skull. But still they'd slept alone, curled up like miniature crescent moons on either side of the fire.

Finally their ore wagon trundled into the outskirts of Denmor, and she looked around with interest. The city had changed since the last time she'd been there. Only a decade before, Denmor had been a village situated on the Strof Harbor, one of the few naturally sheltered bays on the Riorcan coast. When Emperor Lucien had granted control of Riorca to the Obsidian Circle, the Circle had abandoned their mountain shelters, named Denmor their headquarters, and settled there. The village had grown into a city—too quickly, as the roads lagged behind in development.

The wagon was headed for a smelter on the west side of town. She hopped down without a word to Rayn.

He landed lightly beside her. "Where to?"

She pointed to a tower in the distance that rose above every other building in Denmor. "The Enclave building. That's where the authorities are."

She walked in its general direction, trailed by Rayn through muddy, rutted streets. Old-style village pit houses lay interspersed with larger, more recently built dwellings. Some of these newer structures were built upright in the Kjallan style rather than dug into the ground for warmth. The road swarmed with pedestrians and pony carts.

The Riorcans had completed their construction of the Enclave building only a year ago. She'd never seen it before. Even so, it was impossible not to recognize. A red stone tower spiked into the sky and descended sharply into wings on either side, each one curved like a parabola. The tower was ostentatious and unlike any building in Kjall. She had the impression that the Riorcans were, in designing this building, asserting their independence. She liked the building's mathematical symmetry.

Spindly trees had been planted along each side of the road. The Imperial Palace in Riat had a treelined avenue leading to its main gates—perhaps the Riorcans were imitating it? The trees at the Imperial Palace were grand and stately, reflecting the compound's age and grandeur. In a few dozen years, these young trees might look similarly majestic.

"No guards," commented Rayn as they reached the front steps of the Enclave building.

"They're hidden," said Celeste. "Riorcans don't like heavy-handed displays of power."

"A people after my own heart."

A man emerged from the building just as they approached the door. "Welcome to the Enclave building. Are you looking for anyone in particular?"

"Governor Asmund," said Celeste. "Or Bayard. Or Ista." Those were the three Riorcans she trusted the most. Governor Asmund had negotiated with her brother on many occasions, including during the vulnerable time when Lucien was out of power, and she knew him to be fair in his dealings. Bayard was Vitala's trainer from her assassin days. The relationship between the two of them was complicated, perhaps a bit strained, but Celeste would rather deal with him than a stranger. Ista was a former assassin who'd once tried to kill Celeste, but had later teamed up with her and Vitala to kill Cassian.

"Ah—" began the guard, clearly uncomfortable with this request.

"I'm Celeste Florian Nigellus, and this is Prince Rayn Daryson of Inya."

His mouth gaped. He blinked and looked at her more closely. "One moment." He headed inside.

He returned a few minutes later, trailed by Ista. Celeste hadn't seen Ista in a couple of years, but she'd never fail to recognize the onetime assassin. Ista wasn't dangerous now, at least not overtly. She'd traded in her magical death-dealing Shards for an assembly robe—although Celeste wouldn't be surprised if she still carried the Shards, just in case.

"Three gods," cried Ista. "How did you get here? Your ship never arrived—it returned to Riat. The emperor signaled us and said both of you went overboard."

Lucien already knew? Oh, no—he would be in mourning unnecessarily. "What else did he say?"

"That we should look for you," said Ista. "We sent search parties to the coast, but now I can recall them." She inclined her head to Rayn. "Your Highness. Let's get you two inside and the news of your arrival onto the signal network. Everyone thinks you're dead!"

She ushered them indoors and set them to climbing an enormous spiral staircase.

"Did Lucien say anything about my bodyguard Atella?" asked Celeste. "Did she survive the attack?"

"I'm not clear on that," said Ista. "I'm told that one of the Legaciatti managed to kill all three assassins, but not before they threw you into the Great Northern Sea—"

"Thank the gods, that will be her," said Celeste.

"How did you survive?"

Celeste and Rayn explained how they had returned to shore and, afterward, how they'd made their way through the Riorcan wilderness to civilization. Privately, she feared that she and Rayn were not entirely out of danger. If the assassins were part of an organized group, there could be more of them. In addition to that, Kjallans—especially royal ones such as herself—had never been particularly welcome in Riorca.

Celeste's legs burned as they reached the. final flight of the stairway. It ended at a heavy wooden door, which Ista pushed open. Celeste followed her onto the roof of the tower.

"Jorray," Ista called to a man huddled in a three-walled shelter in the center of the roof. He was warming his hands over a heat-glow. "What's the turnaround for a message to the Imperial Palace?"

He scanned the skies. "We've got almost no visibility. Only the nearest towers will see a signal in this haze, so we'll need more relays than usual. I'd guess that a message sent now would take an hour and a half to reach Riat."

Ista turned to Celeste. "Slow, but there's no help for it."

Celeste prepared a message for the signaler about the assassination attempt on the *Goshawk*, her trek with Rayn through rural Riorca, and their safe arrival in Denmor. The signaler coded the message, and with a blast of pyrotechnic magic—colors and shapes launched high into the sky—he transmitted it to all signal towers in visible range.

"Now we wait," said Ista.

While Ista spread the word to the other Enclave members, ordering them to an emergency assembly, Celeste availed herself of the baths on the lowest floor of the building and changed into a fresh syrtos. Ista rejoined her and Rayn in a small dining room. Celeste and Rayn were wolfing a meal of broiled potatoes and lobster cakes when a runner arrived.

"Message from the signal network?" said Ista.

The runner nodded and handed Celeste a folded slip of paper. Celeste opened it and read.

Dear Sister,

GODS ABOVE! Have never been so happy to receive a signal in my life. Sit tight in the Enclave building. I am dispatching a ship immediately to fetch you and Prince Rayn. I look forward to hearing the rest of your story in person. Until I arrive, since you are without protection, please seek wise advice.

Yours with love,

Lucien Florian Nigellus

P.S. Inyan ship arrived last week with a message for Prince Rayn and proceeded to Denmor. Expect it as well.

She smiled at the kind sentiments. *Wise advice*, however—that was a code phrase. He wanted her to make contact with the Order of the Sage and gain the organization's protection. "It's from Lucien," she told the group. "He's on his way here."

Ista's brows rose. "The emperor is coming?"

The former assassin didn't seem happy about it. Celeste was aware that the Riorcans liked as little interference from the Kjallan imperial government as possible. "He says he's coming to fetch me and Rayn." She caught the prince's eye. "An Inyan ship arrived in Riat for you, bearing a message. It's also on its way to Denmor."

Rayn set down his spoon. "What was the message?"

"Lucien doesn't say."

"When will the ship arrive?"

"He said it turned up in Riat last week and proceeded here. It's roughly a six-day journey on a fast ship, so I think we could expect it any day."

Rayn, looking pensive, returned to his food.

"I hope fetching you is all the emperor intends," said Ista. "The last thing Riorca needs is a bunch of imperials running around."

"I can't see any reason they'd need to stay." And in the meantime, she needed to find an agent from the Order of the Sage. She didn't know who any of them were. Perhaps she should signal Lucien again and ask. No, Lucien would never divulge their names on the signal network; it was not secure. She would have to wait until someone approached and gave her the code phrase.

A second runner popped into the room. "The assembly is ready."

Celeste was sorry to leave her meal. She followed Ista down several staircases to the Enclave's assembly room on the bottom floor. A great circular table, seating over twenty, occupied the center of the room, but some chairs stood empty. She counted fourteen men and women at the table. Ista took one of the empty chairs and directed Rayn and Celeste to the two beside her.

Celeste recognized Bayard, the aging battle master who had, years ago, trained the empress in combat and assassination skills. He'd trained Ista as well. And there sat Asmund, the governor of Riorca. Riorca was ruled by Enclave consensus, but when consensus could not be reached, Asmund had the power to make unilateral decisions.

Asmund spoke. "Imperial Princess Celeste Florian Nigellus and Prince Rayn Daryson of Inya, as the governor of Riorca, I celebrate your successful return to civilization and congratulate you for surviving what must have been a harrowing journey. I'm sorry to ask you to come before this assembly so soon, when you are weary from your travels, but the attempted assassination of an imperial princess and a foreign dignitary requires our immediate attention. Have your needs been sufficiently tended to so that you can address this assembly?"

"Yes, Governor," said Rayn and Celeste in succession.

"Please provide the Enclave with an account of the events which took place on the *Goshawk* the night of the Major Reconciliation."

Celeste glanced at Rayn.

He spoke. "On the night of the Major Reconciliation, the Imperial Princess and I went together to my cabin after the party. Three assassins were lying in wait for us. Two of them attacked me, and the other grabbed Celeste. They covered our mouths to keep us from crying out, and their hair and clothes were soaked through with water, a common defense against fire mages. Celeste's bodyguard engaged the assassins, but the assailants threw Celeste out the ship's window into the open ocean, and I jumped in after her."

"Why did you jump in?" asked Asmund.

"Because otherwise the cold would have killed her," said Rayn. "I'm a fire mage. I possess the ability to warm the water around myself."

Celeste stared at him. She hadn't realized Rayn had *jumped* in after her. She'd assumed the assassins had thrown him in, as they had her.

A man at the far end of the table, whom Celeste didn't know, spoke up. "How did you get to shore?"

Celeste picked up the tale. "Rayn kept us warm in the water with his fire magic. I signaled the ship, but it didn't respond. After that, we swam for shore." She decided not to mention the shark. Lucien and Vitala liked to keep the nature of her magical talents quiet. "From there we walked to the nearest village and took a wagon to Denmor."

"What village?" said Asmund.

"It was called Waras," said Celeste. "A family there helped us. I'd like to send them a gift."

Asmund nodded. "We can arrange that."

"Governor," said Ista, "the Imperial Princess has contacted the emperor over the signal network. He's coming here personally."

Asmund's face became carefully expressionless. "Then we will prepare for an imperial visit. Prince and Princess, what services can we render you?"

"I don't suppose you have any coffee," said Rayn.

Asmund raised a brow. "What's coffee?"

"Never mind," said Rayn. "Has an Inyan ship arrived for me?"

"No."

"I'm expecting one," said Rayn. "Please inform me immediately when it is sighted."

Asmund turned to Celeste. "Princess?"

"I just need a place to stay while I await the emperor," said Celeste.

Bayard spoke. "We have staterooms here in the Enclave building, but you'll need protection. I can assign you each a door guard and a bodyguard."

"Thank you, no," said Rayn. "I don't care for guards."

Celeste didn't entirely trust these Riorcan guards, but for now she'd live with them. She hoped her contact found her soon. "I accept your offer. Thank you."

Asmund motioned to a man standing just inside the door. "See the prince and princess to their rooms and make sure they have everything they need."

13

Celeste was shown to a state apartment on the second floor. Just inside was a small anteroom and, beyond it, the bedroom proper and a small dressing room. Weary to her core, she pulled back the sea blue blankets on the bed. After several nights of sleeping on the hard ground, the bed looked inviting. But her belongings were still on the ship, which was now in Riat, and she didn't want to sleep in her clothes. In the dressing room, she found a mirror on a stand and two cabinets full of clothing. She sorted through the cabinets and located a sleeping shift of appropriate size. Though it was only afternoon, she felt she could sleep an entire day.

She had no lady's maid here. She'd be granted one if she asked, but for now she'd manage without. Twisting her arms behind her, she managed to unfasten the hooks on the back of her syrtos. She stripped out of her clothes and reached for the sleeping shift. She was uncomfortably aware of the mirror. Reluctant but compelled, she glanced at herself.

Ugly girl, Cassian the Usurper had said, after stripping her bare on their wedding night to ridicule her in front of his mistress. *Look at you, flat as a hay field. You're lucky you're a princess; otherwise no one would want you.*

She'd been thirteen and not fully developed. She wasn't flat anymore, but neither did she consider her body impressive. Her left breast was larger than her right—what strange deformity was that? Her belly was too round, her hips wider than her chest. She had an ugly scar on her thigh from when she'd fallen off her horse as a child. Not a good enough body for Cassian, as he and his mistress had told her on so many occasions. Nor for Gallus. Nor, apparently, for Rayn.

Swallowing a wave of bitterness, she pulled the shift over her head and felt a little bit less disgusted. Now her defects were hidden.

Someone rapped at the door.

She started, embarrassed to be caught in a sleeping shift. "Who's there?" She checked the angles of the dividers between rooms to make certain she could not be seen.

The door creaked open. "It's a tax auditor," called the door guard.

Why in the world would a tax auditor seek her out? "Let him speak from the door."

"Imperial Princess," called a voice she'd never heard before. "My name is Justien. I wonder if I could consult with you about a tax issue. I've got an importer who may be falsifying his records, possibly even smuggling illicit goods, though he claims to import only lemons in winter."

Lemons in winter. This was her contact. "One moment." She looked around frantically for a robe, found one in a cabinet, and flung it on. She checked the mirror to make sure she was presentable and headed into the anteroom.

A huge, bearded man stood in the doorway. More than huge—he was a giant, half a head taller than Rayn, and broad through the chest. She couldn't tell where he was from—eastern Kjall was her best guess, since with his auburn hair he certainly wasn't Riorcan. He looked more like a barbarian than a man who worked with numbers, but she supposed tax dodgers who saw this fellow at their door would be inclined to rethink what they owed the state.

He saw her robe and looked chagrined. "My deepest apologies, Your Imperial Highness. Have I come at a bad time?"

"Never mind," said Celeste. "We can't let smugglers have their way."

Justien stepped inside. The door guard took up a position inside the anteroom, but Celeste ordered him back outside. If Justien was her contact, he was no danger to her.

Celeste motioned Justien to a chair and watched as he folded his great body into it. "I have your message," she said softly. "Aulus Helividius and Gaius Cinna."

"Ah," said Justien.

She had no idea what the message meant, other than its being a pair of names. But the lines of Justien's face changed. Apparently it meant something to him.

He rose. "Thank you for your time."

Celeste motioned him to sit back down. "Stay. Please. Lucien suggested I seek *wise advice*."

"Did he?" Justien leaned back in his chair.

"You're aware that Prince Rayn and I were the victims of an attempted assassination?"

"I have eyes in the assembly room."

"I've two problems," said Celeste. "I'm alone here, and I need personal protection. I'm not sure how much I can trust these Riorcan guards."

"You should not trust them," said Justien.

"Second, Prince Rayn was offered protection and declined. He hates guards. It's an Inyan thing—they believe that only bad kings need bodyguards. But given that someone's trying to kill him, I think he needs protection. *Discreet* protection. If he doesn't know about it, he can't complain."

Justien looked thoughtful. "I can arrange that. It's not as good as having a bodyguard at his side, but he can be watched from a distance."

"And for me?"

"I'll act as your bodyguard until the ship arrives."

Much as that idea appealed to her, she knew it wouldn't work. "You can't do that. You're undercover. If you start acting as my bodyguard, it'll be obvious you're more than a tax auditor."

"I know," said Justien. "But consider my position. An attempt has been made on the Imperial Princess's life—an attempt that almost succeeded. I can't delegate this job. If I did, and something happened to you, I could never live with myself."

"All right, then. Thank you." It took a load off her mind to know that this man would be watching her back. Vitala had handpicked every member of the Order of the Sage, not just for combat ability, but for intelligence and trustworthiness. And even though she'd just met Justien, she instinctively liked him. "Why do you say the Riorcan guards can't be trusted?"

"Most of them probably can be," said Justien. "But I'm tracking a breakaway enclave, and I'm certain someone here in the building is involved. There's just no telling—"

"Wait. What do you mean by a breakaway enclave?"

"You remember how the Obsidian Circle used to operate, before Lucien pardoned them and they became Riorca's ruling party?"

"Of course," said Celeste. "They were an underground organization of many independent enclaves. Collectively, they incited rebellion and assassinated Kjallan leaders."

"It turns out a few of the enclaves didn't like the idea of Riorca accepting Kjallan rule in exchange for the concessions granted them, and they've broken off from the larger organization. My team tracked down one of the breakaway enclaves last summer and broke it up. But I know there's at least one more out there. Probably two. We've had threats, even assassinations. We had a bomb go off in Cuttleshore."

"Those names I gave you—did they have to do with the breakaway enclave?"

"I can't talk about that," said Justien. "But let me be clear: while most people in the Enclave building are law-abiding and trustworthy, the enemy's eyes and ears are present. Until I identify the responsible party, you should be careful what you say."

Rayn sat on the bed in his assigned state apartment, feeling lonely. He'd slept part of the afternoon and joined the Riorcan leadership at dinner. They'd seated him next to Celeste, but she didn't exchange a word with him all night. The Riorcans had peppered him with questions about his country and his family, and Celeste had swapped stories with Ista and Bayard, with whom it was clear she had a shared history. He and Celeste might have been at two different dinners for all they'd interacted.

He'd driven the woman away. Maybe it was for the best; he couldn't commit to an alliance with Kjall, and sleeping with her had been a colossally bad idea. Still, it would be nice if he could at least talk to her.

He missed Lornis, too; he'd rarely been separated from the man for this long. How had Lornis reacted when he'd learned Rayn had gone overboard? Did he know yet that Rayn had survived? Surely Lucien had passed the word on to the Inyans when he'd found out. Otherwise they'd still be mourning his death in Riat, maybe even heading back to Inya without him.

Celeste had a new bodyguard. The man was enormous. He looked like a savage from some distant land. Oddly, Celeste had seated the man at dinner with them instead of having him hover behind her in the manner of the Legaciatti. The bodyguard had said almost nothing to the group at dinner, but a couple of times he'd leaned over and spoken quietly to the princess, which made him wonder how long the princess had known this man and just how intimate they were.

Lucien said a message had arrived for him from Inya. It was impossible that this could be good news. A ship would have been dispatched for only the gravest of reasons: foreign attack, volcanic eruption, death of a family member.

He rose from the bed and began to pace. He needed his message. And he needed to return home.

Celeste was trying to make the best of being trapped in Riorca. With Justien's help, she tried to make sense of the assassination attempt that had taken place on the *Goshawk*.

Without access to the *Goshawk* itself, her investigation was necessarily limited. She could, at least, communicate with the Imperial Palace via the signal network. Lucien had already departed for Denmor, and Vitala was with him. So she spoke to Lucien's adviser Trenian.

What investigations have you made into the event on the Goshawk? she signaled.

By return signal, delayed several hours, Trenian told

her that once they'd learned what had happened on the ship, they'd taken the entire crew into custody and begun interrogations. These, unfortunately, had revealed little of significance. The three assassins had been taken on board as ordinary sailors in Riat. The practice of taking on new sailors to replace those lost to death or desertion was commonplace, and the ship's captain, who'd had no idea of their ill intentions, was not held to be at fault.

Celeste verified that her bodyguard Atella had survived the attack. But Atella had no intelligence to offer either. She'd killed all three assassins. Searches of their bodies had yielded no significant evidence, and she knew no more than Celeste about who they were.

She and Justien puzzled over this information. The assassins had boarded the ship in Riat, which suggested they were Kjallan. But why would a group of Kjallans want to assassinate an Inyan prince?

Her theory was that the assassins were Inyan and had followed Rayn to Kjall. Possibly they'd even come on his own ship, the *Magefire*, and from there taken up service on the *Goshawk*. She ought to ask Rayn if their faces had looked familiar to him. But he would surely have mentioned it if they had, and after their argument in Waras, she was staying away from the man.

It was the third day of Rayn's stranding in Denmor. Yesterday he'd requested and been granted a tour of the city. Governor Asmund had escorted him personally through the city streets, pointing out the docks and harbor, a recently constructed shrine to the Vagabond, a public park, shops, and eateries.

He'd come here ostensibly to see how Kjall was treating this conquered province. He'd heard nightmarish stories about Riorca: bodies impaled on stakes in the center of town, desperate poverty, townsfolk enslaved by death spells. While he was sure Asmund had shown him the best of Denmor, steering him away from the seedier spots, the stories he'd heard appeared to be untrue or exaggerated. Riorca might be cold and bleak, but the province was thriving in its modest way.

Now, back in his rooms, his thoughts returned to Celeste. Perhaps he'd been wrong to hold her accountable for her father's crimes. As she'd pointed out, she'd been only eight years old when Florian had invaded Mosar. She could not have stopped him. As an adult, she was calm, rational, and kind, obviously more interested in scholarly studies than in war. He probably owed her an apology.

But the problem of Lucien remained. He'd seen enough of Celeste to know that she did not share her father's propensities, but he could not say the same about the young emperor. Celeste vouched for him, but they were brother and sister. He probably showed her a better side of himself than he showed others.

Someone rapped at his door.

"Come," he said dully.

It was a runner. "Your Highness," he said, bowing. "An Inyan ship has arrived."

"What sort of ship?"

"A clipper," said the runner. "Name of *Water Spirit*."

Finally. That was his cousin's ship. This must be the message he'd been waiting for.

He dismissed the runner. Thanks to Governor Asmund's tour, he knew the way to the docks. It was an easy walking distance, and plenty of daylight remained. He left the Enclave building and set out into the city.

He feared the message would have something to do with his father. King Zalyo had deteriorated badly in the last year. The disease or madness, which had taken over his mind, seemed to be accelerating. It was beginning to affect his body: he looked older than he ought and walked with a shuffling gait. The man was fifty-two years old, far too young to be dying, yet clearly he was doing just that.

The bustling streets that bridged the gap between the Enclave building and the harbor were Rayn's favorite part of the city. They were lined with shops and restaurants. The tang of frying fish and the homey scent of baking bread wafted through the air. There was a bookshop across the street, and a chocolate shop on the corner ahead. After he got his message, perhaps he'd stop in and buy some chocolate for Celeste. His apology might be better received with a gift. He carried no money, but perhaps he could borrow some from his cousin, if indeed Tiannon had come personally.

Something slammed into his back.

The dirt road rushed toward his face, but he caught himself and stumbled against the wall of the chocolate shop. Pain erupted between his shoulders, searing, burning— the worst pain he'd ever felt. It tore a cry of agony from his throat.

Knife or arrow in his back, he could not tell.

Townsfolk were fleeing the scene in every direction. He had to find cover. He was a dead man if he stayed where he was.

He stumbled toward the chocolate shop door.

Someone charged toward him through the scattering civilians. He reached for the hilt of his sword, but his arm wasn't working. The attacker crashed into him, knocking him to the ground. A crossbow bolt slammed into the wall where he'd been.

"Stay where you are."

The person who'd knocked him down was a woman — he could tell by her voice. She was enormous, easily as tall as he was, and she held a longbow. Quick as lightning, she drew back the bowstring and released an arrow. It dropped a man standing on a rooftop across the street.

Two more men came running. The woman nocked another arrow. She swung around as if to select another target, but did not loose the arrow.

"We're friends," called one of the men as they approached. He dropped to Rayn's side. "I'm a Healer, and Tomas is a war mage. Are you wounded anywhere besides your back?"

"No," Rayn gasped.

Tomas spoke to the archer. "You see any others?"

"One," said the archer. "I think he's running."

"Should I give chase?"

She shook her head. "Stay."

The Healer pulled out a knife and cut off Rayn's tunic around the bolt wound. "I'm going to get this out. Stay calm."

"Won't I bleed to death if you take it out?" He'd heard it could be more dangerous, sometimes, to remove an arrow or bolt than to leave it where it was.

"I know what I'm doing," said the man. "You won't bleed to death."

The streets had cleared after the attack, but a few civilians were returning now to stare at the scene.

"Get out of here," growled the archer, threatening them with her bow.

She and Tomas began to speak about the dead man on the rooftop, but Rayn soon lost the ability to focus on their words. The Healer was tugging at the bolt in his back, and the pain flared so badly he went blind with it, clenching his fists and grinding his teeth.

"Hold still," said the Healer.

He lost consciousness.

When he came to, the archer still stood above him with an arrow nocked in her longbow, but Tomas was gone. The rooftop assassin lay at the archer's feet; apparently someone had fetched him. Rayn saw that he wasn't dead after all. The assassin was breathing, though he had an arrow in his side and was bleeding copiously.

Rayn gave an experimental twitch and discovered his back didn't hurt nearly as much as before.

"Take it easy." The Healer rose to his feet at Rayn's side and gently helped him up. "I'll need to work on that wound some more later, but you can stand. No sudden movements."

Rayn reeled, dizzy, as his body came upright. He'd lost blood, all right—there was a pool of it where he'd been. Not as much as the other man had.

The Healer handed him a bloody crossbow bolt. "Souvenir?"

Rayn shuddered and pushed it away. "Who are you?"

"We're friends," said the Healer.

That didn't answer his question. Where had they come from?

The Healer nudged the wounded assassin with his boot. "You want me to fix him up? What are we going to do with him?"

"Interrogate him, I'm sure," said the archer. "You might need to take the arrow out so we can move him."

Were they Riorcan city guards? He doubted it. They weren't uniformed. Maybe he'd been assigned a protection detail without being aware of it. He might be inclined to complain about that if they hadn't just saved his life.

Civilians were gathering again, this time watching from a distance. He heard footsteps—a group of people running toward them. He shivered, still jumpy from the attack. The archer aimed her bow in the direction of the newcomers. A group of six people rounded the corner, and she lowered the weapon. Rayn recognized three of them immediately: Tomas, Princess Celeste, and her new bodyguard.

"Oh, thank the gods," panted Celeste as her eyes fell on him.

"My cousin's ship has arrived," he said. "I know I can't go to the docks in this condition, but can someone fetch my cousin and bring him back here?"

"Your cousin's ship?" asked Celeste. "Is that the one bringing your message from home?"

"No ship arrived at the harbor today," said the huge bodyguard.

"Are you certain?"

"Quite certain," said the bodyguard.

Soldier's Hell. The whole thing had been a ruse. He turned to Celeste. "Who are these people?"

"Let's get you back to the Enclave building," she said. "I'll explain there."

14

Back at the Enclave building, Celeste followed Justien downstairs to the underground prison. Ahead of them strode the tall, powerful-looking woman with the longbow slung over her shoulder. She held the captured assassin, who remained conscious but weak. The Healer had already removed the arrow.

The archer carried the assassin into a cell. Guards swarmed around the pair, blocking Celeste's view.

Justien halted outside the cell, and the archer came out to meet him. "Your Imperial Highness," she said to Celeste, dipping her head.

"This is my wife, Nalica," said Justien.

Celeste clasped wrists with the archer. Clearly this woman was another member of the Order of the Sage. "Thank you for what you did. I'm sure you saved the Inyan prince's life."

Rayn came up beside her. "Yes, thank you." He clasped wrists with Nalica as well.

Celeste looked him over. He stood awkwardly, one shoulder raised a little higher than the other. "You should go and finish with the Healer."

"In a moment. I want to see what you learn from this man, since apparently he wanted me dead."

Celeste turned to Justien. "Are you going to question him?"

Justien nodded. "It won't be pretty, but it needs doing. We'll want a mind mage. Would you . . . ? I hate to ask, Your Imperial Highness, but I'm not sure I trust anybody else."

Celeste swallowed. She'd never done this sort of work before, never even viewed an interrogation, though she knew they took place beneath the Imperial Palace. An interrogation was only as reliable as the mind mage who sat in and used magic to determine whether the prisoner was telling the truth. Prisoners would say anything when subjected to torture—lies, truths, half-truths, whatever made the pain stop. Without a trustworthy mind mage, one who honestly reported what her magic told her, interrogation had little to no value. "I can serve as your mind mage. We need a writ, though, or it's not legal."

"I'm authorized to write those. Have you done interrogations before?" asked Justien.

"Not as such—"

One of the guards inside the cell cried out in a frantic voice, "Justien!"

Justien darted into the cell, followed by Nalica. Celeste trailed after them as far as the doorway. Inside the cell, the prisoner convulsed on the stone bench.

Justien turned from the prisoner and cried, "Healer! Kasellus, where are you?"

The Healer who'd helped Rayn shoved past them into the cell, followed by more guards. They surrounded the assassin. From the door, Celeste craned her neck but couldn't see what was going on. Though dying to ask questions, she held her tongue. The men were obviously trying to save the assassin's life.

The noise and frantic activity around the assassin

slowed. Then it ceased, and the men who'd been standing over him stood up, their shoulders slumping.

"That's it," said Kasellus. "He's gone."

"He's dead?" cried Celeste from the door.

"Fucking deathstone," snarled Justien. "That's enough. Get out."

The men filed out of the cell, leaving only Justien and Nalica and the assassin. Celeste went in, followed by Rayn. The assassin lay pale and still on the bench.

"He had a deathstone?" asked Celeste.

Justien lifted the assassin's head and indicated a spot on the back of his neck. "Feel."

Hesitantly, Celeste touched the place. There were two lumps, one for the riftstone and one for the deathstone. The assassin's body was still warm. Her skin crawled. It was not often she saw a dead man, let alone touched one.

"What's a deathstone?" asked Rayn, touching his own fingers to the spot.

"A bit of Riorcan magic," said Celeste. "It's attuned to the person in whom it's implanted. That person can activate it at any time to release a death spell upon themselves."

Rayn blinked. "Why would they do that?"

Justien ran his hands over the victim's clothes, searching him. "For exactly the reason this man did it. To avoid interrogation."

"I know about it because the empress has one," said Celeste. "It was implanted in her when she was a girl. Ista has one too."

"They're not generally used anymore." Justien fumbled in a pocket he'd found sewn into the assassin's tunic. "The Circle once used them, back in the day—ah." He retrieved a folded piece of paper. "Here's something, maybe."

"What is it?" asked Celeste.

Justien unfolded the paper. He looked at it, and his triumphant smile faded. "It's in code. I can't read it."

A frisson of excitement buzzed through Celeste. "Let me see."

Justien handed it to her. On the paper was a series of unreadable Riorcan letters, all uppercase, with no spaces or punctuation. "Can your team break ciphers?" she asked.

Justien's brows rose in bewilderment. "Are you joking?"

"No," said Celeste. "If your people can't break it, I might be able to."

Rayn peered over her shoulder at the letter. "How can you decode it without the key?"

"I'm a mathematician. I can break most ciphers, given sufficient time and a long enough message."

"But they're just random letters," said Rayn.

"In fact, they are not," said Celeste. "They mean something, and the fact that they do should give me a foothold in deciphering them. I can't say for certain whether I can break this particular message—it's less than a page long. But it's worth trying."

"Gods know we've nothing else at this point," said Justien. Snarling at the dead assassin, he aimed a kick at the prison bench.

Rayn turned to Celeste. "I'd like to talk to you."

"About what?" She was wary of anything Rayn might have to say to her, now that she knew how he felt about her family. "Shouldn't you see Kasellus and get that wound healed?"

"It can wait," said Rayn.

"We'll be called to assembly soon," said Justien. "The Riorcans will want to hear about the attack. You should see Kasellus before they drag you off to the assembly room."

"We'll talk after the assembly," said Rayn.

Rayn spent an hour with Kasellus, a skilled Healer who managed to remove every last vestige of pain from his arrow wound. Then, knowing he smelled of sweat and blood, he visited the baths in the basement level of the Enclave building, and was summoned to the assembly just minutes after he'd returned. It was a smaller group than usual. They convened in a dining room and were served luncheon: a salad course followed by a chowder of seafood, root vegetables, and spinefruit. Celeste and Justien and Nalica were present, along with several members of the Riorcan leadership. One seat was empty; they were waiting for Governor Asmund, who'd been away from the building at the time of the attack and had to be fetched by a runner.

Rayn tucked into his food, happy to be alive. While it was clear someone—Celeste?—had arranged discreet protection for him against his expressly stated wishes, he could hardly complain about it. He'd been wrong, and she'd been right. He might not need bodyguards at home in Inya, a civilized country, but he certainly needed them here.

He turned to Celeste and spoke in a low voice. "Were you the one who arranged for me to be followed by Nalica and Kasellus?"

She stiffened. "Yes."

"Thank you."

She met his eyes briefly, looking relieved, before returning to her food.

He'd been a fool to push her away. The more he thought about it, the more embarrassed he felt. He knew so many families where the son or daughter was entirely unlike either parent. He'd spent time with Celeste. He'd talked to her, relied upon her in the Riorcan wilds, exchanged stories with her. He *knew* her. Why had he ignored the evidence before his eyes and blamed her for the crimes of an entirely different person?

And after he'd pushed her away, she'd taken steps to save his life. Possibly she'd done it for political reasons; Kjall didn't want a foreign prince assassinated on their territory. But he could not deny that she'd taken action to safeguard his life when it would have been easier for her to do nothing at all.

Governor Asmund entered the room and took the remaining seat. "Sorry I'm late."

Greetings were exchanged, and Asmund asked Rayn to describe the events that had taken place on the street where he'd been attacked. With some help from Nalica, Rayn did so. Then the conversation turned to what had happened in the prison below.

Asmund eyed Bayard and Ista. "What do you make of the fact that the captured assassin had a deathstone?"

Ista shrugged. "It means the assassin was Riorcan. Someone from an old Circle enclave in the mountains, I imagine."

"The Obsidian Circle?" Rayn was confused. "The organization you're a part of?"

"Yes and no," said Bayard. "Not all of our people approved of the Circle's new role in governing Riorca as a Kjallan province. Some of the Circle members left the organization. This assassin could have been one of them."

"A mercenary, perhaps?" asked Justien. "Paid to carry out this assault?"

Bayard shrugged. "It's possible."

"Could be money is the motive," said Ista. "Gods

know the enclaves trained enough of us, and an assassin's job skills don't transfer well to other professions."

"Might be the breakaway enclave," said Justien.

"What's that?" asked Rayn.

"One of the groups which broke away from the Circle."

"Why would an Obsidian Circle breakaway enclave want to murder Rayn?" asked Celeste. "He's prince of a nation that has nothing to do with them."

"For the money," said Ista. "Fund-raising's not so easy when you can't bully the local villages into coughing up tetrals. Or they may hope to provoke Kjall and Inya into war. If that's the case, they'll want Rayn killed *here*, on Kjallan soil or a Kjallan ship." She turned to Rayn. "You might be safer if you returned home."

Rayn eyed Celeste. "Our treaty negotiations are not complete."

"I'm still trying to work out the political motives," said Celeste. "If money was the cell's motive, someone had to hire them. Rayn, if you're assassinated, who takes your place as heir to the Inyan throne?"

Rayn hesitated. "At the moment, it would be my illegitimate daughter, Aderyn. She's an infant, so a regency council would be appointed to rule in her stead until she comes of age and marries."

"Who would be on the regency council?"

"The Land Council appoints three people."

Ista spoke. "So the Land Council arranges to have you assassinated overseas where the blame is likely to fall on Kjall or Riorca rather than upon them. Then your daughter becomes queen and they name three of their own people for the regency council, thus seizing control of your country."

"That scenario is plausible," said Rayn. "But it's only speculation."

"Speculation is all we've got," said Ista. "With the captured assassin dead, we've no one to interrogate."

Rayn's eyes went to the Imperial Princess. They had no one to interrogate, but they did have an enciphered letter. Could Celeste break the code?

Celeste returned to her room with an inkpot, a quill, a stack of paper, and a mug of chocolate. She sat in the middle of the bed, spreading her writing tools around her, sipped her chocolate, and began analyzing the encoded letter. The preliminary work of decryption was rote and tedious, yet satisfying in its way. She began by making a list of every symbol that appeared in the ciphertext and marking down how many times it appeared. From the start, she observed something that gave her pause: there were many more distinct characters in the ciphertext than appeared in any language known to her. Frowning, she began calculating the percentages of how often each character appeared.

A knock came at her door, and Rayn was announced. After a moment's nervous hesitation, she called, "Enter. I'm in the bedroom."

She heard his heavy steps through the anteroom. He appeared in the archway, and as always, her heart dropped at the sight of him. It was unfair. Someone should pass a law against men this gorgeous.

"Working on the cipher?" he asked.

She nodded.

"Any progress yet?"

"No, I'm just beginning frequency analysis."

"May I see?"

She beckoned him closer, wishing that having him near didn't bring back those memories of the pool in the Riorcan wilds and how he'd worshipped her body—so it had seemed. Of course he hadn't *seen* her body. She'd been underwater until the end, and by that point he'd been too preoccupied to notice her flaws.

He looked through her lists of characters and frequency percentages. "I don't understand what any of this means. But it looks impressive." The bed sank as he sat on the edge. "Who are Justien and Nalica? I mean, *what* are they? They don't wear uniforms like the Legaciatti."

"I can't talk about that."

"Well, I owe you an apology," he said.

Her face flushed, and she turned away. "For what?"

"For not trusting you. For holding you accountable for your father's crimes, and for judging you based on Inyan ideas about bodyguards that don't apply in Kjall. After all that, you still looked after me. I believe you saved my life."

"Well, you saved mine when you jumped out of that ship. Thank you for that." She licked her lips and turned back to her percentages. "Anyway, you know I couldn't allow an Inyan prince to be assassinated on Kjallan soil."

He was silent for a moment. "Is that the only reason you helped?"

"I'm not certain what you're asking."

He sighed. "Do you suppose we might start over? Let me court you the way I ought to have done the moment Lucien proposed the match."

She frowned at the papers on her bed. Challenging as the cipher was, it was easier to lose herself in a complex problem than it was to open her heart to all these messy emotions. In mathematics and cryptanalysis, she either solved a problem or didn't. There was no betrayal, no confusion, no heartbreak. Just a stepwise process. "We've got assassins to track down."

"That will not occupy your every waking minute."

"Actually, it will. This ciphertext is the only lead we have."

"What if I stay and help you with the cipher? After all, it's my life at stake."

Celeste hesitated. She craved his company, but Rayn was a distraction. Not that he tried to be. It was just that with a body like his, he couldn't help it. "You don't know how to break ciphers."

"There's rote work, isn't there?" He picked up one of her frequency lists. "Counting up letters and whatnot?"

"Yes . . ."

"Give me the rote jobs, then. Save the hard stuff for yourself." He smiled. "And when you get tense, I can help you relax."

Don't tempt me. The thought of his hands on her body again, his magical heat flowing through her . . .

She was going to stay focused. But it made sense to let him help with the cipher. "All right. You can help."

15

By evening, Celeste was ready to throw down her quill in frustration. Frequency analysis was getting her nowhere. She'd tried it using every language she knew: Riorcan, Kjallan, Inyan, even Mosari. But nothing had yielded results. Now the letters blurred before her eyes, and she couldn't concentrate. She sank into the sheets, defeated. "There's no getting around it," she said. "This is a homophonic cipher."

Rayn eyed her. "What does that mean?"

"A nonhomophonic substitution cipher is where you substitute one letter for another. Say you replace the Riorcan letter *vert* with the letter *hinan* everywhere it appears. Each letter in the alphabet is mapped to some other letter, and that letter replaces it in the cipher. That sort of cipher can be broken by frequency analysis. See here." She sat up and grabbed one of her papers. The bed looked messy, but she knew exactly what each paper was and what purpose it served. "In the Riorcan language—or any other language—some letters appear more commonly than others. For example, *olov*, a common letter, represents eight percent of all letters in written Riorcan. In the ciphertext, if *hinan* appeared twenty times, that would be eight percent of the total letters. So I would guess that *hinan* is the mapping for *olov*."

"But it's just a guess. Right?"

"An educated guess. It may be wrong, certainly—as it turns out, in this case it is wrong—but if it failed, I could try the letter *yertia*, which represents seven percent of all Riorcan letters, or *riach*, which represents six percent. Essentially, I would make educated guesses and see what they yield."

"But the other two didn't work."

"No, and in fact no character in this cipher appears twenty times." Celeste sighed. "We're dealing with a more sophisticated cipher."

"A homophonic cipher?"

She nodded. "A cipher designed to defeat frequency analysis. I suspected it was homophonic when I saw how many symbols it used. See, instead of assigning just one symbol to a high-frequency letter like *olov*, the cipher creator assigns it several different symbols and uses them all in turn. That means no letter appears much more frequently than any other, and I can't tell *olov* apart from a low-frequency letter."

"Are you saying it can't be solved?"

"No." She bit her lip. "There are ways to break homophonic ciphers. But it's harder, and I can't guarantee success."

"How do you break a homophonic cipher?"

"I look for patterns. Letter combinations. For example, in Kjallan you often see the letter combination *kj*, but you never see the reverse, *jk*."

"I see." His brow wrinkled. "Looking for those patterns sounds like tedious work. Especially if you have to attempt it in multiple languages."

"Indeed." She flopped backward on the bed, closing

her eyes. "But it will be worth it if I can get this decoded."

"I think you need a break, *karamasi*."

That word again. "I need to get back to work. Those assassins are still out there."

"Not as many as there were before," said Rayn. "And you've been working on this for hours. Your mind needs rest. Come here and let me relax you."

She hesitated, uncertain of his intentions and also still drawn to the cipher. She *had* to break it. She'd worked on it all afternoon and accomplished nothing except to determine that it was immune to frequency analysis. And yet Rayn was right. Her mind was blurry and unfocused, like her eyes upon awakening in the morning.

The bed sank beside her, and she felt the warmth of Rayn's huge body. "Here," he said. "I insist." He pulled her onto his lap.

She tried to straighten herself out, untangle her rag-doll limbs, but he placed her where he wanted her, in the crook of his thighs, and massaged her shoulders. His magic began to flow, a gentle breath of heat, warming and unknotting tense muscles. She groaned and leaned into his hands. Bliss.

"You need this," he said.

"I can't imagine why I'm so sore. I've been sitting on the bed all afternoon."

"You need to take breaks," said Rayn. "Maybe take a walk with me every few hours."

She sighed. A walk sounded nice, but the sun had surely gone down by now, and she needed to stay focused on the cipher. Anyway, they couldn't walk freely around Denmor with assassins at large.

"Tell me something," said Rayn. "When you were in Cassian's power, was he cruel to you?"

She shivered. "I told you. He beat me."

"Was there more?"

"Why do you ask?"

"Because you shudder when I mention his name." Rayn shifted to the tender muscles of her neck, working out the knots with warmth and gentle pressure.

Ugly girl. "Cassian hated me. Hated my brother, really, but he couldn't get to Lucien because Vitala had stolen him away. He took his frustrations out on me."

"How did he take out these frustrations?"

If you weren't a princess, you'd be nobody, girl. Do you think a man would want you, with a body like that? She swallowed. "Sometimes he locked me in a cold room overnight."

Rayn's hands stiffened. "A cold room? You mean a larder?"

"It was a prison cell," said Celeste. "He had one set aside for me. In the Imperial Palace, the prison cells aren't served by the hypocaust, and if no heat-glows are provided, they get cold, especially at night. Our interrogators use the cold cell as a means of softening prisoners up. Cassian would throw me in there with only my shift to wear, and I'd shiver all night long."

He was silent for a moment. "Is it true you killed Cassian?"

"Not really," said Celeste. "Vitala and Ista killed him. I helped."

"Ista? The assembly representative?"

Celeste nodded. "That's her."

"I wish I could kill him again for you. He likes to freeze his political enemies? I'd watch him burn." Rayn's magic intensified, and she felt a surge of warmth. "You'll never be cold with me."

"I wouldn't ask you to be my personal heat-glow," said Celeste.

"*Karamasi*, I'm better than a heat-glow." He turned her, lifted her chin, and tilted her mouth toward his.

She could not help herself. She parted her lips in silent invitation, and he kissed them. It astonished her that a man as big as Rayn, with so much muscle and power, could be this gentle. She'd experienced his roughness too, at the pool in the forest, and liked it. But now he held her, stroked her, and kissed her as softly and lovingly as if she were made of glass.

This was not the primal passion they'd experienced in the Riorcan wilds. It was something quieter, something deeper. And Rayn was right—no heat-glow could compare.

Two days into the decoding work, Rayn was getting the hang of things. Deciphering a coded message was a puzzle, essentially—an extraordinarily difficult puzzle requiring a great deal of tedious work. It was one-third mathematics, one-third linguistics, and one-third intuition. Also three-thirds patience. Whenever Celeste became fatigued or frustrated, he took her in his arms, warmed her, rubbed the knots out of her shoulders, and kissed her senseless.

He loved warming her with his magic. He'd warmed other people before—friends, family members. Usually there were no sexual overtones. But Celeste enjoyed it so much more than anyone else he'd plied his magic upon, perhaps because of what she'd been through with Cassian. For her, heat was comfort. While she worked on the cipher, he settled himself behind her, pulling her against his chest. "Pay no attention to me," he murmured. "You concentrate." He laid hands on her, warming her from the core first and working his way to her extremities, avoiding the erogenous zones. Her neck and shoulders began to unclench.

His cock, shoved up against her through several layers of clothing, was like iron. But for now he wasn't going to do anything about that. He realized now that he'd slept with her too soon. Some women leapt right into bed, and it didn't matter what kind of relationship you had with them. But Celeste wasn't that way. What they'd done at the beach had been impulsive, a desperate coupling born of a harrowing experience in the ocean. The pool had been more or less the same thing. But they hadn't been ready; at least Celeste hadn't. There was something deeply vulnerable about her. Perhaps it was the fault of Cassian or that mathematician fellow. Or it could be just her nature—tough as she was on the outside, she had a soft inner core.

He'd broken her trust, and he needed to rebuild it, strand by strand. What they had between them was fragile, a weaving too delicate yet to take off the loom. For now, he would help her with the cipher and court her gently.

Celeste had tried all her deciphering techniques, beginning with the assumption that the destination message was in Riorcan. When that hadn't yielded fruit, she'd tried the same techniques assuming that the message was Kjallan. Then Inyan. No luck with either. Now she was trying Mosari as the destination language.

Rayn couldn't help her with the mathematical work, but he had some linguistic gifts. He spoke all the languages they'd tried except Riorcan. He spoke Mosari better than Celeste did, and that was potentially helpful.

"Gods." Celeste flung a piece of paper across the bed. "I'm getting nowhere."

"The *na* prefix isn't working?"

"No. If it's in there, I can't isolate it."

"Try the *alhe* pronoun," he suggested. "It's a common word in Mosari, and the *lh* combination should be frequent while the reverse *hl* is not found at all."

"I'll try." With a sigh, she took a fresh sheet of paper and laid it on the bed in front of her. "I've got the gods-cursed ciphertext memorized now."

"You're not the only one," said Rayn. "I think I'll be dreaming about it."

Celeste stared at the cipher. Her eyes glazed over, as they often did when she was thinking. Then she set the paper aside. "Rayn, what are we doing?"

"Breaking the cipher," he said.

"No—you and me."

"I'm courting you," said Rayn.

She let out a shaky breath. "I thought you weren't interested in a Kjallan alliance."

"I've changed my mind."

"Didn't you say the trade agreement was horrible for Inya?"

He paused. "I'm not wild about sending brimstone to Kjall. But you say it's for peaceful reasons. Surely if we talk it over, we can work something out." He ran a hand down her side. "Perhaps I am enchanted by your beauty and no longer care about brimstone."

She melted into his arms. "Look, the brimstone is because of Sardos."

"Your brother's going to war with Sardos?"

"Gods, why would he want that? No, there's been a series of assassinations within the First Family. They've been hushed up, but Lucien thinks someone is maneuvering for the position of First Heir."

"I know," he said. "My people are following the situation."

"Before the current First Heir rose to power, Sardos behaved aggressively toward Kjall. The First Heir is a strong ruler. He's kept his country peaceful for decades, but if the man is assassinated, there's no telling what could happen. Lucien has reduced the size of our military, but not by much, because the threat of Sardos looms. That's why he wants brimstone. An attack could come quickly if the First Heir dies, and we have to be prepared."

He wrapped his arms around her. "Thank you for telling me the reason for the brimstone. It gives me some peace of mind."

Celeste picked up her quill and began to write.

"You know what we need in Tiasa, our capital city?" Rayn continued. "A mathematical society. You could found one—and open it to women."

Celeste straightened, obviously intrigued. "I like that idea. You know, I've been interested in this marriage from the beginning. But I don't have the power to negotiate the treaty. That's between you and Lucien."

"Are you always this pragmatic?" asked Rayn.

She swallowed. "I have to be. What I do affects my country. My life is not my own, nor will it ever be."

"I believe you think a great deal about how to please your brother," said Rayn.

"I owe everything to him and the empress."

Rayn lowered his head to her shoulder and spoke quietly into her ear. "Do you spend as much time thinking about what pleases you?"

She squirmed within his arms. "I think about that some. But like I said—"

"Your life is your own," said Rayn, "imperial princess or not. I think you are not quite so pragmatic as you claim. Inside, you want love. You want passion."

Her cheeks colored. She swallowed hard, picked up her quill with trembling fingers, and began to write.

Too soon. He lifted her hair and kissed the back of her neck. He held her as she worked, and gradually she relaxed in his arms.

Suddenly her body stiffened and became electrified. Her quill scratched rapidly on the paper, filling in letters above the ciphertext. "Three gods," she said. "I think I've got something."

16

Celeste saw it now: the message *was* written in Mosari. But not very good Mosari. Whoever had written it lacked an understanding of the Mosari pronouns and had used only *alhe* and its variants, ignoring the other six pronoun forms. Now that she'd figured that out, it was merely a matter of time before she cracked the entire message. She scratched at the paper with her quill, making educated guesses and trying them out, occasionally filling in a letter above the ciphertext when she became certain it was correct.

Rayn sat behind her, watching over her shoulder. He was quiet and didn't disturb her, but she felt the gentle breath of his warming magic as she worked, the safe harbor of his body cocooning hers. Being able to relax completely helped her to focus.

It took her three hours to finish deciphering the message.

AM SENDING THE REQUESTED SUPPLIES
EXPECT A COURIER WITHIN THE NEXT
WEEK REGARDING THE MURDERED SCOUT
DID YOU FIND HIS BODY WAS IT WOLVES
OR ENEMIES HOLD OFF ON SENDING OUT

THE NEW RECRUIT WE'RE GOING TO NEED
SOME PEOPLE IN RESERVE WE'VE TAKEN
LOSSES AND I'VE IDENTIFIED SEVERAL
MORE TARGETS COUNTRY FIRST KEEP
FAITH BAYARD

"Bayard," she said flatly. Could it be Vitala's old trainer? It was not impossible, especially since Justien had told her the breakaway group he'd been tracking had eyes in the Enclave building. A shiver ran through her. Who else might be involved? Asmund? Ista? She couldn't see why they would be, but then she hadn't suspected Bayard either. Could anyone in the Enclave building be trusted?

Rayn leaned forward, speaking softly as his stubble grazed her cheek. "It might be a different Bayard."

"Could be." She doubted it.

"Why would he sign his own name in a message that could be intercepted?"

"People do it all the time," she said. "Ciphers instill a false sense of security. The writer believes his code is unbreakable, so he freely spills his secrets."

"What now?" said Rayn. "Bayard's an assembly representative. He has more practical authority here than you or I. We can't report it to Asmund or Ista. Anyone in the building could be involved, for all we know."

"True." The only people she knew she could trust, besides Rayn, were Justien's team. "Let's talk to Justien. He'll know what to do."

She called to Justien, who was guarding her door, and the huge man came into the anteroom.

"Excellent timing, Your Imperial Highness," he said. "A runner just stopped by with some news."

"What news?"

"The *Soldier's Sweep* has arrived. It's dropping anchor

in the Denmor harbor along with the Inyan ship *Water Spirit*."

Relief flooded her. "The *Sweep*—that's Lucien's ship, is it not?"

"It is," said Justien.

"The *Water Spirit* would be the ship I've been waiting for, the one bearing a message from home," said Rayn. "But it's late. It ought to have arrived ahead of the Kjallans."

"Well, it's here now," said Justien. "Your Imperial Highness, I suggest we head to the docks and meet the emperor."

Celeste waited on the pier with Rayn. She couldn't see much, since the pier was crowded and Justien had surrounded her and the prince with a protective escort. She craned her neck in an attempt to peer into the harbor, her stomach knotting with excitement. The two ships had dispatched boats, which were delivering their passengers to shore. Celeste squinted at the *Sweep*'s boats, trying to spot Lucien or Vitala. As the first craft neared the dock, a crowd of Riorcan guards pushed their way forward, further blocking her view.

She heard a joyful bark and grabbed Rayn's hand. "Patricus!"

The prince turned to her in confusion.

"The dog, remember?" She felt a little sheepish at having taken Rayn's hand, especially in this public place. But he didn't seem to mind, so she held on to it.

Patricus squeezed through the circle of guards and gamboled about the pier, sniffing the air as he wove through the maze of human legs. He spotted Celeste, barked again, and galloped toward her.

She reached down to receive an ecstatic sea retriever, who wagged his tail frantically as she stroked his ears.

"Patricus, get back here," called an authoritative voice.

Boots thumped and swords jangled in belts as Legaciatti in full uniform marched up all around them. Celeste rose to receive her brother the emperor. Lucien's eyes were bright and stern. Celeste, never frightened by her brother but often awed by him, dipped into a curtsy. Lucien seized her arm and pulled her into a hug. "Gods, Celeste," he said. "Could you possibly have frightened us more? I nearly had apoplexy." He squeezed her hard enough to choke the breath from her lungs.

When he released her, Celeste turned to Vitala, who stood next to him, and embraced her—gently, since the empress was expecting. "We've done some investigation while we waited for you. I'll tell you more once you're settled in at the Enclave building."

In the crowd of Legaciatti surrounding them, Celeste spotted her bodyguard. "Atella! Three gods, I'm happy to see you." She beckoned the woman forward and embraced her. "I heard you killed every one of those assassins."

Atella shook her head ruefully. "Not quickly enough."

"I'm still standing here, aren't I?" said Celeste. "It was three against one. You were superb."

Lucien turned to Rayn and clasped wrists. "Prince of Inya, the gods have blessed us twice over that we have lost neither you nor my sister. I apologize that you suffered an attempt on your life while traveling on one of my ships."

"Your Imperial Majesty." Rayn inclined his head. "I don't hold you responsible."

"We'll find out who was behind the crime," said Lucien. "This I promise."

"Thank you for your courtesy and diligence," said Rayn.

"On our way over, we came upon your ship *Water Spirit*," said Lucien. "It's the one I'd dispatched to you earlier with a message from home. The ship had been damaged in a storm. We provided assistance with their repairs, and they ended up sailing alongside us the rest of the way. That man over there—" He turned, indicating with the angle of his head an Inyan man just disembarking onto the dock. "He claims to know you."

"Indeed he does," said Rayn. "That's my cousin Tiannon. If you'll excuse me . . ."

"Of course," said Lucien.

"Wait," said Celeste. "Bring him over here, if you would. Stay with the guards." After two nearly successful attempts on Rayn's life, she didn't want him separated from their escort.

Rayn called to his cousin. "Tiannon, over here."

Tiannon seemed nervous at being in the presence of the Kjallan emperor and empress and so many Legaciatti. He bowed to the imperials and said to Rayn, "I've news from home. It's important."

"Can you speak of it here?" asked Rayn.

"It's for your ears only, sir," said Tiannon.

"Then let's return to the Enclave building. Did Magister Lornis come with you?" he asked Lucien.

"He did," said Lucien. "He'll be on the next boat from the *Sweep*."

Celeste looked out into the harbor. The second boat was already plying its way toward them through the smooth waters. "Let's wait for him, and we can all head back together."

*   *   *

The Riorcans wanted to call another assembly now that the imperials were here, but Celeste insisted on meeting with Lucien, Vitala, and Justien alone. She wasn't ready to face Bayard yet, nor was she certain how to proceed with the information she had uncovered. Lucien and Vitala would know what to do.

The servants were still carrying the emperor's and empress's things up to their rooms, so for the sake of privacy, Celeste invited everyone into the anteroom of her own apartment—an awkward fit, especially with enormous Justien. She'd invited Rayn as well, but he'd declined, saying he needed to talk to Tiannon and Lornis first.

"You didn't bring Prince Jamien?" she asked her brother as they took their seats.

Lucien shook his head. "The heir is safer at home. Let's begin with the assassination attempt. What happened on the ship?"

"Actually, Justien and I have been investigating a second assassination attempt, and—"

Lucien blinked. "There's been another?"

"Yes, but in this case only Rayn was attacked. I was not present. I'll catch you up on those details later—or Justien can do it—but first let me give you the most important piece of information. I know who one of the assassins is."

Justien straightened, his eyes coming alight. "You do? How?"

"Who is it?" asked Vitala.

"I broke the cipher," she explained to Justien. "Let me get the translation." She'd hidden the translated message beneath her mattress. Now she went to the bedroom and retrieved it. Back in the anteroom, she handed it to Lucien. "Bayard is involved."

Vitala gasped. She leaned over and read the message

in Lucien's hands. Her cheeks colored. When they had finished reading, Lucien passed the message on to an impatient Justien.

"I don't know for sure it's *that* Bayard," she added. "It could be another man with the same name."

"I doubt it," said Vitala.

Lucien frowned. "Who knows about this so far?"

"The people in this room plus Prince Rayn."

"Why the prince?"

"He helped me decipher the message."

"We've got to move on this right away," said Lucien. "Before word gets out."

"Let me handle it," said Vitala. "I know Bayard well. Justien, I'll write up an imperial writ for you. Have him arrested, and I'll be the one to question him."

Lucien nodded. "Do we arrest anyone else? There might be others in this building who are part of the plot."

Justien said, "We can't arrest the whole building."

"Certainly not," said Vitala. "Just Bayard for now. If he's involved with this, my hope is that I can talk him into giving up his fellows."

"Tread carefully," said Lucien. "He's got a deathstone."

"I know it. And he knows that I know it," said Vitala. "I don't think he'll use it if we just talk."

"I fear that if he docs have allies, they may run when Bayard is arrested," said Justien.

"Can't be helped," said Vitala. "If they run, at least we'll know who they were."

"What about the assembly meeting?" asked Lucien.

"Make our excuses," said Vitala. "This is more important."

"Very well," said Lucien. "Arrest him, Justien, and Vitala will question him. In the meantime, I want Celeste to tell me everything that's happened since she left Riat."

*   *   *

When Rayn returned to the Enclave building, he learned that the *Water Spirit* was the second ship dispatched to bring him this message. The first had never arrived. Tiannon had suspected it wouldn't, so he'd sailed on his own authority to make sure Rayn received the news before it was too late.

Now Rayn had to figure out what to do about it. Wanting some fresh air and the space to collect his thoughts, he grabbed Lornis and headed out to the Riorcan beach. They were trailed by Nalica and a few other guards. Much as he disliked being followed around, he accepted the necessity of it, at least while he was away from home.

Seagulls wheeled overhead. The beach here was not at all like the ones at home. Riorcan beaches were austere, their colors muted. Gray sand, gray oceans, sometimes even a gray sky. The cliffs looked savage, the forests thick and deep, hiding secrets. Nevertheless, the smell of the sea air sent a dizzying wave of homesickness through him.

He dug a shell out of the sand and flung it into the water.

Lornis hung back from the lapping waves. "When do we sail home?"

"I think this evening," said Rayn. "Or tomorrow on the tide. Certainly no later." The news from home was a shock: his father had abdicated the throne. Had done so, in fact, less than a week after Rayn's departure from Inya. Rayn needed to be present at his ratification vote forty days from the date of abdication if he wanted to ascend the throne. Many of those forty days had already passed. Even if he sailed immediately, he'd have little time to convince the people of Inya that he was worthy of being their king.

"It was deliberate, I'm sure," said Lornis. "The council's timing."

"No doubt," said Rayn. "They pushed him into abdicating when they knew I'd be away. And then their message to me went astray. Funny coincidence, that."

"Not a coincidence at all."

Rayn nodded. "If Tiannon hadn't suspected mischief and come here on his own, I'd have never known I was up for ratification. I'd have missed my vote and lost my chance at the throne."

"Do you think we could finish negotiating the trade treaty before we go? The emperor's here, after all."

"I think it's unlikely we could negotiate it that quickly." Waves ran up the beach like watery fingers, splashing over Rayn's boots. He now regretted not having taken the treaty more seriously when he'd had the opportunity. Instead he'd wasted his time on this trip to Denmor.

"What about the princess?" said Lornis.

What about her, indeed? He'd been courting her slowly, trying to allow some trust to develop between them. She needed time to forgive him for the accusations he'd leveled at her about her family, and he needed time to settle his own feelings. But time was a luxury, and they'd run out. He had to make a decision now: marry her or go home without her.

Lornis stepped up beside him on the wet sand. "You should accept the proposal. Think what it would mean to our people if you returned with a Kjallan princess at your side. Not only will the townsfolk be excited by the prospect of a royal wedding—it gives them assurance that Kjall will not declare war on us."

As usual, Lornis was thinking strategy. Yes, it would strengthen Rayn politically to return with Celeste. But having spent time with her in the Riorcan wilds, and here in the Enclave building, he could not think of her just as a political asset. She was a person, and he wanted her to be happy. Would she be happy with him in Inya?

He'd like to consider how she would adapt, but he was out of time, and he had to make a decision. "I'll marry her, if she'll have me."

"Think again, because—" Lornis cocked his head. "Did you just say you'll marry her?"

"You heard me."

"So you changed your mind," said Lornis. "I thought I was going to have to talk you into this."

"Yes, I changed my mind."

Lornis smiled. "What did you two get up to in the Riorcan wilds?"

"None of your business," said Rayn.

"I'm glad you've come to your senses. This will really boost your odds at ratification."

Rayn shook his head. "It's not about politics."

"What about the trade agreement?"

"I think it will have to wait until after ratification."

Lornis frowned. "I'm not sure the emperor will accept that."

"We won't know until we talk to him." Rayn turned to his friend. "Do you remember what the emperor said that first evening we talked to him? About the legacy he wanted to leave his people, not just during his reign, but after he was gone?"

"Yes. He said he wanted peace for Kjall."

"Well, consider my father," said Rayn. "He ruled wisely and well for years—and then this madness struck, and the country's falling apart."

"You exaggerate."

"He would have sold off the King's Lands—"

"He didn't, because you stopped it," said Lornis.

"But if I hadn't been there . . ." Rayn forced himself to exhale. He looked down as a wave tickled his boot. "Lornis, what if it happens to me?"

"If what happens to you?"

The words stuck in his throat. "I might go mad like my father."

"Oh, Rayn," said Lornis.

"It could be happening," he said. "How would I even know? Father's decline was so gradual. If it were happening to me, would I even be aware of it? Would you say something?"

"Of course I'd say something," said Lornis. "It's not happening. Your mind is as sharp as it's ever been."

"Maybe I shouldn't take the throne. And maybe I shouldn't marry Celeste. Because it could happen, and then what would my legacy be? Madness, like my father's."

"Your father's legacy is *you*," said Lornis. "He raised you. He taught you everything you know. What do you think really happened when you rallied the people against the Land Council? That wasn't you opposing your father. That was you defending him, protecting him—doing what you know he would have wanted you to do. *You are his legacy*. And you must take the throne."

"I'm frightened," he admitted.

"Of course you are," said Lornis. "Ruling a country is a big responsibility. If you didn't find it intimidating, I'd think less of you."

Rayn reached out and clasped wrists with him.

"You won't be alone," said Lornis. "You'll have me to advise you, and if you marry Celeste, you'll have a strong queen by your side. The biggest mistake your father made was marrying Kin-Lera. She's beautiful, but she hasn't any fire inside."

"Celeste has it."

"Then the path ahead of you is clear," said Lornis.

Rayn nodded. "Let's go back to the Enclave building."

17

Back at the Enclave building, Rayn found the halls crowded with Kjallan soldiers. Something was going on. Maybe they'd arrested Bayard or were about to. He headed up the stairs, trailed by Lornis and his guards. Should he speak first to Celeste or to the emperor?

Celeste first, he decided. He headed for her apartment.

Someone called his name. He turned, and a knot of Legaciatti opened to reveal Emperor Lucien.

He dipped his head in acknowledgment. "Your Imperial Majesty."

"Your Highness," said Lucien. "I'm glad you happened by. We need to talk, just the two of us."

Rayn's eyes slid to Celeste's door halfway down the hall. He'd rather speak first to her and see if she was still interested in the marriage. But one didn't refuse a meeting with the emperor of Kjall. "Of course."

Lucien led him back to his imperial apartment, which was much like Rayn's except decorated in red and gold rather than green and silver. There was a small dining room, which Rayn's room didn't have. He took a seat in the anteroom. *Just the two of us* turned out to be him and Lucien and half a dozen Legaciatti. He eyed the guards with annoyance. Did the Kjallan emperor ever have a moment of privacy? How aggravating it must be to be surrounded by armed guards for the entirety of one's life.

Lucien lounged in his chair, clearly more comfortable with the security than Rayn was. "The message from home. I hope it wasn't bad news?"

"Neither good nor bad," said Rayn. "My father has abdicated the throne."

Lucien sat up. "That's a surprise. So you'll be ratified as king."

Rayn nodded. "The vote takes place forty days after abdication. There's little time left, so I must sail for home."

"I find your country's voting ritual curious," said Lucien. "Why bother with it when you are your father's only heir? Is it ceremonial in nature, like a public coronation?"

"Well, the process is more meaningful when there are several heirs to choose from. But there have been occasions in Inyan history when a single heir was rejected and the throne passed to a more distant relative. This is, in fact, how my direct ancestors came to possess the throne. Some cousin, centuries back, was passed over."

Lucien stared at him. "Are you saying it's uncertain whether you'll become king?"

"No one can know for sure until the vote is cast." Had the Kjallan emperor not known this? The workings of Inyan politics were no secret.

"I thought that in your case it was merely a formality."

"It's not a formality," said Rayn. "The vote is important."

Lucien looked flustered. "There hasn't been an Inyan succession in my lifetime. But never mind. I asked you here to discuss something else. I'm relieved that you plan to sail home, because I was going to suggest that you do exactly that. After two assassination attempts, it's clear that Kjall is not safe for you. There is some reason to believe that the assassins want you killed on foreign soil; therefore you will be safer in your homeland."

"I believe Celeste is quite close to finding the assassins."

"She has done admirable work, but it appears there are a number of people involved in this conspiracy. It will take time for us to root them all out."

Rayn doubted that Lucien cared all that much about his safety. The emperor just didn't want the scandal and embarrassment of having a foreign national assassinated in his country. Or was the emperor more worried about Celeste? She had nearly been killed during the first assassination attempt, just because she'd been in his company at the time.

He hadn't thought about it, but the fact that he was being targeted by a group of assassins might be a problem as far as the marriage was concerned. "I'm truly sorry about what happened to Celeste during that first attack. I did everything in my power to protect her, even leaping overboard to save her from the cold water."

"For which I am profoundly grateful," said Lucien. "The least I can do is see to it that you come to no further harm."

Rayn frowned. "I need to leave by tomorrow morning. But I'd like to settle some things first. Regarding the offer of Celeste's hand—"

Lucien shook his head. "Treaty and marriage negotiations will take far longer than a single day. There won't be time."

Rayn stared at him. Had Emperor Lucien just quietly

withdrawn the marriage offer? It was because of the assassins, he supposed—Lucien didn't want his sister marrying a man who was being repeatedly attacked. Maybe it was also because Lucien hadn't understood the ratification vote and that there was no guarantee he would be king of Inya.

But those were temporary problems. If his suit was not welcome now, perhaps it would be in a month or two if he won ratification and the assassins were captured. "I perfectly understand your reluctance to send your sister into an uncertain situation. But when the problems are resolved—"

"My sister mentioned that you had some reservations about marrying into the family of Florian Nigellus Gavros," said Lucien coolly. "I would not ask you to contaminate your immaculate bloodline."

A chill ran through Rayn. "Since then, I've experienced a change of heart. I've apologized to Celeste."

Lucien pinned him with his gaze. "My sister was forcibly married to a usurper of the throne at the tender age of thirteen. He was not kind to her. She suffered greatly."

"She told me," said Rayn.

"I doubt she told you all that there is to know," said Lucien. "Even I don't know exactly what happened. Neither does the empress. Celeste has chosen to keep the details to herself."

Rayn swallowed. Celeste had told him a little, but he knew she was holding back.

"Thus I hesitate to place her in the power of any man who does not cherish and appreciate her," said Lucien.

"You offered her to me—"

"I'm withdrawing the offer."

Rayn swallowed. "But I love her."

"If that were true, you would not care whose blood

runs in her veins." Lucien sniffed. "For your safety, my guards will provide you with an escort for the remainder of your stay here. You will not leave the safety of your rooms except to return to your ship, and you will depart my country no later than tomorrow morning."

"At least let me speak to Celeste before I go." If he left without saying a word to her about what had happened, what was she going to think? That would be twice he'd courted her and then unexpectedly abandoned her.

Lucien turned to his guards. "Help the prince of Inya to prepare for his journey. He is not to visit my sister." To Rayn he said, "We have enjoyed your visit, Your Highness. Please convey my regards to your father. Perhaps we'll speak again at some future date."

"Your Imperial Majesty—" he began, but the guards crowded around him, blocking his view of the emperor and leaving a single opening: a pathway to the door. The interview was over.

Celeste waited with Vitala in the stone hallway of the belowground prison. The empress had promised her that the interrogation wouldn't be violent. This was just a preliminary talk, to establish how cooperative Bayard might be. Still, having never done this before, she felt anxious and out of place. "Has his riftstone been taken away?"

"No," said Vitala. "We'd take it if we could, but it's not on a chain around his neck like yours is. It's implanted in his body."

Celeste blinked. That changed everything about this interrogation. "So he still has his war magic?"

"He's in restraints."

"That's not what I'm worried about," said Celeste. "If he has his war magic, I can't use my own magic. No suggestions, no truth spells."

Vitala frowned. "I was hoping that maybe, since you have that talent with animals—"

"No," said Celeste. "I've tried using suggestions on mages before. It doesn't work."

"That's unfortunate," said Vitala, "but my understanding is that mages can choose to submit to a truth spell, if they so desire. Whether he permits your truth spell or not will tell us how willing he is to cooperate. And if he won't cooperate, that suggests guilt."

Celeste nodded.

"We can't torture him," said Vitala. "He's got a death-stone."

"Could you . . . remove the deathstone and riftstone from his body?" She made a face, realizing what an ugly procedure that would be.

"I'd rather not risk it. He might figure out what we were up to and activate the deathstone before we can remove it. We can try it if all other methods fail, but let's not start with that option."

Celeste was glad there wouldn't be any torture or surgical removal of deathstones as yet, but it seemed they had little leverage over the man. "How will you convince him to talk?"

"I'm not sure," said Vitala. "Whether he submits to your truth spell will tell us something. At this preliminary stage, I just want to feel him out, get an idea what we're dealing with."

A guard approached and bowed to Vitala. "The prisoner's ready, Your Imperial Majesty."

"Thank you, Arrius."

Celeste followed Vitala through the press of guards and into the cell where Bayard sat on a chair, his wrists and ankles shackled. There was an empty chair across from Bayard and another next to him. Vitala took the one and gestured Celeste to the other.

Feeling a little shaky, Celeste sat beside the prisoner.

Bayard glared at Vitala. "This is ludicrous. I've done nothing wrong—only aided and protected the Inyan prince and Princess Celeste."

"If that's so, you've nothing to worry about," said Vitala. "Celeste is going to use a truth spell on you. I suggest you submit to it."

Celeste placed a hand on Bayard's arm. He flinched.

Truth spells were invasive and ugly. She didn't like using them, because to spy on someone's inner thoughts, even in this limited way, could be more violating than stripping him naked. Yet the Kjallan justice system relied on these spells heavily. How else could they definitively sort truth from fiction?

She closed her eyes and called upon her magic. From the Rift, her magic poured forth, invisible in this world, but she'd seen it in the spirit world and knew what it looked like there: impossible shapes, impossible colors. She sent the magic into Bayard. At her urging, it grew like a vine, dividing and spreading, sending tendrils through his chest, his limbs, and upward into the vast sea of his mind.

Then something went wrong. As quickly as new tendrils sprouted, the older ones withered. Her magic unraveled, bit by bit, and the vines disintegrated into dust.

She opened her eyes and saw Vitala's expectant gaze. "He's resisting the spell."

"So much for your being innocent," said Vitala to the prisoner.

"Perhaps I just don't like having my thoughts spied upon," said Bayard.

"Should I try again?" asked Celeste.

"Don't bother." Vitala held the original enciphered letter before Bayard. "Did you write this?"

"No," he said.

"That's funny," said Vitala, "because you signed your name at the bottom."

"Stuff and nonsense," said Bayard. "The whole thing is gibberish. There's no name at all."

Vitala pulled out a second piece of paper—the translation. She cleared her throat and began to read. "*Am sending the requested supplies. Expect a courier within the next week regarding the murdered scout. Did you find his body? Was it wolves or enemies?* Don't keep me in suspense, Bayard. *Was* it wolves?"

Some of the color left Bayard's face. "I haven't the faintest idea what you're talking about."

"I've got a team of investigators at your house," said Vitala. "They're tearing the place apart, searching your belongings. What do you think, Bayard? Will we find more messages like this one?"

Bayard shook his head. "You were the most promising student I ever trained, and look what you've become."

"The empress of Kjall?" said Vitala.

"A shill for the enemy."

Celeste felt a little awkward watching this exchange, and yet she was fascinated. Vitala spoke little enough of her experience being trained by Bayard as an assassin, and even less about how she felt when she'd rebelled against him and abandoned the Obsidian Circle.

"You haven't answered my question," said Vitala. "Perhaps I should rephrase: *how many more* messages like this will my investigators find? And how many people will they incriminate?"

Bayard shifted in his chair. His muscles bulged as he tested his restraints. "I answer none of your ridiculous questions. You think what you've done for Riorca is a victory, and that this is freedom? My people bowing before your precious emperor, signaling him at all hours to ask his advice for this, his permission for that?"

Vitala folded her arms. "Yes, Bayard, this *is* freedom. Freedom from slavery, freedom from war and strife. This dream you have of excising all Kjallan influence from Riorca—it's a chimera, a grotesque imagination. You think that by killing innocent people you can create something beautiful, but it's a lie, Bayard. My *precious emperor* has done more for Riorca than you ever did."

"You watch," said Bayard, "and see what you've wrought. Within a generation, two generations, Riorca will no longer exist. It'll be just another province of black-haired soldiers. Another cog in the Kjallan machine of war."

"Kjall isn't a machine of war anymore." Vitala held up the letter. "Do you deny that you wrote this?"

"Of course I deny it," said Bayard.

"You are a liar," said Vitala, "and I'm going to prove it."

"You betrayed me," said Bayard.

"And you've disappointed me," said Vitala.

Celeste had barely returned to her state apartment when the emperor arrived at her door. He and his security escort crowded into her anteroom.

"Any luck interrogating Bayard?" asked Lucien.

Celeste took a seat. "He refused my truth spell and admitted to nothing. Mostly he spat a lot of accusations at Vitala. Vitala's sent a team to search his house."

Lucien nodded. "What sort of accusations?"

"Stuff and nonsense," she said, borrowing Bayard's phrase. "That Vitala had betrayed Riorca, that she was a disappointment to him. She didn't seem bothered."

"She hides it well," said Lucien, looking grim. "I came to tell you that I've sent the prince home to Inya."

Celeste clutched the armrests of her chair. "Why?"

He gestured at her to sit back. "It's nothing you need worry about. He's received news from home that his father has abdicated the throne."

His father had *abdicated*? She thought back to the snippets of information Rayn had given her about his father. She didn't have the impression that abdication was something the man was capable of making a decision about on his own. "Do you think the man was manipulated into stepping down?"

"I don't know, and it doesn't matter."

She realized something. "So Rayn isn't a prince anymore. He's king of Inya."

"No, it turns out that Inya has a ratification process for their potential rulers. The people have to vote whether or not to accept him as king."

"They will, won't they?" Then she remembered what Rayn had told her about the Land Council conspiring against him.

"I couldn't say, not knowing that much about Inyan politics." Lucien shifted in his chair. "I have to admit fault here. I didn't research this as well as I should have, and I made the same assumption you just did—that of course he would be ratified and it was merely a formality. The process is normally used to select between heirs, if a king has two or more sons. But Rayn is his father's only potential heir; thus I assumed . . . Well, obviously I shouldn't have assumed anything."

"Perhaps we could help him win ratification."

Lucien shook his head. "It's not our business."

Her mind raced, working out the implications. Why had the Land Council pushed Rayn's father to abdicate now rather than at some later date? Probably because Rayn was away in Kjall, and they believed they could stop him from winning. "When does the ratification vote happen?"

"Soon," said Lucien. "Which is why Prince Rayn has to leave."

"I'll go with him," she said.

"The contract cannot be negotiated that quickly."

"We can work out the trade details later. Right now the important thing is to make sure Rayn becomes king."

Lucien leaned forward. "Rayn thinks our bloodline is tainted because of Florian."

"I wish I hadn't mentioned that to you. He never said our bloodline was *tainted*; just that he was concerned about my being Florian's daughter. And your being Florian's son."

"It means the same thing," said Lucien.

"He apologized."

"Just words." Lucien waved his hand. "I've spent half my life trying to undo the mistakes my father made. I don't enjoy being blamed for those mistakes."

"Rayn lives far away," said Celeste. "He's never met Florian, and until now he'd never met you. Is it so wrong that he assumed father and son would be alike? It's personal for him. His aunt died during the invasion of Mosar."

Lucien's brows rose. "Are you making excuses for him?"

"I'm saying he made an honest mistake, for which he apologized. You shouldn't hold it against him. I don't. Not anymore."

"He seems to have changed his mind about you at a most convenient time," said Lucien. "Now that he faces a ratification vote at home, earlier than expected, he's had a sudden epiphany about the benefits of an alliance with Kjall."

"No," insisted Celeste. "He apologized to me *before* he heard about his father's abdication."

"Because he thought about it and realized that he needed you politically."

She fell silent. Lucien was managing to instill some doubts in her about Rayn's intentions, yet none of what he said matched her impression of the prince. Lucien saw him as a schemer and manipulator who played on her affections when he thought he had something to gain from her and otherwise resented her for her ancestry. But the man she knew was one whose genuine concerns about a Kjallan alliance had been slowly alleviated as he came to know her better. Still, Lucien was seldom wrong about people. And this wouldn't be the first time she'd been fooled by someone feigning interest in her.

"He's got enemies in the Land Council," added Lucien. "And he's got a group of assassins after him. I don't want you caught in the cross fire again, and there's no guarantee he'll win the throne. I want him gone. I've placed him under guard and had him escorted to his ship."

A wave of panic washed over her. "I have to see him before he goes." Lucien could be wrong. Maybe Rayn *did* love her. And what would he think if she let him go without saying a word?

Lucien smiled wearily. "I know you want to talk to him, but believe me, it's not a good idea. He seems to know the right things to say, and I would be remiss in my duty as your protector if I let him take advantage of you."

"He loves me," she said, not at all certain it was true, but hoping. Surely those afternoons where he'd warmed her and kissed her while she'd worked on the cipher meant something. And what about those days in the Riorcan wilds?

"I should never have offered him your hand," said Lucien. "I didn't know him nearly as well as I thought I did."

Perhaps she'd never really known him either. Had the things he'd said been genuine, or had he said them to manipulate her? She'd been inclined to believe Rayn, but if Lucien doubted him, she had to wonder about her own judgment. Was Rayn like every other partner she'd known, using her for material gain while secretly or even openly despising her?

Her cheeks heated with shame. Images swam through her mind: Cassian stripping her naked and looking on her with scorn. *Ugly girl. What man would ever want a creature like you?* Lucien was right. Prince Rayn was acting in his own political interest. He didn't love her. Why would he?

18

Rayn leaned out of the rowboat, taking care not to upset it. He craned his neck for a better view of the shore. In the moonlit darkness, everything was shadowy gray. "Not the pier," he ordered the sailors who manned the oars. "Land us on that beach over there."

"In the middle of nowhere, sir?" asked the lead rower.

"I don't want to be seen."

The sailors dragged their oars, and the boat swung toward the beach. Earlier that afternoon, Lucien's men had escorted Rayn to his ship. He was supposed to stay there overnight and sail to Inya on the morning tide, but he couldn't leave without speaking to Celeste. All through the evening, he'd watched the pier. It had swarmed with Kjallan imperial guards, and even after the sun had set, they had not left. No doubt they had instructions to intercept him if he made an appearance.

The murky outline of trees loomed ahead, and the boat dragged as it scraped bottom. Two sailors leapt out, grabbed the towrope, and pulled the craft up onto the sand.

Rayn stood, balancing as the boat rocked on its keel, and stepped out on the beach.

"Shall we wait for you here, sir?" asked one of his men.

Rayn considered. Several men would be more visible than one, but after two failed assassination attempts against him, he was not going to make the mistake of traveling alone. These sailors weren't the equivalent of trained and magically talented guards, but they carried weapons and knew how to fight. "You and you," he said, selecting two. "Come with me."

The chosen sailors fell in behind him as he sneaked across the beach toward Denmor and the Enclave building, giving the pier a wide berth. He expected trouble when he reached the building itself, but if he could get as far as the door to Celeste's apartment, so that she heard his voice, he had a chance.

He'd nearly reached the tree line when a voice called out from the darkness, "Halt."

His head snapped in the direction of the sound, but he could see nothing. His first thought was to run, but he knew nothing about how many men were there or what capabilities they possessed. He halted.

Figures emerged from the shadows onto the moonlit beach, five—no, six of them. Swords and pistols dangled from their belts. He placed his hand on the hilt of his own sword, ready to draw it and call fire in case these were assassins, but as they approached, he recognized the sickle-and-sunburst insignia of the Legaciatti.

"Your Highness," called a Legaciattus, "for your safety, the emperor has ordered that you remain on your ship."

He gritted his teeth. For his safety, indeed. "The risk I take is entirely my own. I must speak to the Imperial Princess."

"I'm sorry, sir. My instructions are to keep you on your ship." The Legaciattus was close enough now that Rayn could see his narrow face and lump of a nose. The other guards stepped forward, surrounding Rayn.

"All I ask is ten minutes with the princess."

The Legaciattus stood firm. "By imperial order, you must return to the *Water Spirit*."

Rayn considered whether he could outrun or evade these men. To fight would be the height of foolishness. No, he was caught. He'd have to turn to his secondary plan. "I've written the princess a letter." He reached into his tunic pocket and withdrew a sealed envelope. "If I return to my ship, will you see that it reaches her?"

The Legaciattus hesitated, uncertain. After a moment, he took the envelope. "I'll see that it reaches the right person."

The *right person*—that sounded suspicious. "It's for the princess."

"Yes, sir."

He wished he could be certain it would reach her, but with the guards crowding around him, Rayn had little choice but to return to his boat. The Kjallans stood on the shore, watching, as his sailors rowed him back to the *Water Spirit*.

At dawn, Celeste climbed the long spiral staircase to the top of the Enclave building. Lucien would never allow her to go to the pier, not with Bayard's team of assassins still on the loose. Indeed, she doubted he'd allow her out of the building at all until they were in custody. But there was no reason not to go up on the roof, and from here she could see Rayn's ship.

He'd made no attempt to contact her.

Lucien had probably forbidden him from speaking to her, and yet a part of her wished Rayn had tried. She still wished she'd gotten his assurance that his feelings for her had been genuine, that his sudden interest in her had not been merely a shift in political strategy. Yes, he had much to gain from an association with the most powerful ruling family in the world. But she still hoped that maybe, just maybe, it wasn't the only reason he liked her.

To be the sister of the emperor of Kjall was, in many ways, a blessing. She was not blind to the doors her position opened for her. She'd never have been welcomed into the Mathematical Brotherhood without Lucien's influence. But there was a price to be paid for her status. She'd paid it once before, when the usurper Cassian had forcibly married her in order to claim the throne, and she would continue to pay it. It was her lot in life to make a political marriage.

This was not an unreasonable sacrifice to make in the service of her country, when her country, after all, had given her so much. When she considered her situation in this light, she realized that even if Rayn's interest in her had been feigned, her feelings ought not to be hurt. What did it matter if he wanted her only for political reasons? By its very definition, that was what a political marriage was.

Now Lucien would find her another husband, one less prejudiced against Kjallans and less vulnerable to assassins, and she would trade one loveless marriage for another.

When her legs began to ache from standing, she paced back and forth across the rooftop. When she tired of that, she called for a chair. A guard fetched her one, and she sat facing the harbor. Rayn's ship was coming to life. Sailors spilled onto the deck and swarmed about the capstan. The *Water Spirit* was weighing anchor for departure.

Her limbs felt leaden. She'd thought there had been something more between her and Rayn. For a few short days, she'd known, or thought she'd known, the experience of being loved. Now she wondered if Rayn had contrived the whole thing. His act had been convincing.

Karamasi, he'd called her. Intentionally or not, he'd voiced an undeniable truth. There *was* something inside her: a desire, a yearning. For all that she tried to deny it, the feeling wouldn't go away. She didn't want to be bartered away for brimstone in a Kjallan treaty. She wanted the one thing her position as imperial princess denied her: someone to love, who would love her in return. The more she tried to convince herself that a political marriage would suit her, the more she became aware of the deep gulf of emptiness inside her, a sadness that she had never, until now, allowed herself to feel.

Out on the water, Rayn's sailors strained at the capstan. From this distance, she couldn't hear their grunts of effort or the songs they sang to keep the rhythm, but she could see that they had the anchor most of the way up. Rayn would be off to Inya, never to see her again.

Behind her, the stairway door opened. "Celeste?"

It was the empress. Celeste turned. "Your Imperial Majesty."

Vitala looked out into the harbor at Rayn's ship and frowned. "Why are you on the roof?"

"I needed fresh air."

Vitala's brow furrowed. "I need you downstairs. Justien's team has been searching Bayard's home, and they've found a packet of enciphered letters. They're hoping you might be able to decipher them."

On Rayn's ship, the sails were unfurling. Celeste tore her eyes away from them. More cryptanalysis—this was what she needed. A stepwise problem of mathematics and linguistics. Nothing that would awaken any uncomfortable feelings or make her wish for things she couldn't have. "I'll have a look."

*   *   *

Sitting in her apartment's anteroom, Celeste leafed through the packet of letters. "These are all in the same hand."

Vitala nodded. "I noticed. Bayard seems to have had a single, highly prolific correspondent. Can you decipher them?"

"Probably." She studied the letter on the top of the pack. Like the previous letter she'd deciphered, it used more characters than were found in any single alphabet. There were a few new characters she hadn't seen yet, but most were familiar. "There's a good chance it's the same cipher as the one before."

"And that means?"

"That I can decipher these quickly," she said. "I'll be right back." She went to her bedroom and fetched the written key she'd assembled that matched ciphertext letters to real letters. She grabbed a few sheets of blank paper, her inkpot, and her quill, and returned to the anteroom.

She began by attempting a straight translation of each known ciphertext character to its real text letter. Right away, words formed under her quill. They were Mosari words, but she understood the language well enough to recognize them.

Vitala leaned forward, intrigued.

"It's working," said Celeste. "I'll have a translation soon." As the message began to take shape, she feared the empress would be disappointed. This was no letter between conspirators, but something more mundane. The words said nothing about assassinations. When she'd translated all the known characters, she was able to fill in the unknown ones through context. She added them to her key. "Done." She handed the translation to Vitala.

MISS YOU SO MUCH KLARA HAD A FEVER BUT IS FEELING BETTER THIS AFTERNOON THE WEATHER WAS MILD I TOOK HER OUTSIDE FOR A SHORT WHILE AND LET HER SKIP LETTERING PRACTICE NOAK DROPPED BY AND WE HAD A TALK HE SAYS HIS BUSINESS IS DOING SO WELL HES HIRED ANOTHER BOAT

The letter went on for a while longer, detailing the minutiae of someone's day. At the bottom, it was signed Stina, a Riorcan woman's name.

"Three gods," said Vitala. "I think Bayard has a lover."

"Or a wife?" said Celeste. "They seem to have children. Or, you never know, it might be a sister and his nephews and nieces."

"If he has family, I've never seen them. And officially he's a bachelor. But there's something going on here. *Miss you so much.* This is not a business letter."

"I fear it's not what you'd hoped for."

Vitala's brow furrowed. "It's not what I expected. But maybe we can work with it. There are a lot of names in here and some little details that might help us find this woman, wherever she is. She and Bayard are writing to each other in code—at least she's writing to *him*; I assume he writes back to her, and those letters will be in her possession, if she has retained them. But if they're using code, that suggests Bayard doesn't want her to be discovered."

"You think she's aware of the conspiracy?"

"If she's not, then it's because Bayard wants to protect her and the children. Either way, we may have some leverage over him." She smiled grimly.

"Shall I translate the remaining letters?"

Vitala nodded. "Please."

For several hours, Celeste deciphered letters, occasionally adding a new character to her key. All the letters used the same cipher, the one she'd broken before, and all were from Stina. They were similar in content to the first letter—routine goings-on and various milestones with the children, a lost tooth from the eldest, a new word from the youngest. There were three children, she determined: two girls and a boy. Other names were mentioned, which seemed to be those of friends and neighbors. These might be useful for tracking down the location of the family.

Atella rapped at the door and poked her head inside the anteroom. "There's a woman here to see the empress."

Vitala, who was studying translated letters and scribbling notes on a blank piece of paper, answered without raising her head. "Who is it?"

"She says her name is Treva Salonius."

Vitala froze midstroke, with her quill in hand.

"Empress?" asked Atella. "Are you all right?"

"I'm fine." Vitala swallowed and lifted her quill from the paper. She dipped it in the inkpot. "I don't know any Treva Salonius. Send her away."

"Yes, Your Imperial Majesty." Atella withdrew.

"Salonius is your surname," said Celeste. "Is this Treva a relative from when you lived in Riorca?"

Vitala's mouth was a tight line. "I've put those days behind me."

"Don't you want to at least find out who she is? I'm curious about her."

Vitala said nothing.

Now Celeste understood. "You already know."

"Let's stick to business," snapped Vitala. "I'm the empress of Kjall. There's no reason I should have to show myself to some peasant who shows up claiming a connection. She probably just wants money."

Celeste returned to the letter she was deciphering. It was unlike Vitala to react with such hostility, or to speak condescendingly of peasants. "You and I have this in common—no family remaining except Lucien and Jamien. My eldest brothers were assassinated, my father is imprisoned on Mosar, my mother passed away when I was a girl—"

"Our situations aren't the same at all," said Vitala. "Your family didn't abandon you by choice; they were murdered or forcibly removed. But my family sold me to a resistance group. For money."

Chastened, Celeste began filling in letters above the ciphertext. For several minutes, they worked together in silence.

Vitala raised her head. In a milder voice, she said, "I'm sorry to snap. None of this is your fault. It's just that I'm not in the same position as you at all. You miss the family members you've lost—"

"Not Florian," put in Celeste.

Vitala shrugged. "You miss the others. In my case . . . they were not good to me. They never expected me to amount to anything. And now they come calling, when I'm the empress? Maybe they want money, maybe they want . . . I don't know. You can tell a person's character by how they treat you when you haven't any power. These people showed their colors years ago. I'll have nothing to do with them."

Celeste slumped, feeling melancholy. How sad it must be to have living family nearby and want nothing to do with them. She had never realized how much resentment the empress was carrying around. "Have you considered that they might regret what they once did? Maybe they desire your forgiveness."

Vitala gave an unladylike snort. "Forgiveness is for people who forget your birthday. It's not for people who sell their daughters." She looked up. "You know what I mean better than most. Would you forgive Gallus? Would you forgive Cassian?"

"No," she said softly.

When Celeste had finished deciphering the letters, Vitala took the translations and left to deliver them to Justien and his team for analysis. The hope was that Justien would be able to locate Stina and the children. Then they could arrest the lot of them and bring them before Bayard, who might be persuaded to talk if his family were in custody.

Meanwhile, Celeste took dinner with Lucien and Patricus. The dog lurked under the table, waiting for choice morsels to fall, while her brother caught her up on the palace gossip. Jamien had learned how to catch a ball. Trenian had read some book by a Mosari philosopher and crowed about its brilliance for days. The Legaciatti were organizing a retirement party for the oldest of their number, a man named Fulvianus.

The guards at the door snapped to attention, and Vitala entered the room. "Celeste, have you got a moment?"

"Sit down and eat, love," said Lucien. "You're in no condition to work this hard."

"I believe I will." Vitala took a place at the table. Servants rushed forward to supply her with a plate, a glass, and utensils, and then brought the dinner dishes around. Vitala loaded her plate.

"Has Justien's team found you-know-who yet?" asked

Celeste, not wanting to tip off a guard or servant who might, for all she knew, be part of Bayard's conspiracy.

"No, but they believe they're close," said Vitala. "I came to see you for another reason. Justien's recovered a second packet of letters from Bayard's residence." She pushed the packet across the table at Celeste.

This packet was smaller than the other, but the handwriting on the topmost letter looked identical to the ones she'd deciphered before. "More of the same, you think?"

"Probably," said Vitala. "Still, they might have new information. I was hoping you could decipher them when you're finished here."

By now, Celeste had the key memorized. "I could decipher them now, if someone brings me paper and a quill."

Vitala called for a servant to do so, and when the items were delivered, Celeste settled into the work, snacking on Riorcan wafers as she deciphered the first letter. Within fifteen minutes, she'd handed the translation off to Vitala—it was more daily minutiae from Stina—and begun the second. In this second letter, a familiar name took shape beneath her pen. She bit her lip and finished the translation:

MESSAGE ARRIVED FROM ZOE TODAY SHE LOST AN AGENT AND NEEDS A REPLACEMENT

She pushed the translated letter across the table to Vitala. "Isn't this curious? *Zoe* is not a Riorcan name."

"Of course it's not," said Vitala. "Neither is *Vitala*. The Obsidian Circle gives its people names based on where they will be operating."

"It's an Inyan name," said Celeste.

"Am I supposed to recognize it?"

"Zoe is the name of the woman Rayn had the illegitimate child with. I met her briefly on the *Goshawk*."

Vitala read the translation and frowned. "Well, I don't think it's the same person." She handed the letter to Lucien. "Do you?"

He read it. "We shouldn't discount the possibility. We know that the child may be used as a political pawn if the assassins kill Rayn. What if this Zoe deliberately seduced Rayn with her wards down, hoping he'd sire a baby on her which she could use for political purposes?"

"That still doesn't explain why Rayn's wards were down," said Celeste.

Vitala's eyes lit. "Actually, it might."

"How so?" asked Lucien.

"Zoe could be a wardbreaker," said Vitala. "This Zoe mentioned in the letter is one of Bayard's people. She may be an assassin trained in exactly the way I was—by the same man, in fact. If that's the case, it's not necessary for Rayn to be careless with his wards. Zoe can *break* his fertility ward, using her magic, thus making pregnancy likely."

"So she produces an illegitimate child ...," mused Celeste.

"And the next step is to assassinate Rayn," said Lucien. "Someone wants the Inyan throne, but it cannot be Bayard. He's Riorcan."

"Someone hired him to produce the child and perform the assassination," suggested Vitala. "Someone on the Inyan Land Council, perhaps."

"What could they offer that Bayard would want?" said Lucien.

"Arms, riftstones, maybe even just money," said Vitala. "These breakaway enclaves have no funding now that the rest of the organization's gone mainstream. And consider this: if this plan succeeds, he'll have placed a half-Riorcan on the Inyan throne."

"If Zoe's a wardbreaker," said Celeste, "is she armed with Shards?"

"Of course," said Vitala. "Why wouldn't she be?"

"Don't wardbreaker assassins typically seduce their victims and kill them in bed?"

"Only if the victim is a war mage. In that case, they need the distraction of sex in order to make the kill," said Vitala.

Celeste noted her use of the pronoun *they*. Vitala had once been a wardbreaker assassin. She apparently didn't include herself in that group anymore.

"And since Rayn is a fire mage," continued Vitala, "she doesn't need to sleep with him in order to kill him. She just needs to get close enough to stick a Shard in him without him noticing. Mind, we're all just speculating. This may not be the same Zoe at all."

Celeste felt certain they had the right Zoe. "The servants Rayn brought with him to Kjall—where are they now?"

"They came up with us on the *Soldier's Sweep*," said Lucien. "And they'll have left for Inya with Rayn on the *Water Spirit*."

"So at this very moment, Rayn is on a ship with a ward-breaking assassin."

"We don't know for sure," said Vitala. "As the emperor says, we're speculating."

"We have to tell Rayn," said Celeste.

"I'll dispatch a message at once," said Lucien.

Celeste blinked. "On the post? It won't reach him on the ship. He needs to be told *now*."

"You ask the impossible," said Lucien. "He's on a ship in the open ocean. Even the signal network cannot reach him there."

"He left this morning," said Celeste. "If we sent a ship right now—"

"We cannot send a ship right now," said Lucien. "And if we did, there's no guarantee we'd find him. The ocean is a big place. There are many routes to Inya."

The thought terrified her, that Rayn could die on the boat at Zoe's hands, and there wasn't a thing she could do about it. "Then we meet him at the Inyan docks. We can't protect him on the water. But if he survives the journey, we can protect him when he lands."

"You're trading on a very big assumption right now," said Lucien. "I'm not going to commandeer a ship based on a conjecture—"

"You don't need to commandeer anything. Send the *Soldier's Sweep*."

"My private ship? Out of the question," said Lucien. "Give Justien's team more time. They'll break Bayard, and when they do, he may confess everything. Then we'll learn exactly who this Zoe is and what she intends."

"There's no time for that!" Her hands trembled. Rayn could be dead inside of a week if they didn't stop this. He could be talking to Zoe, maybe even following her into her cabin, right this moment. They had to warn him of the danger.

"Rayn is not our responsibility," said Lucien. "When he was on Kjallan soil, it was my duty to protect him. Now he's on his own ship, Inyan territory, and he's got to look after himself."

"It is our responsibility," said Celeste, "because the assassin is Kjallan."

"Riorcan," said Lucien.

"Riorca's part of Kjall."

"Indeed it is," put in Vitala. "You can't collect taxes from Riorca and then disavow responsibility for it."

"I can't be responsible for the actions of every rogue citizen in my empire. And besides, we don't even know if it's the same Zoe," said Lucien. "Celeste, you're mixing political and personal desires. You like Rayn and want to protect him. But it's not your job, nor is it mine, to go chasing after the man every time we think he might be in danger."

"It may not be our job, but it's common decency!"

"We are not sending a ship after Prince Rayn," said Lucien. "And that's final."

19

The next morning, Celeste woke to a knock at her door. She didn't answer it, and the empress was announced. "I'm not dressed," Celeste called, pulling a pillow over her head.

The door swung open. That was the problem with the empress. She and Lucien could do whatever they wanted, and generally did.

Vitala marched into the bedroom, oblivious to the fact that Celeste was hiding under her bed linens. "Get something on," she said. "A few hours ago, Justien found Stina and her children—"

"What?" Celeste threw the pillow off her head and sat up, blinking the sleep out of her eyes. But she kept the bedspread pulled up to cover her inadequately clothed body.

"They're in custody now, in separate cells beneath this building."

Celeste gathered up the linens, wrapped them around herself, and trundled to the dressing room to fetch her robe.

"And what do you think of this?" called Vitala. "No deathstones or riftstones on any of them."

In the privacy of her dressing room, Celeste dropped

the linens. She grabbed her robe and slung it around her shoulders. "So they can be interrogated."

"That's the idea. Are you up for it?"

"When?"

"Now."

"Of course I'm up for it. After I get dressed."

"Meet me in the prison," said Vitala.

Celeste washed and dressed and, though she wasn't hungry, ate a quick breakfast just in case. While she had never performed an interrogation, she knew they could take a long time. When she felt ready, she headed down the stairway to the underground prison. Vitala and Justien were standing in the aisle, speaking in whispers.

Vitala beckoned. "There you are. We're ready."

Justien inclined his head. "Your Imperial Highness."

Celeste glanced about the prison hallway, curious about the prisoners, but all the cell doors were closed. Since they were made of solid iron with no windows, she couldn't see through them. "What do you want me to do?"

"Since she's not magical, I'd like you to try a suggestion," said Justien. "See if you can get her talking freely. If that doesn't work—"

"It should work," said Celeste. She hoped it did. Manipulating the woman with a little mind magic would be far better than having to torture her.

"If it doesn't, we have backup plans." Justien gestured to a guard, who pulled a ring of keys from his pocket and unlocked the door nearest them. Justien entered the cell first. Celeste filed in after.

A tall blond woman sat on the prison bench. She was fettered, with some slack in her chains. Her face pinched with worry. "Where are my children?"

"Answer our questions and you'll be with them again soon," said Justien.

"I've done nothing." Stina's voice trembled. "*They've* done nothing."

Justien nodded at Celeste.

Celeste reached out with her magic and planted a suggestion. *I want to tell these people everything I know.* "Who is Bayard?"

The woman smiled, and her face radiated warmth. "Bayard's my husband. He's so good to me—"

"How can he be your husband?" asked Justien. "He claims to be unmarried."

Stina's brow tightened. "It's a secret." She put a hand over her mouth. "I wasn't supposed to tell."

Celeste sent another suggestion. *I can tell these nice people anything, even things that are secrets.*

"But I'm sure it's all right if you know." Stina's face crumpled in confusion, but she went on. "He said we had to keep it secret, because he had enemies, and if they found out about me, they might use me against him."

"Tell me about Bayard's friends. Did you ever meet any of them?"

"I've met many of his friends," said Stina. "Sometimes I stay at the enclave in the mountains, and I see them there."

Celeste and Justien exchanged a look.

"Tell us more," said Justien. "What are the names of some of these friends?"

"There's Anton," said Stina. "He's a war mage, but he's very kind. He studies poetry in his spare time. Gota takes care of the horses. They don't have many horses, on account of the grain expense. I think Gota does something else too, but I can't recall what. And there's Petronella. . . ."

Stina prattled on, prodded by Celeste's suggestions, spilling name after name. By the end of the interrogation they had not only a working list of two dozen conspirators but the location of the enclave.

Celeste was finished with the interrogation by lunchtime. She headed back to her apartment with Vitala on her heels. In the second-floor hallway, they came upon Lucien, who was surrounded by his guards and talking with Governor Asmund.

He called to them the moment he saw them. "Exactly the two women I've been looking for." He disengaged from the governor and gestured for Celeste and Vitala to follow him to the end of the hall for privacy. "How did the interrogation go?"

"Easiest thing in the world," said Celeste. "I used suggestions, and she told us everything."

He held out a hand to Vitala. "What did she say?"

Vitala took his hand, hugged him with one arm, and kissed him lightly on the cheek. "She really is his wife. They concealed their marriage in order to protect her and the children. We know where the assassins are hiding; it's an old enclave in the mountains about half a day's ride from here. Justien and Nalica are assembling a team to head out and make arrests. There are a lot of conspirators—more than twenty—so they need a lot of men."

"Are you going with them?"

Vitala nodded. "I have to. There aren't many people who can read the old Obsidian Circle's signs and find the enclave. Without me, they might walk right past it."

Lucien placed a hand on her belly and frowned. "I don't like your being out there. Perhaps if I came with you—"

"No need for that," said Vitala. "Justien and his people will be more than adequate protection for me."

"I'll go," offered Celeste.

"No," said Lucien and Vitala in unison.

Lucien continued. "There's no sense risking you. You can't locate the enclave the way Vitala can. And we don't need your mind magic or your cryptanalysis skills to make arrests."

"There might be more coded letters at the enclave—"

"Justien's team will recover them and bring them back to you," said Vitala.

Celeste nodded. Much as she'd like to take Vitala's place in this, she couldn't. Vitala had skills she did not possess.

"I figure Justien and Nalica won't be ready to move for at least an hour," said Lucien. "In the meantime, you two can take lunch with me."

Celeste assented, recognizing, now that he mentioned it, the hollow feeling in her stomach. She was feeling better now that the interrogation was over, and breakfast had been a while ago.

Lucien led the way down the hall. Glancing over his shoulder, he said, "I have a guest who'll be dining with us—a friend I'd like you to meet."

"Who?" asked Vitala.

"You'll see," said Lucien. "Is Justien going to confront Bayard about his captured wife and children?"

"Yes," said Celeste. "But not right away. He wants to capture the conspirators at the enclave first. He says that once we have all his people in custody, Bayard should break. When he starts cooperating and giving us names, Justien will round up the stragglers." And she could find out for certain whether Zoe was among the conspirators. Stina had mentioned a Zoe and given a physical description that roughly matched, but there were a lot of blond women in Riorca. She still wasn't certain it was the same Zoe.

The guards outside the imperial apartment snapped to attention and opened the door to admit them. Lucien and Vitala's apartment was larger than Celeste's and featured an intimate dining room. Places were set for four, and a woman Celeste had never seen before sat at the table, waiting for them. She was an older woman, a little careworn, and probably Riorcan since she was blond. The woman turned anxiously to the group, her hand shaking where it sat on the table.

Vitala came to a sudden halt. "No."

"Dearest—" began Lucien.

"I told you I wasn't going to do this."

He took her hands in his own. "I have no father anymore. My mother passed away when I was young. I miss her every day."

"I *don't* miss mine." Vitala flung his hands back at him and stalked out of the apartment.

Lucien followed on her heels. "I have no other family. Will you deny me a mother-in-law?"

His voice faded as he passed out of hearing range. Celeste, standing in the dining chamber and feeling awkward about being caught in the middle of this family drama, met the eyes of the nervous woman sitting at the table. So this was Vitala's mother. She curtsied. "It's nice to meet you, Treva Salonius."

Vitala's mother stared at her with a wrinkled brow. Then she said, in Riorcan, "Pardon me. I don't speak Kjallan."

Celeste repeated her greeting in the woman's own language.

"Are you a friend of my daughter's?" asked Treva.

"I'm her sister-in-law," said Celeste.

"My daughter is an extraordinary woman," said Treva.

"That she is."

"But she will not talk to me."

Celeste had little to say about that. She knew as well as anyone that for all Vitala's good qualities, she wasn't the most forgiving of individuals. "I'll just see how things are going outside."

She went out into the hallway. Lucien and Vitala were inches from each other's faces, puffed up like threatened house cats as they exchanged words.

"You set me up," said Vitala. "You knew I didn't want to see her, and you dragged me in there without even a hint of what you had planned—"

"It's for your own good," said Lucien. "It's time you made peace with her. Shouldn't my feelings count for something? What if I want to know the woman who birthed and raised the woman I love?"

"She *didn't* raise me; that's the whole point."

"For eight years, she did," said Lucien.

"And four hundred tetrals she was paid for it. You want to have lunch with her, go ahead. You're the gods-cursed emperor of Kjall; I can't stop you. But don't drag me into it." She stormed down the hall.

Lucien turned apologetically to Celeste. "That didn't go so well."

Celeste only raised her brows. Vitala wasn't a woman who could be forced into anything; Lucien ought to know that by now.

The emperor held out his arm. "Shall we?"

She took it and headed back into the imperial apartment to have lunch with Vitala's mother.

For the rest of the day, Celeste waited anxiously for news about the assault on the mountain enclave. The team was away all afternoon and all evening, and when Celeste gave up on them and went to bed, they were still out at the enclave, and no word had been received from them in Denmor.

In the morning, she learned that Justien, Nalica, Vitala, and the others had returned to the Enclave building in the wee hours with a herd of prisoners in tow, so many that Celeste wondered how the Riorcan authorities would manage to house them all.

A few hours later, Justien came to fetch her. "It's time," he said. "We're going to confront Bayard."

She followed him out of her apartment and down the hallway. "Is the empress coming?"

"She's already there," said Justien. "The emperor too."

They descended to the underground prison. Vitala and Lucien were standing in the hallway, surrounded by Legaciatti. They turned as Celeste and Justien approached.

"Are we ready?" asked Lucien.

"Yes." Justien gestured to one of his men, who opened a cell door and led out Stina and three young children. The oldest child looked perhaps eight or nine years old; the youngest was a toddler. All but the toddler were shackled.

"Must we chain the children?" asked Celeste.

"It's for effect," said Lucien. "Lives are at stake here, including perhaps Prince Rayn's. You don't want him assassinated, do you?"

"No." He was right, of course. And no harm had been done to the children, nor the wife, since Celeste had been able to accomplish the entire interrogation with magical suggestions. Still, she felt uneasy.

"Here we go," said Justien. He unlocked the door to Bayard's cell.

Bayard, who still possessed his war magic, was shackled tight to his chair. Celeste wondered what they did with him when he wasn't being interrogated—surely he couldn't be immobilized all the time. Wouldn't it do him harm? But he hadn't been beaten or tortured; she saw no physical signs of abuse. He just looked sullen and angry, as any prisoner would.

The cell became crowded as they filed in: first Justien; then Vitala, Lucien, and herself; then Stina and the children, followed by the guards who were escorting them.

Bayard didn't react to Justien, Vitala, Lucien, or Celeste, but when his family entered, he sat up straighter in his chair. He swallowed, as if to moisten his tongue, and said, "They have nothing to do with any of this."

"On the contrary, Bayard," said Justien. "The letters we found suggest that your wife, Stina, was heavily involved in the conspiracy. We found references to Zoe, to Frode and Mattias and Sander. Others too."

"I'm sorry," said Stina. "They forced me to talk."

Justien gestured to a guard near the back of the cell. "Get the woman and children out, and bring the prisoners from room five."

Bayard's family was escorted out. Shortly afterward, three shackled men entered the room. None were familiar to Celeste.

"Last night, we assaulted your enclave," said Justien. "We have twenty-six of your people in custody—I'm showing you just these three. If you don't believe me, I can show you the rest. It's over, Bayard. Your organization is destroyed. All that remains is to determine who shall be punished, and in what way."

Bayard's eyes were on his men. He looked grave. "I've seen enough. Send them away."

Justien nodded to the guard, who escorted the three prisoners out of the cell. He closed the door, sealing those who remained inside. "Well?"

Bayard licked his lower lip. "Let Stina and the children go."

"That's not going to happen," said Lucien. "We have unanswered questions about who else might be involved, particularly anyone who might be overseas in Inya. We have concerns about a woman named Zoe. We cannot interrogate you, but we can interrogate the others."

"My wife doesn't know anything beyond the enclave location and some of the people's names, and you already have those," said Bayard.

"We'll see for ourselves," said Lucien.

"No one knows where Zoe is except me," said Bayard. "If I use my deathstone right now, you'll never find her."

"She's on the *Water Spirit*; we already know that," said Lucien. "Using your deathstone won't save your family. We'll interrogate them, using any means necessary. And once we have everything out of them that we can get, we'll stake them."

"For what crime?" snarled Bayard. "The children are guilty of nothing!"

"Treason," said Lucien.

Bayard turned to Vitala. "Do you see? This is what happens when you join forces with the enemy. Simon is but three years old!"

"Perhaps we could work something out," said Vitala.

"I don't bargain with traitors," said Lucien.

"If you were to tell us everything you know," said Vitala, "we would have no need to interrogate your family or any of your conspirators from the enclave."

"You think I'm going to fall for that?" said Bayard.

"It's not a trick," said Vitala. "It's a bargain. You give us what we need, under truth spell, and we'll spare your family from any unpleasantness."

"Why should I do any of this if you're just going to stake them anyway?"

"To save them unnecessary pain," said Lucien.

"Perhaps we could spare their lives," suggested Vitala.

"Out of the question," said Lucien.

"The woman has no riftstone, no magic," said Vitala. "Neither have the children."

"The woman has to die," said Lucien. "And when she's gone, and Bayard too, the children will be orphans. There is no one to care for them."

"It was the Inyans!" cried Bayard. "They planned everything. They wanted an heir from Rayn, and then they wanted him dead."

"Which Inyans?" asked Vitala.

Bayard said nothing.

"What are Zoe's intentions on the *Water Spirit* and in Inya?" asked Celeste.

The old battle master shook his head. "I've said all I'm going to say. You want more, offer me a deal. One that allows Stina and the children to live free."

"You have to tell us *everything*, under truth spell," said Vitala.

"Deal," said Bayard.

"And you publicly denounce the Inyans behind all this," she added.

"For that, you have to make a better offer."

"You publically denounce them," said Vitala, "and you get to live. You do as you're told, go where you're told, and say what we want you to say. In return, you can watch your family grow up. Not as a free man, but as a prisoner below the Imperial Palace in Riat. We'll relocate your family to Riat, and they can visit you periodically as long as you keep your end of the bargain."

Bayard sagged in his chair, though whether it was a gesture of defeat or relief, Celeste could not tell. "It's a deal."

Justien beckoned to Celeste.

She stepped forward to administer the truth spell.

20

Though it was early yet, Celeste crawled exhausted into bed. The interrogation of Bayard had taken all day. Her part in the interrogation had not been difficult — not in and of itself. It was like riding a horse, an undemanding activity unless one had to do it all day long. Then one got tired and sore.

She'd had to sustain a truth spell on Bayard and report to Justien anytime the man lied or evaded a question. Sustaining magic continuously for hours on end drained her. By lunchtime, she was exhausted, and since there wasn't another mind mage available whom Lucien trusted, she went back and sustained her spells for another six hours.

It had been worth it. Justien had pulled many important details out of Bayard. It turned out that Justien and Vitala's sweep had missed two of the conspirators, both of whom had been away from the enclave at the time of the assault. Bayard gave them the details on who those men were and where to find them, and Justien dispatched his people to intercept them.

Bayard confessed that about five years ago, Councilor Worryn had approached him and promised aid to his resistance movement in the form of money and gunpowder in exchange for Bayard training an assassin to target Prince Rayn. Later, when the Inyans had learned the chosen assassin was a woman, they'd come up with the idea of having her seduce Rayn first. That way the prince might produce an heir that Councilor Worryn could later use to control the throne.

Part of that plan had succeeded.

The Inyans had insisted that the assassination take place outside of their country. This had to do with Inyan laws mandating the use of truth spells on all political officials, including Land Council members, when a public figure was assassinated in Inya. Plans were put in motion to send Rayn to Kjall and assassinate him there.

Prince Rayn traveled to Kjall as intended. Zoe and three of the war mages on her team went with them, Zoe traveling openly and the others in secret. The assassins found the Imperial Palace impregnable, but when Rayn traveled to Riorca on the *Goshawk*, they made an assassination attempt there, which failed and resulted in the loss of the war mages. Later, while Zoe was en route to Riorca again, this time on the *Soldier's Sweep*, another team of Bayard's tried to assassinate Rayn—and failed again.

Now Zoe was on the *Water Spirit* with Prince Rayn.

Would she make another attempt on Rayn's life?

Yes, Bayard had said, but only if she could get Rayn alone and distracted. Rayn was a fire mage. In a fair fight, he was more than a match for her. She would attempt to seduce him or otherwise throw him off his guard rather than attack him openly.

This was Celeste's worst fear. No matter what she did, she could not protect Prince Rayn during his journey on the *Water Spirit*. All she could do was hope and pray that he didn't put himself into a situation where he was alone with Zoe.

But she could, if Lucien allowed her to take the *Soldier's Sweep*, travel to Inya and tell him about the danger when his ship made landfall. Once Rayn arrived on Inya, he might be safe from the assassins if they were unwilling to kill him within his country's borders. But she was not going to count on that.

She'd cajoled Lucien, yelled at him, and finally begged, but he'd remained firm. He would send word to Rayn on the post, but he would not chase after the prince with his personal ship, even though they now knew with certainty that Zoe meant to kill him.

For now, Celeste needed sleep. Tomorrow, she would take matters into her own hands.

Rayn stood in the driving rain, looking southward toward home. Just a few weeks ago, he couldn't wait to set sail for Inya. Now it was the last place he wanted to go. Once again he'd have to deal with the corrupt Land Council, his addled father, his self-absorbed mother. Once again it would be him and Magister Lornis against the world—and with high stakes, now that he faced a ratification vote.

Having Celeste at his side would have made all the difference. He could have looked forward to showing her his homeland. Inya was beautiful by anyone's standard, and he had many favorite spots he wanted to share with her. Without her, he feared they would be empty pleasures.

He heard footsteps behind him, and Lieutenant Tonas joined him at the rail. "I suggest you go to your cabin, Your Highness," he said. "The weather's worsening."

Rayn looked up at the nighttime sky. The lieutenant was right; the wind was picking up. The sailors swarmed into the tops to reduce sail. "All right."

He headed to his cabin, opened the door, and stepped inside.

And jumped in surprise. Zoe was sitting on his cot.

"What are you doing here?" he said. "You're not to be in my cabin without permission."

"You decided not to marry that princess they tried to foist on you," said Zoe.

Rayn frowned. "You've got your facts twisted up."

"So tell me the story. The rain's going to continue for a while." She rose to her feet and walked toward him. "We'll have to stay in our cabins. Why not pass the time in an agreeable way?"

"You mean in conversation?" He raised his brows. Zoe had never been much for talk.

"If you like," said Zoe. "I have other ideas."

The floor tilted as the ship heeled over, and he leaned to compensate. "Go back to your own cot. I'm not interested tonight."

"That's not what your body's telling me." Zoe eased up next to him and slid an arm around his waist. Firm breasts pressed against him.

For a moment, he tolerated it. He liked being touched, and she did have a lovely body. And yet so much had changed. A year ago, his cock would have stiffened in eager anticipation when she'd slid up against him like this. But not today. Nor ever again, he suspected. He was truly over women like Zoe.

He pushed her away—gently, because the floor was moving beneath their feet. "No. We're finished."

Anger flashed in her eyes. "That princess can't suck you off the way I can."

Now she'd done it. Her words had summoned the mental image of Celeste taking him into her mouth. He nearly groaned at the eroticism of that image. Their lovemaking had been limited in scope and opportunity, and they hadn't tried that particular sex act yet. But it was fantasy material. *Now* he had a cockstand.

Zoe reached for his belt. "Let's go to your cot, where the storm won't knock us off our feet."

He pushed her hand away. She might have felt his physical response, but she had no idea what had actually inspired it. "Go to your own quarters and leave me alone."

Outside, the sailors shouted, and the wind groaned in the sails. The cabin lurched. He fell heavily to one side and caught himself, but Zoe wasn't so lucky. She lost her balance and windmilled her arms. He reached for her, but snatched only empty air as the ship's bucking tossed her halfway across the cabin.

"Are you all right?" Struggling as the floor tilted and heaved beneath him, Rayn made his way haltingly toward her and picked her up off the floor. "Here, hold on to something." He spotted some handrails mounted on the wall, perhaps intended for this very situation. He steered her toward them.

The floor lurched again, and he grabbed her more firmly, placing one hand on her arm and another on the back of her neck. He maneuvered her to the railing and she grabbed hold of it.

His thumb found something on her neck: a lump. No, two lumps, one next to the other. He'd felt them before, years ago, and thought nothing of them at the time. But now they piqued his curiosity. Where had he felt something similar?

In the belowground prison at the Enclave building. The Riorcan assassin had lumps in his neck just like these, for his implanted riftstone and deathstone.

"Stop," she said. "You're hurting me."

He jerked his hand away. As the wind howled outside and rain drummed on the cabin roof, the hair rose on his own neck. Who *was* this woman, really? "What are those lumps on your neck?"

"Where?" She placed her hand on the spot. "You mean my neck bones?"

Rayn knew what neck bones felt like, and those weren't them. Was Zoe an assassin, like those men who'd assaulted him in Denmor? The thought boggled his mind. Yet it would explain a great deal. He'd always wondered why she'd dogged him so persistently in the face of continued rejection. "I don't think that's what they are."

The muscles in her arm jumped beneath his fingers. She was frightened.

She yanked her arm from his grip and staggered toward the door. Despite the bucking of the floor, she managed to open it and leave. Windblown sheets of rain, nearly horizontal, assailed his cabin.

He went to the still-open door. Should he go after her? She might be an assassin—but then, she might not be. As suspicious as her behavior was, a couple of lumps on her neck weren't evidence of anything.

And really, how could she be Riorcan? She spoke Inyan without even the trace of an accent. He'd been to her home and seen her family.

He shook his head. The more he thought about it, the more confused he became. He could only conclude that he knew next to nothing about this woman he'd sired a child on. Pushing against the wind and grunting with the effort, he shoved the cabin door closed. From now on he was going to keep his distance.

The sky shone opalescent pink when Celeste reached the pier. Mist crept along the still waters, and the fog shone with the diffuse light of a rising sun. Out in the harbor, the masts and spars of the *Soldier's Sweep* were barely visible, a trio of bony skeletons rising from the haze.

Atella was following closer than usual, which was her habit when nervous. "This isn't a good idea. What if the assassins are about?"

"There aren't any," said Celeste. "Justien rounded them all up night before last." Except for two stragglers he was still searching for, and Zoe, and the other two in Inya, of course.

"You could see the sunrise from the Enclave building," said Atella hopefully. "If you went up on the roof."

"It's prettier here." Celeste glanced around the foggy harbor. "It will be even prettier on the water. What's the point of coming all the way to Denmor if I can't see the beauty of the frigid north?" A couple of sailors stood watch over the rowboat that ferried passengers to and from the *Sweep*. "You there," she called to one of them. "Ready that boat and take me out into the harbor."

He bowed his head in obeisance. "To the *Sweep*, Your Imperial Highness?"

"Just into the harbor. I want to see the sun rise from the water."

"Absolutely, miss." He called to his fellows and they prepared the boat, removing some cargo, bailing out the bilge water, and uncoiling the rope from the pier. Soon four strong men sat in the boat, manning the oars, and two more waited on the pier to help Celeste and Atella in.

Celeste took the sailor's hand and stepped on board. A grumbling Atella followed.

The sailors plied the oars, and the boat slipped into the harbor. Celeste shivered in the chill morning air. Tendrils of fog washed over her, leaving her skin damp. She wouldn't mind a little Inyan fire magic right now. Or the company of a certain Inyan prince.

"Not much of a view here," said the sailor, looking up into the mist-shrouded sky.

"Take me to the *Sweep,* then," commanded Celeste. "Perhaps the view is better there."

The boat changed direction. Celeste wrapped her arms around herself as the hull of the *Soldier's Sweep* emerged from the fog, at first in patches, and then all at once, an enormous wooden wall that loomed out of the haze. The sailor called to his fellows on the ship, and a rope ladder was dropped down to them. The sailors spun the boat and dragged their oars until the boat just kissed the side of the hull below the ladder.

"Will you need help with the ladder, Your Imperial Highness?" asked the sailor.

"Not at all. I'll go first, and Atella after me."

She seized the highest rung she could reach and hauled herself upward until she could step onto the bottom rung. The ladder lurched sideways, but clung to the hull. Taking a deep breath, she began to climb, one rung after another, not looking down. An icy plunge into the ocean would be most unwelcome, especially with no fire mage to warm her. The ladder seemed endless, but she kept moving. When she reached the top, two sailors took her arms and gently lifted her on board.

"Thank you," she said. As Atella joined her on deck, she projected a suggestion into the first sailor's head, and then the second: *I will do whatever the Imperial Princess tells me to do.* Then she said, "Haul up the anchor. We're setting sail."

The sailors snapped their thumbs to their chests in salute. "Right away, Your Imperial Highness," said one of them.

"What?" cried Atella.

"We're going to Inya to help Prince Rayn," said Celeste.

"No. *Please* tell me you're not stealing the emperor's ship," said Atella.

Celeste shook her head. "Don't worry. He won't be angry with you. Just with me." And three gods, was he going to be furious when he learned what she was doing. She'd never defied him before, had never wanted to. He was good to her, and she loved him. But she was not going to leave Prince Rayn to fend off three assassins alone, especially when he didn't know that his former lover was one of them.

"You can't do it," said Atella. "You can't use your magic on this many people at once."

She rather suspected she could. Suggestions lasted a reasonable length of time; she just had to refresh them periodically. She moved among the ship's sailors, projecting her suggestion to each one in turn, ensuring their compliance with her plans.

"Imperial Princess!" called an unfamiliar voice.

Celeste turned. It was one of the ship's lieutenants. This fellow might be trouble. He was probably a mage, and thus immune to her magic. "Good morning, Lieutenant."

"What's going on here? This ship isn't scheduled to depart."

She tried her suggestion on the lieutenant, just in case: *I will do whatever the Imperial Princess says.* "We're sailing for Inya," she said. "Rouse your men."

"We are *not* sailing for Inya. I've had no such order."

Pox it. "*I'm* giving the order. As the Imperial Princess."

"You are not authorized to make it," the man hissed.

"Imperial Highness!" The captain was hurrying toward her.

The captain was a sea mage; there was no way her suggestions would work on him. Rather than waste her time arguing, she moved toward the capstan, projecting her suggestion on every sailor she saw. The bosun, she found, was vulnerable to her magic. "All hands up anchor!" he shouted to his men. "Rig the capstan."

"Avast!" cried the captain. "Avast rigging capstan!"

The men ignored him.

The captain stormed over to her. "You're controlling them with magic. But this is the emperor's ship, not yours. We haven't enough water. We haven't enough food—"

"Not true," said Celeste. "Lucien always keeps his personal ship stocked in case he needs to leave someplace in a hurry." She'd gone belowdecks and checked the supplies, just in case. She wasn't going to let them get halfway to Inya and run out of water.

"We're not scheduled to sail at this time," he said.

"We're sailing whether you like it or not, Captain," said Celeste.

Later, one group of sailors was catting the anchor while another had run up into the tops to make sail. Celeste was nervous. The fog was burning off. She could easily see the pier and shore now, which meant the guards at the dock could see the ship. They might report her mischief to Lucien. Much as she wanted to stand at the rail, keeping a watchful eye on the dock, it wasn't possible. She was controlling nearly a hundred people with mind magic, and her suggestions needed frequent refreshing.

The captain and his lieutenants had grown troublesome. She'd ordered some of her magicked soldiers to lock them in the captain's quarters. This was going to be a difficult journey. She'd have to keep the captain imprisoned the entire time; otherwise he might turn the ship around while she slept. Sleep might be impossible for her except in short stretches, because what was going to happen when her suggestions wore off and she wasn't there to refresh them?

Tense with worry, she shook her head. If only Lucien had been sensible, she wouldn't have had to steal his ship. They could be sailing to Inya under his authority, with the captain and his lieutenants up on deck applying their considerable skills.

Instead, they would be conspiring against her, thinking up ways to retake the ship. And poor Atella, pacing nervously on deck, was caught between two loyalties. On the one hand, she wanted to report Celeste's malfeasance to the emperor. On the other hand, as Celeste's bodyguard, she couldn't leave her charge unprotected.

"Rig the fish," called the bosun.

Celeste had no idea what a *fish* was, except that it clearly was something other than a sea creature with scales. They'd put a second line on the anchor, with which they had hooked the bottom of the anchor and were drawing it up so that it lay horizontal against the ship. Soon the *Sweep* would be off to Inya, and then it wouldn't matter if someone reported her to Lucien. She would be out of reach.

"Princess!" called a sailor from up on the yards. "There's a boat down yonder." He pointed to the place where Celeste had climbed up the rope ladder. She hurried in that direction. Fortunately, she'd had the good sense to pull the ladder up behind her.

As she approached the rail, she heard a dog bark. Patricus? Her stomach tightened.

Below, in a rowboat, was Vitala, accompanied by six Legaciatti and the black-and-white sea retriever, whose tail wagged frantically when he saw her.

Celeste retreated from the rail, hoping the empress had not seen her.

"Celeste, let me up!" called Vitala.

Pox it all. Celeste returned to the rail and called down, "I'm sorry, but I'm going to Inya. I have to warn Rayn."

"Let me up," cried Vitala. "I won't try to stop you. I swear."

Celeste gritted her teeth. She couldn't let Vitala up on the *Soldier's Sweep*. She didn't trust that the empress wouldn't interfere with her plans. Plus she wasn't kidnapping her pregnant sister-in-law and taking her to Inya. Her men nearly had the anchor up.

"I want to go with you!" cried Vitala.

Celeste blinked down at the boat. "Why?"

"Because you need help," said Vitala. "I run the Order of the Sage—did you think I didn't have eyes on you? That I wouldn't find out what you'd done almost as soon as you did it?"

Celeste said nothing.

"I could have told Lucien, but I didn't." Vitala spread her arms. "See? It's just me and Patricus. You shouldn't do this alone. Let me help."

"Why do you want to help me?"

"Because you're doing the right thing. Because Rayn needs to be warned about the assassins."

Celeste glanced back at the captain's quarters, full of mages who would be trying everything in their power to seize the ship from her and sail it back to Denmor. She threw down the rope ladder.

21

Celeste stood by the rail at the front of the ship. A sea breeze caressed her face and teased her hair. They were away at last, out of the harbor and into the open ocean. The empress, once aboard, had freed the captain and his officers and ordered them to proceed to Inya with all haste. Celeste didn't need to use her mind magic on the sailors anymore.

Now that she'd solved the problem of traveling to Inya, she turned to fresh worries. Would Rayn survive his voyage on the *Water Spirit*, with Zoe on board? And would her ship arrive in time to help him? Celeste's greatest nightmare was that she would arrive in Inya just in time for a royal funeral.

Assuming Rayn survived, how would he react to her unexpected arrival in Inya?

Rayn was uncomfortable with her family and her ancestry, yet he'd insisted that since their squabble in Waras, his feelings on the matter had changed. It wasn't the love they'd shared in the Riorcan wilds that had done it—after all, that had happened before Waras. As far as she was concerned, those had been physical acts without much meaning. And while part of her felt she ought to be angry that he had slept with her while secretly harboring a hatred of her family, when she tried to whip up some self-righteous fury about that, it didn't materialize. Her memories of Rayn on the beach and at the forest pond were sweet, and even if she never saw the man again, she would treasure them.

Even now, just thinking about the way Rayn had made love to every inch of her body in the pond made her squirm with unfulfilled desire. Tonight, in the privacy of her cabin, she would relive those memories in detail. She'd retrace the route his hands had made, calling to mind the heat and strength of his body.

But something entirely different had happened after the second assassination attempt in Denmor. When she'd worked on the cipher and he'd held her and massaged her shoulders—that hadn't been purely physical. She'd felt appreciated, supported. Loved?

So why had he left the country without a word of explanation? Lucien had forced him to go; she knew that. But surely if Rayn cared for her the way he claimed, he would have made some effort to contact her. Perhaps she had misread his intentions after all.

Would she be unwelcome when she turned up?

She wished this were a math problem, something she could figure out in logical, stepwise fashion. But there was no logic to this situation, no solution that she could see. Numbers and ciphers made sense. People were gods-cursed confusing.

She heard a patter of paws on the deck that could only be Patricus. The dog sidled up to her and leaned into her leg. She obliged his blatant bid for affection by rubbing his ears. Was there anything more comforting than a dog? Patricus was never shy about his love for her, or for anyone. With the sea retriever, she always knew where she stood.

Just as she had started to relax a little, she heard footsteps behind her.

"I talked to the captain," said Vitala. "He's steamed at you, but I think I've got him settled down."

"Thank you." She grimaced. "I'm not looking forward to what Lucien's going to say when he catches up to us."

"He's a reasonable man," said Vitala. "He'll get over it."

"Will he be mad at you too?" Celeste glanced sidelong at the empress. She hated to think that she might be driving a wedge between her brother and his wife.

"Mad as a stuck boar," said Vitala. "But only because he worries. He feels it's his job to protect the women in his charge. That's the real reason he doesn't want you to go. Or me." She placed a hand over her rounding belly.

"I wish I hadn't stranded him in Riorca."

"I *love* that you stranded him there." Vitala chuckled. "It serves him right. Anyway, he's not truly stranded; he'll commandeer another ship."

"It serves him right for what? For not letting me go?"

"Yes," said Vitala. "And for trying to shove my mother at me."

"Oh." Celeste felt a pang, deep in her chest. "He meant well, with that."

"I'm sure he did. That doesn't make it right."

Celeste swallowed. She didn't agree, but she didn't want to cause offense. Vitala had done her an enormous favor in coming on board and authorizing her voyage. "I had lunch with Treva. I thought her rather nice."

"*Nice,*" said Vitala mockingly. "You didn't grow up with her."

"Was she cruel to you?" asked Celeste.

"She was weak," said Vitala.

"Is that so terrible?"

"Yes," said Vitala. "A mother has no business having children if she hasn't the strength to protect them. When I was a little girl, everyone hated me—my father, my brothers and sisters, the neighbors. It wasn't just name-calling either; some of the kids threw rocks at me. And she never defended me, not once."

"I think Treva had a hard life," said Celeste. "My people did not treat yours very well back then."

Vitala sniffed. "They certainly didn't. For that matter, sometimes they still don't. But it's no excuse for Treva."

"Perhaps she was weak," said Celeste, "but she loved you."

Vitala shook her head. "It's not love, letting your daughter be treated in such a manner."

"Are you certain?" said Celeste. "Is it a crime to lack the strength to stand up for another?"

Vitala's eyes were hard and narrow as she stared out to sea. "Yes."

"I pity her," said Celeste.

When Prince Rayn's ship sailed into the Bay of Tiasa on a fine cloudless morning, the harbor and its environs exploded into activity. A pyrotechnic stationed atop a palace tower broadcasted the news of his return with an exuberant display of airborne shapes and colors. On the docks, a crowd gathered, watching and pointing at the ship as it anchored. By the time Rayn had disembarked and been rowed to shore, a welcoming party had gathered to receive him.

As Rayn stepped onto dry land, his mother, Kin-Lera, stepped forward to embrace him. She was the queen of Inya. No—not anymore. Now that her husband had abdicated the throne, her status and rank were uncertain. Rayn's own status was clearer. As a candidate for the throne, he retained the title of prince as a courtesy until the ratification vote.

"Rayn," she murmured. "So much has happened since you left."

"So I hear. It's good to see you, Mother." He drew back to study her. He hadn't been gone more than about a month, but it seemed to him that she had a few more gray hairs than when he'd left.

"You should have come earlier," she said. "You've barely any time before ratification."

"I'm aware of that." Councilor Worryn had engineered it that way, hoping Rayn would miss his ratification ceremony entirely, in which case he would almost certainly lose the vote. "How is Father? Why did he abdicate?"

She shook her head. "I don't know. I can't bear to be around him, the way he is now."

Rayn frowned. His father needed her, yet she lacked either the courage or the compassion to face his illness. For the past few years, she'd confined herself to her rooms, refusing to involve herself in politics. She would not help him fight the Land Council. For that, he needed someone tougher, someone ready and willing to throw herself into the fray. Someone like Celeste.

Rayn's fourteen-year-old sister, Rilia, pushed forward and threw her arms around him. "I missed you!"

"Hey, Gills." He tousled her hair, and she fake punched him in the arm. She pretended to hate the nickname he'd coined for her years ago for her habit of diving deep into ocean gullies and staying down so long people thought she'd drowned. He knew she secretly liked the name.

"We had a tremor," said Rilia.

"Did we?" His eyes rose to craggy Mount Drav, which

towered above the city. It was shrouded in mist and looked quiescent, but that could be an illusion. "How long ago?"

"Two days," said Rilia. "I wasn't scared."

"Of course you weren't," said Rayn.

"Mom was," said Rilia.

He nodded absently. Tremors were common in Tiasa, and not a good sign. They often preceded a lava flow. He frowned at the mountain.

Standing a short ways behind his mother and sister was Kima, his daughter's wet nurse. She had eleven-month-old Aderyn in her arms. He strode forward to meet them. "How is she?" he asked, taking the baby from her.

Kima beamed. "Talking up a storm, Your Highness."

He bounced Aderyn gently. "Are you a talker, little one?"

"Da," she said.

Still carrying her, he walked to the end of the pier, where the royal carriage waited, guarded by a palace servant. "Ishyo," he said, greeting the man with a clasp of the wrist.

Ishyo inclined his head. "Your Highness." He opened the carriage door.

Rayn rode to the palace in the company of his family, Kima, and Magister Lornis. The carriage windows were flung open, as they ought to be on such a fine day. While he was not pleased about having been forced out of Kjall without concluding his business there, it was impossible not to enjoy Inya's pleasures. Celeste would love this weather. There were no cold nights in Inya. Not often, anyway. And it wasn't unbearably hot. A brisk breeze blew in over the ocean during much of the daylight hours, freshening the air.

There were so many things he wanted to show Celeste: the ocean so blue that it outshone the sky; the ominous but awe-inspiring Mount Drav, sitting above the city like a god in residence; the smell of flowers on the breeze.

Ahead was the Tiasan Palace, where he had been born, and where one day, gods willing, he would die. It was a magnificent, open-air structure of quartz and limestone, all columns and arches and bridges and breezeways. In every hidden nook stood a fine tree, or a bush as tall as a man. Flower-laden vines twined up the columns. And there were not nearly so many guards here as there were in Kjall and Riorca. In Kjall, he thought he'd suffocate from them—but the empire had always been a more violent nation than Inya. Here, one could relax and be a man, not some guarded, sequestered thing who needed an escort just to relieve his bladder.

As they left the carriage, he handed Aderyn back to Kima.

Lornis hurried to his side as they passed beneath the archway and into the main gallery. "We have much to do," he said. "You should start by lining up support from the Fireturners. After that, the Merchants' Guild. Some of the councilors, too—not all of them oppose you."

Rayn turned left, toward his quarters. "I think I should freshen up first. And I want to talk to my father."

"Of course," said Lornis. "But then—"

"Your Highness," called Ishyo from behind them. "You're going the wrong way."

Rayn turned, annoyed. "My quarters are this way. You think I've forgotten where they are?" A shiver of fear ran through him. Maybe he *had* forgotten. Was his mind going, like his father's? No, of course not. He was absolutely in the right hallway.

"Since your father's abdication, your rooms have been moved."

"What?" said Rayn. "Why?"

Ishyo clasped his hands, looking nervous. "Councilor Worryn said your rooms should be moved to the Hibiscus Tower, since you're no longer the king's son."

"But I'm up for ratification in ten days!" cried Rayn.

Ishyo lowered his head. "Yes, sir."

"It's true, Rayn," said his mother. "The whole family's been moved."

"Did you not tell them—" He cut himself off. His mother never talked back to the Land Council.

"I can show you the way," offered Ishyo. "Fastest route is up to the third floor, across the suspension bridge—"

"I know where the Hibiscus Tower is." Rayn took a deep breath. The situation was infuriating—humiliating!—but he couldn't blame it on poor Ishyo. The man only followed orders. And while he knew where the tower was, he didn't know which room he'd been assigned. Through gritted teeth, he said, "Show me to my new rooms."

Ishyo nodded. "Yes, sir." He led Rayn to the spiral staircase in the middle of the gallery.

Rayn traipsed up the stairs, down a long hallway, and out onto the suspension bridge that led to the tower. It was pretty out here. A stream wound through the palace grounds, and he was above it now, inhaling the sweet scent of frangipani flowers blended with mangoes from a tree that overhung the stream. The pleasant nature of his surroundings didn't change the fact that he'd been placed in no-man's-land with the minor nobles and visiting dignitaries. Councilor Worryn was sending him a message: *In the corridors of power, you are not welcome.*

"Well," said Lornis, stiff with affront, "I suppose Worryn thinks you should be grateful to have a room at all."

"And a beating heart," said Rayn. He had a feeling Councilor Worryn had never meant for him to come home from Riorca at all.

22

After settling into his new quarters, Rayn headed for his father's room. Already he was annoyed at these new lodgings. The Hibiscus Tower didn't have enough arches and windows, and the air didn't circulate well. If he was ratified as king, perhaps he could fix that—open up a few key passageways to let the air flow. Furthermore, his rooms were on the south side of the grounds and overlooked the island interior instead of the harbor. The view was pleasant, but in his old room on the north side he'd enjoyed being able to watch the ships come and go. It was a simple way of keeping up with the goings-on of his people, since most local trade passed through the Tiasan harbor.

Rayn's father had been moved to the Hibiscus Tower as well. One of his caretakers stood outside the door to his new room.

"Konani," said Rayn, greeting the man by name, "how is he?"

Konani grimaced. "Not well."

Rayn lowered his voice. "Were you here when he decided to abdicate the throne?"

"Yes, sir."

"Why do you think he did it?"

"Well," said Konani, also in a low voice, "I think it was about time, sir. He ought to have done it years ago. He had some discussions with Councilor Worryn, and then he signed the papers."

"I find it curious that the decision was made while I was out of the country."

"Ah." Konani looked uncomfortable. "That is curious."

"I want to see him," said Rayn.

"He's not in a good mood," said Konani.

"Nonetheless." Rayn gestured for him to step away.

"Yes, Your Highness." Konani complied.

Rayn went inside.

Zalyo Daryson, former king of Inya, sat by the window, looking out. Rayn, who'd been spindly as a child, now resembled his father in ways that both pleased and worried him. The two men were about the same height and had the same large build and blond hair. Zalyo's hair was fading now, but in an attractive way, almost to a platinum color. Rayn might age similarly, he knew, but that was what frightened him. He did not want to follow his father into madness.

Zalyo spoke without turning around. "Konani, this window isn't right."

"Excuse me, Father," said Rayn. "It's Rayn, not Konani."

Zalyo spun around and looked at him. He blinked twice and furrowed his brow as if deep in thought. "Rayn?"

"Yes, Father. It's me."

Zalyo's breath quickened, and he raised a shaky hand. "You've come to take my window."

"No, Father. I've returned from a diplomatic visit to Kjall. I've come to talk to you."

"You want my window," said Zalyo. "But you won't have it. Konani! Help!"

Konani entered the room and held out his arms placatingly. "Rayn is not taking anything, sir. He's your son, come to speak to you."

"It's the wrong window," said Zalyo. "It's supposed to look out on the harbor, so I can watch for the attack ships."

"There are no attack ships," said Rayn gently.

"There are. You don't want me to see them," said Zalyo. "That's why you changed my window." He turned to Konani and pointed at Rayn. "It's his fault. *He* took my window."

Konani's brow wrinkled. "No, sir. The prince wasn't here when it happened. Councilor Worryn is the one who moved you to this room."

"But he ordered it. The councilor told me." Zalyo turned to Rayn. "You want to steal my throne. I had to sign those papers to stop you. If I didn't, you'd have let the attack ships come, same as they did in Mosar. I was watching for them. I was watching for the ships, but now the window is wrong and I can't see. How will I know if they're coming?"

Rayn shifted on his feet. He couldn't react to his father with emotion—he'd made that mistake in the past, and it had only worsened the situation. But it was hard to suppress the rage and grief that welled up within him. Councilor Worryn was poisoning his father's mind, addling him further, turning him against his own family members so that he feared to trust the very people who protected and cared for him.

He swallowed the lump in his throat, took a deep breath to calm himself, and said, "You're confused, Father. I'm your son, and I'm not trying to steal anything. Those papers you signed were something else."

"He said you would deny it." Zalyo wagged his finger at Rayn. "He told me you would. Didn't he?" He turned to Konani.

"Rayn had nothing to do with any of this," said Konani.

"You weren't in the room," said Zalyo.

Konani and his mother were right: his father was worse. Maybe it was just the natural progression of his madness, but the change in room might have contributed to his paranoia. Rayn was plenty annoyed at having been moved from his quarters. How did it feel for Zalyo, who'd lived in his old rooms for much longer, and who didn't have a lot of mental reserves to call upon? "You want your window back, the one that overlooks the harbor?"

"I have to watch for the ships," said Zalyo.

"I'll talk to Councilor Worryn and see what I can do," said Rayn. "I haven't much influence now, but if I'm ratified—"

"You see?" hissed Zalyo. "He wants to steal my throne. I told you."

"No, Father." He glanced helplessly at Konani, who shrugged, looking sad.

"Get out," said Zalyo. "Get out!"

Rayn left the room, trembling all over.

By the time Rayn had crossed the suspension bridge again and reached the bottom of the spiral staircase, his hands had stopped shaking. He was still furious, and the back of his neck was hot, but he had sufficient control for a confrontation. Councilor Worryn would be, no doubt, on the first-floor hallway of the main gallery, in some of the very rooms from which he'd ousted Rayn and his family.

As Rayn approached the hallway, a pair of guards stepped forward and blocked his way.

Rayn rose to his full height. "You know who I am."

"Your rooms have been relocated," said one of the guards, "by council's orders. The council has ruling authority until a new king is ratified."

"I'm here to talk to Councilor Worryn," said Rayn.

"He's not available."

Rayn peered down the hallway. He was certain the councilor was there somewhere. What a coward. "My father, the king, is agitated—"

"Your father is no longer the king," said the guard.

Rayn sighed heavily. "My father, the former king, is agitated because he's been displaced from his chambers and can no longer see the harbor from his window."

"Those chambers are reserved for the king."

"And there is no king at the moment," said Rayn. "My father just wants to look out his window. If he could just be placed there until ratification, or perhaps in another room that overlooks the harbor—"

"You must take that up with the councilor," said the guard. "When he's available."

"And when will he be available?"

"I don't have that information, sir."

Rayn clenched his fists. "There's something else I need to discuss with him, and it's urgent. I'm told we had a tremor in Tiasa two days ago, and that often precedes a lava flow. There are settlers in the Four Pines valley who need to be evacuated. He needs to issue an emergency order—"

"You'll have to speak to him about it," said the guard.

"Yes, exactly!" said Rayn. "So let me through."

"Councilor Worryn isn't available at this time," said the guard.

More than ever, Rayn wished for Celeste. Justien too. Those two strategists would know how to handle a councilor who abused his father, insulted his family, and didn't have the cods to speak to Rayn in person. He did, at least, have Lornis.

He found Lornis's door, also in the Hibiscus Tower, and knocked.

No one answered.

"Come on, Lornis, I know you're in there." Lornis left his door open when he was out, so there was no question that the man was at home. Rayn pounded on the door.

The door squeaked open. A man who was not Lornis peered out at Rayn.

"Oh, Magister Donyl." Rayn held out his hand. "Are you well?"

Donyl clasped his wrist. "I am, thank you, Your Highness. Your adviser's indisposed. He'll be here in a moment."

"Right." He should have anticipated this. Magister Donyl was Lornis's longtime lover—of course Lornis would want to see him after such a long absence.

Lornis came to the door, looking flustered. "What is it?"

"Sorry to interrupt," said Rayn, "but I need your counsel. There's a problem with my father, and I need to evacuate Four Pines because of the tremor. Councilor Worryn won't see me, so I can't get authorization."

"He won't authorize the evacuation of Four Pines?"

"I can't even get in to see him. So, no."

Lornis lowered his brows. "Who's the leader here, you or him?"

"He has the official authority," said Rayn.

Lornis gave him a *look*.

"The law says—"

"He wants you to look weak and ineffective," said Lornis. "And you're letting him do it. You've opposed him before, and with great success. Forget what's official, for the moment. Who's the leader here, you or him?"

"I am," said Rayn.

"Exactly," said Lornis. "Get out there and evacuate Four Pines. Who cares if you have his authorization? Show these people you are prepared to lead them."

Rayn nodded. Lornis had the right of it, as always.

Rayn rounded up six of his fellow Fireturners. It wasn't the whole group, but a half dozen should be enough. One of them was his cousin Tiannon, whom Rayn trusted implicitly. They wouldn't be fighting a lava flow; they just needed to order the settlers of Four Pines to evacuate. Still, he insisted on everyone wearing their uniforms.

They assembled at the Tiasan Palace stables. Rayn mounted his blood bay stallion and took his place at the head of the group. The other Fireturners trotted in pairs behind him, dressed in their red-and-blacks.

As they entered the streets of Tiasa, civilians turned and stared. Children darted through the crowd to spread the word, and merchants came out of their shops to watch them pass. Some of them chanted: "Rayn! Rayn!"

Tiannon, who rode just behind Rayn, kicked his horse up alongside. "I think you were missed, while you were away in Kjall."

"I'm glad they didn't forget me," said Rayn, sitting straighter in his saddle. Lornis was right: it was time for him to step up and lead this country. Inya hadn't known an effective king for years now. His people were desperate for leadership. He would evacuate the settlers from Four Pines. He would protect the King's Lands. He would open trade with Kjall.

Four Pines was well outside Tiasa. After they'd left the city streets, he urged his mount into a canter, then leaned back in the saddle and inhaled deeply. Inya bloomed year-round—not everything at once, but always something was in flower. He'd missed the sweet, heavy scent of the air. Riorca's scent had been clean and fresh, like salad greens. But Inya's scent was decadent, a rich dessert.

Now that they were on country roads and no longer being observed, the riders of his troop loosened their formation, and he found himself riding alongside Tiannon and Faydra, another cousin and one of the few female Fireturners.

Faydra was looking up at Mount Drav, which loomed over them, larger and more intimidating here than in Tiasa. "You think it's going to blow?"

"You felt the tremor," said Rayn. "What do you think?"

"Yes," said Faydra. "The tremor was substantial."

Rayn turned to Tiannon.

"I missed the tremor, as you did," he said.

"Don't leave town," said Rayn. "I think I'll recall all the Fireturners to the palace. If Drav blows, we don't want any delay in rounding people up."

Four Pines was a wild place, only recently settled. Rayn felt it should never have been settled at all—what sort of fool builds a house in the shadow of a volcano? If he became king, he would order these settlements abandoned and allow the land to revert to its wild state. As a hunting preserve, the land had value to his people. But its primary use was as a reservoir for sending lava flows, so that his Fireturners could continue to turn fires away from Tiasa.

The valley was named for four ancient Island Pines that had survived countless lava flows from Mount Drav. The valley was mostly grass and scrubby, fast-growing

plants that spawned quickly after a fire. The four old
trees weren't beautiful. They were enormously tall—
Rayn estimated their height at fifteen to twenty stories—
and their trunks were almost entirely bare, except at the
very top where each sported a crown of leaves, just high
enough to be safe from the leaping flames.

Farmers had torn up the grassland and plowed it into
neat rows. Some of the plots were already producing.
Rayn recognized sweet potatoes, onions, and sugarcane.

"This is ridiculous," he muttered to Faydra.

"A waste," she agreed. "It'll all be destroyed in the
next lava flow."

"Councilor Worryn thinks we can stop the flow up on
top of the mountain," said Rayn.

She raised an eyebrow. "Has that man *seen* a lava flow
from Mount Drav?"

Rayn suspected the councilor hadn't. He was the type
to hide away in the Tiasan Palace, leaving the dirty work
to everyone else. *Coward.* He called his Fireturners together and assigned each of them a nearby farmhouse to
visit and deliver the evacuation order.

"It's not an official order, is it?" said Tiannon.

"It's official," said Rayn. "It's coming from the prince
of Inya."

They fanned out, and each Fireturner galloped toward a farmhouse. For the next few hours, Rayn knocked
on doors and informed farmers that their land was in
imminent danger of a lava flow from Mount Drav, and
they were to gather their belongings and leave immediately.

"For how long?" the farmers asked.

He wanted to say forever. No one had any business
farming this valley or building houses on it. If Mount
Drav did not erupt within the next couple of weeks, it

certainly would within the next couple of years, and all of this would be destroyed. But he looked at their half-grown plants and realized they had sunk a great deal of effort and investment into these lands already. They should never have planted in this valley, but they had, and he had a feeling that at least some of them wouldn't be heeding the evacuation order. Not until the mountain blew. He told them two weeks.

At least he'd given the order. It was more than Councilor Worryn had done.

23

Rayn's new apartment was smaller than his old one, but aside from the stuffiness, it was comfortable. He left the balcony doors open overnight to improve the air flow and slept in just his smallclothes. It had been a while since he'd slept in a room that wasn't sealed tight as a wine jug, and the feeling of the island breezes caressing his skin was pure bliss. If only he had Celeste to hold close while he slept, his nights would be perfect.

He woke rested, pleased about having delivered the evacuation order to the settlers in Four Pines. Councilor Worryn should never have placed those civilians' lives at risk. Defying him hadn't been precisely legal, but it had been the right thing to do.

After breakfast and his morning coffee, someone knocked at his door.

"Come." Rayn threw a gauzy robe over his shoulders. The skies were overcast. They might have rain later.

Lornis stepped inside, looking annoyed. "Shunting you off to the Hibiscus Tower is an insult. Councilor Worryn is treating you like a visiting dignitary."

"I think that's the message he's trying to send," said Rayn. "He wants me to think my presence here is temporary."

Lornis folded his arms and looked about the room, frowning. "I'll grant that your accommodations aren't *too* unpleasant. Perhaps Worryn hopes to lull you into a hibiscus-scented stupor."

Rayn took a seat on the bed. His apartment lacked an anteroom and had only one chair, which he left for Lornis. "Hibiscus has no scent."

Lornis glanced at the chair but declined to sit. "Frangipani, then."

"I'll look petty if I make a fuss about the room change," said Rayn. "It's temporary. If I'm ratified next week, I'll kick *him* out of the first-floor hallway."

"And if you're not ratified, he'll probably remove you from the palace grounds entirely."

"If it's the will of the people not to ratify me, I won't gainsay him," said Rayn. "I'm more upset about his moving Father. The move has aggravated his paranoia. From his old room he watched the ships coming and going from the harbor, and now he's convinced there are attack ships coming and he can't see them."

"It bothers me too that Worryn can be so petulantly cruel to a sick old man," said Lornis. "But I think you're right to wait this out. It's only a week. Evacuating Four Pines is more important."

"I did that last night."

"Excellent," said Lornis. "Without Worryn's authority?"

"Correct."

"This afternoon I want you to speak with the leaders of the Merchants' Guild. They're very influential, especially here in Tiasa, and if you can secure their support—"

A pair of guards appeared in the doorway. "Prince Rayn," called one of them.

"Yes?" said Rayn.

"The council demands your immediate presence."

Rayn exchanged a look with Lornis.

"They're upset about the evacuation," Lornis guessed. "You could refuse to see them."

"I *want* to speak to Worryn," said Rayn.

Lornis lowered his voice. "Do you think you should go alone?"

Rayn eyed the sword belted to Lornis's hip. Perhaps it was time he belted on one of his own. "You'd better come along."

Ten minutes later, the guards admitted them into the first-floor hallway, which had, until recently, been Rayn's own stomping grounds. Now it was enemy territory. The unfamiliar weight of a sword tugged at his belt. Inya wasn't a violent country, and normally he felt safe enough just with his fire magic. But given recent events, it seemed sensible to carry a weapon and to have a companion at his side.

He'd never seen so many guards here before. A pair of them stood before every door, a practice similar to what he'd seen in Kjall, though it had never been Inyan custom. *Bad king,* thought Rayn.

The council room was adjacent to the throne room, on the north side of the hallway. The two chambers, one home to the king and the other to the council, were connected to each other by a side door, reflecting Inya's long tradition of shared governance.

The guards showed Rayn and Lornis into the council room.

Nine councilors sat around the outside of a U-shaped table. So that he could see all the men at once and address them easily, Rayn stepped into the opening of the "U." He'd addressed the council on many occasions in the past and, before that, stood audience as his father addressed them. Public speaking did not frighten him, but today a prickle of unease crawled up his neck. Five of these men were his enemies. Some of them might have hired assassins to kill him on foreign soil.

The five councilors who voted in a bloc were Worryn, Burr, Chagar, Beltan, and Seph. The other four, Quar, Roth, Delard, and Aryack, operated independently; their votes were unpredictable. Within the group of independents, Rayn might have a friend or two, but since those four men were in the minority, they had little power.

"Rayn—" began Councilor Worryn.

"*Prince* Rayn," corrected Lornis. "Or *Your Highness*."

"He has no rank," said Worryn. "His father abdicated the throne."

"As the son of a king awaiting ratification, he does have rank," said Lornis. "Look it up in the law books if you're unclear on the matter."

Councilor Worryn frowned. It was a subtle change. To those unfamiliar with the man, Worryn appeared to wear the same facial expression all the time—a slightly strained and disapproving look, as if he needed to visit the privy. But Rayn had, over the years, acquired the ability to read him. The man's moods varied between only three states that he could identify: miffed, angry, and furious. One could tell the difference by observing minute changes in the architecture of his face. Worryn had just transitioned from *miffed* to *angry*.

"Nobody invited *you* here," said Worryn to Lornis. "You sully this room with your presence."

"You want to speak with me, you speak with Magister Lornis as well," said Rayn.

Worryn turned his gaze to Rayn. "You evacuated Four Pines yesterday without authorization."

"I tried to speak to you beforehand, but I was denied

admittance to this council. Since the matter was urgent, I had no choice but to proceed on my own authority."

"Since your father's unfortunate abdication, I have been responsible both for Land Council business and the king's business," said Worryn. "I am not at your beck and call, princeling."

"Your Highness," corrected Lornis.

"It's unfortunate you're so overworked," said Rayn. "I assure you the situation is temporary. In a week, I will relieve you of half of those responsibilities."

Worryn's barely visible frown deepened. *Angry* to *furious.*

"The people will decide that," said Worryn. "I cannot imagine they will ratify a king who governs so recklessly."

"There's been a tremor," said Rayn. "Mount Drav could erupt at any time, and the Fireturners need that land cleared of civilians. It would be reckless *not* to evacuate."

"I have instructed you not to direct lava flows into Four Pines."

"During an eruption, the Fireturners take instruction from no one but me," said Rayn. "If we cannot stop the lava flow on the mountain, we will direct it into Four Pines. There is no other place to send it. Anyone occupying that valley has to leave."

"Those settlers have farms in Four Pines," put in Councilor Burr.

"They should never have built them." Before any of the councilors could protest, Rayn added, "I have another matter to bring before this council."

"We are not finished with the first," said Worryn.

"My father is ill," said Rayn, "and he has been moved to a room where he cannot see the harbor. Since it gives him comfort to see the harbor, I would like to relocate him—"

"All harbor-facing rooms are occupied," said Worryn.

By whom? Rayn wondered. "After my father's long years of service to this country—"

"Your father is mad!" cried Worryn.

"He served this country well before he became so afflicted, and it quiets him to look upon the harbor. It is cruelty to deny him this simple comfort."

"The prince is right," said Councilor Roth. "Why not grant the former king a harbor-facing room? It's the least we can do."

Rayn met Roth's eyes in silent gratitude. He had at least one friend on the Land Council.

"We'll put it to a vote," said Worryn. "Those in favor of moving the former king to a harbor-facing room, declare yourselves."

Councilors Roth, Quar, Delard, and Aryack each held up a finger. The other councilors' arms disappeared to their sides. Rayn gritted his teeth in exasperation. This was just petty meanness on Worryn's part.

"Opposed?" said Worryn.

The four fingers went down, and the five men of Worryn's voting bloc raised theirs.

"Denied by vote of the Land Council," said Worryn. "As for your illegal evacuation, as regent-in-standing while Inya is without a king, I order you to return to Four Pines and rescind the evacuation notice. If the settlers have left home, find them and tell them they're to return."

Rayn had wondered, before, why this issue was so important to Councilor Worryn. Now he had a theory: Worryn was setting him up. If Mount Drav erupted, and Rayn led his Fireturners to direct the lava flow into Four

Pines, and people were killed because the area hadn't been evacuated, who would be blamed for the tragedy? Not Councilor Worryn, but Rayn and the Fireturners. Worryn was a nasty, selfish man; he was not above staging a real-life tragedy if it benefited him politically. And the people would never ratify Rayn if they believed he was responsible for civilian deaths.

"No," said Rayn. "I will follow no order that places my people in danger."

Councilor Worryn banged his fist on the table. "Princeling, you have no authority to make that decision!"

"Your Highness," Lornis corrected again.

"This interview is over," said Rayn. He gestured to Lornis and headed for the door.

24

Rayn changed clothes for his meeting with the Merchants' Guild. Around a black silk shirt and pants he belted the gold chain his father had given him for his fifteenth birthday. For luck, he added his favorite necklace, a pendant featuring a sea green peridot as large as his thumb. The stone had been found in the volcanic ash near the base of Mount Drav—a gift from the fire spirits. He finished with soft leather boots and, as a nod to practicality, his sword belt and weapon.

The meeting was at the Merchants' Guild headquarters, a large building in the center of Tiasa, and a short ride from the palace. Rayn met Lornis at the stables and swung up on Copperhead, his blood bay stallion. Lornis mounted the brown gelding Whiskey.

"You did well in front of the council," said Lornis as their horses jogged down the cobbled streets of Tiasa.

"When I was a child, I was awed by Worryn," said Rayn, "but he doesn't scare me now. He's a *small* man. Not physically; I mean in the way he sees the world."

"Stand strong and don't let him cow you," said Lornis. "The man is yellow to the core. He's only as dangerous as you allow him to be."

Lornis spoke sense, and yet there was something

about Worryn. He wasn't frightening when confronted directly, but Rayn was a little worried about what the man might do when no one was looking. After all, assassins had tried to kill Rayn twice in the past month. He knew the Riorcan breakaway enclave was responsible, and yet he couldn't rule out some degree of involvement by Worryn. It seemed like just the sort of sneak attack Worryn would orchestrate.

"What's this?" Lornis reined his horse over to a glow post. He peered at a handbill posted there and ripped it away. He trotted back to Rayn and handed it to him. "Someone's causing trouble."

The handbill read:

RATIFY PRINCE RAYN?
WHEN INYA NEEDED LEADERSHIP,
PRINCE RAYN WAS SIRING AN ILLEGITIMATE CHILD.
WHEN INYA NEEDED A TREATY WITH KJALL,
PRINCE RAYN CAME HOME EMPTY-HANDED.
INYA DOES NOT NEED PRINCE RAYN.

Rayn frowned. There was just enough truth in there to sting. Had Councilor Worryn posted this, or someone in his employ? It was true he'd sired an illegitimate child, but at the same time he'd been standing up to the Land Council to protect the King's Lands. As for coming home empty-handed from Kjall, yes, he had. But he'd been recalled early because Councilor Worryn had bullied his father into abdicating the throne.

He returned the handbill to Lornis. "What worries me is that not one statement in here is an outright lie."

"The last one is," said Lornis. *"Inya does not need Prince Rayn."*

"I meant the ones in the middle."

"They're not lies, but they're intended to deceive," said Lornis. "He makes you sound ineffective, when you were the only person capable of stopping the council's abuses."

"I wish I'd finished negotiating that Kjallan treaty." He wished even more that he'd made things right with Celeste. Already her absence made him feel as if he were missing a limb. He kept thinking she was there, and then feeling the ache anew when he remembered she was not.

"I did warn you about that," said Lornis, who folded up the handbill and stuffed it in his pocket. "Still, you might have done it if you hadn't been called back prematurely."

At the Merchants' Guild, they hopped down and handed off their horses to a pair of grooms. A steward showed them inside. This was to be a luncheon meeting, and food was set out for them: boiled carp in a sauce of jackfruit and coconut milk, rice steamed in banana leaves, bitter melon soup, and other Inyan delicacies.

He worked the room, clasping wrists with each man. They took seats at the common table, and food was passed around. Lornis sat several seats away, allowing Rayn access to more merchants. Rayn filled his plate.

"Prince Rayn," began a merchant who traded in coffee, "during your trip, did you find the Kjallans amenable to opening trade with our little nation?"

"Very amenable," said Rayn. "They're particularly interested in brimstone, but my impression was that they were eager to open trade for all goods."

"Do you worry," asked another merchant, "that their intentions are duplicitous? That they might send their ships here under pretense of trade and instead launch an attack?"

"No." To his surprise, Rayn realized he felt confident

about that now. The Kjallans were no longer strangers to him, and despite his annoyance at Lucien for sending him away, he could not see the man ordering an attack on his country. "I think we need to be cautious, because Kjall has a worrisome history, and I'm concerned about trading them brimstone, with which they can manufacture gunpowder. But Lucien has been, thus far, a peaceable ruler. While he remains in power, I believe we have nothing to fear from Kjall."

"What are the terms of the treaty they're offering?" asked a third merchant.

"It's under negotiation. I had to leave Kjall abruptly because of my father's abdication, and we hadn't settled everything."

"We need this market opened," said an older, bearded merchant. "How hard can it be to settle upon some mutually agreeable terms?"

Rayn wondered if this man had seen the handbill from the glow post. In truth, he was at fault with regard to the treaty; he'd wasted a lot of time in Kjall by not taking the negotiations more seriously. It was a mistake he wouldn't make again. "Negotiations were proceeding before they were interrupted by the necessity of my returning home. Once I'm ratified, I'll complete them and finalize the treaty."

"How are we to have confidence in you," asked a thin-faced man, "when thus far you have produced no results?"

"Sir, I'm taking the issue of Kjallan trade seriously, unlike any other Inyan political leader. My father never visited Kjall. Neither has any council member, excepting Burr, who accompanied me on this trip only for the purpose of obstructing the negotiations. I've met with the Kjallan rulers and opened a dialogue with them, something no Inyan has done for nearly a century."

There were nods around the table, but Rayn didn't see a lot of enthusiasm, and he couldn't blame these people. His arguments were weak. Merchants cared about results. Trade goods sold or they didn't. Coffers filled up with coin or they didn't. Vague promises would not satisfy people who dealt in physical reality every day.

Back at the Tiasan Palace, he and Lornis dropped off their horses at the stable and headed toward the main gallery.

"That didn't go as well as I'd hoped," said Rayn.

"Don't lose heart," said Lornis. "It wasn't a disaster, and you *are* the right leader for Inya—I'm convinced of it. We need only convince the rest of Inya, and I don't think that will be hard. Ever since you stopped the Land Council from selling off the King's Lands, you've been popular."

Rayn nodded, somewhat mollified.

As they reached the base of the spiral staircase, Lornis halted. "I have a thought. I'm going to speak to a handbill printer."

"You're going to print some handbills of your own?"

"Yes, exactly." Lornis's eyes darted in the direction of the stable. "Will you be all right getting back to your room, or would you prefer company?"

Rayn waved him away. "I'm fine. Print your handbills." If Worryn meant to try once more to assassinate him, he would not do it in the middle of the palace where there were so many witnesses.

He trudged up the two long flights of stairs, down the hallway, across the suspension bridge, inhaling mango scent. He needed to meet with the Fireturners to work up a plan of action in case the mountain blew. For that, he wouldn't need his finery. He headed into the bedroom.

The wet nurse Kima was standing in the entryway, holding Aderyn. She bobbed in a curtsy. "Your Highness."

He nodded. "Kima. Is everything all right?" He took Aderyn, who wrapped her arms around his neck.

"I'm sorry to bother you, but I thought you might want to know. Zoe's disappeared."

The hair rose on the back of his neck as he remembered those two lumps he'd found. After he'd asked her about them, Zoe had stayed away from him. "You mean she didn't show up for work?"

"Right. Not yesterday, and not today either. Her supervisor came looking for her in my room, thinking she might have come to see her daughter. But she hasn't been by, sir."

The situation was curious. Had she left on purpose, or had something happened to her? "I'll send someone to her father's house to inquire after her. Tell me if you hear anything else."

He blinked. Something felt wrong. The bed was moving.

No, the whole room was moving. The whole *tower*.

"Tremor," he said shortly. He grabbed Kima's arm and, still carrying Aderyn, dragged the wet nurse across the floor to his writing table. He shoved her underneath and then folded himself into the too-small space, shielding his daughter with his body. There was a grating noise — he always heard it during tremors — like two enormous stones being rubbed together.

Kima was calm beside him. She had no doubt ridden out many a tremor like this one. But poor Aderyn was screaming her head off.

A chair scraped the floor as it inched, unbidden, across the room. Something fell and shattered, showering them with shards of clay. Then, as suddenly as it had begun, the tremor ended. He crawled out from under the table with a terrified but unhurt Aderyn and helped Kima up.

"What do you think?" he asked, bouncing Aderyn to calm her. "Was that much like the last one?"

"A little stronger," said Kima.

Lornis appeared in the doorway, coming to a sudden stop after what appeared to have been a full-out run. He gave Kima a quizzical look and turned to Rayn. "Mount Drav's erupting," he said. "You're needed on the mountain at once."

25

As the *Soldier's Sweep* hove to outside the Tiasan harbor, Celeste stared, awestruck, at the first volcano she'd ever laid eyes on. She stood at the rail with Vitala, her face damp with the afternoon's fine drizzle, watching the mountain while the ship's signaler tried to contact the Inyan authorities. Inya had a strong navy. Their harbor was well defended with shore batteries and warships, and a lone Kjallan ship dared not enter without permission.

"It must be Mount Drav," said Celeste. "Do you suppose it always looks like that?"

"I would think not," said Vitala.

The mountain was shrouded in mist—or was that smoke? She couldn't tell from this distance; the mountain was inland, beyond the city of Tiasa. Red lines trailed down the mountain, glowing like the iridescent trails of fireworks. One thick ribbon of fire wound down the left-hand side of the mountain, forking in two places. Elsewhere, the fiery lines were slimmer, like glowing filaments, or pinpricks of red light. It was a beautiful sight, but some primal instinct within her screamed danger.

The ship's captain joined them at the rail. "We haven't been able to contact Prince Rayn."

Celeste gripped the rail so hard, her fingers hurt.

Please don't let him be dead. "Who did you talk to, and what did he say?"

"Some harbor official. He said Rayn was unavailable."

She loosened her grip a little. *Unavailable* didn't sound like dead. "Can you talk to someone else? The Land Council, perhaps?"

"I was told they couldn't authorize our entering the harbor at this time, because Tiasa is in a state of emergency."

Celeste turned to Mount Drav. "The volcano."

"That was my assumption," said the captain.

"You don't suppose we could just sail in?" suggested Vitala. "We're obviously not an attack fleet. Surely they won't open fire."

"With respect, Empress," said the captain, "we cannot take that chance. They would be foolish to fire upon us, since that would be an act of war. But our sailing in unauthorized could also be interpreted as an act of war."

Vitala sighed. "We can't just heave to and wait. It's obvious the volcano isn't an immediate danger; look at all the Tiasans at the docks just going about their business. I don't see anyone panicking. I've a feeling the Land Council doesn't want us landing and assisting Rayn."

"Contact them again," said Celeste to the captain, "and ask for Magister Lornis this time."

"I'll try that, Your Imperial Highness."

"I'll go with you," said Vitala. "See if I can talk some sense into someone."

The captain and the empress departed, and Celeste returned her gaze to the volcano. If this was an eruption—and that seemed likely; what else could explain those glowing red lines?—Rayn might be up on the mountain right now. How tiny he must be in comparison to that red ribbon of lava. She could see the lava flow from here, but she certainly couldn't see anything as small as a person. She tried to guess where he might be. Near the top, where the ribbon began? Or perhaps at the bottom, diverting the tail end.

For half an hour she watched, shaking raindrops off her face. Then, behind her, someone began shouting orders, and the ship's crewmen swarmed into the tops. Vitala returned to the rail and said, "That was a good idea, to contact Magister Lornis. He's granted us authorization to anchor."

A frisson of excitement ran through Celeste. She was about to set foot on Inya—Rayn's home country—for the very first time. Neither Lucien nor Florian had ever been here. She and Vitala would be the first Kjallan imperials to visit this country in decades.

Inya wasn't a single island but an archipelago. The island upon which the capital city of Tiasa sat was called Rul Linaran, which in literal Inyan translated to "island of people." As the ship sailed into the harbor, she marveled at what a beautiful island Rul Linaran was. Despite the rain, the sea was brilliant blue and the beaches pale and sandy. Tiasan buildings clustered around the harbor with nary a space between them, like soldiers cozying up to a campfire. Some were built of pale stone and others of painted wood. Despite the lack of open space, plants were everywhere. Ivies climbed the walls, trees rose up alongside buildings to shade the streets, and flowering bushes hid in every nook.

Anchoring the ship took over an hour, during which time she waited impatiently, eager to see the city of Tiasa up close and to hear about Rayn. Had Zoe tried to attack him? Was he up on the mountain? Had his ratification vote taken place?

The sailors rowed her ashore in the company of Vitala, Patricus, and an escort of Legaciatti. Magister Lornis met them at the docks as they disembarked. The air smelled of dampness and flowers, and it wasn't even spring.

Lornis bowed first to the empress and then to Celeste. "You can't imagine how happy I am to see you."

"Where's Rayn?" Celeste asked. "Is he all right?"

Vitala shot her a scolding look, and Celeste closed her mouth. This wasn't proper diplomatic etiquette.

"I apologize for our arriving unannounced and uninvited," Vitala said to Lornis. "Thank you for allowing us to anchor."

"The pleasure's all mine." Lornis turned to Celeste. "Prince Rayn is up on the mountain with the Fireturners, controlling the lava flow. I'm sure he'll be ecstatic to see you when his work is done."

Thank the gods he was safe—as safe as any man could be on an erupting volcano. But Celeste didn't worry overmuch about the mountain. Rayn was trained to handle that. Her real concern was Zoe. "How long will he be up there?"

"Days," said Lornis. "It's no small feat, turning lava."

Celeste gazed upon the glowing red ribbons on distant Mount Drav. "That's fire, isn't it? The glowing red."

"It's stone that's so hot it melts and glows red," said Lornis. "It sets fire to everything it touches. But you needn't worry. It's far away, and the Fireturners are adept at handling it."

"Do you think I could go up on the mountain and watch them?" Then she realized how unreasonable a request that was. "I'm sorry; I shouldn't ask such a thing."

"Actually, I'd love to see that myself, if it's possible," said Vitala.

Lornis looked uncertain. "It may be too dangerous

for spectators. I'll contact the base camp and ask how stable the flow is right now; perhaps we can arrange something. For now, please accompany me to the Tiasan Palace. We have rooms prepared for you, and once your needs have been seen to, we should discuss a few things."

Celeste nodded. "I have urgent news for you. But I can't tell you here." She didn't feel comfortable speaking about Zoe on the docks, where any bystander could listen in. Even so, Rayn needed to be warned as soon as possible.

Celeste had grown up in the Imperial Palace, easily the loveliest building in Kjall with its marble domes and gilt roofs, yet she was unprepared for the sight of the Tiasan Palace. It looked like a delicate piece of latticework. Everywhere Celeste turned, she saw windows and breezeways and open-air plazas. Her Kjallan eyes instantly picked out its vulnerabilities—the stately old trees whose branches afforded access to windows and balconies, the twining ivy that might allow an intruder to scale the walls. Inya had always possessed a strong navy. As an island nation, they feared no land invaders, and for that reason, perhaps, they had built their palace not for defense but to please the eye.

She was delighted to spot a stream flowing through the palace grounds. It snaked around the buildings, which were connected to one another by suspension bridges.

As she entered the palace, she realized the building was practical in at least one respect: the open, airy structure helped to keep it cool. Inya was a warm country— really, it was *hot*, even on a day when the sun wasn't shining. At home in Kjall, cold winters were the bigger problem, and the Imperial Palace had a system of underground heat-glows that kept it warm. No one had yet managed to invent a "cold-glow," so the Inyan building's many openings were strategically placed to funnel in the island's prevailing breezes. Without them, the palace would have been unbearably stuffy. As it was, she found it pleasant and comfortable.

The palace was not a single building but a complex, with spires of all shapes and sizes jutting up around a large central building. She could make out no pattern to the arrangement of towers. Possibly they had just been added over the years. She thought of building sand castles on the beach as a girl, upending her bucket to mold tower after tower in an arrangement that, though it seemed random, nonetheless satisfied her sense of aesthetics. The Tiasan Palace was disorganized, yet its apparent lack of planning did not diminish its beauty.

This is a wild place, she thought. Something about Tiasa exhilarated her.

Magister Lornis led them into the main building, where they entered an open-air gallery with a polished floor. To the left was a single hallway and to the right were two others. She smiled: not symmetrical.

Her companions paused as a group of men approached them from across the open gallery. Lornis stiffened at their approach, and she took his reaction to mean that these weren't friends.

"Your Imperial Majesty and Your Imperial Highness." One of the men inclined his head. "My name is Worryn. I serve on the Inyan Land Council. Your visit is an unexpected honor."

Worryn. Celeste studied him warily. This man was a criminal. He had paid Bayard's enclave to assassinate Prince Rayn.

"Thank you for allowing us to anchor our ship," said Vitala.

"I'm sorry for the confusion earlier. The situation is an awkward one," said Worryn. "I'm sure you noticed we're experiencing an emergency. Mount Drav has erupted, and while hosting you would be a great honor for our country, Tiasa is unsafe for visitors at this time. My conscience demands that I send you back to your ship."

"We accept the risk of the volcano," said Vitala. "Don't your Fireturners direct the lava away from the city?"

"Leadership is wanting among the Fireturners," said Worryn. "I cannot be certain they will succeed."

Celeste suppressed an eye roll. If Worryn truly feared that the lava flow would reach Tiasa, she guessed he'd be the first to leave town. But he wasn't evacuating, and neither were the others. The townsfolk were going about their business, apparently with total confidence that the Fireturners would keep them safe.

"Our business here is urgent," said Vitala. "I'm sure the Fireturners have the situation under control."

Worryn tilted his head. "What is the nature of your business?"

Vitala glanced at Celeste, who spoke up. "When Prince Rayn visited Kjall, we were in the middle of some negotiations regarding a trade agreement between our countries. He had to return home unexpectedly, leaving our talks incomplete. We are here to continue them."

"How interesting." The expression on Worryn's face didn't change, and Celeste couldn't tell if he was indifferent or openly hostile toward this proposal.

"If you'll excuse us," Lornis broke in smoothly, "our imperial visitors are weary from their journey."

Worryn remained unreadable. He bowed to Vitala and Celeste. "When you are recovered from your travels, we'll discuss this further."

Celeste hoped he didn't make good on that threat. She wanted nothing to do with the man.

Lornis led them to a spiral staircase, and they began to ascend.

"I've placed you in the Hibiscus Tower," he said. "It's not where visitors of your stature would normally be housed—typically you'd be in that hallway on the left." He pointed. "But Rayn and I are in the tower right now, and given the unstable political situation we're in, I think it's safest for you to be near us."

"I agree," said Vitala.

So did Celeste. She wanted to be close to Rayn, not to that treacherous snake. They ascended another flight and walked down a pillared hallway with open archways along the sides. The hallway opened up into a balcony. Before her was one of the suspension bridges she'd seen earlier. From the ground, the bridge had looked appealing, a little arc in the shape of a smile. She had not anticipated what it would look like from up here. The bridge curved steeply downward. It had handrails, but no supports at all to keep it upright.

She halted uncertainly at the edge. "Is this safe?"

Lornis walked out onto the bridge. "Absolutely safe, Your Imperial Highness."

She followed with a couple of tentative steps. The bridge wasn't stable; it shifted and jounced beneath her feet. Lornis didn't seem to mind. He strode forward with no concern for the bridge's movement. She decided she was being silly to worry about this, and trotted across the wooden slats to catch up to him.

Her room in the Hibiscus Tower was lovely, though a little stuffy and woefully insecure compared with her rooms in the Imperial Palace. Her bedroom opened through a double archway onto a balcony overlooking a garden. The Inyans seemed not to use window glass; their windows were artfully shaped openings exposing them directly to the weather, and potentially to enemies. She was several stories up and saw no trees offering access to her balcony—that was a relief. Nor did the ivy climb this high.

Vitala joined Celeste on the balcony and frowned. "We're going to have to put Legaciatti up here."

"We have guards patrolling the grounds," offered Lornis.

"Not enough for imperial security," said Vitala.

Lornis nodded. "Do as you deem necessary. Inya is a smaller country and not as security-minded as Kjall."

It wasn't just that Inya was smaller, Celeste thought. It was different in character. These rooms would never have been built in such an open way if political assassinations and coups were common here. While she accepted the need for placing Legaciatti to make up for the room's defensive shortcomings, she envied Inya for not needing such precautions, at least most of the time.

And yet political scheming was not unknown here.

"We've learned some important things we need to share with you," she told Lornis.

The Legaciatti took up positions around the room, ensuring that they would have privacy, and Celeste and Vitala told Lornis what they'd learned from Bayard: that Councilor Worryn had arranged for the assassination attempts, that Zoe was no Inyan woman at all but a Riorcan assassin sent to Inya first to produce an illegitimate heir, then to remove Rayn from the line of succession.

Lornis looked grave as he took in these facts, but he did not seem surprised. "Councilor Worryn is a known enemy," he said, "but Rayn needs to be warned about Zoe. She recently abandoned the palace."

"She's gone?"

"Just up and left, yes," said Lornis.

"That might be good, or it might be bad," said Celeste. "Take me up on the mountain, and I'll tell Rayn what I know. He may be in danger."

Lornis nodded. "I'll contact the base camp and see what I can do."

26

Celeste had never felt as small as when she looked upon the lava flow on Mount Drav. When she'd seen the mountain from a distance and observed the glowing red line of lava, she'd imagined something akin to a river. Now that she was up on the mountain, viewing the flow from up close, she realized that she'd vastly underestimated its size. It was nothing like a river. It was a slow-moving beast of colossal size, well over ten feet tall and wider than she could see from her vantage point. Everything it touched, it devoured utterly. Trees in its pathway burst into flame; bushes vanished in puffs of steam.

Her horse, borrowed from the Inyan stables, shifted uneasily on the mountain trail and tossed its head. Its muscles tensed beneath her, and she could tell the animal wanted nothing more than to turn around and head back to the lowlands.

For all its power, the lava flow was eerily quiet. Flames crackled and spat when it set the vegetation afire, but the lava itself was silent, inevitable death. Mostly all she heard were the shouts of the Fireturners.

Rayn's voice rose above the others, sharp and crisp as he gave orders. The other men—and some women, she realized—responded with equal brusqueness, putting her in mind of a military operation.

How could they stand being so close to the lava? She was a hundred yards away at least, on a rocky trail overlooking the scene. Even at that distance, heat spilled off the lava in an asphyxiating wall. Much closer, and the air would be stifling. She understood now how important the fire mages' magic was—without their ability to heat or cool the air around them, they wouldn't be able to do this work at all.

"How do they turn the lava in the desired direction?" she asked Magister Lornis, who sat beside her on his horse. Vitala was also present, staring at the spectacle.

"They cool it at the edges," said Lornis. "When lava is cooled, it hardens into rock. Do you see how they're building a wall along that ridge?"

Indeed they were. It was hard to tell, since most of the Fireturners were clustered about that area, blocking her view. But she saw that a wall of cooled lava was in fact taking shape.

Sometimes the Fireturners walked directly over the lava. There was a man up on the flow now, gesturing at the people on the ground. When he spoke, Celeste realized that man was Rayn.

Rayn lifted his head and spotted Celeste. For a moment he stood completely still. Then he spoke to his people again—words Celeste couldn't make out from this distance—and hopped from the lava to a rocky ledge, then from the ledge to the ground.

He jogged toward her.

Celeste dismounted from her horse and ran to him, heedless of the wall of sweltering air that engulfed her.

He held up his arms. "I'm filthy, covered with ash—"

Celeste flung her arms around him. Yes, he smelled of brimstone and fire, but he was her Rayn, and it was nothing a good bath wouldn't take care of.

"You came for me," he murmured into her ear, hugging her so tightly she could barely breathe. A wave of wintry air surrounded her, countering the heat of the lava. Rayn's magic was at work again, this time cooling her instead of warming her.

Suddenly she remembered that she was uncertain of her welcome—that Rayn had left Riorca abruptly with no word of where the two of them stood. "Why did you not come to see me before you left Riorca?"

"I tried." He pulled back just enough to stroke her face. "Did you not receive my letter?"

"What letter?"

Rayn's brows lowered. "Lucien's men intercepted me when I tried to come from the *Water Spirit* to speak to you. They forced me to return to my ship, but I gave them a letter that they were to deliver to you."

Gods, a letter? It would have made all the difference in the world. "I never received it."

He frowned. "I think somebody must have decided they didn't want you to have it. Never mind—you're here. That's all that matters." He glanced back at the lava flow. "What do you think of Inya so far? This is, I suppose, a rather rude introduction."

"It's beautiful and fascinating." She studied him, noting the weary cast to his face. He must be exhausted. "How long have you been up here fighting the lava?"

Rayn shrugged. "I lose track of time on the mountain. Two days? Maybe three?"

"Do you sleep in shifts?"

"Yes, at the base camp. As little as we can get away with and keep our magic strong. It takes many of us, working together, to cool the lava enough to build the walls that will contain it. This is no trivial bit of magic."

"How in the world do you walk on top of the lava?"

Rayn glanced back at the massive flow. "Fire magic isn't just about warming things. We can also draw the heat out of things—cool them down. I just cool the surface of the lava where my feet step, enough that it hardens a little and becomes walkable. I have to keep moving when I'm doing it, because the hardened bits of lava tend to sink."

"What about the other lava flows? When I was in Tiasa, looking up at the mountain, I saw quite a few of them—smaller ones, I mean."

"This is the only one that matters," said Rayn. "The others won't even make it off the mountain."

"They'll dry up on their own?"

"Yes, they'll cool and harden into rock, right here on the mountainside. My people are monitoring a couple of the larger ones, but I don't think we'll have to do anything about them."

"So this big one—it's not going to stay on the mountain like the others?"

He shook his head. "This one we have to send into Four Pines. The good news is that Mount Drav tends to erupt in a similar way every time, and we've directed many flows to Four Pines over the centuries. We know the critical places where our walls have to be built up to divert the flow, and in most cases those walls are already in place. We just have to shore them up and make sure the lava doesn't overrun them."

One of the Fireturners shouted Rayn's name. Rayn turned, looking torn.

"I won't keep you. This is important work," she said.

"When I'm done here, I'd like to talk to you," said Rayn. "At length."

"Absolutely," said Celeste. "Let me tell you one thing, though. Zoe is a Riorcan assassin."

Rayn's mouth twisted. "I thought she might be. She's disappeared of late. I was going to send someone to look for her—"

"I'd be very careful if you did that. She may have joined her fellows. She's got two other assassins with her, here on Inya."

"Soldier's Hell," he said. "I'll tell you what little I know when the eruption is over, and you can fill in the blanks for me."

"If you see her, keep your distance. She's got Shards. Like the empress."

His brows rose.

"Also . . ." Perhaps now was not the best time to tell him that Zoe was a wardbreaker. "Never mind. I'll tell you later."

Rayn nodded to Vitala, who was still on her horse. "Your Imperial Majesty."

"Your Highness," answered Vitala. "This is quite a spectacle. I've never seen the like."

"It's a dangerous spectacle for those without fire magic," said Rayn. "Do keep well back—I wouldn't want harm to come to you or your sister-in-law."

"Nothing would induce me to go any nearer," said Vitala.

Rayn turned to Celeste. "Kiss for luck?"

She'd been hoping for such an invitation. She threw her arms around his neck, heedless of the ash that smudged his face. He tasted of fire, and his skin was hot against hers. Muscles flexed as he wrapped her in his arms, and she felt his strength—the strength of a man who could tame a mountain.

As their lips parted, he stroked her cheek with a gentleness that belied the power of his body. "I wish I could stay," he murmured.

She shook her head. "Go. We'll settle everything later."

When it was over, and the lava flow had been safely directed into Four Pines, Rayn washed the mountain's filth from his body and slept for sixteen hours straight. The fires would burn in Four Pines for a while, and needed to be managed so that they did not get out of control, but his cousin Tiannon had volunteered to organize the shifts for that work so that Rayn could prepare for his ratification vote. When Rayn awoke the next morning, he could think of nothing but Celeste. He dressed with a great deal more care than usual and went in search of the Kjallan princess.

He found her at breakfast with Empress Vitala and Magister Lornis. Though his heart beat a tremor against his rib cage just at seeing her, he was frustrated that she had company. He wanted to speak to her alone.

Celeste's eyes lit up when she saw him. "Rayn!"

"Princess." He inclined his head in formal greeting, yet couldn't stop himself from pasting a huge, sloppy grin on his face. Lornis would scold him for the diplomatic impropriety. He took a seat at the table. A servant delivered his coffee, which he sipped gratefully. "Are you enjoying your stay in Inya?"

"It's a beautiful country," said Celeste. "I love everything about it."

The words warmed his heart. If she loved it, maybe she'd be willing to stay. He took a seat, and a servant placed his favorite breakfast in front of him, seasoned rice topped with a fried egg and surrounded with crisp vegetables. "Has Lornis shown you around?"

"He offered," said Celeste. "But I felt . . . Well, I was hoping *you* would do it."

Rayn grinned again. She'd just handed him the perfect excuse for spending some time alone with her. "Princess, I would love to show you my favorite places around Tiasa." Then he realized he could hardly exclude the empress of Kjall. "And the empress as well."

Vitala gave him a sly smile. "Much as I'd like to spend the day touring, Lornis and I have business to attend to."

Praise the gods—she was on his side.

"Rayn," said Lornis, "I have plans for you. Now that the Kjallans are here, we need to visit the Merchants' Guild again. Plus I'd like you to make some public appearances with Celeste. And you should talk about the lava flow that went into Four Pines. Those farms are burning. You did the right thing, but we need to make sure the people of Tiasa don't draw the wrong conclusions."

Lornis was right about Four Pines; there was no doubt Councilor Worryn would try to paint his successful fire-turning in a negative light. But to make appearances with Celeste was premature. He hadn't even established yet why she'd come all this way to visit him. "Tomorrow I'll put myself at your disposal, Lornis. But today I'm spending time with Celeste."

"Your ratification is in five days—" began Lornis.

"I know that," said Rayn. "This is important."

"Let them go," Vitala urged Lornis. "Rayn's been up on the mountain for days, and Celeste has eagerly awaited his return. They have much to discuss. Let them have a day to themselves."

Lornis grudgingly agreed.

Rayn was glad of it, since nothing was going to stop him anyway.

27

Rayn presented her with a dozen interesting ideas for where they could go, but Celeste wanted to start with something simple: a visit to the beach. Ever since she'd seen that pale white sand near the Tiasan harbor, she'd been dying to feel it between her toes.

Rayn wanted to take her to a different beach, however: one he said was more private. Celeste decided to bring Patricus, who would enjoy a swim in the ocean.

Rayn frowned when Atella and a second Legaciattus trailed them to the stables. "Must we bring your guards?"

"Lucien would have my head if I went anywhere without them," said Celeste.

"But it's not Inyan custom," said Rayn. "In fact, it carries a stigma here. *How do you tell a good king from a bad king?*"

"*The bad king is surrounded by bodyguards*—you told me. But I'm not Inyan. Your people must understand that Kjallans operate by a different set of rules." She'd never been without bodyguards in her life, excepting those few days in the Riorcan wilds. And with a known group of assassins targeting Rayn, she wasn't going anywhere without an escort. While she doubted anyone would attempt to harm her, Rayn was certainly in danger. By bringing along a Kjallan escort, ostensibly for herself, she could offer a measure of protection to Rayn that for Inyan cultural reasons he could not provide on his own.

However, she shared his disappointment that they would have no privacy. That had been part of the magic of the Riorcan wilds, a time that had been physically stressful and frightening, yet which she nonetheless regarded with wistful longing. For once in their lives, she and Rayn had been entirely on their own. They'd made their own decisions with no one watching, no one protecting, no one judging.

At the stables, Rayn mounted his blood bay, and Celeste swung up onto the smoke gray gelding she'd ridden on the mountain during the volcanic eruption. The grooms produced two additional horses for the guards, and they set off. Patricus loped at their side.

They wound their way through the streets of Tiasa. The Tiasan townsfolk did not scatter aside in fear, but actively engaged Rayn, calling his name and waving to him. He answered them with waves of his own and the Inyan greeting, *"Gama!"* It had no translation in Kjallan but meant something along the lines of "I see you." This interaction with the people in the streets was a new experience for Celeste. When Kjallan imperials rode into Riat, their bodyguards surrounded them, and everyone scrambled out of their way. Most Kjallan civilians, especially those living outside of Riat, wouldn't recognize their rulers on sight, since the imperial family left the palace grounds infrequently and rarely spoke to anyone outside the nobility and the military command structure. Lucien's profile was on the Kjallan tetral, but the iconic representation didn't look much like him.

Yet Rayn was known to his people not as an image on

a coin but as a living, breathing man. The townsfolk recognized him and apparently liked him. He must have spent a great deal more time in Tiasa than she or Lucien ever had in Riat. The thought intrigued her. What would it be like to be queen here, in a country where the people would actually know her?

She steered her horse alongside Rayn's. "The people here seem to like you."

"I've been popular since that business with the King's Lands," he said. "And it doesn't hurt that I'm a Fireturner."

Of course Rayn would be loved by his people when he served them in such a direct and useful way. Sadly, she could think of no equally visible service that Lucien and Vitala provided for the people of Kjall. Not that they weren't excellent rulers; they were some of the best Kjall had ever possessed. But their work wasn't so visible. They kept Kjall out of wars, rebuilt its neglected infrastructure, weeded out corrupt bureaucrats, and trained retired soldiers in new skills.

She had no idea what the people of Kjall thought of her or of Lucien or of Vitala. Maybe her family could take some lessons from the Inyans. They could be less aloof and more personable toward the townsfolk. Perhaps the men of the Mathematical Brotherhood had rejected Celeste not simply because she was a woman, but because she was an *imperial*, and the imperials weren't popular in Kjall.

They left the city and cantered down a road of soft dirt, riding abreast. Trees overhung the road, while ferns and bushes crowded close to the edges. The jungle loomed over and around them, not overtly threatening, yet quietly asserting its power. She felt the jungle would, given half an opportunity, swallow up this road entirely.

Rayn turned his horse off the main path, and she fell in behind him since there was no room to ride abreast. They traveled a ways, and Rayn pulled up his horse. She yanked on the reins as her horse ran up against the blood bay's hind end.

They were pinned between two rocky cliffs, each overhung with vegetation. The cliffs converged on their position, blocking further progress, but ahead, a rock tunnel carved its way through the cliff face. A pair of guards stood before the tunnel, which surprised Celeste since Inya used so few guards in general. Why station two of them way out here? Rayn spoke to one of them in rapid-fire Inyan. He glanced back at Celeste with a nod of invitation and urged his horse forward into the tunnel at a walk.

She followed. It was cool in the cave, but not dark. She could see daylight up ahead. The clops of her horse's footfalls changed to pats as the ground beneath them transitioned from stone to sand. They emerged from the tunnel into the sun. Celeste sneezed at its bright glare and blinked at the white sand beach that lay before them. Beyond it, the ocean glittered as if a thousand sapphires were strewn across its surface.

Patricus, upon spotting the water, barked in delight. He dashed forward a few yards and turned to stare at Celeste, his head cocked and his body poised for action.

"Go," she said, granting him permission, and he raced for the water.

Rayn grinned as he awaited her reaction to the scenery.

"It's beautiful," she said.

"And it's private," he said. "Reserved for the exclusive use of the royal family."

"Are these King's Lands?" she asked.

"No, the King's Lands are public," said Rayn. "This is something else. Look, you'll see there's no access to this beach at all except through the tunnel. Or by boat, I suppose, if you want to sail around all this way."

She clucked to her gelding, who stepped out onto the beach. The animal's hooves sank into the deep sand. Right away she saw what Rayn was talking about. This wasn't an open beach, stretching away endlessly on either side, but a sheltered cove enclosed by two rocky cliffs. Nearby was a cluster of palm trees, providing a bit of shade. "Let's put the horses over there," she suggested. She wanted to feel sand between her toes.

Beneath the palm trees, they dismounted and handed their reins to the Legaciatti. "Stay here," Celeste ordered them. "I want to walk with Rayn by the water, alone. I don't think we're in any danger."

"Your Imperial Highness—" Atella protested.

"Look around," said Celeste. "The whole place is enclosed. No one can touch us here."

Atella nodded grudging acquiescence.

Celeste kicked off her shoes.

Rayn took her hand and led her out onto the sand. "Let's see if the ocean has left us any gifts."

The sun, still low in the morning sky, was warm but not blistering. Later she might wish for Rayn's magic to cool them down, but for now the air was pleasant. Patricus, spotting them, came in from the ocean, shook off the seawater, and gamboled about the beach, sniffing at everything.

Celeste's feet sank into the sand as they walked, but as they neared the water, the sand became firmer. They reached the water's edge. A shallow wave rolled over her feet, tickling her toes.

Rayn glanced back at the guards, who were out of

hearing range by now. "I think we've enough privacy to talk now. Will you tell me why you came to Inya? When I left Riorca, your brother was adamantly opposed to our having any further contact."

"I wish I could say he'd changed his mind, but the truth is I'm here without his consent. He wouldn't let me come, so I stole his ship."

Rayn stared at her. "You *stole his ship*?"

"I did."

"But the empress is with you."

"She caught me stealing it and decided to go with me. That makes this trip somewhat official, I suppose. But we don't have Lucien's support, and I expect he will come looking for me as soon as he manages to find a way here. When he arrives, he's not going to be happy."

Rayn eyed her. "Why did you want to come?"

"You know already that Bayard was behind the assassination attempts. After you left, we persuaded him to confess, and we learned a few things. One of them was that Zoe was in his service. I felt we had to warn you immediately."

"You came here to warn me about Zoe."

"Yes."

A line appeared in the middle of his forehead. "Was that your only reason?"

Celeste's cheeks warmed as she looked down at the sand. "I might have had another reason."

Rayn lowered his hand into the shallow water. He grasped something and shook it in the water to rinse off the sand. "I believe the ocean *did* give us a gift." He examined the object, and then, smiling, he placed it in Celeste's hand.

It was a shell of a variety she'd never seen before, flat on one side and rounded on the other. The flat side opened into what looked like a toothy mouth. The rounded side was smooth and glossy white, encircled with a bright band of gold.

"It's a ring cowrie," said Rayn. "My ancient ancestors used them as currency."

"Cowrie? Isn't that the word for the Inyan coin?"

"It is," said Rayn, "and now you know why."

Celeste turned the shell over and over in her hands. It did make a nice makeshift coin, of sorts. It was small and pleasant to hold and distinctively marked with that gold ring. She could imagine carrying a pocketful of these as currency.

"This is the actual coin." He reached into his pocket, pulled out a silver Inyan cowrie, and handed it to her. "See the ring on the back?"

She turned the coin over. It was marked with a golden ring, like the shell. "How interesting. I couldn't tell you where the Kjallan tetral comes from." She handed both coin and shell back to Rayn.

He accepted the coin but pressed the shell into her hand. "Keep it. It's my gift to you."

Though it was a small thing, she felt oddly touched. As an imperial princess, she was no stranger to gifts. On her birthdays she was practically buried in expensive presents by nobles and military officials hoping to curry imperial favor. Yet none of those gifts had any meaning. She would have traded them all for this tiny shell, because Rayn had found it and freely offered it to her.

"How did you get Bayard to confess?" asked Rayn.

Celeste told him the story: how the Order of the Sage had searched Bayard's house and discovered the letters from his secret wife, which Celeste had deciphered. How she'd interrogated the wife using mind magic. How Justien and his people had found the hidden enclave and arrested Bayard's coconspirators, and Bayard had agreed to talk so that his wife and children might go free. "He also told us he'd been hired by Councilor Worryn to assassinate you. Be careful around that man. He's not just a political enemy—he literally wants you dead."

Rayn stopped walking. "So Worryn's behind everything?"

"Bayard said as much under truth spell. Worryn paid Bayard to somehow secure an heir from you and then assassinate you on foreign soil. It was planned well in advance. Zoe was sent here years ago as part of a plan that was to unfold over a long period of time."

"But Zoe—the heir—are you telling me Zoe's not even Inyan?"

"Correct," said Celeste. "She's Riorcan. She was born in Riorca and trained as an assassin there, by Bayard himself—the same man who trained the empress. She was taught your language by an Obsidian Circle enclave. And she's a fully qualified mage."

"What sort of mage?"

"Wardbreaker. Like Vitala, she carries Shards, tiny weapons that she keeps hidden in the Rift until she needs them. The Shards are spelled. If she stabs you with one and breaks the ward on it, the spell takes effect. Usually it's a death spell. And she'll have learned other skills at the enclave as well."

"Such as what?" His mouth twisted. "Seduction?"

Celeste swallowed. "I was thinking combat skills. I don't really know what else." Vitala was rather guarded when talking about her Obsidian Circle training.

"This is a lot for me to think about." He looked out at the ocean. "Will you give me a moment?"

"Of course." She'd had the entire voyage, plus several additional days, to accept this new reality herself—and it didn't affect her personally as much as it did Rayn. She couldn't imagine how he must feel, knowing that a woman he'd once loved, or at least been attracted to, had seduced him entirely for the purpose of doing him harm. That the woman had lied to him from the first day she'd met him. "I can go back to the trees if you like." She glanced at the Legaciatti, who watched them from beneath the stand of palms.

"No, just . . ." He gestured vaguely. "Away from the water."

Celeste retreated inland past the tide line and sat in the soft sand.

Rayn waded through the waves into deeper water, where he stopped and stood motionless. His back was stiff, his muscles rounded and tense. She wished she could rub his shoulders and release some of that tension, but she'd promised to leave him alone.

He reached into the water and pulled something out—a rock or a shell. He drew back, winding up with his whole body, and flung the object out into the sea. It landed with a faint splash in the distance. He reached into the water and swirled his hand around again. This time he came up with a handful of dripping sand. He flung that.

Celeste dropped her gaze to the sand. It felt wrong to stare.

A translucent crab, no wider than the tip of her thumb, skittered sideways past her foot. Clutching a single large claw defensively across its body, it raced across the sand and disappeared into a tiny hole. She watched the hole, curious to see if the crab would come out again. Staring closely at the ground, she saw that much of what she thought of as sand was actually minuscule seashells.

At length, she heard footsteps, and Rayn dropped his huge body onto the sand beside her.

"I'm sorry," she said.

"I'm going to kill her," said Rayn. "I'm going to wring that woman's *gods-cursed neck*."

"We'll find her," said Celeste, "and bring her to justice."

"I can't believe I had a baby with her!" he cried. "That's the worst of it. I feel like the biggest fool who ever walked this island, first of all for getting involved with her, and second for letting my fertility ward drop—"

"You didn't let your fertility ward drop," said Celeste. "She broke the ward. She's a wardbreaker."

"Three gods," he groaned. "Of course she did." He dropped his head into his hands. "I always took her for a sapskull, which shows how much I know. That woman played me like a lute."

Celeste took his hand, interleaving her fingers with his. "You were young, and you were conspired against by people who were well practiced in the art. The Circle's been doing this kind of thing for decades. Remember that my brother was fooled in exactly the same way by Vitala, when she worked for the Obsidian Circle. And Lucien's the smartest man I know."

"You know why I feel like such a sapskull?" Rayn shook his head miserably. "I thought I was helping her. Saving her, you know? I found her in that bar, with that black eye her father had given her—gods, even the black eye and the father must have been a lie!—and I thought, here is something I can do. I can help this woman. I can turn the lava for her, keep her safe." He sighed heavily. "She must have known that would draw me in, the desire to save her. She must have been laughing at me the whole time."

"She exploited one of your best traits," said Celeste. "That doesn't make you a sapskull. It makes her a bad person. And consider this: she hasn't succeeded. Every assassination attempt thus far has failed, so how much do you think she's really laughing right now?"

He squeezed her hand. "You're a kind woman, to still want to help me after all this."

She bumped his hip with her own. "Kindness has nothing to do with it."

His forehead wrinkled. "I don't think Zoe's actually attempted to assassinate me yet. I've seen her twice, once here and once in Riorca, and she didn't pull any Shards on me either time."

"Did you let her get close? You're big and strong, and your magic is powerful. She could never kill you in a fair fight. She'd want to get close and distract you so that she could strike without your having the opportunity to fight back."

Rayn frowned. "You have a point. She constantly tries to lure me back into bed."

"If you'd slept with her, you'd probably be dead now. Tell me about Inyan law. How do we bring treason charges against Worryn?"

"Through the court system. Lornis will know; he's a magister. But I can't do it yet. I've no proof."

"What proof do you need?"

Rayn shrugged. "A confession from Worryn would do it. Or physical evidence, like letters he wrote to Bayard. Or a witness who condemns him."

"I could be your witness," said Celeste.

"Not good enough," said Rayn. "You heard Bayard accuse Worryn, but you didn't see Worryn himself do anything or confess to anything."

"That's true," she admitted. "What about Bayard as a witness?"

"Bayard might suit," said Rayn. "Even better if he

could lead us to some physical evidence, like letters exchanged between the two of them."

Now Celeste felt like the sapskull. If only she'd brought Bayard with her on the *Soldier's Sweep*. Instead he was back in Riorca, where he could do them no good at all. And they could hardly walk into Worryn's private rooms and start looking through his letters.

"Let's talk about your ratification vote," she said. "How can I help you win it?"

"You want to help?"

"Of course I do! I want *you* to be in charge of Inya, not that treasonous worm."

"Lornis will have all kinds of ideas for you. The Tiasan merchants, for example, want a trade agreement with Kjall, and if you talked to them, you could assure them we're making progress on that front." His brow wrinkled. "I hate to overpromise. *Do* you think a trade agreement might be possible? Maybe with some limits on the amount of brimstone traded? Your brother was upset with me in Riorca."

"Lucien may be upset, but he absolutely wants the trade agreement."

Rayn squeezed her hand. "And what about the marriage?" he asked softly. "Does he still want that?"

Celeste tensed. "I'm not sure."

Rayn looked down at the sand. His eyes followed the translucent crab, which had emerged from its hole and skittered to a position not far from his feet. "And your feelings: are they the same as his?"

She swallowed. "They are not."

For a moment, he was so silent, she thought he'd stopped breathing. "Are you saying that if I asked you to marry me — and we ignore, for the moment, the fact that your brother doesn't approve — you might say yes?"

She spoke quietly. "That's what I'm saying."

"*Can* we ignore the fact that your brother doesn't approve?"

She licked dry lips. "I don't think so."

He grinned. "You're too much the good sister. Come here." He lifted her off the sand and placed her in the space in front of him, between his legs, with her back against his chest. "You stole your brother's ship. I don't think you're entirely opposed to doing things he doesn't approve of."

Celeste said nothing. She was torn between her love for Rayn and her esteem for her brother. It had not pleased her to steal the emperor's ship.

"I won't propose to you now," said Rayn. "I may fail my ratification vote, and if I do, I'll be a nobody for the rest of my life. A Kjallan princess cannot marry a nobody."

She twisted in his arms to look into his face. "You'll never be a nobody. I wouldn't marry your role. I'd marry *you*."

"If I can't take my country back from Worryn, I'm not worthy of you," said Rayn. "Here's what I'm going to do. First I'll win the ratification vote and take back the Inyan throne. Second, I'll expose Worryn's treason. And third, I will spend the rest of our time together, until your brother arrives, convincing you to firewalk with me."

"Firewalk?"

"An Inyan custom," he said. "When one of our fire mages takes a wife—or a husband—the two of them walk through fire. That's how we marry." When she shuddered, he added, "It's safe. The fire mage protects both of them from the heat."

"Are there accidents?"

"None in living memory."

Though it was frightening, she found herself intrigued by the idea of stepping through fire with Rayn at her side. "And how will you convince me to firewalk with you?"

"I have some ideas." He enveloped her in a hug, cocooning her within his powerful body, and ran a hand down her arm. His touch licked like fire across her skin, awakening and sensitizing her flesh. Her body remembered him. It was like when she jumped into the water and instantly knew to swim. Like when she galloped a horse and instinctively moved her body in ways that kept her in the saddle. When Rayn touched her, she didn't think, but opened for him like a flower unfurling to the sun.

"Gods, I've missed you," he murmured.

One taste of Rayn, and desire flared. His breath tickled her ear, and she turned her head to capture his lips. He tasted of coffee from breakfast, and just a hint of ash.

He stroked her cheek and then her neck. She thrust her bosom at him, thinking with shuddering pleasure of his mouth upon her breasts. He took one of her breasts through the fabric of her dress and cupped it in his hand. Sensation shot from her nipples to her core.

"Someday," he said into her ear, "I am going to take you right here on this beach."

"Not *someday*," she breathed. "Now."

He slipped a hand beneath the fabric of her dress. He found her firm nipple and stroked it. She gasped.

"I am going to lay you out on this sand," he said, "down by the water where the waves tickle your feet. I'm going to enter you slowly, so that you feel every inch of me as I fill you."

Her whole body quivered as she pressed herself into him.

"Someday," he said again, removing his hand from her dress.

"Now," she said.

"Not with an audience." He pulled the fabric of her dress back into place, covering her.

"Rayn, you are the worst kind of tease."

"That wasn't a tease. It was a promise. We'll come back sometime without guards, or leave them outside the tunnel. I perform only for you, *karamasi*."

Her skin cried out for his touch, but much as she hated to admit it, he was right. She didn't want to make a spectacle of herself in front of the Legaciatti. "I think you've ruined me for beaches forever. Every time I see one, I think of loving you."

"I rather like that," said Rayn, kissing her. "Maybe I should love you in some other places—in the jungle, up on the mountain. Maybe I should love you everywhere we go, so that you're thinking about me all the time."

"How about in an actual bed sometime?" said Celeste.

"That can be arranged," said Rayn. Shifting his body so that he shielded her from the view of the Legaciatti, he drew up her dress, reached between her legs, and touched her.

She writhed against him, moaning.

"Feel how wet you are for me," he said.

"I *know* how wet I am for you," she gasped.

Rayn stroked her lightly. It was just enough pressure to turn her to jelly, but not enough to bring her to climax. "Tonight you and I have a date with a bed," he said. "I'm going to have a cockstand all day just thinking about it. Your ripe breasts, waiting for me to suck them. Your swollen sex, waiting for my cock."

"Rayn, you're making me crazy."

He removed his hand, smoothed her dress, and grinned. "That's the intention."

"We could go back to the palace now. Find a bed."

Rayn shook his head. "I want you thinking about me for the rest of the day. I know I'll be thinking about you." He rose to his feet and offered her his hand. "Let's keep walking. We've given the Legaciatti enough of a show."

"I don't think my legs work anymore."

He pulled her up, and while she was weak in the knees, she found she could in fact walk.

"Let's find you some more shells," said Rayn.

There were no more ring cowries, but the cove yielded a brindlecat-striped spider shell as large as Celeste's hand and two white and orange speckled ram's head shells.

When they'd combed the beach in its entirety, they headed back to the palm trees, where the horses and Legaciatti waited. Celeste blushed as she considered what the Legaciatti must have seen. But Atella was circumspect and said not a word.

Celeste swung up onto her smoke gray gelding. "Where are we going now?"

"Are you hungry?" asked Rayn.

"Yes."

"I've got a place in mind."

28

They cantered through the jungle back to Tiasa, trailed by the Legaciatti, and slowed their mounts when they entered the city streets. They steered around pony carts and mule carts and hand-drawn carts, around pedestrians and knots of chattering civilians. Tacked onto glow posts and the walls of buildings were printed handbills advertising shops and services and meetings. These were new to Celeste. Handbills were not used in Riat.

"How many Tiasans can read?" she asked Rayn.

His forehead wrinkled. "Four in ten? Maybe five in ten?"

"That's a lot." Which explained the handbills.

"It's not the same in Kjall?"

"Only our upper classes can read. With some exceptions."

"Hmm," he grunted. "Most of our merchants can. Of course, they're city dwellers. Out in the countryside, in the rural villages, the numbers won't be so high."

She slowed to read some of the handbills. The one on the nearest glow post advertised a lost dog. Poor creature—she hoped the owner found him.

Rayn, who was ahead of her, halted his horse. "You

get used to the handbills after a while. I barely notice them."

"I like to notice them." She moved on to the next and was startled to see Rayn's name at the top.

RATIFY PRINCE RAYN
HE WILL PROTECT THE KING'S LANDS
HE WILL ESTABLISH TRADE AND A
LASTING PEACE WITH KJALL
FIRM HANDS, STRONG HEART, PRINCE RAYN

"I agree with the firm hands part," said Celeste.

"What?" Rayn steered his horse to the handbill and read it. "Oh—Lornis must have put that one up."

"Here's another." She rode up to one posted on the side of a building. "Wait. It's different."

RATIFY PRINCE RAYN?
HE LET FOUR PINES BURN
RESIDENTS LOST THEIR HOMES AND FARMS
IS THIS THE LEADERSHIP WE WANT FOR INYA?
VOTE NO ON RATIFICATION DAY

A prickly feeling ran across her skin, as if she'd overheard someone talking about her.

Rayn rode up next to her and read in silence. "Lornis warned me that would happen."

"It's unfair," she said. "You had no choice but to send the lava into Four Pines. What did the settlers expect when they built their homes in the volcano's path?"

"The handbill is meaningless," said Rayn. "It's just Councilor Worryn trying to prevent me from being ratified."

"But it makes you look bad. And it's not fair."

"It's Inyan politics," said Rayn. "Pay it no mind. Lornis will have me respond soon enough, probably tomorrow, but for now I need to *establish a lasting peace with Kjall*. That means spending time with you." He smiled.

"Right," said Celeste, steering her horse away from the handbills. "We'd better get to work on establishing some peace." She wasn't sure she liked Inyan politics, in which it seemed common practice to bad-mouth their leaders. She wouldn't like it if handbills were posted around Riat, criticizing her brother. On the other hand, she was certain that the Kjallan people did talk about her brother behind closed doors, and that Lucien wished he knew what they said. Her father, Florian, who'd impoverished Kjall through his ill-conceived policies, might have benefited from knowing how negatively he'd been perceived.

Were handbills the solution? She was of two minds about it.

Rayn led the way to a bakery with a sign above the door reading VOLCANO BREAD. The name amused Celeste. How many shops, she wondered, were named directly or indirectly for Mount Drav?

Rayn seated her at a table and went to buy their food, while the Legaciatti hovered unobtrusively one table away. He returned with a loaf of soft bread and a knife resting on a large platter. A second, smaller platter held a crumbling white cheese surrounded with mango slices. Celeste had eaten mango a couple of times at the Tiasan Palace while Rayn had been on the mountain turning the lava. It was an acquired taste, but she was beginning to like it.

"I'm afraid it's peasant food," said Rayn as he set the platters on the table. "Hardly suitable for a princess. But you get finer stuff at the palace, and I thought you might like to taste something different. This is volcano bread."

"I thought that was the name of the shop." The bread was flecked with herbs but otherwise looked ordinary.

"It's the name of the shop because volcano bread is what they sell," he said. "It's baked in the volcano."

"Don't be silly."

"I'm serious." Rayn prepared a plate for her, layering a slice of cheese over a slice of volcano bread and spooning on some mango. "There are places on the mountainside where the ground is quite warm. You can walk on it without harm, but if you start digging, you reach areas that are hot as an oven. Since ancient times, my people have used this natural heat to bake their bread. Nowadays it's more convenient to use an oven—you don't have to trudge up the mountainside and dig a hole. But in rural villages near the volcano, farmers still bake their bread this way. And so do a few places like this bakery, for those of us who like the idea of eating the way the ancients did."

Now she was curious. She took the bread and cheese and mango he'd prepared for her and lifted it to her lips. "Does it taste different?"

"Not really." Rayn finished preparing his own plate and took a seat next to her.

She bit into her "peasant food." The bread was smooth, almost melting in her mouth. The tang of the cheese offered a nice counterpoint to its muted flavor, and the herbs added interest. "I've never tasted bread like this."

"Have you not?" Rayn spread the cheese over his own bread.

"The texture is unusually smooth."

"Well, it's not wheat bread," said Rayn. "It's manioc. I confess, wheat bread is not my favorite—so coarse and chewy. We make both kinds in Inya, but manioc is more popular than wheat."

Celeste took another bite and chewed thoughtfully. When she'd considered the ramifications of marrying abroad, she had not fully understood how different Inya would be from Kjall. She'd known the weather would be warmer, and that the people spoke a different language, but she had not imagined that even small things like the fruits they ate and the bread they baked would be unfamiliar. Or that there would be handbills on the streets insulting Inya's leaders. It was intimidating to be in a world so full of practices that were unknown to her. But it was also exhilarating. If she'd lived out her life in Kjall, she might never have tasted a mango. And she would never have known there was such a thing as bread baked in a volcano.

The baker approached, grinning and bowing, with two mugs in his hand. "A gift for my royal guests."

"Thank you, Reus; that's very thoughtful," said Rayn.

The baker set one mug before each of them and departed.

"Gods above, I'm thirsty," said Celeste as she picked up her mug. "What is this?" She eyed the cream-colored liquid, wanting to sniff it but refraining in case the Inyans thought it rude. "Doesn't look like coffee."

"It's kava," said Rayn. "Expensive stuff."

She took a sip and nearly spat it back out. She squeezed her eyes shut and forced herself to swallow. It tasted like watered-down mud.

Rayn chuckled. "I should have warned you. Many people don't like the taste."

"Your people pay money to drink this? It tastes like dirt."

"If you stay in Inya, you'll probably develop a taste for kava," he said. "But for now . . ." He gestured to the baker, who returned to their table. "Would you mind flavoring hers?"

The baker scooped up Celeste's mug and left.

"What's he going to do to it?" she asked.

"Add lime and sugar," said Rayn. "Foreigners often like it better that way."

The baker returned a moment later and set the mug gently on the table.

Celeste regarded it warily. Then she picked it up and sipped the kava. It tasted a tiny bit better.

Rayn took his own kava mug and tipped it back, draining the whole thing in several large gulps.

Celeste gaped at him. "You like this stuff?"

He shrugged. "I'm not wild about the taste. But this is how kava should be drunk."

She lifted her mug dubiously. "If I don't drink it, I'll be insulting the baker, won't I?"

"You don't have to drink it," said Rayn.

Bracing herself, she brought the mug to her lips and poured the muddy-flavored kava down her throat. Once it was down, she placed her mug on the table and shook her head involuntarily, a reaction to the foul taste.

The baker smiled from behind the counter.

"Well done," said Rayn.

She followed the kava with a bite of bread and cheese, to get the taste out of her mouth. "I have to ask. Why drink something so repulsive?"

"You'll see," said Rayn.

"Is it alcoholic?" Her lips and tongue were tingling— an unfamiliar feeling.

"No."

"Then why does it make me feel strange?" Her stomach felt odd. It wasn't nausea, but a feeling she'd never experienced before.

"It's a numbing agent," said Rayn. "It makes you feel relaxed."

"My stomach feels weird."

"A harmless quirk. You'll get used to it."

"Where does it come from?"

"It's made from the root of a plant," said Rayn. "The kava plant."

As they ate volcano bread and talked, she began to understand kava's appeal. Her muscles unwound, and her body sank deeper into her chair. She felt calm and deeply contented, yet she wasn't experiencing any of that fogginess of mind she associated with being drunk. "I'm beginning to understand why Inya isn't a violent country."

Rayn laughed happily. "It's a special-occasion drink. Too expensive for everyday use."

"Is this a special occasion?"

"The most special of all occasions."

When they had eaten their fill, they returned to their horses and headed out of Tiasa, toward the outskirts of town. Celeste had learned in her studies that Inyan words did not always translate perfectly to Kjallan. Inyan possessed two directional words that had no Kjallan equivalents, and which the Inyans used constantly in lieu of north, south, east, and west. These were *bamedra*, which meant toward the ocean, and *fomedra*, which meant away from the ocean. Rayn told her they were heading *bamedra*, but it wasn't the same direction that had led them to the secluded beach.

It was a long ride, well over an hour at a trot and canter, and Celeste was glad to have the kava in her belly for the duration. She sat loose in the saddle, with her limbs relaxed and rubbery, and breathed in the scent of flowers as they rode.

The path climbed, which was odd since normally when one traveled *bamedra*, one was heading downhill toward sea level. She knew they were getting close to wherever Rayn intended to take her, because she could hear the roar of the surf. Then they emerged from the jungle. Daylight burst out around them. Shielding her eyes from the tropical sun, she saw that she was on a high cliff overlooking the ocean. Out in the water sat an is-land—if it could be called that, since it was essentially a column of rock. It had no beaches that she could see. The rock cliffs, bare and encrusted with moss, rose a hundred feet out of the ocean, where they gave way, on top, to an explosion of vegetation, like hair upon an unusually tall head.

The island was connected to the cliff she stood on by a suspension bridge. The moment she saw that bridge, she hoped she would not be asked to cross it. It was like the one she'd crossed to reach the Hibiscus Tower, but far longer. It looked sturdier than the Hibiscus Tower bridge, and did not have so much downward arc. But there was no getting around the fact that it possessed no support beams whatsoever.

"Please tell me we're not crossing that," she said to Rayn.

He dismounted from his horse. "Are you afraid of heights?"

"No. It's just . . . there are no support beams."

He smiled. "It doesn't need them. See?" He left the horse and went to the bridge, wrapping his fingers around the thick cords of metal that served as handrails. "These coils are solid steel. They hold up the bridge. Support beams aren't necessary."

She frowned. It seemed unlikely that those cords could support an entire bridge on their own. "Are we taking the horses across?"

"No," said Rayn. "It's a walking bridge."

That helped. People were lighter than horses. "What's on the other side?"

His eyes twinkled. "You'll find out when we get there."

She slid off her horse and led the animal to a hitching post. "Are you sure it's safe?"

"Trust me," said Rayn.

She tied her horse and walked to the bridge entrance. Rayn took her hand with a smile of encouragement and stepped out onto the wooden slats. The wood was firm and thick, and it didn't appear to move much under his feet. If only the bridge weren't so frighteningly long.

"Come on," he urged.

She gripped the handrail and stepped onto the bridge. Another step, and another. She didn't know where she should cast her gaze. Looking down didn't work, because she could see the ocean through the slats. Looking forward, she saw how far away the island was, and how much bridge she had yet to travel.

Patricus, behind them, whimpered at the bridge entrance. Frustrated, he spun in circles.

"Come on, Patricus," called Celeste.

The sea retriever tested the bridge with a tentative paw and, apparently satisfied, stepped out onto it. The bridge was enclosed along the sides with protective netting, so there was no chance of his falling off. He trotted to catch up to them.

Rayn squeezed Celeste's hand and pulled her gently forward. "Living in Rul Linaran, especially in Tiasa, one can easily forget that Inya is an archipelago. After all, you can buy almost any Inyan product in Tiasa. But much of our industry takes place on the other islands: mining, farming, textile weaving. Inya has always needed ways to transport goods from one island to another."

"You have boats," said Celeste.

"Bridges are better," said Rayn. "Two of our larger islands are accessible to Rul Linaran by bridge, and from those you can hop to several more. We still have some that use a ferry system, because we're not yet able to bridge them. Our engineers work constantly to better our bridge designs."

She had never studied bridge engineering, but she was aware it was an interesting topic involving complex mathematics. Perhaps she should speak to the Inyan bridge engineers sometime.

Patricus, confident now, dashed ahead of them. He ran all the way to the end of the bridge and watched them from the new island, his ears erect and jaunty.

"Surely you don't transfer goods on this bridge," said Celeste. "It's too narrow."

"This is strictly a walking bridge," said Rayn. "No goods to be transferred. The island we're heading to is called *Rul Kejaban*."

She translated the literal Inyan. "Island of Wonders?"

"Yes, exactly. Rul Kejaban has no industry. No one lives here."

"Why build a bridge to it?"

"You'll see," said Rayn.

The end of the bridge was closer now. It sloped slightly upward, which made her feel more secure than when she had been heading downward to its nadir.

Finally she stepped out onto the island of Rul Kejaban. Trees, thick with hanging moss, crowded around them, and a stony dirt path headed inland—*fomedra*, she reminded herself. Patricus dashed ahead on the trail. She and Rayn followed. It was midafternoon and hot. The trees here were old, perhaps ancient. In the grounds surrounding the Kjallan palace, she had ridden through old-growth forests and cultivated forests and learned to distinguish between them. This one was old-growth and so thick that she wondered if it had ever seen an ax.

Ahead of them, Patricus gave a bark of alarm.

"Is it safe for him up there?" Celeste asked Rayn.

"Yes."

Patricus sprinted back to them, his ears low and his tail pinned between his legs. He circled behind Celeste, whimpering. "Something scared him," she said.

"It's all right," said Rayn. "He saw something he didn't expect."

Curious, she quickened her pace. They rounded a corner, and she saw what Patricus had stumbled upon: a giant brown lizard, half-hidden by the trees. It was easily twelve feet long, including tail, and several feet high.

She stopped short. "Three gods."

"Besarkadal," said Rayn. "The great lizards."

Patricus barked sharply at the creature from behind Celeste's legs.

"You say it's not dangerous?"

"I know it looks frightening," said Rayn. "But it's a plant eater. It's not aggressive at all. Watch." He walked into the jungle, straight toward the lizard.

Celeste bit her lip.

The lizard paid him no mind, even as he walked close enough to touch it—and then he patted the creature on its shoulder. "Come and see," called Rayn. "The *besarkadal* are scared of nothing."

Curiosity won out over fear, and she followed Rayn into the trees, right up next to the creature. It started to walk as she approached, its great legs crunching the vegetation underfoot. She almost turned and fled, but the animal only took a few steps to the nearest fern and bent its head to tear off a mouthful of leaves. It chewed rhythmically, with a not unpleasant grating sound. She laid a hand on the creature's shoulder. It felt dry and leathery, like the skin of the shark she'd grabbed onto in the Great Northern Sea.

"This is the only place they are found," said Rayn. "On Rul Kejaban. They used to be on all the islands— their bones turn up from time to time—but they disappeared everywhere except here."

"Why did these survive when all the others died out?"

"We're not sure. Maybe because there are no people here. No one has ever lived on Rul Kejaban—it's inaccessible by water unless you go to great lengths to scale that cliff. About a century ago, someone did exactly that and discovered the *besarkadal*, which for countless years had been known only in stories and legends. The Inyan king—my great-great-grandfather—claimed this island as King's Lands, making it a public space, and built the bridge so people could visit whenever they liked. There are a couple of guards who keep an eye on the place. It's against the law to harm the lizards. Look, there's another one."

She turned and spotted a second lizard partially hidden behind some trees. And a third, farther away. "Do the *besarkadal* ever cross the suspension bridge?"

"It hasn't happened yet," said Rayn. "I don't think they like that bridge."

Celeste didn't blame them.

Rayn offered Celeste his arm. "Shall we keep walking? The trail circles around. It doesn't cover the entirety of Rul Kejaban—the island is larger than it looks—but there's plenty to see."

She took his arm and they headed farther into the Island of Wonders.

29

When Celeste returned with Rayn to the Tiasan Palace, a little daylight remained, but they'd missed the supper hour. Rayn ordered food to be sent up to his room. Celeste, who'd been riding and walking and exploring all day, ate ravenously.

Strangely, she didn't feel tired. The sights Rayn had shown her had breathed new life into her. Her mind could not stop thinking about the things she'd seen. From the moment Lucien had suggested this marriage, she'd been intimidated by the thought of moving to a foreign land and leaving everything she knew behind. And there *was* a cost. She would miss many things that she loved in Kjall, not just her family, but comforts and interests, like the food and the oak forests and Riat and the Mathematical Brotherhood.

But there was much to be gained by living in this new world. She was learning about coffee, and kava, and volcano bread, and great lizards living on an island. About cowrie shells and handbills and suspension bridges — surely there was much she could learn from the Inyan bridge engineers. Her mind craved stimulation, and she'd been granted it in abundance. An archipelago of exploration and experience awaited her, if she settled here with Rayn.

For today, she'd had her fill of the Inyan sights. There was only one more experience she wanted. She'd been waiting all day for this cherished moment of privacy—and she could tell by the look in Rayn's eyes that he felt the same way.

She pushed back the remains of her dinner. The effects of the kava had worn off, but she didn't miss them. Her body was pleasantly weary, in a well-used sort of way, and she had a good meal in her. She felt happy and contented, and the evening's pleasures were only beginning. She hoped before long to be well used indeed.

"Did you have a good day?" he asked.

"The best."

"I'm glad to hear it." Rayn rose from his chair and held out his hand. "I promised you some privacy and a date with a bed."

She went to him.

He folded her into his embrace, turning her so that her back was against his chest. Framing her shoulders with great hands, he stroked downward along her arms. She sighed and leaned into him, laying her head backward on his shoulder.

"It's a pity we don't need your fire magic anymore," she said.

"I still have it, *karamasi*." As he said it, his touch on her body changed. His fingers traced fire along her skin, enough to stimulate but not to burn. "My people once worshipped not just the Three," Rayn whispered, "but sea spirits and fire spirits. Fire mages such as myself were considered priests to the fire spirits."

"I cannot envision you as a priest."

"It was centuries ago. We've since come to realize that the fire spirits are not gods and have no interest in being worshipped."

"Of course not," said Celeste. "They don't exist."

"They do exist. Just because you haven't seen them doesn't mean they're not out there." Rayn's hand reached her thigh, where he marked her with fiery patterns. "This bit of magic I'm using—fire touch—was thought to have healing properties."

"I believe it," said Celeste. "Keep doing it."

"It restored fertility to the barren," said Rayn. "It cured fevers and pox boils. It was the blessing of the spirits—so my people believed."

"Continue," she gasped, "and I will believe anything."

"Kiss me," commanded Rayn.

She turned her head and parted her lips. While he tasted her, as if sampling a fine wine, his hands moved, bestowing the blessing of fire on her skin. He traced circles of fire on her chest and neck.

He reached for the fastener on the back of her dress.

"Wait." Fear spiked through her, breaking the spell of his touch. The sun had not yet sunk beneath the horizon. Light spilled in through the open balcony, and she felt exposed. "Can we close the curtains?"

"They need to stay open," said Rayn. "Otherwise the air won't circulate."

"Please," she said. "Until the sun goes down."

Rayn released her and went to the balcony. He unfastened the ties of the gauzy curtains, and they flowed loose over the entrance to the balcony, shrouding them in near darkness. Celeste's stomach began to unknot.

Rayn crossed the room and activated a pair of lightglows.

"N-no," she stammered. "Please. No light."

He turned to her, bewildered. "I want the light, *karamasi*. I want to see you."

She shivered. "I . . . don't like to be seen."

He deactivated the light-glows, returning the room to near darkness. But she could see, or at least sense, his frown. And he did not come to her. "Why does the light frighten you?" he asked. "Do you not know how beautiful you are? It gives me pleasure to look at you."

Celeste shivered, crossing her arms. She wanted to give him pleasure, but he was wrong. She was not beautiful. He hadn't really seen her body, not up close and in full light.

Rayn activated a light-glow. He went to the bed and sat on its edge. "Come here. Let me show you how beautiful you are."

"I am not beautiful," she choked out.

"Karamasi!" he cried. "Why do you say such a thing?"

Her eyes swelled, and she blinked back the tears. "I say only what is true."

Rayn rose from the bed, crossed the room, and picked her up, sweeping her off her feet in one swift motion. He carried her to the bed and laid her on it, sitting next to her. "Who told you that you weren't beautiful?"

"Nobody," she whispered.

Rayn's cheeks flushed with anger. "Was it your brother?"

"Gods, no."

"That horse's ass of a mathematician."

"Not Gallus."

"It was somebody," said Rayn, "because you *are* beautiful, and you would know it if someone hadn't tried to convince you otherwise. Was it Cassian?"

Celeste stiffened as if slapped.

"Cassian," said Rayn. "That *bastard*. I thought you said he didn't sleep with you."

Ugly girl. "He didn't," she said in a small voice.

He growled under his breath. "I assumed he didn't sleep with you because you were thirteen and he had a sense of decency. Was there another reason?"

She bit her lip. Her throat felt swollen, her chest thick and heavy. She could not speak.

"What happened, Celeste?"

Look at her. Scrawny and flat as a hay field. No curves at all.

Her curves will come, but they'll never be like yours.

Stop covering yourself up, girl. We're looking at you.

Lucky for her she's a princess. Otherwise, no one would marry her.

Celeste screwed her eyes shut.

Rayn gathered her into his arms. He stroked her hair, running his fingers through it like a comb. "Do you know that your hair has fascinated me from the moment I saw you?"

Celeste opened her eyes. "I'm not blond like your kinsmen."

"I see blond hair every day," said Rayn. "I see it on my own head. Your hair is dark and shining and lustrous. I love the way it curls around your shoulders. Did you know that on the beach in Riorca, when I was half out of my senses, I almost took you for a sea spirit?"

She shook her head.

"And gods, your face." Rayn ran his hand reverently down her forehead, her nose, her cheek. "How can I describe it? I am no poet, but the lines of your face are a work of art." He leaned down and kissed her gently. "I love the way your lips pink up when I kiss them."

Celeste swallowed. Her emotions were in a jumble. Rayn's loving words about her body were like scraps tossed to the starving. She devoured them and craved more. Yet the idea of his scrutinizing her, part by part, was terrifying. He would get to the flaws soon enough.

"Let's have a look at the rest of you." He rolled her onto her side.

"Rayn—" she protested.

"Trust me." He unfastened her dress and pulled it down, exposing her breasts. His breath hitched as he stared. "Now that is the most beautiful sight in the world."

She hauled her dress upward, covering herself.

"You deny me the pleasure of looking?" he said.

She sank into the bed, feeling hopeless. What was the use in stalling? He was going to discover the truth sooner or later. Averting her eyes, she lowered her dress and allowed him to look his fill. "They're not beautiful. See? The one on the left is larger than the one on the right."

He looked perplexed. "It is?"

She thrust her bosom at him. "It's plainly obvious."

He studied her breasts. "I think you're right. It's a little bit bigger." He smiled. "You think that's a fault?"

"It's practically a deformity," she said.

"My left foot is bigger than my right. Do you call me ugly?"

She shook her head. "You are the handsomest of men."

"None of us are created perfect," said Rayn. "We are mortals, not gods. And this mortal, when he sees breasts as lovely as these, doesn't measure and compare. He drinks in the sight, grateful for the gift that has been given him." He lowered his mouth to her left breast.

Pleasure suffused her as he took her nipple in his mouth. He took her other breast in his hand and rubbed it in gentle circles. He wasn't using his fire magic, yet she was burning up from the inside. She grabbed him, one hand tightening on his broad shoulder and the other on his braid, and moaned, half out of her senses.

He lifted his head.

"Gods, Rayn. More."

He turned his attention to her right breast, tasting it, sucking it, and rubbed the other with his hand. A blaze of heat kindled between her legs.

Once more Rayn lifted his head. "I assure you that these breasts are, in fact, perfect. But I may need to play with them some more to be certain."

"Don't tease," she complained.

"I am not teasing." He rolled her onto her side and tugged her dress downward. "Let's get this off of you."

She cooperated, not from a desire for him to see the rest of her body, but because she wanted him inside her, and that wasn't going to happen with her dress on. In a moment, she was completely naked, and he was looking on her with frank admiration.

He ran a hand down the curves of her body. "Surely you can find no fault here."

"I'm shaped wrong," she said. "I'm wider in the hips than in the chest."

"That's a fault?"

She wasn't certain anymore. "Isn't it?"

"Every woman has her own shape," said Rayn. "Yours is beautiful."

"Look, there's a scar here on my thigh."

He studied it. "How'd you get that?"

"Fell off a horse when I was a girl."

Rayn smiled. "Evidence of a life well lived. I'll bet you never even noticed my scars. You'll have more of them before your life is done, and if you deign to marry me, I'll love each and every one of them. Tell me, did Cassian convince you that these entirely normal features of your body made you ugly?"

She looked away. "Sort of."

"Tell me," said Rayn.

"He had a wife," said Celeste. "Not officially—he had to divorce her in order to marry me. But they remained lovers. She was jealous of me."

"The wife is the one who said these things?"

"No. Well, a little bit. Mostly it was Cassian, to reassure her that he wanted her and not me. They would strip me naked and tell me everything that was wrong with me. Then they'd leave and go to the bedroom to make love."

A line appeared in the middle of Rayn's forehead. "But you didn't *want* him to make love to you. Right?"

"No, I didn't." Fresh tears sprang to her eyes. "I know it doesn't make sense. I'm *glad* he didn't sleep with me. I'm *glad* he found me ugly. And yet it still hurt, knowing I was not desired. He said I would never be desired by anyone."

"He lied," said Rayn.

A fat tear tracked its way down her cheek, and she wiped it away. "I shouldn't be so upset. It's stupid. Obviously I didn't want him to rape me, so why does it bother me that he didn't want to? I *hate* him for making me feel so mixed up. I *hate* him."

"That's right, *karamasi*," said Rayn. "Hate him, because that's what he deserves. He is dead, and I am here. Let his words drift into obscurity, unremembered. You are beautiful and very much desired." He stripped off what remained of his tunic and pants. "Look at me. Do you see how much I desire you?" He was thick and erect.

"I do."

Rayn rose from the bed stark naked and went to the curtains. He pulled them back from the balcony, letting the sun's waning light filter into the room. She envied him for feeling so at home in his own skin.

Gentle sunlight fell upon her body, while a cool breeze caressed her skin.

"The light only enhances your beauty," said Rayn as he returned to the bed. "Don't be afraid to let it shine on you."

He entered her—as promised, slowly, letting her feel every inch of his length. He kissed her, feasting upon her mouth. He sucked one breast and then the other while tracing circles on her skin with his fire touch. And he moved inside her, filling her, making it clear just whom she belonged to.

When his gentle movements were no longer enough, and she gasped with need, he sped his pace. He was so *big*. His muscles flexed with exertion; his body glistened with sweat.

"Oh, *karamasi*," he groaned.

Her body spilled over into wave after wave of burning climax. She gripped him as her body clenched, and closed her eyes in ecstasy. He moved against her in an ever-increasing rhythm. Then he groaned again. His body went rigid and his hands held her in a grip of iron.

As she quaked with the aftershocks, he lay beside her and gathered her into his arms. The light of the setting sun spilled over the two of them, and for the first time in her life Celeste welcomed its illumination.

30

The next day, Rayn gathered the Fireturners, and they went as a group to the public square in the middle of Tiasa. There Rayn addressed a crowd of gathered civilians and told the tale of the weeklong battle against the lava flow on Mount Drav. He explained the history of Mount Drav eruptions and how lava flows had always been directed into Four Pines. He described the size and boiling heat of the lava flow, since few Tiasans had seen one up close. He explained how the Fireturners had opposed the Land Council's decision to open Four Pines for farming and warned them that the next major eruption could destroy those farms. And how he'd evacuated the Four Pines settlers despite having been denied permission to do so by the Land Council.

Then his Fireturners took the stage, one by one, to add their experiences to the tale and confirm the validity of Rayn's words.

It was hard to gauge the mood of the crowd, but Rayn felt he'd made his points clear. It was up to the people of Inya to judge who was to blame for the destruction in Four Pines. He hoped they would reflect, additionally, on the role of the Land Council in the debacle.

After his public appearance, he collected the Kjallan

imperials, who'd watched the speech from the plaza, and escorted them to the Merchants' Guild. There Celeste and Vitala mingled among the Inyan distributors and shopkeepers, assuring them in accented but serviceable Inyan that they were highly interested in opening trade with Inya. A few tradesmen inquired about the brimstone issue—would they consider a trade agreement that didn't include brimstone? Celeste and Vitala were noncommittal in response to that query, saying only that they were certain something could be worked out to everyone's satisfaction.

They returned to the Tiasan Palace for lunch. On their way, Rayn spotted a new set of handbills. Lornis had been busy in their absence.

WHO IS TO BLAME FOR FOUR PINES?
LAVA FLOWS HAVE BEEN SENT TO
FOUR PINES FOR CENTURIES
THE LAND COUNCIL AUTHORIZED
SETTLEMENT OF FOUR PINES
BUT DENIED AUTHORIZATION TO
EVACUATE WHEN THE LAVA CAME
PRINCE RAYN DEFIED THAT ORDER TO KEEP INYA SAFE
RATIFY PRINCE RAYN

"I like it," said Celeste.

"I don't know what I'd do without Lornis," said Rayn.

Lornis joined them for lunch. Everyone complimented him on his handbills, and the conversation turned to the trade agreement.

"You told the merchants that Kjall is interested in trade," began Rayn, addressing Vitala. "But Emperor Lucien isn't here. Can we hammer out an agreement without him?"

"We cannot sign it without him," said Vitala. "By law, Lucien's authority exceeds mine. In practice, the two of us rule by consensus. But there can be no consensus without him."

"You believe he's on the way here?"

"There is no doubt in my mind," said Vitala. "The only question is how long it will take. We stole his ship, so he has to procure another one."

Rayn had seen several suitable ships in the Riorcan harbor. He doubted it would take Lucien long to seize one of them. "How angry is he going to be?"

"Very," said Vitala. "But not at you."

Rayn frowned. "He won't harm Celeste, will he?"

"Not physically," said Vitala. "Nor would he harm me, not even if he wished to."

It sounded like Celeste was in no danger of being beaten. But Lucien could hurt her in other ways. Confine her, send her home to Kjall. Burn her math treatise.

Could Rayn protect Celeste from Lucien's anger by marrying her before he arrived? No—that might make matters worse. Stealing her brother's ship was bad enough; eloping would compound the crime. Besides, he didn't want to propose marriage until the people of Inya ratified him as king. Celeste deserved better than the political exile he would become if he failed his ratification vote.

"While I can't authorize a trade agreement without Lucien," said Vitala, "we can still negotiate one. Don't you think it would cheer Lucien considerably if he arrived on the island to find a mutually beneficial trade agreement prepared and awaiting his signature?"

"There's an idea," said Lornis.

"I don't think it would be hard to work one out except for the one problem," said Rayn.

Vitala smiled wryly. "Brimstone."

"I've explained to you my objections," said Rayn. "Would Lucien sign a treaty that excludes brimstone?"

"No," said Vitala. "We need it. We're Sardos's nearest neighbor, and you know as well as I do that the country isn't stable."

Rayn nodded. All indications were that Sardos was on the verge of a coup. For thirty years, the First Heir of Sardos had kept his nation quiet and peaceful. But some of the Heir's detractors openly expressed their desire to recapture territories they'd lost to Kjall ages ago. If the Heir were assassinated, there was no telling who would rise to power in his place, and what policies that person might advocate. Inya was fortunate in that Kjall sat between them and Sardos, acting as a buffer from possible Sardossian aggression. If Inya's brimstone, converted to gunpowder, served the purpose of keeping Sardos contained, that would benefit Inya.

The problem was that there was no way to guarantee that Kjall would use the gunpowder for the purpose of containing Sardos. To make this deal, he had to *trust*—something he was leery of doing when it came to ambitious nations with a history of invading their neighbors.

"We must have it one way or another," said Vitala. "If you will not supply us, we will get it from Dori."

"You'll never get a consistent supply, not until they rebuild their nation."

"We will do what must be done to ensure the safety of Kjall," said Vitala.

Rayn considered the implications of her words. Kjall was quite capable of invading Dori. Would they do so, if that was the only way they could secure a supply of a resource they deemed essential to their national security?

"Would you feel better," inquired Celeste, "if Kjall traded you weapons in return?"

"Are you suggesting we need them?" said Rayn.

"I have no idea," said Celeste. "I was just thinking that would equalize the trade. Arms for arms."

Celeste's offer was well intended, but it rubbed him the wrong way. His country was sufficiently armed. He saw no need to stockpile weapons. No, this came down to thinking not just about Inya but about the world as a whole. It would be better for Inya if Kjall stood firm against an uncertain Sardos. It would be better for Inya if Kjall didn't invade an already unstable Dori. He just had to trust the Kjallans. That was the hard part, but less so than when he'd first met them. He knew the Kjallans now, had dealt with them and relied on them in matters of importance. And there was one particular Kjallan whom he trusted completely.

"If you want brimstone, there's only one thing I'll accept in trade for it," said Rayn. "The hand of the Imperial Princess."

Vitala blinked. "Isn't that what we offered in the first place?"

"At the time, I didn't fully appreciate the merits of the offer." He caught Celeste's eye and smiled.

"Celeste, what say you?" asked Vitala.

"I am one hundred percent in favor," said Celeste.

"We've no quarrel, then," said Vitala. "Not among the people sitting at this table."

"Let's draft the agreement," said Rayn. "We'll make it contingent on my winning ratification." What was a king for except to make judgments in uncertain situations? There were no easy answers here, no guarantee that he'd chosen correctly in throwing his lot in with the Kjallans.

But his gut told him that these were the people who would help him keep his archipelago safe.

"Of course it will be contingent on your winning ratification," said Vitala. "If you don't win, you won't have the authority to make the agreement. So Lornis and I will handle the drafting, and you work on winning your ratification vote. We'll present the agreement to Lucien when he arrives: everything's done, all he needs to do is sign the paperwork. Trade agreement and marriage alliance — and we pray he accepts them without a fuss."

"And I'll present the agreement to the Inyan people," said Rayn. "It gives them more reason to ratify me."

"Clasp wrists on it?" said Vitala.

Rayn reached across the table and sealed the deal.

That evening, Rayn took Celeste back to his bedroom and made love to her, slowly and gently. He laid her on the bed and worshipped her with his hands and mouth, telling her all the while how beautiful each part of her was. She was tense at first, but relaxed under his ministrations. It was going to take a while to banish the memory of Cassian's lies. He might have to remind her every single day that she was beautiful. It was a job he willingly embraced.

Now it was morning, and he was taking his coffee with her in his room, too greedy to share her with the others yet. Another busy day lay before him. He had a speech to give and meetings to attend. This was the calm before the storm, the last quiet moment he would have with Celeste until evening. Only two days left before his ratification vote.

Someone knocked at his door. There went his quiet moment.

"Come," he called.

Lornis entered. His hair was mussed and his clothes rumpled.

"Are you all right?" asked Rayn.

"Your Highness, I need to speak with you privately."

Celeste, who was wrapped in a gauzy silk robe, set down her spoon and rose from her chair. "I'll go. I need to get dressed."

Rayn looked at her half-eaten breakfast and held out his hand to stay her. "If something's happened, tell both of us. Has Emperor Lucien arrived?"

Lornis shook his head.

Something was wrong. Normally Lornis's stiff posture suited the man; it looked natural on him. But now he looked wrong all over, like a marionette with twisted strings. Rayn grabbed an empty chair and pulled it to the table. "Have a seat, man. Whatever the problem is, we can fix it."

When Lornis hesitated, Rayn took his arm and led him to the chair. He pressed lightly on his shoulder, and Lornis sank reluctantly into it.

Lornis placed a folded piece of paper on the table and shoved it toward Rayn. "I'm tendering my resignation."

"What?" Rayn snatched the paper from the table and read. It was indeed a resignation letter, with Lornis's signature at the bottom. "This is ridiculous. I do not accept."

Lornis swallowed. "I cannot fulfill my duties as your adviser any longer, Your Highness. I am leaving whether you accept it or not."

"But why?" said Celeste.

Rayn rose from his chair. "Lornis, my ratification vote is the day after tomorrow." He couldn't believe this. Twelve years of service, and Lornis was abandoning him on the eve of the most important day of his life? He stared with foul hatred at the resignation letter, and then snatched it from the table and tore it in half. "What inspires this treachery?"

Lornis flinched.

"There's got to be a sensible explanation," said Celeste. She turned to Lornis. "Why do you feel the need to resign?"

"My reasons are my own. Your Highness, Your Imperial Highness: I wish you success and happiness." He turned to go.

"You can't just walk away." Rayn grabbed him by the arm and yanked him around. "Who got to you? Was it Worryn? Zoe?"

"Nobody has threatened me," said Lornis.

"You can't tell me nothing happened to provoke this," said Rayn.

Lornis's gaze went to Rayn's hand on his sleeve. "Let go of me."

"Not until I get some answers."

Lornis yanked his sleeve out of Rayn's grip and walked away.

Rayn followed him. "Something happened. At least give me the courtesy of letting me know what I've done to lose your service. You don't want to say it in front of Celeste? I'll grant you the privacy you asked for."

Lornis paused. "Sir, you are the finest man I've had the pleasure of advising, and it is my deepest desire that you be ratified as Inya's next king. There is nothing more I have to say on the matter."

"But it doesn't make sense," said Rayn.

"It will," said Lornis. "Good-bye, Your Highness."

As Lornis walked away, Rayn was tempted to grab him again, to haul him bodily back to the room and reinstate him whether he liked it or not. But respect stayed his hand. As a magister, Lornis could make a good living any number of ways. He chose to be an adviser because he believed in Rayn. Rayn could not force him to do the work he did.

"What did I do?" Rayn called desperately.

"Nothing, sir."

31

Celeste headed to her own room to dress, turning over in her mind the mystery of Magister Lornis. There had to be a reason for his resignation. That left her and Rayn with a dilemma of pragmatics. Should they investigate Lornis's reasons for resigning, or keep the appointments Lornis himself had arranged for them? Celeste was of the opinion that they should keep the appointments. Ratification was in two days; any missed opportunities could not be made up. But Rayn was going to be distracted now that he'd lost his adviser.

She put on the prettiest dress she could find, knowing she would be onstage with Rayn for his speech, and headed back to Rayn's rooms.

She found him still in his bedclothes, drinking *uske* from the bottle.

She took the bottle from him. "What are you doing? You've got a speech this morning, and more going on besides."

He regarded her through hazy eyes. "I can't do this alone."

"You're *not* alone," she said. "You've got me. You've got Empress Vitala. You've got the Fireturners and the whole Inyan population—"

"I do not have the whole Inyan population, or this would be easy," said Rayn. "When my father's mind was riddled with holes, Lornis helped me stand up to the council. When my self-absorbed mother took to her bed, unable to cope, Lornis remained to advise and reassure me. Everyone else abandoned me, and he was there. Do you understand? And now *he* leaves. What am I supposed to think when I'm the man everyone abandons?" He reached for the *uske* bottle.

She held the bottle out of his reach and walked out on the balcony with it. She tossed it into the garden below.

"There's a law against that," said Rayn.

"I'll tell you what you're supposed to think," said Celeste. "You're supposed to think he had a good reason for doing what he did, one that probably has nothing to do with you. For the years of service he's given you, the least you can do is make it through these last few events before your ratification vote." She returned to Rayn and tugged him out of his chair. "Get dressed."

Rayn rose reluctantly and stripped out of his bedclothes. While he put on tunic and pants, Celeste went to the door and spoke to Atella, who was standing guard along with a second Legaciattus. "Fetch the empress."

"Yes, Your Imperial Highness." Atella departed.

Celeste returned to Rayn.

"I don't understand why he'd do it," said Rayn, adjusting his belt. "Something has upset him, but I can't imagine what."

"We'll find out," said Celeste.

Vitala arrived, and while Rayn continued to dress, Celeste conferred privately with her at the door. "Lornis just resigned, and we don't know why."

"*Lornis?*" Vitala looked so stunned that it was clear she didn't know anything either.

"Rayn's got a speech this morning, and I'm going with him. Would you get to the bottom of this for us? Rayn won't be himself until we understand what happened."

Vitala nodded. "Of course."

At the palace stables, Celeste and Rayn mounted their horses. Then, followed by an escort of three Legaciatti, they rode into Tiasa. The crowd in the street thickened as they approached the plaza. Most people were going in the same direction they were. The Legaciatti cleared a path through the crowd—she could see Rayn's back stiffen as they did their work; he still didn't like bodyguards—and they found the plaza packed with humanity. Celeste hoped it was a good sign that so many more people had come to hear this speech than the one he'd given the day before.

Rayn took the stage and spoke about his efforts at bringing Kjallan trade to Inya. Celeste, shy but no stranger to making public appearances, said a few words of support. Her prince then went on to speak at length about the King's Lands and his desire to protect them from any further abuses by the council. This got a round of applause. As Rayn headed into the conclusion of his speech, someone in the crowd shouted, "What about your adviser?"

Rayn stopped short. Celeste, standing at the side of the stage, felt her heart race. How did this heckler know that Lornis had resigned? Rayn recovered from his stunned silence and said, "I'm not taking questions on that subject."

"Is he a sodomite?" called the heckler.

Rayn went very still. Celeste, watching him, was reminded of a lion that goes motionless just before it springs, but he only said, "I'm not taking questions about my adviser," and continued his speech. He was a professional—

his voice did not waver, though Celeste was certain he was deeply disturbed.

As he moved through his concluding words, Celeste scanned the crowd and spotted Vitala near the edge, conspicuous with the orange-garbed Legaciatti surrounding her. She hoped Vitala's presence meant that she'd tracked down some information.

When the speech was over, Rayn descended into the plaza and spoke to individual civilians, many of whom had their own private complaints with Inyan governance. Celeste accompanied him. Rayn was gracious but honest, making promises when they seemed reasonable and responding noncommittally when they weren't. Several people asked him the sodomite question. Rayn was chilly as he informed them he would not answer. The plaza was emptying. Vitala and her guards made their way over to them.

Rayn spotted her. "Thank you all," he announced to the townsfolk who remained. "I've got another engagement. Thank you for coming." He stepped away from the dwindling crowd.

"Did you find anything?" Celeste asked Vitala.

Rayn looked confused, and she explained that she'd asked the empress to look into the reasons for Lornis's resignation.

"I talked to Lornis's friend Magister Donyl," said Vitala. "He gave me this." She held out a folded sheet of paper.

Rayn took the paper and unfolded it. It was a handbill.

RATIFY PRINCE RAYN?
HE WAS EDUCATED BY MAGISTER
LORNIS, A KNOWN SODOMITE
WHAT ELSE DID LORNIS TEACH THE KING'S ONLY SON?
VOTE NO ON RATIFICATION DAY

"Vagabond's Breath," said Rayn. "Are these posted around Tiasa?"

"All over the place," said Vitala.

Rayn took a deep breath, and Celeste saw him swell with fury. His face flushed and his muscles bulged beneath his tunic. He crumpled the paper and threw it on the ground. He looked like he was about to erupt in a tirade of swearing, but there were civilians around, some of them idly watching. She took his hand and folded her small fingers around his large ones.

He exhaled and spoke in a tight voice. "Is Magister Lornis back at the palace?"

"Donyl said he'd left town," said Vitala. "He didn't think Lornis would be gone for more than a few days."

Rayn's hands curled into fists. "I'm going to destroy that man."

"Who?" said Vitala, looking surprised.

"Councilor Worryn." Rayn's eyes narrowed. "Did Lornis take his horse? Did he tell anyone where he was going?"

"Yes, and no," said Vitala. "I used my discretion in this matter and sent a team of Legaciatti after him. He can't have gone far, and I don't think he anticipates being chased. I told my people to bring him back peaceably."

"Thank you, Empress." Rayn clasped wrists with Vitala. "That's exactly what I needed done."

Vitala nodded. "I'll return to the palace and await news from the Legaciatti."

Rayn led Celeste away from the plaza and to their horses.

"At least we know," said Celeste.

"Yes," said Rayn, pulling himself into the blood bay's saddle. "But it creates a political dilemma."

Celeste mounted her gray gelding. "How so?"

"Some people will be bothered by those handbills," said Rayn. "I understand why he resigned. Lornis's living arrangements have been an open secret in the Tiasan Palace for over a decade. Some people disapprove, but until now they've minded their own business. Now that Worryn's dragged it into the open, he's turned Lornis into a political liability."

"How much will it affect your chances at ratification?"

"Hard to say," said Rayn. "I don't think the insinuation that Lornis and I were involved with each other will stick. My scandalous and well-known affair with Zoe gives it the lie. But the rest of that handbill is true."

"Why should it matter that your adviser sleeps with a man?"

"Some here think it unseemly. Why, is it accepted in Kjall?"

"Actually, no," said Celeste. "It's illegal. But during Lucien's reign the law has not been enforced. I know some people who live openly that way."

"It's not illegal in Inya, just frowned upon. Lornis did what he felt he had to do. He hoped to mitigate the damage." He scowled. "I hope Donyl's not in danger. Generally Inyans don't get violent about this kind of thing. But you never know."

"I can assign him a guard," said Celeste.

Rayn smiled at her. "You're such a Kjallan. Guards are your solution to everything."

Celeste shrugged. "They work."

Rayn couldn't afford to obsess about the situation with Lornis—he had a full afternoon of meetings ahead of him, where he would exchange small talk and not so small talk with influential Tiasans. He put Lornis out of his mind as best he could and redirected any questions he received about his adviser. His anger had ebbed since that initial burst of rage, but the injustice of this treatment of Lornis gnawed at him all day, making him testy.

Celeste was wonderful. Seeing her today as she made conversation with strangers in meeting after meeting, he would never have guessed she was at heart a shy woman. Her black hair and exotic look appealed to Inyan eyes. While the Tiasans had mixed feelings toward the Kjallan Empire, they did regard the empire with awe, and she was by far the most sought-after conversation partner in the room.

She was calm, kind, and gracious. He knew she was smoothing over a lot of his rough edges today.

When they rode back to the palace in the evening, he asked, "How do you do it? You were so quiet when I met you in Kjall."

She ducked her head. "That situation was different. You didn't know it, walking into that dinner, but I knew that Lucien intended to offer me to you as a marriage partner. And I hate being scrutinized, especially in that way."

"I hope my scrutiny doesn't bother you now," said Rayn.

"No, you've . . . changed my attitude about that quite a bit." Her cheeks flamed. "But this is different. Mingling, making conversation—back in Kjall, I did these things at imperial events at least once or twice a week. It's easier when I don't care deeply what the people think of me. It's a performance, you know? An act. Inside I'm the quiet girl who wants to go home and work on her math treatise. But I can pretend for a little while."

Vitala was waiting for them at the Hibiscus Tower. "We've got him," she said shortly.

"Please tell me you mean Lornis," said Rayn.

"My people caught up with him on a bridle path just outside the city. He's waiting in your room."

He felt as if a weight had been lifted from his shoulders. "Thank you."

Celeste made her excuses and departed. Rayn suspected she wanted to give him the opportunity to speak privately with Lornis, and he appreciated that.

A knot of Legaciatti waited at his door. Rayn was ironically amused. He hated door guards, but he'd thrown his lot in with the Kjallans, and now he seemed to be stuck with them everywhere he went. Celeste had even reassigned two of her own guards to him, fearing a last-minute assassination attempt.

The guards parted to admit him—imagine, needing authorization to enter one's own room—and he went inside to find Lornis sitting alone at the breakfast table, looking forlorn.

"I saw the handbills," said Rayn.

"I did what had to be done," said Lornis.

"You're not leaving," said Rayn. "I forbid it."

Lornis sighed. "Think about it, Rayn. Ratification is the day after tomorrow. Worryn's had this in his back pocket the whole time. He's been waiting to spring it on us, this ugly last-minute attack. There's a very real chance you could fail ratification because of me. And I've worked so hard—for twelve years, Rayn!—to make you king of Inya."

"The damage is already done." Rayn pulled out a chair and sat across from his adviser. "You think I can feign ignorance, pretend I didn't know about you and Donyl? The whole palace knew. Nobody cared until Worryn decided to make an issue of it."

"It doesn't matter that the palace knew," said Lornis.

"It matters what the people knew. You must disclaim me. Disown me. The people who are bothered by it will be satisfied—"

"They won't," said Rayn. "They'll think I'm trying to cover something up. If I lie and cut you loose, they'll know I'm a man who doesn't stand behind his people, a man who drops his closest friend at the barest whiff of a scandal. You think I'm that sort of man, Lornis?"

"You can hire me back after ratification," said Lornis.

"Pox that," said Rayn. "You've stood with me for over a decade. Now I stand with you."

"I want you to be ratified," said Lornis. "It's been my life's work, this past twelve years."

"I'll be ratified with you or not at all," said Rayn. "I refuse your offer of resignation."

"But you already accepted—"

"No, I didn't. I ripped it in half. I'm ordering new handbills to be posted tomorrow, declaring my support for you. So you'd better stay. I'll be taking the heat for it whether you do or not."

"Your Highness—"

"Not another word about it," said Rayn. "Clasp wrists?"

Reluctantly, Lornis extended his hand.

"Let's go to dinner," said Rayn.

32

The morning before ratification, Celeste was at breakfast in Rayn's apartment. By virtue of sleeping in the prince's bed every night, she was learning about him. Small things, like the fact that he preferred to eat the same breakfast every single morning: coffee and a rice dish with vegetables and a fried egg. She found she wanted to know every little thing about him. What were his favorite activities? Did he like books, sports, horses? How did he get that scar on his right elbow?

She had been eating the same breakfast as Rayn, only substituting chocolate for coffee. She had a feeling she could develop a taste for coffee if she tried—certainly it had a lovely smell—but she had no desire to do so, as long as chocolate continued to exist.

"You haven't introduced me to your family yet," she said.

Rayn winced. "I know. I'm putting it off."

"You already told me about your father's illness and your mother's disinterest in caring for him. There are no secrets beyond that, are there?"

He shook his head. "No secrets. I'll introduce you, but can it wait until after ratification? I don't think my family will reflect well on me. Except my sister—you'll probably like her. I need to ask you, though—how do you feel about Aderyn?"

"Your daughter? What do you mean, how do I feel about her?"

"I know she's illegitimate, but I'd like to raise her within the family, if we marry, and if . . . well, if you approve." His forehead wrinkled.

"I've no experience with babies," said Celeste.

"You won't have to raise her," said Rayn. "She has a nurse who looks after her full-time. I just don't want her to feel unwelcome, especially once we have children of our own. *If* we have children of our own."

She rather hoped they would. "If we marry, Aderyn will be welcome as part of our family."

Rayn smiled. He seemed about to say something when a knock came at the door and Lornis was announced. Rayn shook his head ruefully. "We're never going to have a quiet morning."

"Maybe after ratification." She reached over and squeezed his hand.

"Come," Rayn called to the door guards.

Lornis didn't look distraught this time, and he wasn't holding a folded piece of paper. He entered the room with a quick stride and an alert look that made Celeste want to roll her eyes. She was never so bright and eager this early in the day.

"News?" asked Rayn.

"A Riorcan ship sailed into the harbor this morning," said Lornis.

Celeste sat up straighter, suddenly more alert herself. "Is it Lucien?"

"He's on board, yes."

Something fluttered in her chest. She'd missed her brother terribly, but her excitement at seeing him again was mixed with trepidation. She was going to have to face the consequences of stealing his ship. "Have you told the empress?"

"I'm going to her room next," said Lornis.

She glanced regretfully at her half-finished chocolate. "I'll go with you."

Rayn rose from the table. "I'll go as well."

Celeste laid a hand on his arm. "Finish your breakfast. I'll handle this on my own."

"You've stood by me. The least I can do is stand by you in return."

"If you come, Lucien will think I'm using you as a shield. He won't feel at liberty to say what he needs to say."

"Which is exactly why I should be there."

She shook her head. "I need to make things right with him, and that means letting him speak his mind. He won't be able to do that if you interfere."

Rayn growled his displeasure. "This is my country, not his. When I was in Kjall, I obeyed his laws. Now he is a guest in my archipelago, and he must obey mine. I won't tolerate his treating you ill."

"He won't treat me ill," said Celeste.

"Are you sure? He may not beat you, but there are other ways to hurt a person."

"It was my own decision to come here—"

"Pox that," said Rayn. "You came for my benefit."

"It's not as if you twisted my arm. The conversation will go better if it's handled as a family matter: just me, Vitala, and Lucien."

"Well . . ." He scowled. "I won't gainsay you. You know your family better than I do." He maneuvered his big body around the table, slipped an arm around her, and kissed her. "But if the meeting goes badly, summon me at once. No matter what happens, you will always have shelter in Inya."

Celeste smiled. Brave words, considering that if he sheltered her from Lucien, he'd be defying a country with an army many times the size of his own. Fortunately, her brother had no interest in war.

"If you're ready?" prompted an impatient Lornis.

Celeste turned to him. "Has the emperor been rowed to shore?"

"He was still on the ship when I spoke to him by signal," said Lornis. "But I don't expect he'll remain there much longer. Let's meet him at the harbor before the Land Council gets to him. Not that they'll do him any harm, but they might whisper some lies into his ear."

"Agreed," said Celeste.

Last time Celeste had been at the Tiasan docks, it had been raining. Even then she'd been struck by the beauty of the Inyan archipelago. Today the sun was out, and the colors dazzled her eyes. Never had she seen ocean water so light blue in color. How was it possible? The oceans were all connected, so why were they dark blue or gray or greenish around Kjall, but light blue here? Someday she'd have to find a naturalist and ask.

In the distance, well beyond the tall ships in the harbor, lay a long green peninsula, hazy in the sun: another of Inya's islands. Someday, when she and Rayn were not so busy, she would ask him which one it was. She'd heard Inya called the land of a thousand islands. Were there really that many? How many were inhabited? More questions to ask at some later date.

Lucien's ship was easy to identify. The Riorcan ship *Quarrel* was dark and squat and heavy, built to withstand cannon fire and the assaults of the Great Northern Sea.

It was quite unlike the taller, lighter Inyan ships. A boat was loading up alongside the *Quarrel*, and Celeste was fairly certain Lucien would be on it.

"This is a beautiful place," said Vitala, looking around at the harbor.

"I know." Celeste sighed.

Vitala glanced at her. "Are you in love with the man, or with the country?"

"If not for the man, I wouldn't have come here in the first place."

"Don't let the beauty of this place lull you into believing it's a paradise," said Vitala. "Inya has problems. The people here cling to outmoded ideas—for example, the notion that bodyguards make a bad king. That's an idea that makes sense in a small, self-policing community. But not in a country the size of Inya."

"Inya is smaller than Kjall."

"Its population is growing rapidly," said Vitala. "And Inya is settling some of its islands that were once thought uninhabitable. Its policies must adapt to its growing size and influence."

"I agree," said Celeste.

"You'll be part of that process," said Vitala. "If you become the Inyan queen."

She nodded. Vitala was right; Inya's apparent peace and tranquillity overlay some troubling problems: political corruption among the Land Council, the hiring of mercenaries to assassinate a prince they found inconvenient, a need for personal protection when formerly it had been unnecessary. Such problems were like the molten lava that lay within Mount Drav, simmering beneath the surface, quiet and unseen, until they erupted in sudden violence and harmed everyone in their path.

But the Inyans had found ways to keep the mountain's fits of temper from incinerating their cities. Perhaps Rayn—with her help?—could also mitigate these political problems.

Vitala tugged Celeste's sleeve. "Look, he's almost here."

Lucien's boat bumped against the pier, and they hurried to meet him. Celeste caught a glimpse of the boat before the guards crowded around and was pleased to see not just Lucien but Justien as well.

Guards blocked her view again. Then she heard the distinctive thump of Lucien's artificial leg on the wooden slats of the dock. "Where's my wife?"

"I'm here, Lucien." Vitala pushed her way through the guards. They stepped aside, giving her room.

"Thank the gods." *Thump, thump* went Lucien's leg, and he had Vitala in his arms. "What am I going to do with you?" They hugged each other so tightly they appeared melded together on the dock, two sides to the same body. Lucien's hand reached down to cradle Vitala's belly. "How's the baby?"

"Perfectly all right," said Vitala.

Lucien looked around. "Where's Celeste?"

Celeste stepped forward, nervous. "Here."

He raised an eyebrow at her. "It was one thing to take my ship. But did you have to take the dog?"

She flushed. "Actually, I didn't. That is, it was . . ." She trailed off, not wanting to get Vitala in trouble.

"A ship is just a pile of wood nailed together. I can always commission another." He gave her a stern look. "*Never* take the dog."

Vitala slung an arm around him. "Let's get you to the palace."

Celeste stared distastefully at the cup of milky white liquid that had been sent up to Vitala's room in the Hibiscus Tower, where Lucien intended to settle for the duration of his visit. Patricus lay under the table across Lucien's foot, panting. He'd finished his greeting ceremony, which consisted of spinning in ecstatic circles, and had worn himself out.

"So this is the famous kava." Lucien regarded it dubiously. "Have you read Plinius's *Travels in Foreign Lands*?"

"I have not." Celeste had tried reading Plinius. He was an insufferable bore, and his ideas on math and astronomy were sadly outdated.

"He says some interesting things about this drink."

A servant had delivered the kava on Rayn's orders, ostensibly to honor the emperor's arrival. Celeste suspected Rayn had sent it for another reason: to calm the emperor if his temper flared.

Lucien didn't seem angry, but perhaps he was saving his wrath for when they had privacy. Which they now had. He'd dismissed every last one of the Legaciatti to just outside the door.

"It's mind-altering," said Celeste. "I feel you should know that."

"Mind-altering in what way?" asked Lucien.

"It makes you feel relaxed."

"Like wine?"

She shook her head. "It won't fog your mind or make you clumsy. But if you're planning to have it out with me over my stealing your ship, you might want to do that before you drink the kava." If he was going to yell at her, maybe punish her, she would accept that—within reason. She understood Rayn's desire to protect her from the emperor's anger, but it wouldn't help matters to drug an unwitting Lucien into a better temper. That would only postpone the inevitable.

Lucien frowned into his still-full cup. "I am not going

to *have it out* with you. Still, I'm disappointed that the two most important women in my life saw fit to abandon me in Riorca, a country where I'm not the most popular of men."

"You were not being reasonable," said Vitala.

"Was I not?" said Lucien. "The prince came falsely represented. He didn't tell me that his ascending the throne was dependent on his winning some ridiculous vote by the Inyan people—"

"He thought you knew," said Celeste.

"Well, I didn't," said Lucien. "Furthermore, he didn't tell me he was the target of an organized assassination plot—"

"*Nobody* knew that," said Celeste. "Least of all him. And by the way, Rayn said he wrote me a letter before he left Riorca. I never received it. I have a feeling you intercepted that letter."

"Ah," said Lucien, looking sheepish. "I burned it."

"What did it say?" she cried.

He shrugged. "I didn't read it."

Celeste glared at him.

"If I may," said Vitala, "your concerns about the prince are being addressed. Rayn's ratification vote is tomorrow—we'll know then whether he is to be king of Inya or not. And we caught most of the assassins in Riorca."

"Except for the ones who came to Inya," said Lucien. "And you two deliberately exposed yourselves to those assassins in coming here."

"There have been no attacks," said Celeste.

"Why not?" said Lucien. "Do you think the assassins have given up?"

Celeste frowned. Bayard had said the assassins would only kill Rayn on foreign soil, so the prince might be safe now. But if the assassins wouldn't touch him on Inya, why had they come here at all? She suspected that they were in fact planning another attempt, and it was likely to happen before the ratification vote took place. That was why she'd assigned him some of her guards. "I had to warn Rayn about Zoe. So I did."

"You were under no obligation to do so. Leave Inya's problems to Inya."

"Rayn's problems are my problems," said Celeste.

"They certainly are not," said Lucien. "He is a foreign national."

"They are"—Celeste swallowed—"because I'm in love with him."

Lucien set his still-full kava mug on the table. Silence descended.

The emperor broke it with a pained sound. "I was afraid you might say that. Nothing less would have induced you to fly to Inya. I have some experience, you know, with normally sensible women who behave irrationally when their men are in danger."

"Come, now," said Vitala. "I have never behaved irrationally in my life."

He turned to Celeste. "You want to marry him? I give my approval on three conditions. One, he wins his ratification vote. Two, all the assassins involved in the plot are found and brought to justice—*all* of them, including Zoe. Three, we work out a mutually agreeable trading pact between Inya and Kjall."

"That last one's already done," said Vitala.

"I have neither seen nor signed such a document. As for you . . ." He scowled at Vitala. "*You* didn't run away because you were mooning over some prince with a blond braid."

Vitala sniffed. "Of course not."

"Was it because I brought your mother to lunch that day?"

"I ran away with Celeste because I recognized that this was something she had to do," said Vitala.

"You weren't at all influenced by the fact that we'd had an argument the day before?" said Lucien.

Vitala shrugged. "Not at all."

"Well, your mother's on board the *Quarrel*."

"What?" yelped Vitala.

"I promised her a place at the Imperial Palace," said Lucien. "She's got nowhere else to go. Her children have grown up and left; her husband's dead. I told her she could stay. And we're not going back to Riorca from here; we're going straight home."

"Straight home?" put in Celeste. "When?"

Lucien waved a hand. "After this ratification business."

She hoped he wasn't planning to pack her on board the *Quarrel* the moment Rayn won or lost the vote. They still had the assassins to track down. In fact, she wasn't planning on going home at all.

"I won't see her," said Vitala.

"Don't, then," said Lucien. "I won't force you. But I hope someday you'll change your mind." He turned to Celeste. "I'm going to put Justien and his team on the trail of these assassins—if there's any trail to be picked up. Also, I brought Bayard. We can expose Councilor Worryn's crimes. That should help Rayn, don't you think?"

"You brought Bayard?" Gods, that changed everything. They could bring charges against Worryn. How was such a thing done in Riorca, when the man being targeted was the head of the Land Council? She had little sense of Inyan law. Lornis would know better how to proceed. "Brother." She rose from her chair and went to Lucien, taking his hand in her own. "I thought you'd come to punish me. Thank you for instead coming here with help and good sense."

He stood and pulled her into his arms. She squeezed him so hard she could feel his heartbeat.

He sighed when he released him. "I was angry at first, but I've had time to think things over," he said. "I'm the emperor of Kjall—in essence a tyrant, since my power is near absolute. But I won't be a tyrant over my family. Florian chose that route, and look where he is now: deposed and alone, hated by his closest relatives. A sister is not to be ruled over." Glancing at Vitala, he added, "And neither is a wife."

"A good attitude," said Vitala, "when the wife carries Shards."

Lucien sat down and picked up his kava mug. "Shall we try this in celebration of our reunion? See if Plinius's words have merit?"

Celeste returned to her seat. Shuddering in anticipation, she raised her kava mug to her lips and downed its contents in four long swallows.

Lucien and Vitala followed suit.

"Aggh," said Lucien, shaking his head and wrinkling his nose. "Is it supposed to taste like mud?"

33

Rayn, after worriedly watching Celeste head off to collect her sister-in-law and face the wrath of the emperor of Kjall, spent the early morning at the handbill printer's. There he had a new page assembled:

PRINCE RAYN SPEAKS ABOUT
MAGISTER LORNIS:
MY ADVISER'S WORK IS BEYOND REPROACH
I STAND BY HIM WITH PRIDE
AS I STAND BY ALL OF INYA
VOTE YES ON RATIFICATION DAY

The printer cranked the windlass, and freshly inked handbills came off the press one by one. Satisfied with their look and contents, Rayn arranged to have them posted all over town.

He'd missed one of the appointments Lornis had scheduled for him, but it couldn't be helped. He might miss more than one, depending on how things went between Celeste and the Kjallan emperor. He didn't like that Celeste had excluded him from the meeting. She had protected him in coming here; now it was his turn to protect her. Still, he understood that some matters needed to be kept within one's immediate family, and he wasn't family yet, though he hoped to be.

When he returned to the Hibiscus Tower, he found all three Kjallans waiting for him in his room, along with Magister Lornis. They were sitting at his tiny breakfast table. Emperor Lucien was the first to rise in greeting.

Rayn inclined his head. "Your Imperial Majesty."

"Your Highness," said Lucien, clasping wrists. "Forgive my ignorance: is it still *Your Highness*, after your father's abdication?"

"Until the vote, yes, I retain the title." Studying the emperor, he saw no sign of anger. Lucien had an ease about him that Rayn had not expected to find in such a powerful man, but he was getting used to it. Lucien was like the lead dog in a hunting pack. Rayn had hunted with packs before, and while many men assumed that the most aggressive dogs were the dominant ones, Rayn had observed that the opposite was true. The subordinate or middle-ranking dogs, anxious and uncertain of their position, were the ones most likely to snap and growl. The lead dogs were calm and confident. The others deferred to them and followed them without quarrel.

Lucien had that sort of aggression-free confidence. He struck Rayn as a man who knew exactly who he was and what he wanted and felt at peace with himself.

Even so, Rayn had taken the precaution of dosing him with kava.

The others rose from the table to greet him. He returned their greetings politely and automatically, turning a surreptitious eye to Celeste. Her eyes were bright, and she appeared to be at ease. But that too could be the kava.

"The imperials are here to discuss a matter of Inyan law," said Lornis.

"What's that?" Rayn pulled up a chair. Now that most

of the eyes were off him, he raised a brow at Celeste. *Are you all right?*

She smiled and pressed a thumb to her chest in the Kjallan salute.

"I have Bayard in custody," said Lucien. "I brought him on the *Quarrel*. He's willing to give evidence implicating Councilor Worryn in the two attempts on your life."

"They are asking how to proceed," said Lornis.

Rayn laid his hands on the table, stunned by the implications of this surprise gift. Could they really bring up Councilor Worryn on treason charges? They had a witness to his crimes. But the timing was awful. If Worryn was arrested for treason this afternoon, the scandal would send Inya topsy-turvy until the case was resolved, which would take days if not weeks. How would the disruption affect his ratification vote? The Inyan citizens, who wouldn't know the merits of the case right away, might think it a publicity stunt. "I think we should wait until after ratification."

Lornis nodded. "I was explaining to them how our King's Court works. The victim of the crime must be the one to bring the case to the court—in other words, Rayn himself, since he was the assassination target. Therefore this case will be highly political in nature. It cannot be resolved before ratification even if Rayn brings the charges immediately, because Worryn will be given several days to prepare his defense. Many Inyans will be horrified that the prince of the realm is bringing treason charges against a Land Council member. It could affect the ratification vote."

"I quite understand," said Celeste. "So we wait. One more day won't change anything. But, Rayn, I want guards on you constantly between now and ratification."

Rayn hated guards, but the woman had a point; if Worryn's assassins were going to strike again, it would happen soon. "Agreed."

Ratification day dawned cloudy, with a smell of rain in the air. Celeste thought it an inauspicious omen, but Rayn didn't seem bothered. They took breakfast together. Rayn left his rice untouched and drank only his coffee.

"Are you all right?" she asked.

He gave her a rueful smile. "My stomach's tied up in knots."

"Can I do anything to help?" She didn't feel nervous, exactly, but then she wasn't the one facing the ratification vote. If anything, she felt relieved. They were done with the public appearances. Done with handbills and meetings and speeches. Either their efforts had proven effective, or they hadn't. It was too late to change anything now.

Rayn shook his head. "I just need to get this over with."

"I'll rub your shoulders." She rose from her chair and circled around him. He was still in his robe—no point in getting dressed, since there was some special outfit he had to wear for the ratification ceremony later this morning. She slid the robe off his shoulders and placed her hands on his smooth, tanned skin.

He wasn't an easy man to massage. He was big, and her hands were small. Kneading his shoulder muscles felt like shaping iron with her fingers. Still, her efforts seemed to help. He slumped in his seat and sighed.

She continued to work his muscles, expanding her range to his neck and upper back. "I don't think you have anything to worry about today."

He shook his head. "I had so little time to make my case."

"You made your case years ago, when you stood up to the Land Council's abuses. Your people remember that."

"Worryn's been smearing my name."

"And it's not sticking," said Celeste. "I think it's not what you say to the people that matters. It's what you *do*. Everything you've done has been in Inya's best interest—even when you originally declined the trade agreement and marriage because you had concerns about a country you didn't trust. It exasperated me at the time, but now that I understand it, I respect that choice."

"Come here," he rumbled, pulling her around the back of his chair and into his lap. "I just thought of something that will help me relax."

"What, last night wasn't enough?" she teased.

His hand slipped beneath her robe and found her breast. She gasped, and his mouth covered hers.

She turned molten in his grasp, like the liquid stone beneath Mount Drav, as his mouth had its way with hers. Maybe this *was* the best way to spend the morning prior to a ratification vote. She stroked his hair. Last night he'd let her unbraid it so she could run her hands through it. There wouldn't be time for that this morning, but there might be time for other things.

He knew just how to touch her. When she'd been with Gallus, she hadn't liked having her breasts touched because he liked to mash them around. But now she understood why women liked this sort of touch. Rayn stroked her breasts, alternating light touches with firmer ones. She made little mewling noises as the sensations shot through her like miniature lightning bolts.

It wasn't that Rayn was a man of superior sexual skills—though perhaps he was; she had little basis for comparison. Rather, it was a matter of awareness. A lover like Gallus did as he pleased and was indifferent to how his partner responded. But Rayn was exquisitely aware of her response. Every time they were together, he found ways to drive her to greater heights of pleasure.

Someone rapped at the door.

"Go away," called Rayn. He lowered his head and took her nipple into his mouth.

The knocking continued. "Prince Rayn!" The voice was unfamiliar to Celeste.

"Come back later!" said Rayn.

"We're here to prepare you for the ceremony," called the voice.

Rayn lifted his head from her breast with a noise of exasperation. "Gods-cursed ratification vote." He pulled her robe back into place, covering her up. "Tonight, we finish this."

"I should hope so, after you've put me in such a state." She climbed off his lap, smoothed her clothes, and returned to her seat at the breakfast table. She felt warm all over, and her sex was swollen with need. She sipped her chocolate, hoping the mundane act would return her to a less obviously aroused state.

"Come in," called Rayn.

A quartet of servants entered the room. One carried a red, jewel-studded robe and a crown woven of live flowers. Another carried a basin and a razor, and the other two, a small box apiece—she wasn't sure what was inside.

"I'll go back to my own room," she said. "I need to get dressed."

Rayn nodded, looking with trepidation at the servants. "I'll see you shortly."

She left her breakfast behind, but took the unfinished glass of chocolate.

Lucien had been exceedingly thoughtful in planning his trip to Inya. Not only had he brought Bayard with him; he'd brought Celeste's complete wardrobe—everything, at least, that had been on the *Goshawk* before she and Rayn had gone overboard. The clothes had since been brought up to her room. She sorted through them, hoping to find something that wouldn't leave her stifling in the Inyan heat. Her syrtoses and formal dresses were all long-sleeved and made of heavy fabrics. Pox it—if she'd thought of this earlier, she might have had one of them altered.

Never mind; she'd wear something Inyan. Sipping her chocolate, she sorted through her borrowed Inyan gowns, looking for something striking.

Her stomach cramped as she worked. Nerves, perhaps, or had she eaten something she shouldn't have? The latter was certainly a possibility. Inya was full of new-to-her foods.

She put down her glass of chocolate, no longer interested in finishing it, and continued searching through the gowns.

A stomach cramp bent her double, and her mouth flooded with saliva. Abandoning the dresses, she made her way to the chamber pot. Weak and dizzy, she lowered herself to the floor. The room was blurring. She had some idea that she ought to be concerned about what was happening. She ought to be yelling for help. But she seemed to lack the will to open her mouth. Despite the nausea, she felt contented. Even blissful.

She was floating on a bed of air. She lay flat, staring up at the ceiling. Holding her eyelids open seemed like too much work, so she closed them, and drifted away on a cloud of mist.

34

Inyan ratification ceremonies were rare. The last one had taken place before Rayn was born. He had not realized there was so much ritual involved: a special robe, a crown of flowers, war paint on his face. War paint! Such adornment had not been used in the archipelago for centuries. The ceremony was old and apparently hadn't changed much. He supposed there was little reason to modernize it when it was such an infrequent event.

Celeste was taking longer than he'd expected to get ready.

Several robed magisters had arrived and were walking him through the ceremony and what was expected of him. It wasn't complicated. There would be music. He'd make a speech. After that, the Inyans in attendance would vote, yes or no, as to whether they wanted him to be their next king.

Tiasa's population had swelled in recent days. People from the outlying villages and other islands had come into town to attend the ceremony and cast their votes.

"Check on the Kjallan princess," he ordered one of the servants. "Tell her we're almost finished here." He was shaved and painted and wearing his ceremonial robe. The servants had done something curious with his hair—they'd separated it into three parts and dyed one part black and another red. The third they left in his natural blond. Then they'd braided them together.

"Yes, Your Highness." The servant left the room.

The officials were teaching him some ritualistic words he was supposed to recite at the beginning of the ceremony. They were in the Old Language, but not difficult to memorize. He repeated them mindlessly.

The servant came dashing back. "The Kjallan princess is missing."

Rayn stood up so fast he had to catch his chair. "What do you mean? Explain that."

"She's not in her room. The door guard is in a panic because she says she was standing in front of the door the entire time, and no one came or went."

"Are you sure she's not just in the dressing room? She can be shy." He turned to the magisters. "Excuse me for a moment." Feeling ridiculous in his ceremonial garb, he jogged down the hallway to Celeste's room.

The door stood open, and Vitala and Lucien were already there. Vitala was searching the room while Lucien spoke to a tearful Atella.

"Sage's honor," said Atella. "I never left her door. I stood right here the entire time. Nobody came to the door, and she never cried out, never left the room—"

"Well, obviously she left the room," said Lucien.

"Not through this door!" cried Atella.

Vitala moved to the balcony and looked outside. "Where were her balcony guards?" she called.

"She reassigned them," said Atella. "They're watching Rayn's balcony."

Lucien turned to Rayn with a look of fury.

Rayn felt hot all over. This was his fault? He swallowed. It was no use casting about for blame; first they needed to find Celeste. "What do we know so far? Is there any sign of violence?"

"None," said Vitala, returning from the balcony. "She's simply missing. It may be harmless, but I don't think so. Atella says she came in here to get dressed, and when your servant came by and inquired as to when she'd be ready, she knocked on the door and got no response. She looked inside and Celeste was not here."

He stepped into the room. *Stay calm,* he told himself. *Keep sharp and figure this out.* First he went to the balcony. Unless the room had a secret exit he didn't know about, the balcony was how she'd been taken. It was three stories up from the ground, but that problem was solvable with a ladder or even a rope. "You," he said, pointing at a servant. "Go into the garden and look for ladder marks."

"Yes, sir." The servant ran off.

She'd come to her apartment to get dressed. He turned the corner into the alcove that served as her dressing room. One of the cabinets holding her dresses stood open. On the floor next to it was Celeste's mostly empty chocolate mug. "She was in here recently," he called.

Lucien hurried into the alcove.

"See?" He pointed at the mug. "That's her morning chocolate."

Lucien picked it up. "Why would she leave it sitting here?"

Rayn, spotting another servant, called out, "Fetch Magister Lornis."

The servant ran off.

The man he'd sent to the garden returned. "Your Highness, there are deep grooves in the ground below the balcony. Would you like to see?"

"In a moment." So the kidnappers had fetched her

from the balcony with a ladder. Maybe they'd left some tracks he could follow.

"Found something!" cried Vitala. "There's a note wedged under the chamber pot."

Rayn and Lucien ran into the bedroom and crowded around Vitala to read.

I HAVE HER. COME AND FIND HER.

"Oh, gods," said Rayn. "*Who* has her?"

Magister Lornis skidded into the entryway. "What's going on?"

Rayn took the note from Vitala's hand and pressed it into Lornis's. "Celeste is missing. Read this."

Lornis read it, and his face went ashen. "Who's got her, and what does he want with her?"

"I haven't the slightest idea."

"What are we going to do about it?"

"Find her," said Rayn.

"Well, you can't do that," said Lornis. "That's what the kidnapper wants you to do. Besides, you've got the ratification ceremony."

"I realize the kidnapper wants me to come looking for her, but what else can I do? I can't just leave her there." Furthermore, if his racing heart and sweaty palms were any indication, he was in no condition to give a speech this morning. Not until he'd found Celeste and assured himself that she was all right.

"We can't delay the ceremony," said Lornis. "People arrive hours before it starts just to get a good view of the proceedings. And if you don't show up—well, think of Prince Turon."

"Yes, I know." Prince Turon had been a candidate for the throne centuries ago, who'd been passed over because in his arrogance he'd been three hours late to the ceremony.

This unseen enemy had forced on him the worst possible choice: lose Celeste, or jeopardize his sole opportunity to win the Inyan throne. He saw now that he was going to lose Celeste no matter what he did. If he didn't win ratification, he'd become a powerless political exile, and Lucien would never allow him to marry her. But at least in that case she'd be alive.

"Let's consider who's behind this," said Magister Lornis. "It's obviously Councilor Worryn. I don't see that he has anything to gain from harming Celeste. He intends only to use her for the purpose of manipulating *you*. Which is why you have to go to the ceremony. If you're not ratified, you know full well what's going to happen. Worryn will seize control of the throne using your illegitimate daughter. You can't allow that to happen."

Lucien pushed his way in between them. "Did I hear you right? Did you say you're going to sacrifice my sister so Rayn can win his ratification vote?"

"I'm saying they've no reason to want her dead," said Lornis. "They just want to manipulate Rayn."

"How do you know they won't hurt her?"

Lornis hesitated. "I'm making an educated guess."

"My sister's well-being cannot be hazarded on a *guess*," snarled Lucien.

Vitala stepped forward. "Why are we letting Worryn manipulate anybody? We know he's behind this. Arrest him! Make him pay for his crimes. We've got Bayard, who will testify against him. Take him and force him to tell us where Celeste is."

"We haven't time," said Lornis. "Rayn has to leave in about an hour for the ceremony. Arresting Worryn and getting the story out of him will take days."

"If it's done through your Inyan court system," said Lucien.

"What are you suggesting?" said Lornis.

"I'm not bound by your courts or your laws," said Lucien. "I'm the emperor of Kjall, and my sister has been kidnapped. If I order my troops to take this Councilor Worryn and interrogate him, they'll do it. No one will stop me."

"You haven't an army here to back you up," said Rayn.

"I have two dozen Legaciatti," said Lucien.

Rayn felt profoundly uncomfortable at the thought of the Kjallan emperor arresting a member of the Inyan Land Council. It was practically a declaration of war against Inya. But then, kidnapping the Kjallan princess might be considered a declaration of war itself. If he and his people were not careful, they could end up with disaster—tens of thousands of people dead in a pointless war. "I cannot authorize such an action."

"I don't need your authorization." Lucien turned to one of his guards. "Take a dozen Legaciatti to the council room and arrest Worryn. Bring him here—and bring a mind mage as well."

Celeste awoke with her arms bound behind her back. She was aware of having been conscious for a short time already, in a dazed, uncaring stupor. Now the fog was lifting from her mind. The room was dimly lit, and she had the impression she was underground, perhaps in a cellar. The dirt floor pressing against her cheek was surprisingly chilly. Along the walls sat casks and barrels and lumpy sackcloth bags. The room smelled earthy. She thought the bags might hold freshly dug root vegetables: potatoes and turnips, or whatever their equivalent was in Inya. Rutabagas, perhaps.

Despite the underground chill, she figured she had to be still in Inya. She couldn't have been unconscious long—she wasn't even hungry yet.

She tried to move her legs and get to her feet but couldn't. They were bound. Her arms were twisted behind her at an awkward angle, and she felt almost certain the bindings were cutting into her wrists. Yet she felt no pain. She tried to move by curling and extending her body like an inchworm. Might that accomplish anything? No, it didn't.

"You're awake," said someone behind her.

She angled her head back awkwardly and spotted a woman sitting in a chair, sharpening a knife with a whetstone.

It was Zoe, no longer possessed of that vapid look Celeste had seen before. Now the Riorcan assassin looked determined and cold. "For your information," said Zoe, "we're too far underground for anyone to hear you scream. But if you do, I'm cutting that pretty throat of yours."

"You're after Rayn, not me. Why take me instead of him?"

"You were easier to carry," said Zoe.

Ignoring that flip answer, she tried to make sense of the situation. It was ratification day, and the assassins had taken her. They'd captured her alive, when clearly they'd had the opportunity to kill her. Why? Probably they wanted leverage over Rayn. "Has the ratification ceremony happened yet?"

"Should be starting about now," said Zoe.

Celeste shifted, trying to make herself more comfortable on the dirt floor. Was Rayn at the ratification ceremony? Would he have the sense to win his political vote first and then search for her? Surely these people wouldn't kill her—to do so might start a war. Even

Councilor Worryn wouldn't want that. But then, who knew what these assassins were after? Zoe wasn't Inyan; she was Riorcan, and a rogue Riorcan at that. She'd probably like it if Kjall and Inya went to war. "If I die here, my brother will destroy this nation."

"Wouldn't that be a shame?" said Zoe. *Shick, shick,* went her knife against the whetstone.

"I see. You don't care," said Celeste. "You'd *like* this peaceful nation destroyed. And Kjall embroiled in a meaningless war."

"Honey, I don't give two tomtits," said Zoe.

Above them came a faint sound, a wailing, as if someone were injured. No—after a moment, Celeste recognized it as the sound of a baby crying. "Is that your daughter? Yours and Rayn's?"

"Little brat never shuts up," said Zoe, not moving from her chair.

"I'll quiet her," offered Celeste.

Zoe just laughed.

"A war benefits nobody," said Celeste. "Councilor Worryn wants to control the Inyan throne, and you want your daughter to be queen of Inya. But what good does that do either of you if Kjall invades?"

"Worryn is an idiot," said Zoe. "He wants to rule, but he hasn't the stomach for it."

"What do you mean?"

"He says we can't kill Rayn on Inyan soil. Why should he care about Inyan laws, when he's broken dozens of them? But he didn't say I couldn't kill *you*."

Celeste shivered. "If you wanted to kill me, you'd have done it already."

"What fun would that be?" said Zoe. "Rayn has become such a bore. Now I've got his daughter *and* his lover. He's going to dance for me—you watch."

35

Down in the garden, Rayn searched for clues. There were a few boot prints in the soft mud by the ladder marks, but they disappeared entirely when the mud ended at a paved walkway. He tried to pick them up again on the other side, without success. He searched up and down the walkway, looking for a spot where the prints might resume.

"You'll not find her this way," said Lornis.

"I don't know how else I'll find her." He wished he'd learned tracking skills in his youth. Was there someone he could call upon who was an expert at this? A hunting master, perhaps?

"You're running out of time," said Lornis. "We've got to get you to the plaza."

"First we find Celeste."

"There's no time!" cried Lornis. "Rayn, this is the culmination of everything we've worked for. Think about it—as king of Inya you'll be able to search for her more effectively."

"If they haven't *killed* her," snapped Rayn.

"They're not going to," said Lornis. "It doesn't benefit them."

"You don't know that."

A servant ran up to them and bowed. It was a man Rayn had never seen before. "Your Highness."

"Is this important?" asked Rayn.

"I think so, sir. I went to Aderyn's room to deliver her midmorning meal and found Kima flat-out on the floor, unconscious. The baby's nowhere to be found."

"*Aderyn* is missing?" Surely these two events had to be related. Someone had taken both his lover and his daughter.

"Yes, sir."

"Is Kima all right?"

"She's breathing, sir. I called a Healer. I believe she's been drugged."

"Thank you. Come back if you learn anything else."

"Yes, sir." The servant dashed away.

"It's the same people," said Lornis. "You know it is."

He nodded. "I'll bet they also drugged Celeste. If I find her, I find Aderyn too."

A voice called down to them from the balcony. "Your Highness?"

Rayn looked up. It was one of Lucien's Legaciatti. "Yes?"

"Councilor Worryn is here."

"Let's go," he said to Lornis, and headed for the Hibiscus Tower stairs at a run. Worryn surely knew something about what had happened to Celeste and Aderyn.

Celeste's rooms were crammed with Legaciatti, at least twenty of them, all in their signature orange uniforms with the sickle and sunburst. Emperor Lucien stood among them, as did Empress Vitala. In the middle of the Legaciatti, spitting mad and held firmly with his arms behind his back, was Councilor Worryn.

Worryn flung words at Lucien. "You cannot do this. I am head of the Land Council. This is an act of war."

"The act of war was your abducting the Kjallan Imperial Princess," said Lucien. "This is merely my response."

"I did not abduct or harm the princess!" cried Worryn.

"If you are truly innocent, you'll submit to a truth spell and tell us everything you know."

Worryn hesitated. "The use of truth spells is restricted by law. First you must bring official charges, then—"

Lucien gestured at one of the Legaciatti, who brutally twisted Worryn's arm.

The councilor shrieked in pain.

"Tell me again about Inyan law," said Lucien. "I find that subject so fascinating and relevant."

"Why would I kidnap your sister? There is no benefit to me whatsoever—"

Lucien gestured.

The Legaciattus twisted Worryn's arm more sharply. There was a sickening crack.

Worryn bent over, screaming. He would have fallen, but the Legaciatti held him up.

"Get him a chair," said Lucien.

Someone shoved a chair under Worryn's rear. The Legaciatti released their grip on him, allowing him to sit and cradle his broken arm, rocking back and forth.

Rayn said nothing. He had the creeping horrors just watching this.

"Truth spell?" said Lucien.

"Yes," said Worryn softly.

A woman stepped forward and crouched beside him, placing her hands on his uninjured arm. Her eyes went distant, and she said, "Ready."

"Where is Celeste?" asked Lucien.

"I don't know," said Worryn.

"Truth," said the mind mage.

"Who took her?" said Lucien.

"I don't know."

The mind mage hesitated. "Half-truth."

"Explain yourself," said Lucien.

"I don't know who took her," said Worryn. "But I think it was very likely a group of Riorcan assassins."

"Is Zoe one of those assassins?" said Lucien.

"Yes."

"Truth."

Lucien turned to the mind mage. "Report only if he tells a lie or half-truth. Otherwise you may remain silent." Then to Worryn, "Did you order the attack?"

"No."

"Do you know where these assassins are?"

"No."

"What is your association with these assassins?"

Worryn hesitated. A Legaciattus stepped forward and punched him in his injured arm. Worryn howled, and when the Legaciattus pulled his fist back for a more serious blow, he spoke rapidly. "I hired them initially—paid them for a number of tasks. But they're out of control. They don't take my orders anymore."

Rayn moved to Lucien and whispered in his ear about Aderyn having gone missing and her nurse being drugged unconscious. Lucien's brows rose. He asked Worryn a series of questions about Aderyn and her nurse, but the councilor knew nothing.

Rayn had seen enough. He backed out of the crowd, found Lornis, and pulled him aside. "Worryn didn't take them," he said in a soft voice.

"So I hear."

"Then this gets us nowhere."

"I told you, you've got to go to your ratification ceremony," said Lornis. "If you don't leave now, you may be late, or we'll have to reschedule. And you have no idea how that might affect the vote."

Rayn ignored that. He stepped away from Lornis and returned to the interrogation.

Worryn was crying and confessing his crimes freely as Lucien peppered him with questions. But it was becoming increasingly clear that the man knew nothing about Celeste's abduction, or Aderyn's. He *had* hired the assassins initially. He'd brought them to Inya and harbored them, and ordered them to kill Rayn on foreign shores. But they'd grown tired of his restrictions and stopped following his orders.

Lucien asked Worryn whether anyone else might know where the assassins were. Worryn could not think of anyone who would know. "Hold him for now," Lucien ordered his Legaciatti. He gestured to Rayn and Vitala and Lornis, and they retreated to a corner of the room for a council.

"We've got nothing," Lucien said. "It's clear this man has committed crimes against Rayn and against the state. But he doesn't know where Celeste is."

"Rayn has to get to his ratification ceremony," said Lornis.

Vitala, ignoring that, said, "If the Riorcan assassins have Celeste, and they're now operating independently, they might very well kill her. They won't care if their actions spark a war."

"We have to find her," said Lucien. "There's no other way around it."

"Rayn can't stay any longer," said Lornis. "He's going to be late."

"I don't care if he's late," said Emperor Lucien. "The Inyan people shouldn't care either—we've got a mountain of evidence that a criminal conspiracy is afoot. They'll understand if he has to reschedule."

"They may or they may not," said Lornis. "Some of them will have spent their life savings to be present for the vote."

As Rayn listened to them bicker over what ultimately must be his own decision, he felt increasingly ill. This was his fault. Celeste had loaned him two of her three guards, and so the attack had targeted her instead of him. He'd laughed off her security concerns, even knowing a group of assassins was after him, because he didn't want to believe that Inya had turned into this sort of country—the sort where rulers had to be escorted everywhere and couldn't mingle freely with the townsfolk. He didn't want Inya to be another Kjall.

But corruption was not limited to nations like Kjall. It had come to Inya. He hadn't wanted to believe that, and now Celeste was in danger. Aderyn too.

They could not be far away. The kidnapping had been recent, and the note from the assassins implied they had their eyes on him. Celeste could be found. She *would* be found, if he had to knock on every door in Tiasa.

The others were still arguing.

"Enough!" he cried, loud enough to silence them.

All eyes turned to him.

"I'm not going to the ratification ceremony. I'm going to find Celeste. She cannot be far. We'll track her down."

"But Rayn—" began Lornis.

"No arguments," he said. "I've made my decision." It tore him up inside, knowing that after all he'd been through, all he'd done to oppose the abuses of the Land Council, he might lose his opportunity to rule Inya. But what sort of king would he be if he let the woman he loved die for the sake of his political power? Celeste's safety had to come first.

"I'll get Justien. He can look at the baby's room and see if there are any clues there." Lucien squeezed Rayn's shoulder in passing, adding, "Good man."

"Let's get down to the garden," Rayn said to those who remained, "and see if we can pick up her trail."

Down in the garden, Rayn had no more luck than before. He tried following the boot prints again, and again they led him nowhere. Only to the walkway, and at that point he could discover nothing, not even whether they'd turned left or right. He tried to think which way it most made sense for the kidnappers to go. Either way made sense. The walkway meandered through the palace grounds, spawning a number of side walkways and ultimately joining up with itself. The side walkways led to other buildings or into the city of Tiasa. The kidnappers could have gone anywhere.

Where might they have taken her? Somewhere on the palace grounds? Certainly there were enough outbuildings, and many were not heavily used. There were plenty of places to hide. Or she could be in Tiasa. Perhaps he could organize search parties. They'd look inside every building, fanning outward in an ever-broadening circle, until they found her. That was a last resort, however. It could take days, and the assassins might kill her first.

Justien's team and some of the Legaciatti had looked through Aderyn's room and found nothing. Now they were searching here, looking for any clues that might have been dropped. A thread from her robe, a long black hair. Patricus was sniffing about the walkway.

"Poor fellow." Rayn rubbed the dog's ears. "You know something's wrong, don't you? But you don't know what."

Patricus looked at Rayn quizzically, waving his long tail.

"I bet you'd find her if you could."

Patricus licked his hand.

A wild idea occurred to him: *could* Patricus find her? He'd never heard of a hunting dog tracking a person before — only wild game — but surely the concept was the same, if the dog could be made to understand what was asked of him. And Patricus knew this game already. Celeste had told Rayn they played hide-and-seek with Patricus at home.

"Patricus," said Rayn, suddenly excited but trying to keep his voice calm. "Where's Celeste? Find Celeste."

Patricus's ears flew up. He gave a happy bark and bounded about the garden, sniffing wildly, looking everywhere.

Rayn's spirits fell as he watched. The dog thought they were playing hide-and-seek here in the garden. He didn't understand that this was serious. Patricus wasn't going to find Celeste here. He had to pick up her trail and follow it.

"Here, Patricus," he called, moving to the footprints below the balcony. He directed the dog to the footprints. Patricus sniffed diligently. Rayn waited until the dog had his fill of the scent and said, "Find Celeste. Go on, find her."

Patricus left the footprints and went bounding around the garden.

Pox it, he couldn't communicate what he wanted.

Lucien came up beside him. "What are you doing with my dog?"

"I had a crazy thought," said Rayn. "I thought I could convince him to pick up Celeste's trail for us. But it's not working. He doesn't understand."

Lucien straightened, his eyes going wide. "Three gods, man, that's a *superb* idea. Even better if you've got a trained tracking dog. Do you?"

Rayn shook his head. "The royal dogs track rabbits and foxes, not people."

"It'll be up to Patricus, then. Let's keep trying. Surely he'll get the idea if we keep at it. Patricus!"

The dog raced to the emperor and skidded to a halt in front of him.

"Find Celeste," commanded Lucien.

Patricus bounded away again.

"No," said Lucien.

Patricus halted in midstride. His ears fell, and he looked sheepishly back at Lucien.

"Here." Lucien indicated the footprints with his foot. "Here."

Patricus ran to the footprints, sniffed at them a moment, and looked up at him with cocked ears.

"Find Celeste," said Lucien.

Patricus lifted a foot, torn between an obvious desire to run around the garden and his understanding that Lucien didn't want him doing that.

Lucien indicated the footprints again. "Find Celeste."

Patricus returned to the footprints and sniffed. He looked up at Lucien.

"Find Celeste."

Patricus continued to sniff. He made his way to the walkway and sniffed in one direction, then the other.

"Good boy, Patricus," said Lucien. "Find Celeste."

Patricus angled one eye up to Lucien and resumed sniffing. The path leading to the right seemed to interest him more than the one leading to the left. He worked his way along it a good ways. Then he gave a bark and began to lope down the path.

"He might have it," said Lucien. "Let's follow him. Justien, Nalica, Fenius, Orissian!" he called. "Come with us. Patricus may have her trail."

Patricus was moving fast now, much of the time at a dead run, occasionally slowing to sniff a patch of ground. Rayn and Lucien and a horde of guards followed him. Quite suddenly, without pausing to sniff, Patricus veered off the walkway entirely. Rayn worried that he had lost the trail or even forgotten what he was doing. But even as he moved over the grass, he seemed to still be sniffing and tracking.

Vitala caught up with the group, puffing with exertion. "What are you doing?" she asked Lucien.

"Patricus may have picked up the kidnappers' trail," said Lucien. "We're following him." He glanced at her. Running was awkward for her in her pregnant state. "Look, you stay behind. I don't know how long a chase he's going to lead us or whether it will amount to anything. I've got enough people to handle this."

Vitala nodded and stopped running. The group went on without her.

They'd left the Hibiscus Tower behind. Then they passed a greenhouse and the Melati Tower. Now they came to the stream that ran through the palace grounds, and Rayn worried that Patricus might lose the scent here. The dog followed the bank a short ways, came to a bridge, and led them over it. At the far end of the bridge, he sniffed the area thoroughly, moving from left to right, then nearer and farther from the bridge.

"Come on," muttered Rayn, worried the trail had gone cold. There was no use scolding the dog. It was clear he was working as hard as he could.

Patricus took off again. Rayn and the others were hard-pressed to keep up with him.

"If I'd trained him to do this," Lucien panted by his side, "I'd have taught him to go a little slower."

Rayn just hoped their destination wasn't far. He could

keep up this pace for a while, but not forever, and if they faced a battle at the end, he needed his strength.

They'd reached the outskirts of the palace grounds, an empty field that was periodically mowed down with scythes. It was reserved for future buildings, since the Tiasan Palace had a tendency to expand over the generations. Patricus crossed the field. There he came to a storage building, one of many that lurked along the edges of the grounds.

Patricus ran up to the storage building, sniffed along the bottom of the door, and flopped into a sitting position. He turned his head to bark once at the men following him and then stared at the door as if willing it to open.

36

Rayn hurried to the door, but as he was reaching for the lever to open it, someone grabbed his arm.

It was the Kjallan emperor. "Stand back," he said. "Guards first."

Rayn withdrew, and the Legaciatti crowded into the space where he'd been, weapons drawn. They opened the door and went inside. Almost at once, someone fired a gun. The Legaciatti scattered, spreading out in the wider space of the building's interior.

Rayn reached for his sword and found nothing—his ceremonial garb did not include one. But his fire magic had some value in a fight. He darted in behind the Legaciatti. He couldn't see at first; it was too dark. When his eyes adjusted, he took stock of his surroundings. The interior of the storage building was cluttered, with stacks of crates breaking up the room's otherwise clean lines. Gun smoke drifted upward beside some of the crates. Several Legaciatti charged toward the crates and around them. He heard shouts and the clang of swords clashing. And something else—a baby crying. Aderyn?

Uncertain whether there might be other enemies in the vicinity, Rayn stood where he was, scanning the room. The Kjallan emperor had come inside. He stood on Rayn's right, and Nalica, the archer, was on his left, with her bow in hand and an arrow nocked.

"Move," said Lucien suddenly, shoving Rayn hard to the side.

He stumbled, not expecting an assault from that quarter, and felt something fly over his shoulder. The object crashed against the wall and tumbled to the floor. A knife.

Nalica loosed an arrow, which impaled itself in the wall near another stack of crates. "Pox it," she said. "He was there."

Justien charged toward the crates, sword in hand.

Rayn ran after him. By the time he'd rounded the corner, Justien's sword was impaled in an enemy's abdomen. He watched as Justien lowered his blade and the dying man slid off it and fell limply to the floor.

He could see no other attackers, and the battle sounds had ceased in the other part of the room. "Are there more?" So far he didn't see Celeste. But he did hear a baby crying. He came out from behind the crates. Three Legaciatti were searching the room, and Patricus was nosing the floor. One of the Legaciatti held the baby.

"Gods," he said, rushing toward the Legaciattus. "You've got Aderyn."

"Who?" said the Legaciattus.

"My daughter." Rayn reached for her.

Lucien pushed his way in. "I'll take her. There may be more assassins, and with this leg I'm no good in a fight anyway."

Rayn let Lucien take her. The emperor got around so well on his artificial leg that sometimes Rayn forgot he was an amputee. Lucien had managed to keep up with them as they'd followed Patricus, which was a feat, now that Rayn thought about it. But Lucien was limping badly. The run had cost him.

A bark interrupted the silence. They all turned at once.

The dog had nosed his way to a dark stairway leading down. The guards rushed toward it, and Rayn followed.

They piled down the stairs. The room below was lit, dimly. At the bottom, Rayn nearly crashed into the guard in front of him, who came to a sudden halt. The guard moved aside, and Rayn saw why they'd all frozen in place.

Celeste lay bound on the cellar floor. Zoe stood over her. She had a tiny black Shard in her hand, no larger than an arrowhead. She pressed it against Celeste's neck.

Patricus tried to dart toward Celeste, but a Legaciattus grabbed him by the scruff.

"If you even *lift* a weapon, she dies," snarled Zoe.

Rayn needed no weapon. He called fire into the Shard. It turned from black to red, and Zoe screamed, dropping it.

Zoe cradled her burned fingers. Then with a shout of rage, she wrapped her hands around Celeste's throat. "I don't need a weapon to kill this bitch!"

An arrow buried itself in Zoe's side. Zoe grunted with the impact, her eyes going glassy. Her fingers shook on Celeste's neck.

Rayn's heart beat fast. Had that arrow been just a little bit off, it could have struck Celeste. And yet Nalica, beside him, was calmly nocking a second arrow.

War mage, he reminded himself. *She doesn't miss.*

Nalica loosed the second arrow.

Zoe, his onetime lover, mother of his illegitimate child, and undercover Riorcan assassin, slumped lifeless to the floor.

Celeste, who'd had the sense to remain quiet and still throughout these events, now cried, "Get her off me. Get her off!"

Rayn rushed forward. He hauled Zoe's inert body off Celeste and flung it aside. He reached for his belt knife and realized that in his ceremonial garb, he didn't have that either.

"Here." Justien handed him a knife.

Rayn cut Celeste's bonds. "Are you all right? Can you stand?"

"I think so."

Rayn pulled her gently to her feet.

"What's all that on your face?" she asked.

"Oh. War paint." He grinned.

"There's a baby somewhere in the building," said Celeste.

"Right here," said Lucien, holding up Aderyn.

"Lucien?" She turned and saw him.

He hobbled toward her on his artificial leg, and they embraced. The guard released Patricus, who bounded happily around them.

Rayn rubbed the dog's head. "Good dog," he said softly.

Celeste turned and embraced Rayn. He wrapped his arms around her, relieved beyond measure to feel her body pressed against his, warm and alive and unhurt.

"Pox it," she said. "I've got blood on your ceremonial robe. How did it go? Are you ratified now?"

"I didn't go to the ceremony," said Rayn.

Her eyes widened. "Don't you have to be there in order to win the vote?"

He said nothing. It had been his choice, not hers. He did not want her to feel the weight of the sacrifice he'd made, especially when he'd had the good fortune of finding both her and Aderyn before Zoe had done them serious harm.

"How late are you?" she asked. "Can we still go?"

"Over an hour late at this point," he said.

"Let's get you there right away," said Celeste.

Despite feeling a little weak on her feet, Celeste insisted on accompanying Rayn and his people to the plaza. Lucien offered to take her back to the palace, but she declined. Her limbs still felt a bit woolen—the aftereffects of the drug, probably—and her wrists were raw and sore from the bindings. Otherwise she was all right.

They hurried to the stable. There they found Rayn's horse Copperhead saddled and waiting, looking ill-tempered since he'd been standing in his tack for over an hour. Lornis's horse wasn't present, and since he hadn't been among the party that had freed her from the assassins, she wondered if he might have gone ahead to the plaza. More horses were brought out for the rest of them.

Lucien was still holding Aderyn. Once Celeste was up on her horse, she offered to take the girl. Her brother had enough to deal with; he was limping on his artificial leg, and that was not normal for him.

Lucien handed the baby up. Celeste juggled the reins to find a satisfactory means of holding on to her while riding. She was not the sort of woman who asked to hold babies, generally, and everything about this was unfamiliar to her. Aderyn wasn't a tiny infant, at least; she was nearly a year old and sturdy. She was awake and turning her head in all directions to look at the men and horses.

They set off at a trot, with the Legaciatti flanking them on all sides. Rayn, ahead of her, turned in the saddle and met her eyes worriedly. Clearly he wanted to talk to her about something, but now wasn't the time.

The Tiasan streets were deserted. Celeste thought this must be a good sign. If the crowd of civilians awaiting the vote had given up on Rayn, surely they would have dispersed by now. But the streets were empty, and every shop had a CLOSED sign on its door.

Outside the plaza, they came upon the outer edge of the crowd. The street leading into the plaza was choked with people trying to press their way forward for a better view. Someone was speaking from the plaza. It was a man's voice, familiar to her, though she could not recall where she'd heard it.

"Make way!" cried the Legaciatti in heavily accented Inyan, pulling their swords from their scabbards and sending their horses straight into the crowd. At first there were curses and complaints as the onlookers scrambled out of the horses' path, but then someone spotted Rayn inside the escort. The whispers traveled through the crowd like ripples on a pond. *Rayn's here, Rayn's here.*

The crowd opened up and made room.

From the back of her horse, Celeste had a good vantage point. Once they'd entered the plaza, she saw who was up onstage speaking to the crowd. It was Bayard. Vitala stood beside him.

"We were paid two thousand cowries in the first installment," Bayard was saying. "When the child was born, we received another thousand."

"Who gave you these moneys?" prompted Vitala.

"An agent of Councilor Worryn. His name was Ismos."

The crowd was rapt.

Celeste had not thought to ask where Vitala was during the rescue in the cellar; the empress was pregnant, and of course it did not make sense for her to participate in something so physical. But bless her, she'd made herself useful, had perhaps even saved Rayn's ratification vote, by transfixing the crowd with Bayard's confessions and preventing the ceremony from ending prematurely.

Magister Lornis stood on the other side of Bayard. Perhaps the two of them had worked out this scheme together.

Rayn's approach could not fail to be noticed. He was mounted on an enormous stallion and wearing his ceremonial gear. And if his war paint was a little smeared and his three-color braid unruly, nobody seemed to care. The voices of the people rose in a great cheer. "Rayn! Rayn!"

Celeste's heart leapt. *They love him,* she thought. *They will ratify him.*

"I think we've heard enough," Vitala said to Bayard onstage. "Thank you."

The two of them stepped down, and a band began to play as Rayn dismounted from his horse and ascended the stage. The ovation for him was so loud that it drowned out the music. After basking for a moment in the cheers of the crowd, Rayn patted the air, asking the townsfolk for silence. At that point, the ceremony proceeded as intended, except an hour and a half late.

Rayn and several other men led the crowd in what appeared to be prayers. Their tone was reverent, but the words were in a language unfamiliar to her.

"Da," said baby Aderyn, from within her arms.

Celeste turned to her in surprise. "Yes. That's your da-da."

Next came Rayn's speech. Rayn had made public appearances before, and she knew he was comfortable speaking before a crowd. She did not doubt that in this particular situation he was nervous, because it was such a high-stakes event, but she saw no sign of it from where she stood. His speech was not formal, and she knew he had not memorized it. He spoke as if addressing a handful of friends. He spoke about his love for Inya, his desire to protect its lands, the lessons he'd learned at his beloved father's feet. He spoke of his wishes for Inya's future: to establish trade and a peaceful alliance with Kjall, to eliminate corruption in the Land Council, to keep the country safe from volcanic eruptions.

Lucien, sitting on the horse beside her, said softly, "He needs training in rhetoric."

"He speaks in the Inyan style," said Celeste. "Not like you, I'll grant. But he's a lovely speaker. He makes me feel as if he's talking just to me, in my own sitting room."

Lucien grunted.

When Rayn finished his speech, the townsfolk roared their approval. Rayn was directed off the stage, and several officials came forward, bearing two enormous earthenware jars. One was painted red and yellow, the other black.

"What's this about?" asked Lucien.

"Maybe it's the vote," said Celeste.

A line formed, and one by one, the civilians stepped up onto the stage. Each one carried a palm leaf. As they passed the jars on their way to the other side of the stage and back down, they dropped their leaf into one of the two jars.

"I see," said Celeste. "A leaf in the red-and-yellow jar is a *yes* vote, and a leaf in the black jar is a *no*." She hoped that was how it worked, because most of the votes were going in the red and yellow jar.

So many Inyans had turned out for the ceremony that it took over two hours for all of them to drop their palm leaves into the desired jar. Aderyn became restless and fussy, and Celeste passed her around between herself and Lucien and some of the Legaciatti. Vitala came out into the crowd and joined them, with Bayard and a few more Legaciatti in tow.

"Wonderful thought you had," said Lucien, "coming here to amuse the crowd with Bayard's confessions."

"Thanks," said Vitala. "After all that, I think the Inyans will arrest Worryn. I left him in the care of a few guards to make sure he didn't run away." She turned to Celeste. "You see the vote? Your prince is winning."

"Is it the red and yellow jar?"

Vitala nodded. "And look, it's almost full."

As the final Inyans came up onstage to vote, the red and yellow jar began to overflow. Here there seemed to be some confusion; the officials who had carried out the ceremony were huddled at the side of the stage, talking among themselves. Celeste hoped there wasn't some kind of problem.

Finally one stepped to the front of the stage and addressed the crowd. "Normally this task falls to the head of the Land Council, but he's not present. Men and women of Inya, I am proud to present His Majesty the king of Inya, Rayn Daryson."

The crowd cheered, and Rayn came back onstage, beaming from ear to ear. He hugged each of the officials. One of them wrapped a jeweled mantle around his shoulders, and another produced a fine, glittering sword and presented it to him.

"They don't wear a loros in Inya?" she asked Lucien.

"No, they told me here it's the mantle and the sword," he answered.

When the cheering died down, Rayn spoke once again to the crowd. "I'd like to ask the Kjallan Imperial Princess, Celeste Florian Nigellus, to come up onstage with me."

Celeste's neck heated as thousands of eyes turned toward her. "Oh, gods," she whispered.

"You can do this," Lucien whispered back. "Go."

Celeste dismounted from her horse, conscious of the many eyes on her, and made her way onto the stage. Up close, Rayn looked larger-than-life in his red robe and face paint and jeweled mantle. But beneath all that, she could see the kind, intelligent eyes of the man she loved.

He took her hands and addressed the crowd. "People of Inya, without this woman, the conspiracy against my life would not have been unraveled in time, and I wouldn't be here today." He dropped to one knee before her, and as he did so, every Inyan in the crowd knelt as well. They fell like a wave, rippling out from the stage, leaving only the Kjallans standing upright or sitting on their horses.

Rayn held the jeweled sword horizontally, like an offering, with one hand on its hilt and the other on its scabbard. "I ask you to share with me the burdens of kingship. Will you walk through fire with me, Celeste Florian Nigellus of Kjall?"

For a moment, she was confused. *Walk through fire?* Then she remembered that walking through fire was part of the royal marriage ceremony. Rayn was proposing!

"Rayn Daryson of Inya," she said, "I will walk through fire with you anytime."

Rayn, grinning in delight, thrust the sword toward her. She took it. Rayn rose to his feet, and the crowd rose too, roaring their approval. He pulled her into his arms and hugged her fiercely.

37

In the days that followed, Celeste was so busy, she barely had time to catch her breath. The wedding had been arranged for four months hence, but for now that was the least of her concerns.

Rayn had brought formal charges against Councilor Worryn. The resulting investigation had implicated four more Land Council members who voted with him in a bloc. It turned out they'd been in on the decision to hire the Riorcan assassins, and had helped finance the endeavor.

Suddenly the Land Council had five vacancies, and new candidates were vying for the elected positions.

Celeste and Rayn settled the trade agreement with Vitala and Lucien. It had already been written up and wanted only Lucien's signature, which after some obligatory grumbling he provided. Then there were hugs and kisses and tearful farewells all around, and the Kjallans— everyone except Celeste and her bodyguard—set sail for home. They would return for the wedding.

Celeste and Rayn moved from the Hibiscus Tower into the royal wing. However, they did not take up residence in the king's quarters. Those were, as a courtesy, granted to Rayn's father, who in his increasing madness did not tolerate change well and who was set much at ease by returning to the familiar. For themselves, they claimed the prince's quarters, Rayn's old room.

Rayn's mother and sister were returned to the royal wing, as was Aderyn. Rayn relented and hired a personal bodyguard. Celeste had, with special dispensation from Lucien, arranged to keep Atella with her in Inya. Atella remained a member of the Kjallan Legaciatti and would continue to accrue her years of service. Women Legaciatti served fourteen years before being granted a generous retirement stipend, and Atella was halfway through her term.

As the initial excitement of exploring a new land began to wear off, and her family departed, Celeste began to feel the pangs of homesickness. It was not easy, starting a new life in an unfamiliar place. But Rayn's love and companionship gave her strength. They retained the habit of taking his coffee and her chocolate together every morning, just the two of them, no matter what else they had going on that day. Most days they were together, and on those days when Rayn's business took him elsewhere, they were together at night, Rayn searing her with his fire touch, their bodies straining together for release. During the day, Inya's king belonged to his people. But at night he was Celeste's.

Lucien had promised to bring her personal possessions when he and Vitala returned for the wedding: her horse, Raven; her unfinished math treatise; her clothes and knickknacks. Celeste grew hungry for intellectual stimulation and spoke to the scholars at the Tiasan University. She made arrangements to found the Inyan Mathematical Society, an organization open to both men and women.

Rayn had but one sorrow remaining in his life—his father's deterioration. Though he had moved his father back to his old room and no longer heard complaints about the former king's loss of his window, the former king continued to be suspicious and hostile.

Rayn visited him frequently, despite the usually disappointing outcome. Today Celeste, who had yet to meet Zalyo, offered to accompany him. As they approached the man's door, Rayn turned to her and said, "What you see may disturb you. He's not himself."

"I understand." Celeste was not nervous. She knew not to expect much from the profoundly ill man. But poor Rayn's hands were trembling. This was more emotional for him than it was for her. He had known his father in his prime; thus it was more disturbing for him to see the man's deterioration. But Celeste had never known a sane Zalyo, and did not approach this meeting with any expectations.

"My family is not like yours," Rayn added. "Your relatives—they are all competent, all capable. Mine ... well ..."

"None of us have perfect families," said Celeste. "Your father may be mad now, but at one time he was an excellent king who taught you everything you know. My father, on the other hand, massacred thousands."

Rayn blinked, taken aback. "You make a sound point."

"I am not my father, and you are not yours," said Celeste. "Let's go in."

Konani, the caretaker, ushered them into the room.

Zalyo was sitting at the window, staring out. He glanced at them briefly before returning his attention to the window. "Arrick, is that you?"

"No, it's your son, Rayn," said Rayn. "And I've brought someone else to see you."

"Not now," said Zalyo. "I'm waiting for Arrick."

Rayn looked quizzically at Konani.

Konani whispered, "An old fleet captain, I think."

"Oh, I remember." Rayn addressed his father again. "Sir, Captain Arrick isn't available—"

Zalyo waved his hand. "Go and fetch him. There's an attack ship in the harbor."

Rayn went to the window. "That one?" said Rayn, indicating a ship that was just dropping anchor.

"Yes!" cried Zalyo. "Get Arrick right away."

"Father, that's a Mosari merchant ship."

Zalyo rounded on them. "Is it your place to question me, you . . . you . . ."

"I'm your son." Rayn's voice broke as he said it. "I came to introduce you to my fiancée, Princess Celeste." He'd told her in advance he would not mention where she was from; Zalyo had a habit of becoming fretful at any mention of Kjall.

Zalyo's eyes went back and forth from Rayn to Celeste to Rayn again. "What is this nonsense? You're distracting me when our nation is at war! Why are we not firing on the ship? Get Captain Arrick."

"Sir—" began Rayn.

"Who are you?" demanded Zalyo. "Have you come to take my window? To take my throne? I'll not have it. Konani!"

"Give me a moment," said Konani, rushing to him. "I'll quiet him."

Celeste and Rayn let Konani take over with his soothing voice and moved to the back of the room.

Rayn's voice trembled as he spoke. "I'm sorry. I was hoping this would work, but clearly it's not going to. He's just . . . he's . . . Look, Captain Arrick died six years ago."

"I'm so sorry," said Celeste. "I have a thought. You can tell me no if you're not comfortable with it."

"What's your thought?"

"I can use mind magic on him."

Rayn shook his head. "Absolutely not. I don't want his mind tampered with."

"Before you decide, hear me out," said Celeste. "I can use a suggestion to quiet his fears and remind him who you are. It's true that a suggestion tampers with the mind, but the effects are temporary. It will wear off within the hour, and it may help him remember a few things. I'm not familiar with his particular condition, but I've used suggestions for healing purposes before."

Rayn sighed and looked back at Konani, who was making soothing gestures at a ranting Zalyo. "We'll try it. Just once."

They crossed the room to the window, where Konani raised his hands to warn them off. "Your Majesty, he's not having a good day."

"Let's try just once more," said Rayn.

Celeste projected her suggestion immediately. *Inya is not at war, and there are no attack ships in the harbor. This is my son standing before me, whom I raised from infancy.*

The lines in Zalyo's face relaxed. His stared at them slack-jawed. After a moment, he said, "Rayn?"

Rayn took Zalyo's hand in his own. His voice broke as he answered, "Yes, Father, it's me."

"You've grown, son. Is that the Ormathian Mantle you wear?"

"Yes, Father. I'm king now." Rayn looked apprehensive, and Celeste bit her lip as she awaited the former king's response.

Zalyo shook his head. "I don't remember. I'm sorry. I don't know what's wrong with me these days. I remember so little—"

"Don't apologize," said Rayn.

"You won your ratification vote?" asked Zalyo.

"Yes, Father."

"I knew you would," said Zalyo. "Always, you made me proud."

Rayn's face crumpled. Celeste placed a hand on his shoulder and squeezed gently.

Zalyo looked up at her. "Who is this young lady with you?"

Rayn rose from his kneeling position and slipped his hand into hers. "This is Celeste, my fiancée. I came here to introduce her to you."

Zalyo studied her. "She's beautiful."

"She certainly is," said Rayn.

"You'll take care of my son, won't you?" asked Zalyo.

"Every moment of his life," Celeste promised.

EPILOGUE

Celeste felt both nervous and a little ridiculous as she made her way through the crowd with Rayn, clasping wrists with friends old and new. It was their wedding day, and this time she too was wearing the Inyan face paint. Her wedding dress was lighter in weight than a Kjallan one would be, on account of the weather. It was an elaborate gold-and-white garment of tulle and satin, embroidered with thousands of tiny pearls. Rayn, who followed just behind her, was dressed in silver, the traditional color of Inyan bridegrooms.

It was a fine day, which was fortunate because Inyan royal weddings were held outdoors, and if it rained, they had to be postponed. She and Rayn had chosen for their location the hidden cove where he'd given her the ring cowrie. She greatly preferred the sounds of sand and surf to the hollow echoes of an indoor hall.

Before the ceremony commenced, it was customary for the bridal couple to greet all the guests. That way, they could be spirited away immediately after the ceremony to their private chamber for the all-important consummation of the marriage—not that this particular marriage hadn't been well and truly consummated already.

The inaugural members of the Inyan Mathematical Society were in attendance: five men and three women. She clasped wrists with each of them as she moved down the line.

Near the end, she came to the Kjallans. First Justien and Nalica, and then her family. It amazed her that Vitala had made the trip. She was hugely pregnant now and accompanied at all times by a Healer, in case she went unexpectedly into labor. It was entirely possible that Vitala and Lucien's second child might be born in Inya, or, more likely, on the *Soldier's Sweep* during their voyage home.

She hugged Vitala gently, and then her brother.

"Are you really going to walk through fire?" asked Vitala.

She glanced back at the enormous line of firewood that had been set up on the beach. There was a ramp leading over it, so they wouldn't have to walk directly on the wood, but she supposed the ramp became quite hot when bathed in flames. "As I understand it, yes, we do."

Lucien's brows furrowed. "You're sure this is safe?"

"Rayn insists that it is," she said. "The tradition goes back to the days when fire mages were considered priests to the fire spirits. Walking through fire assured everyone that the spirits approved the match."

"They'd better approve this one," said Lucien, "or they'll have a war on their hands."

"When do the officials light the fire?" asked Vitala.

"At the last minute, right before we walk through," said Celeste. "Otherwise we'd be boiling out here."

At the end of the line, they came to Rayn's family: his mother, Kin-Lera; his younger sister, Rilia; and his older sister, Selda, who had traveled here for the ceremony in the company of her Mosari husband. Aderyn sat babbling happily in Kima's arms. And Zalyo was present, accompanied by two caretakers.

It was clear to Celeste that Zalyo would never recover; the damage to his mind was incurable. But he suffered less now from paranoia and anxiety. Over the years, Councilor Worryn had exacerbated the man's symptoms by whispering in his ear about supposed wrongs that were being done to him. Now that Worryn was out of the picture—imprisoned for his crimes— Zalyo was more at ease. Rayn made a point of visiting with him several times a week to play Knots, a simple tile matching game. Zalyo tended to forget the rules and cheat, but that didn't matter. The point was spending time together. Some days Zalyo recognized Rayn and some days he didn't. When his father's state distressed him more than he could handle, Rayn came to Celeste afterward. They'd learned some mutually enjoyable techniques for quieting Rayn's inner fire. And while thus far Celeste had not used her mind magic on Zalyo a second time—Rayn preferred as little interference with the workings of his mind as possible—they knew it was an option should Zalyo become too confused and agitated to find peace.

Now Celeste kissed Aderyn's cheek and clasped wrists with each of her in-laws, ending with Zalyo. She then left them to Rayn, who hugged them all in turn and whispered in their ears.

They'd reached the end of the line. It was time for the ceremony. Directed by the officials, they walked arm in arm around the line of firewood and took their place on its far side, so that they faced both the firewood and the crowd beyond it. A trumpet sounded, and an official said something in the Old Language. Then he repeated the words in Inyan.

Celeste listened with half an ear. It was a familiar litany of invocations to the gods, remarkably similar to what she'd heard in Kjall on countless occasions, although it was interesting to hear it in another language. She glanced at the ocean, bringer of gifts, and looked up at her fiancé. Would she ever tire of gazing at him? Even now, after knowing him in the most intimate of ways, she was amazed anew by the fact that he was the most beautiful creature she'd ever laid eyes on.

"It's time," whispered Rayn.

The officials standing on the other side of the firewood dipped their lit torches into it. The wood must have been treated with something, because it rushed up in a great wall of flame before them, emitting a blistering wave of heat. Suddenly they were alone. Everyone else was on the other side, and the fire lay in between.

Celeste felt the heat for only an instant, and then she was surrounded by cool air. Rayn was using his magic.

He grinned. "Shall we?"

She nodded nervously. All they had to do was pass through that flame, and they would be married.

They stepped up onto the ramp. She would have shrunk from the flames, but Rayn moved steadily forward, encouraging her with his confidence. In front of them was an inferno. She swallowed.

Rayn stepped directly into the flames, and she went with him. All around them was fire. She felt nothing—even her feet, on the iron ramp, were not hot. Since this would likely be the only time in her life she stood inside a fire, she took a moment to look around.

Her mouth fell open. All around her, the spirits danced. They were red and orange and yellow, their elongated limbs twisting and gyrating to an unheard rhythm. Fascinated, she stared. Their dance was exuberant, and they sang in rushing, crackling voices. She could not make out the words. It was a language foreign to mortals.

"You see them?" asked Rayn.

"I do."

He tugged at her arm. "They are a private people—we cannot stay."

Looking through the flames, she saw the crowd waiting anxiously for them to emerge from the fire. All the people she loved were out there, save the one she loved most—and he was by her side. She stepped forward with Rayn, out of the fire and into her new life.

Dear Reader,

Thank you for reading Prince's Fire*! I hope you enjoyed the book.*

If you'd like to know when my next book is available, you can subscribe to my newsletter at http://www.amyraby.com, or follow me on Twitter at @amyraby, or like my Facebook page at https://www.facebook.com/Amy.Raby.Author.

Prince's Fire *is the third full-length novel in the Hearts and Thrones series. The first book is* Assassin's Gambit, *and the second is* Spy's Honor. *You can find links to these books at http://www.amyraby.com.*

I appreciate all reviews, whether positive or negative. Please consider leaving an honest review at Goodreads or your favorite retailer.

All the best,

Amy Raby

ABOUT THE AUTHOR

Amy Raby is literally a product of the U.S. space program, since her parents met working for NASA on the Apollo missions. After earning her bachelor's in computer science from the University of Washington, Amy settled in the Pacific Northwest with her family, where she's always looking for life's next adventure, whether it's capsizing tiny sailboats in Lake Washington, training hunting dogs, or riding horseback. Amy is a Golden Heart® finalist and a Daphne du Maurier winner.

Read on for a look at the first novel in
Amy Raby's Hearts and Thrones series,

ASSASSIN'S GAMBIT

Available from Signet Eclipse.

PROLOGUE

His body moved against hers, chafing her skin. Vitala shifted beneath him and tried to remember his name. Rennic, maybe. Some spy in training from the practice floor who'd leapt at the opportunity to engage in a different sort of practice.

"Not much into this, are you?" he murmured, pumping away.

Right—she was supposed to act like she enjoyed this. And if she couldn't fool this Rennic fellow, she'd never fool the emperor. She moaned and writhed, convinced, as always, that such obvious fakery couldn't work. And yet it did. He quickened. The hard muscles of his arms tensed against her, and his rhythm accelerated. His eyes fluttered shut.

She ran her hands down his back.

Her mentor's words echoed in her head. *Remember the nature of the emperor's magic. If your timing is even a little bit off, he'll see the attack coming, and you will fail.*

She knew the difficulty of her task and the importance of getting the details right. She would practice until every move had the slick perfection of a well-played Caturanga game.

Rennic grunted, beyond speech. He jerked and gasped. The moment had come.

A touch of her mind and a flick of her finger, and from out of nowhere a Shard glinted in her hand. She stabbed the tiny blade into the soft flesh of his back. He didn't react, probably didn't even feel it. Another touch of her mind, and she released the spell it carried—a benign white-pox spell, easily cured. Not the more fatal alternative.

With a grunt that could have been satisfaction or pain, he collapsed atop her, sticky with sweat.

She yanked the Shard out of his back, and he jerked in sudden awareness. He twisted and stared at the inky Shard, now daubed red with his blood. "You get me with that thing?"

"It's a good thing you're not the emperor," said Vitala, "or you'd be dead."

1

"Vitala Salonius?"

She set down her heavy valise on the dock's oak planking. The man approaching her looked the quintessential Kjallan—tall and muscular, black hair, and a hawk nose. He wore Kjallan military garb, double belted, with a sword on one hip. On the other hip sat a flintlock pistol with a walnut stock and gilt bronze mounts, so fine and polished that Vitala found herself coveting it. His orange uniform bore no blood mark but instead the sickle and sunburst—the insignia of the Legaciatti, which made him one of the emperor's famed personal bodyguards.

"Yes, sir. That's me," she said.

His handsome face broke into a smile. "My name is Remus, and I'm here to escort you to the palace. I'll get that for you." He hefted the valise with ease and gestured at a carriage waiting at the end of the dock.

She followed him, swaying at the sensation of being on dry land after two weeks aboard ship. Remus's riftstone was not visible. Most Kjallan mages wore them on chains around their necks, concealed beneath their clothes. The collar of Remus's uniform hid even the chain. He was certainly a mage—all the Legaciatti were—but she could not tell what sort of magic he possessed. Was he a war mage? That was the only type difficult to kill. She relaxed her mind a little, opening herself to the tiny fault lines that separated her world from the spirit world, and viewed the ghostly blue threading of his wards. He was well protected from disease, parasites, and even from the conception of a child.

They arrived at the carriage, a landau pulled by dark bays. At Remus's gesture, she climbed inside. He handed her valise to a bespectacled footman, who heaved it onto the back and strapped it in place. Remus, whom she'd expected to ride on the back or up front with the driver, stepped into the carriage and sat in the seat opposite her. Of course. The vetting process began here. He would make small talk, and she'd have to be very, very careful what she said to him.

The carriage lurched forward, and the Imperial City of Riat began to pass by the windows—wide streets and narrow ones, large homes and small ones, with the usual collection of inns, shops, and street vendors crammed into the available spaces. She spotted a millinery shop, a gunsmith, a Warder's, an open-air market with fresh imported lemons. A newsboy with an armload of papers cried his wares from a corner. Kjallan townsfolk moved about the streets, buying, flirting, and trading gossip. The citizens caught her eye with their brightly colored robe-like syrtoses, while slaves in gray flitted by like shadows. The city was pleasant enough, but unremarkable. Well, what had she expected? Marble houses? Streets lined with diamonds?

"I hear you're a master of Caturanga," said Remus.

"Yes, sir. I won the tournament this year in Beryl."

"The emperor was impressed by your accomplishment." His blue eyes studied her with a more than casual interest.

"I'm honored by that."

"And you're from the province of Dahat?"

Please don't be from Dahat yourself. It would be a disaster if he were looking for someone to swap childhood stories with. She'd been to Dahat, so she could provide a few details about the region, but she hadn't grown up there. "Yes, sir."

"How are feelings toward the emperor there?"

Her forehead wrinkled. *What sort of question is that?* "Citizens of Dahat have great respect for Emperor Lucien."

Remus laughed. "You think this is a loyalty test, don't you? Tell me the truth, Miss Salonius. Emperor Lucien likes to know how public sentiment runs throughout his empire. Platitudes and blind expressions of loyalty mean nothing to him. He wants honesty."

Vitala bit her lip. "I've been on the Caturanga circuit for more than three years, sir, longer than Emperor Lucien's reign. What little I picked up from my visits home is that while most of the citizenry supports him, there are some who disapprove of his policies and preferred the former emperor. I imagine that would be true in any province."

"Indeed," said Remus. "There are those who miss the old emperor Florian and his Imperial Garden. Have you had the privilege of visiting it?"

"Visiting what?"

"Florian's Imperial Garden."

"No, sir. This is my first visit to the palace." Vitala was puzzled. He had to know that already.

"Ah," he said. "You should seek it out during your visit."

"That would be lovely, sir."

The carriage tilted backward. Vitala looked out her window. They'd passed through the city and started up the steep hill that led to the Imperial Palace. The carriage was navigating the first of half a dozen switchbacks. When she turned back to Remus, his eyes had lost their intensity. Whatever the test was, it seemed she'd passed it. "You are the first woman to win the Beryl tournament," he said. "Pray tell me who you studied under."

Vitala smiled. This was one of the questions she'd been coached on. "My father taught me to play when I was four years old and I showed an aptitude for the game. Within a year, I could beat my cousins. Later, I studied under Caecus, and when I'd mastered his teachings, I studied under Ralla." She droned on, feeding him the lies she'd recited under Bayard's tutelage. Remus leaned back and nodded dully. It seemed he'd lost interest in her. Thank the gods.

As the carriage crested the final switchback, Vitala craned her neck for a look at the Imperial Palace. Three white marble domes, each topped with a gilt roof, rose into view, gleaming in the sunshine. Next appeared the numerous outbuildings and walled gardens that surrounded the domes. A wide treelined avenue directed them to the front gates.

Inside the palace, silk hangings of immeasurable value draped the walls, while priceless paintings and sculptures graced every nook. She'd never been anywhere so boldly ostentatious. What a contrast to Riorca, with its broken streets and ramshackle pit houses! How much of this had been built by Riorcan slave labor?

Two Legaciatti, both women, met them inside the door. Vitala studied them, curious at the oddity of female Kjallan soldiers. Bayard had told her that women made ideal assassins for Kjallan targets because Kjallan men didn't take women seriously. Ostensibly, that was true; Kjall was patriarchal, and women had little power under the law. But as she'd traveled on the tournament circuit, she'd learned the reality was more complicated. Most Kjallan men were soldiers who were often away from home. In their absence, their wives had authority over their households. Women and slaves were the real engine of Kjall's economy; few men had many practical skills outside of soldiering.

"Search her," ordered Remus.

One of the women beckoned. "Come along."

The search took place in a private room and was humiliatingly thorough. Vitala knew what they were looking for: concealed weapons or perhaps a riftstone. They would not find either. She didn't wear her riftstone around her neck; it was surgically implanted in her body, along with the deathstone, her escape from torture and interrogation if she botched this mission. Her weapons were magically hidden where none but a wardbreaker could detect them. And there were no Kjallan wardbreakers; only Riorcans possessed the secrets of that form of magic.

As she put her clothes back on, the Legaciatti emptied her valise, checked it for hidden compartments, and pawed through her paltry collection of spare clothes, undergarments, powders, and baubles. They found nothing that concerned them.

They repacked her things and led her up two flights of white marble stairs. The walls were rounded and concave; she must have been in one of the domes. Her room was the third on the right from the top of the stairway. A young guard with peach fuzz on his chin stood in front of it, wearing an orange uniform but no sickle and sunburst. Peach fuzz. He looked familiar.

The young soldier lay on the cot, his wrists and ankles bound. His blanket had fallen to the floor, a result of his struggles. His eyes jerked toward her, wide with fear, but when he saw her, he relaxed a little. He wasn't expecting a teenage girl.

"Miss Salonius?"

He shouldn't know her name. How did he know her name?

"Miss Salonius?"

And why did he sound like a woman?

Vitala blinked. The Legaciatti were staring at her in concern. "Miss Salonius?" one of them asked.

"I'm sorry." Gods, where was she? Marble walls. The Imperial Palace.

"You stopped moving. You were staring into space."

"Sorry, I was . . . Never mind." Averting her eyes so that she wouldn't see the young man guarding her door, she stepped inside.

Vitala's room was a suite. Just inside was a sitting room with a single peaked window along its curved wall and a pair of light-glows in brass mountings suspended from the ceiling. The room was lavishly furnished with carved oaken tables and chairs upholstered in silk. A bookshelf on the far wall drew her eye. Among its contents, she recognized all the classic treatises on Caturanga and some she'd never seen before, as well as books on other subjects. An herbal by Lentulus. Cinna's *Tactics of War*. Numerous works of fiction, including the notoriously racy *Seventh Life of the Potter's Daughter*. Who had put a book like that on an otherwise erudite bookshelf?

On a table in the center of the room sat the finest Caturanga set she'd ever seen. Pieces of carved agate with jeweled eyes winked at her from a round two-tiered board of polished marble. She picked up one of the red cavalry pieces. The rider was richly detailed down to the folds of his cloak. The warhorse was wild-eyed, his beautifully carved expression showing equal parts fear and determination.

Had Emperor Lucien set up this room just for her? No, of course not. He hosted many Caturanga champions. Probably all of them had been housed here.

The bedroom was equally fine, with a high four-poster bed, silk sheets, and a damask down-stuffed comforter. The silk hangings were blue and red. Was that by design? Blue and red were the traditional colors of Caturanga pieces.

"You will reside here until the emperor summons you," a Legaciatta instructed. "Take your rest as needed, but you are not to wander about the palace. If you desire something, such as food or drink, ask the door guard. If you wish to bathe, he can escort you to the baths on the lower level."

Vitala nodded. "Thank you, ma'am."

The Legaciatti left, closing the door behind them. Vitala went to the window—real glass, she noted—and peered out. Below was a walled enclosure obscured by a canopy of trees, through which she caught glimpses of red, purple, and orange. The famous Imperial Garden? Looking up to take in the broader view, she noticed a patch of too light blue in the sky and picked out the Vagabond, the tiny moon that glowed blue at night but faded almost to invisibility in the daytime. God of reversals and unforeseen disaster, the Vagabond wandered across the sky in the direction opposite the other two moons, and was not always a favorable sighting. "Great One, pass me by," she prayed reflexively.

Leaving the window and lighting one of the glows with a touch of her finger, she pulled *Seventh Life* from the bookshelf. Sprawling on a couch, she waited upon the pleasure of the emperor.